John Hoole

Jerusalem Delivered an Heroic Poem

Translated from the Italian of Torquato Tasso

I0740310

John Hoole

Jerusalem Delivered an Heroic Poem
Translated from the Italian of Torquato Tasso

ISBN/EAN: 9783742830418

Manufactured in Europe, USA, Canada, Australia, Japa

Cover: Foto ©Andreas Hilbeck / pixelio.de

Manufactured and distributed by brebook publishing software
(www.brebook.com)

John Hoole

Jerusalem Delivered an Heroic Poem

ALL'ECC^{mo} ED EMIN^{mo} PRINCIPE

IL · SIG^r · CARDINAL·LUIGI

VALENTI · · GONZAGA · · &c.

IL · DI · CUI · GUSTO

PER·LE·BELLE·LETTERE

E · SEGNALATAMENTE

PER · LE · OPERE · IMMORTALI

DI · TORQUATO · TASSO

SPARGE · NUOVI · ALLORI

SULLA · TOMBA · DEL · POETA

IL QUALE · EBBE · IL · VANTO

DI · MERITARE

LA · PROTEZIONE · E · L'AMICIZIA

DEL · SUO · GRANDE · E · DOTTO

ANTENATO

IL · CARDINAL · SCIPIO·GONZAGA

DE' · SER^{mi} · DUCHI · DI · MANTOVA

QUESTA · VERSIONE

INGLESE

DELLA · GERUSALEMME · LIBERATA

LETTA · CON · PREDILEZIÖNE

DALLA · NAZIONE · BRITANNICA

AMMIRATRICE

DELLE · MUSE · E · DEGLI EROI

D'ITALIA

È · OFFERTA

COME · PICCIOL · TRIBUTO

DI · STIMA · DI · RISPETTO

E · DI RICONOSCENZA

ROMA, 19. NOV: 1792.

JERUSALEM DELIVERED;

AN

HEROIC POEM:

Translated from the ITALIAN of

TORQUATO TASSO,

By JOHN HOOLE.

IN TWO VOLUMES.

VOL. I.

THE FIFTH EDITION,

WITH NOTES.

LONDON:

Printed for J. DODSLEY, in PALL-MALL.

M.DCC.LXXXIII.

QUEEN.

MADAM,

To approach the High and the Illuftrious has been, in all ages, the privilege
of Poets; and though Tranflators cannot
juftly claim the fame honour, yet they naturally follow their Authors as Attendants;
and I hope that, in return for having
enabled Tasso to diffufe his fame through
the Britifh Dominions, I may be introduced by him to the prefence of Your
Majesty.

Tasso has a peculiar claim to Your
Majesty's favour, as a Follower and Pa-
negyrift of the Houfe of Este, which has
one common Anceftor with the Houfe of
Hanover; and in reviewing his life, it is
not eafy to forbear a wifh that he had lived
in a happier time, when he might, among

the

the Defcendants of that Illuftrious Family, have found a more liberal and potent pa-tronage.

I cannot but obferve, MADAM, how un-equally Reward is proportioned to Merit, when I reflect that the Happinefs, which was with-held from TASSO, is referved for me; and that the Poem, which once hardly procured to its Author the countenance of the Princes of FERRARA, has attracted to its Tranflator the favourable notice of a BRI-TISH QUEEN.

Had this been the fate of TASSO, he would have been able to have celebrated the Conde-fcenfion of YOUR MAJESTY in nobler lan-guage, but could not have felt it with more ardent gratitude, than,

MADAM,

YOUR MAJESTY'S

Moft faithful, and

Devoted Servant,

JOHN HOOLE.

ADVERTISEMENT

BY THE TRANSLATOR,

TO THE PRESENT EDITION.

HAVING completed a translation of the ORLANDO FURIOSO of ARIOSTO, with explanatory Notes, and the favourable attention that has been paid to my version of TASSO, making it necessary to give a new edition of the JERUSALEM, I thought it expedient to revise the work, and, in order not only to render it more worthy of the public favour, but to give an uniformity to the two publications, I have added to the present edition such Notes as might be useful for explaining the historical allusions, and some few other passages: but as the JERUSALEM is in itself complete, and wholly independent of every other poem, in which respect it has the advantage of the ORLANDO, and of the three great Poems of Antiquity; and as the historical allusions are rare, compared to those of ARIOSTO, the bulk of the notes

will

will be inconfiderable. It may poffibly at firft be thought, by fome, that I have not dwelt fufficiently on the imitations and ftriking parts of this admirable Poem; but the truth is, I was unwilling to fwell the pages with an unprofitable difplay of criticifm; and I hope I may add, without the imputation of vanity, that little commentary was required to an author with whom my countrymen are now acquainted. But it appeared to me that much was to be faid, on the introduction of fuch a poem as ARIOSTO's, to open fully a poetical character fo new and uncommon to the Englifh reader.

May 23, 1783.

PREFACE.

PREFACE.

OF all Authors, so familiarly known by name to the generality of English readers as Tasso, perhaps there is none whose works have been so little read ; and the few who have read them, have seldom estimated them by their own judgment. As some authors owe much of their reputation to the implicit acquiescence of the many in the encomiums bestowed upon them by some person with whom, for whatever reason, it has been thought honourable to acquiesce ; so others have been rated much below their merit, merely because some fashionable critic has decried their performances ; and thus it has happened to Tasso.

M. Boileau, in one of his satires, had ridiculed the absurdity of " preferring the tinsel of Tasso to the gold of " Virgil :" this sentiment was hastily catched up by Mr. Addison, whose polite and elegant writings are an honour to our nation, but whose greatest excellence was not, perhaps, either poetry or criticism ; and he has zealously declared, in one of his Spectators, that " he entirely agrees " with M. Boileau, that one verse in Virgil is worth all " the tinsel of Tasso." These declarations, indeed, amount to no more than that gold is better than tinsel, and true wit than false ; a discovery which does no great honour to the author : but those, who are accustomed to take things in the gross, and to adopt the judgment of others because they will not venture to judge for themselves, have inferred, that all Virgil is gold, and that all Tasso is tinsel ; than which nothing can be more absurd, whether M. Boileau and Mr.

Addison

Addifon intended the implication or not : it is as true, that
the gold of Taffo is better than his tinfel, as that the gold
of Virgil is better ; and though a verfe of Virgil is better
than all Taffo's tinfel, it does not follow that it is alfo better than Taffo's gold.   That Taffo has gold, no man, who
wifhes to be thought qualified to judge of poetry, will chufe
to deny.   It will alfo be readily admitted, that he has tinfel ; but it will be eafy to fhew, not only that the gold pre-
ponderates, but that the tinfel, mingled with it, is not in
a greater proportion than in many other compofitions, which
have received the applaufe of fucceffive ages, and been preferved in the wreck of nations, when almoft every other
poffeffion has been abandoned.

By tinfel is meant falfe thought, and, perhaps, Incredible
fiction ; and whoever is acquainted with the writings of
Ovid, knows that he abounds with falfe thoughts, that he
is continually playing upon words, and that his fictions
are in the higheft degree incredible ; yet his METAMOR-
PHOSES have ever been held in great eftimation by all judges
of poetical merit.

But if Taffo's merit is to be decided by authority, may
not that of M. Voltaire be oppofed with great propriety to
the pedantry of M. Boileau, and the echo of Mr. Addifon ?
" There is (fays he, in his Effay on Epic Poetry) no mo-
" nument of antiquity in Italy that more deferves the at-
" tention of a traveller than the JERUSALEM of Taffo.
" Time, which fubverts the reputation of common per-
" formances, as it were by fap, has rendered that of the
" JERUSALEM more ftable and permanent : this poem is
" now fung in many parts of Italy, as the ILIAD was in
" Greece, and Taffo is placed, without fcruple, by the fide
" of Homer and Virgil, notwithftanding his defects, and
" the criticifms of Defpreaux.   The JERUSALEM appears,
" in fome refpects, to be an imitation of the ILIAD; but if
" Rinaldo is drawn after Achilles, and Godfrey after Aga-
" memnon, I will venture to fay, that Taffo's copy is much
" fuperior to the original : in his battle he has as much
" fire as Homer, with greater variety ; his heroes, like

5   " thofe

" thofe of the ILIAD, are diftinguifhed by a difference of
" character; but the characters of Taffo are more fkilfully
" introduced, more ftrongly marked, and infinitely better
" fuftained; for there is fcarce one in the ILIAD that is
" not inconfiftent with itfelf, and not one in the JERU-
" SALEM that is not uniform throughout. Taffo has paint-
" ed what Homer only fketched; he has attained the art of
" varying his tints by different fhades of the fame colour,
" and has diftinguifhed, into different modes, many virtues,
" vices, and paffions, which others have thought to be the
" fame. Thus the characteriftic, both of Godfrey and
" Aladine, is fagacity, but the modes are finely varied; in
" Godfrey it is a calm circumfpective prudence, in Aladine
" a cruel policy. Courage is predominant both in Tancred
" and Argantes; but in Tancred it is a generous contempt
" of danger, in Argantes a brutal fury: fo love in Armida
" is a mixture of levity and defire; in Erminia it is a foft
" and amiable tendernefs. There is, indeed, no figure in
" the picture that does not difcover the hand of a mafter,
" not even Peter the hermit, who is finely contrafted with
" the enchanter Ifmeno, two characters which are furely
" very much fuperior to the Calchas and Talthybius of
" Homer. Rinaldo is, indeed, imitated from Achilles,
" but his faults are more excufable, his character is more
" amiable, and his leifure is better employed; Achilles daz-
" zles us, but we are interefted for Rinaldo.

" I am in doubt whether Homer has done right or wrong
" in making Priam fo much the object of our pity, but it
" was certainly a mafter-ftroke in Taffo to render Aladine
" odious; for the reader would otherwife have been neceffa-
" rily interefted for the Mahometans againft the Chriftians,
" whom he would have been tempted to confider as a band
" of vagabond thieves, who had agreed to ramble from the
" heart of Europe, in order to defolate a country they had
" no right to, and maffacre, in cold blood, a venerable
" prince, more than fourfcore years old, and his whole
" people, againft whom they had no pretence of complaint."
M. Voltaire then obferves, that this is indeed the true cha-

racter

racter of the crusades: but " Taffo (continues he) has,
" with great judgment, reprefented them very differently ;
" for, in his JERUSALEM, they appear to be an army of
" heroes marching under a chief of exalted virtue, to refcue,
" from the tyranny of Infidels, a country, which had been
" confecrated by the birth and death of a GOD. The fub-
" ject of his poem, confidered in this view, is the moft fub-
" lime that can be imagined ; and he has treated it with
" all the dignity of which it is worthy, and has even ren-
" dered it not lefs interefting than elevated. The action
" is well conducted, and the incidents artfully interwoven ;
" he ftrikes out his adventures with fpirit, and diftributes
" his light and fhade with the judgment of a mafter: he
" tranfports his reader from the tumults of war to the fweet
" folitudes of love, and from fcenes exquifitely voluptuous
" he again tranfports him to the field of battle: he touches
" all the fprings of paffion, in a fwift but regular fuccef-
" fion, and gradually rifes above himfelf as he proceeds from
" book to book: his ftyle is in all parts equally clear and
" elegant ; and when his fubject requires elevation, it is
" aftonifhing to fee how he impreffes a new character upon
" the foftnefs of the Italian language, how he fublimes it
" into majefty, and compreffes it into ftrength. It muft,
" indeed, be confeffed, that in the whole poem there are
" about two hundred verfes in which the author has in-
" dulged himfelf in puerile conceits, and a mere play upon
" words ; but this is nothing more than a kind of tribute,
" which his genius paid to the tafte of the age he lived in,
" which had a fondnefs for points and turns that has fince
" rather increafed than diminifhed."

 Such is the merit of Taffo's JERUSALEM in the opinion
of M. Voltaire: he has, indeed, pointed out, with great
judgment, many defects in particular parts of the work,
which he fo much admires upon the whole ; but this gives
his teftimony in behalf of Taffo, fo far as it goes, new
force ; and if Taffo can be juftified in fome places where
M. Voltaire has condemned him, it follows, that his general merit is ftill greater than M. Voltaire has allowed.

Having

Having remarked fome fanciful exceffes in the account of the expedition of Ubald and his companion, to difcover and bring back Rinaldo, who was much wanted by the whole army, M. Voltaire afks, " what was the great exploit which " was referved for this hero, and which rendered his pre- " fence of fo much importance, that he was tranfported " from the Pic of Teneriffe to Jerufalem ? Why he was " (fays M. Voltaire) " deftined by Providence to cut down " fome old trees that ftood in a foreft, which was haunted " by hobgoblins." M. Voltaire, by this ludicrous defcrip- tion of Rinaldo's adventure in the Enchanted Wood, infi- nuates, that the fervice he performed was inadequate to the pomp with which he was introduced, and unworthy of the miracles which contributed to his return : but, the en- chantment of the foreft being once admitted, this exploit of Rinaldo will be found greatly to heighten his character, and to remove an obftacle to the fiege, which would otherwife have been infuperable, and would confequently have defeated the whole enterprife of the crufade : it was impoffible to carry on the fiege without machines conftructed of timber ; no timber was to be had but in this foreft ; and in this foreft the principal heroes of the Chriftian army had attempted to cut timber in vain.

To this it may be added, that M. Voltaire has not dealt fairly, by fuppofing that Rinaldo was recalled to the camp for no other intent than to cut down the wood : the Cri- tic feems to have forgotten the neceffity of this hero's pre- fence to the general affairs of the Chriftians : it was he who was deftined to kill Solyman, whofe death was, per- haps, of equal confequence to the Chriftians, as that of Hector to the Grecians : the Danifh meffenger had been miraculoufly preferved and fent to deliver Sweno's fword to Rinaldo, with a particular injunction for him to revenge the death of that prince on the Soldan : we fee further the importance of Rinaldo in the laft battle, where he kills al- moft all the principal leaders of the enemy, and is the great caufe of the entire defeat of the Egyptian army.

M. Voltaire's general cenfure of this incident, therefore,

appears

appears to be ill-founded. "But certain demons (says he)
"having taken an infinite variety of shapes to terrify those
"who came to fell the trees, Tancred finds his Clorinda
"shut up in a pine, and wounded by a stroke which he had
"given to the trunk of the tree; and Armida issues from
"the bark of a myrtle, while she is many leagues distant
"in the Egyptian army."

Upon a review of this last passage, the first sentence will
certainly be found to confute the censure implied in the
second: in the first sentence we are told, "that the forms,
"which prevented the Christian heroes from cutting down
"the trees, were devils:" in the second it is intimated,
that the voice of Clorinda, and the form of Armida were no
illusions, but in reality what they seemed to be: for where
is the absurdity that a demon should assume the voice of
Clorinda, or the figure of Armida, in this forest, though
Clorinda herself was dead, and Armida in another place?
Tasso, therefore, is acquitted of the charge of making Armida in two places at one time, even by the very passage in
which the charge is brought.

To the authority of M. Voltaire, who, at the same time
that he supposes Tasso to have more faults than he has,
thinks his excellencies sufficient to place him among the first
poets in the world, may be added that of Mr. Dryden, who,
in the preface to the translation of Virgil, has declared the
JERUSALEM DELIVERED to be the next heroic poem to the
ILIAD and ÆNEID.

Mr. Dryden was too great a master in poetical composition, and had a knowledge too extensive, and a judgment too
accurate, to suppose the merit of the JERUSALEM to be
subverted by improbabilities, which are more numerous
and more gross in the works of Homer and Virgil. It is
very likely that magic and enchantment were as generally
and firmly believed, when Tasso wrote his JERUSALEM, as
the visible agency of the Pagan deities at the writing of the
ILIAD, the ODYSSEY, and ÆNEID: and it is certain, that
the events, which Tasso supposes to have been brought
about by enchantment, were more congruous to such a
cause

cause than many fictions of the Greek and Roman poets to
the Pagan theology; at least that a theology, which could
admit them, was more absurd than the existence and opera-
tion of any powers of magic and enchantment. If we do
not, therefore, reject the poems of Homer and Virgil as
not worth reading, because they contain extravagant fables,
we have no right to make that a pretence for rejecting the
JERUSALEM of Tasso; especially if the Gothic machines
were more adapted to the great ends of epic poetry than the
system of antiquity, as an ingenious author has endeavoured
to shew: his words are; "The current popular tales of
" elves and fairies were even fitter to take the credulous
" mind, and charm it into a willing admiration of the
" *specious miracles*, which wayward fancy delights in, than
" those of the old traditionary rabble of Pagan divinities.
" And then, for the more solemn fancies of witchcraft and
" incantation, the horrors of the Gothic were above mea-
" sure striking and terrible. The mummeries of the Pagan
" priests were childish, but the Gothic enchanters shook
" and alarmed all nature. We feel this difference very sen-
" sibly in reading the ancient and modern poets. You
" would not compare the Canidia of Horace with the
" witches of Macbeth: and what are Virgil's myrtles
" dropping blood, to Tasso's enchanted forest !" Letters
on Chivalry and Romance, p. 48, 49.

As I think it is now evident that a reader may be pleased
with Tasso, and not disgrace his judgment, I may, without
impropriety, offer a translation of him to those who cannot
read him in his original language. I may be told, indeed,
that there is an English translation of him already, and
therefore that an apology is necessary for a new one. To
this I answer, that the only complete translation is that of
Fairfax, which is in stanzas that cannot be read with pleasure by the generality of those who have a taste for English
poetry: of which no other proof is necessary than that it
appears scarce to have been read at all: it is not only un-
pleasant, but irksome, in such a degree, as to surmount
                                            curiosity;

curiofity; and more than counterbalance all the beauty of expreffion, and fentiment, which is to be found in that work. I do not flatter myfelf that I have excelled Fairfax, except in my meafure and verfification, and even of thefe the principal recommendation is, that they are more modern, and better adapted to the ear of all readers of Englifh poetry, except of the very few who have acquired a tafte for the phrafes and cadences of thofe times, when our verfe, if not our language, was in its rudiments.

That a tranflation of Taffo into modern English verfe has been generally thought neceffary, appears by feveral effays that have been made towards it, particularly thofe of Mr. Brooke, Mr. Hooke, and Mr. Layng: if any of thefe gentlemen had compleated their undertaking, it would effectually have precluded mine. Mr. Brooke's in particular, is at once fo harmonious, and fo fpirited, that I think an entire tranflation of Taffo by him would not only have rendered my tafk unneceffary, but have difcouraged thofe from the attempt, whofe poetical abilities are much fuperior to mine: and yet Mr. Brooke's performance is rather an animated paraphrafe than a tranflation. My endeavour has been to render the fenfe of my author as nearly as poffible, which could never be done merely by tranflating his words; how I have fuccceeded the world muft determine: an author is but an ill judge of his own performances: and the opinion of friends is not always to be trufted; for there is a kind of benevolent partiality which inclines us to think favourably of the works of thofe whom we efteem. I am, however, happy in the good opinion of fome gentlemen whofe judgment, in this cafe, could err only by fuch partiality; and as I am not lefs ambitious to engage efteem as a man, than to merit praife as an author, I am not anxioufly folicitous to know whether they have been miftaken or not.

As many paffages in the original of this work are very clofely imitated from the Greek and Roman Claffics, I may perhaps, inadvertently, have inferted a line or two from the
Englifh

English versions of those authors; but as Mr. Pope, in his translation of HOMER, has taken several verses from Mr. Dryden, and Mr. Pitt, in his translation of the ÆNEID, several both from Mr. Dryden and Mr. Pope, I flatter myself I shall incur no censure on that account.

I have incorporated some few verses both of Mr. Brooke's and Mr. Layng's version of Taſſo with my own; but as I have not arrogated the merit of what I have borrowed to myself, I cannot juſtly be accuſed of plagiariſm. Theſe obligations I acknowledge, that I may do juſtice to others; but there are ſome which I ſhall mention to gratify myſelf: Mr. Samuel Johnſon, whoſe judgment I am happy in being authoriſed to make uſe of on this occaſion, has given me leave to publiſh it, as his opinion, that a modern tranſlation of the JERUSALEM DELIVERED is a work that may very juſtly merit the attention of the Engliſh reader; and I owe many remarks to the friendſhip and candor of Dr. Hawkeſworth, from which my performance has received conſiderable advantages.

Before I conclude this Preface, it is neceſſary the Engliſh reader ſhould be acquainted that the Italian poets, when they ſpeak of infidels of any denomination, generally uſe the word Pagano: the word Pagan, therefore, in the tranſlation, is often uſed for Mahometan; and Spenſer has uſed the word Paynim in the ſame ſenſe.

As the public is not at all concerned about the qualifications of an author, any further than they appear in his works, it is to little purpoſe that writers have endeavoured to prevent their writings from being conſidered as the ſtandard of their abilities, by alledging the ſhort time, or the diſadvantageous circumſtances, in which they were produced. If their performances are too bad to obtain a favourable reception for themſelves, it is not likely that the world will regard them with more indulgence for being told why they are no better. If I did not hope, therefore, that the tranſlation now offered, though begun and finiſhed in the midſt of employments of a very different kind, might ſome-

<table>
<tr><td>VOL. I.</td><td>b</td><td>thing</td></tr>
</table>

thing more than atone for its own defects, I would not have obtruded it on the public. All I request of my readers, is to judge for themselves, and if they find any entertainment, not to think the worse of it, for being the performance of one, who has never before appeared a candidate for their suffrages as an author.

T H E

THE

LIFE

OF

TASSO*.

TORQUATO TASSO was defcended from the illuftrious houfe of the Torregiani, lords of Bergamo, Milan, and feveral other towns in Lombardy. The Torregiani, being expelled by the Vifconti, fettled between Bergamo and Como, in the moft advantageous pofts of the mountain of Taffo, from which they took their name. This family fupported itfelf by alliances till the time of Bernardo Taffo, whofe mother was of the houfe of Cornaro. The eftate of Bernardo, the father of our poet, was no ways equal to his birth; but this deficiency, in point of fortune, was in fome meafure compenfated by the gifts of underftanding. His works in verfe and profe are recorded as monuments of his genius; and his fidelity to Ferrante of San-

---

* All the principal incidents in this Life are taken from the account given by Giovanni Batiſta Manſo, a Neapolitan, lord of Biſaccio and Pinoca. This nobleman was Taſſo's intimate friend; he had many of our Author's papers in his poſſeſſion, and being himſelf witneſs to ſeveral particulars which he relates, his authority ſeems unexceptionable.

                    ſeverino,

feverino, prince of Salerno, to whom he was entirely devoted, entitled him to the esteem of every man of honour.
This prince had made him his fecretary, and taken him
with him to Naples, where he fettled, and married Portia
di Roffi, daughter of Lucretia di Gambacorti, of one of the
moft illuftrious families in that city.

Portia was fix months gone with child, when fhe was
invited by her fifter Hippolyta to Sorrento, to pay her a vifit.
Bernardo accompanied her thither : and in this place Portia
was delivered of a fon, on the 11th day of March 1544, at
noon. The infant was baptized a few days after, in the
metropolitan church of Sorrento, by the name of Torquato.
Bernardo and Portia returned foon after to Naples, with
little Taffo, whofe birth, like Homer's, was afterwards
difputed by feveral cities that claimed the honour of it :
but it feems undeniably proved that he was born at Sorrento.

Hiftorians relate incredible things of his early and pro-
mifing genius : they tell us, that, at fix months old, he not
only fpoke and pronounced his words clearly and diftinctly,
but that he thought, reafoned, expreffed his wants, and anfwered queftions ; that there was nothing childifh in his
words, but the tone of his voice ; that he feldom laughed
or cried ; and that, even then, he gave certain tokens of that
equality of temper which fupported him fo well in his future misfortunes.

Towards the end of his third year, Bernardo his father
was obliged to follow the prince of Salerno into Germany,
which journey proved the fource of all the fufferings of
Taffo and his family. The occafion was this. Don Pedro
of Toledo, viceroy of Naples for the emperor Charles V.
had formed a defign to eftablifh the inquifition in that city.
The Neapolitans, alarmed at this, refolved to fend a depu-
tation to the emperor, and, for that purpofe, made choice
of the prince of Salerno, who feemed moft able, by his authority and riches, to make head againft the viceroy. The
prince undertook the affair ; and Bernardo Taffo accompanied him into Germany.

Before

Before his departure, Bernardo committed the care of his son to Angeluzzo, a man of learning; for it was his opinion, that a boy could not be put too soon under the tuition of men. At three years of age, they tell us, little Tasso began to study grammar; and, at four, was sent to the college of the Jesuits, where he made so rapid a progress, that at seven he was pretty well acquainted with the Latin and Greek tongues: at the same age he made public orations, and composed some pieces of poetry, of which the style is said to have retained nothing of puerility. The following lines he addressed to his mother when he left Naples to follow his father's fortune, being then only nine years of age.

> Ma dal sen de la madre empia fortuna
> Pargoletto divelse, ah di' que' baci
> Ch' ella bagnò di lagrime dolenti
> Con sospir mi rimembra, e de gli ardenti
> Preghi che sen portar l'aure fugaci,
> Che i' non dovea giunger più volto à volto
> Fra quelle braccia accolto
> Con nodi così stretti, e si tenaci,
> Lasso, e seguij con mal sicure piante
> Qual' Ascanio, o Camilla il padre errante.

Relentless Fortune in my early years
  Removes me from a mother's tender breast:
With sighs I call to mind the farewel tears
  That bath'd her kisses when my lips she press'd!
I hear her prayers with ardor breath'd to Heaven,
  Aside now wasted by the devious wind:
No more to her unhappy son 'tis given
  Th' endearments of maternal love to find!
No more her fondling arms shall round me spread;
  Far from her sight reluctant I retire;
Like young Camilla or Ascanius, led
  To trace the footsteps of my wandering sire!

                    The

The fuccefs the prince of Salerno met with in his embaffy greatly increafed his credit amongft the Neapolitans, but entirely ruined him with the viceroy, who left nothing unturned to make the emperor jealous of the great deference the people fhewed Ferrante, from which he inferred the moft dangerous confequences. He fo much exafperated the emperor againft the prince of Salerno, that Ferrante, finding there was no longer any fecurity for him at Naples, and having in vain applied to gain an audience of the emperor, retired to Rome, and renounced his allegiance to Charles V.

Bernardo Taffo would not abandon his patron in his ill fortune; neither would he leave his fon in a country where he himfelf was foon to be declared an enemy; and forefeeing he fhould never be able to return thither, he took young Torquato with him to Rome.

As foon as the departure of the prince of Salerno was known, he, and all his adherents, were declared rebels to the ftate; and what may feem very extraordinary, Torquato Taffo, though but nine years of age, was included by name in that fentence. Bernardo, following the prince of Salerno into France, committed his fon to the care of his friend and relation Mauritio Cataneo, a perfon of great ability, who affiduoufly cultivated the early difpofition of his pupil to polite literature. After the death of Sanfeverine, which happened in three or four years, Bernardo returned to Italy, and engaged in the fervice of Guglielmo Gonzaga, duke of Mantua, who had given him a preffing invitation. It was not long before he received the melancholy news of the deceafe of his wife Portia: this event determined him to fend for his fon, that they might be a mutual fupport to each other in their affliction. He had left him at Rome, becaufe his refidence in that city was highly agreeable to his mother, but that reafon now ceafing, he was refolved to be no longer deprived of the fociety, of the only child he had left; for his wife, before her death, had married his daughter to Martio Serfale, a gentleman of Sorrento.

Bernardo

Bernardo was greatly furprifed, on his fon's arrival, to fee the vaft progrefs he had made in his ftudies. He was now twelve years of age, and had, according to the teftimony of the writers of his life, entirely compleated his knowledge in the Latin and Greek tongues: he was well acquainted with the rules of rhetoric and poetry, and completely verfed in Ariftotle's ethics; but he particularly ftudied the precepts of Mauritio Cataneo, whom he ever afterwards reverenced as a fecond father. Bernardo foon determined to fend him to the univerfity of Padua, to ftudy the laws, in company with the young Scipio Gonzaga, afterwards cardinal, nearly of the fame age as himfelf. With this nobleman Taffo, then feventeen years of age, contracted a friendfhip that never ended but with his life.

He profecuted his ftudies at Padua with great diligence and fuccefs; at the fame time employing his leifure hours upon philofophy and poetry, he foon gave a public proof of his talents, by his poem of RINALDO, which he publifhed in the eighteenth year of his age.

This poem, which is of the romance kind, is divided into twelve books in ottava rima, and contains the adventures of Rinaldo, the famous Paladin of the court of Charlemain, who makes fo principal a figure in Ariofto's work, and the firft achievements of that knight for the love of the fair Clarice, whom he afterwards marries. The action of this poem precedes that of the Orlando Furiofo. It was compofed in ten months, as the author himfelf informs us in the preface, and was firft printed at Venice in the year 1562. Paolo Beni fpeaks very highly of this performance, which undoubtedly is not unworthy the early efforts of that genius which afterwards produced the Jerufalem.

Taffo's father faw with regret the fuccefs of his fon's poem: he was apprehenfive, and not without reafon, that the charms of poetry would detach him from thofe more folid ftudies, which he judged were moft likely to raife him in the world: he knew very well, by his own experience, that the greateft fkill in poetry will not advance a man's private fortune. He was not deceived in his conjecture;

b 4

Torquato,

Torquato, infensibly carried away by his predominant paf-
sion, followed the examples of Petrarch, Boccace, Ariosto,
and others, who, contrary to the remonstrances of their
friends, quitted the feverer studies of the law for the more
pleasing entertainment of poetical composition. In short,
he entirely gave himself up to the study of poetry and philofophy. His first poem extended his reputation through all
Italy; but his father was so displeased with his conduct,
that he went to Padua on purpose to reprimand him.
Though he spoke with great vehemence, and made use of
several barsh expressions, Torquato heard him without in-
terrupting him, and his composure contributed not a little
to increase his father's displeasure. " Tell me" (said Bernardo) " of what use is that vain philosophy, upon which
" you pride yourself so much?" " It has enabled me" (said
Tasso modestly) " to endure the harshness of your re-
" proofs."

The resolution Tasso had taken to devote himself to the
Muses, was known all over Italy: the principal persons of
the city and college of Bologna invited him thither by means
of Pietro Donato Cesi, then vice-legate, and afterwards legate. But Tasso had not long resided there, when he was
pressed by Scipio Gonzaga, elected prince of the academy ef-
tablished at Padua, under the name of Etherei, to return to
that city. He could not withstand this solicitation, and
Bologna being at that time the scene of civil commotion, he
was the more willing to seek elsewhere for the repose he
loved. He was received with extreme joy by all the academy, and being incorporated into that society, at the age of
twenty years, took upon himself the name of Pentito; by
which he seemed to shew that he repented of all the time
which he had employed in the study of the law.

In this retreat he applied himself afresh to philosophy
and poetry; and soon became a perfect master of both: it
was this happy mixture of his studies that made him an
enemy to all kinds of licentiousness. An oration was made
one day in the academy upon the nature of love; the orator
treated his subject in a very masterly manner, but with too

little

little regard to decency in the opinion of Tasso, who, being asked what he thought of the discourse, replied, " that it " was a pleasing poison."

Here Tasso formed the design of his celebrated poem, JERUSALEM DELIVERED; he invented the fable, disposed the different parts, and determined to dedicate this work to the glory of the house of Estè. He was greatly esteemed by Alphonso II. the last duke of Ferrara, that great patron of learning and learned men, and by his brother, cardinal Luigi. There was a sort of contest between these two brothers, in relation to the poem : the cardinal imagined that he had a right to be the Mecænas of all Tasso's works, as RINALDO, his first piece, had been dedicated to him : the duke, on the other hand, thought that, as his brother had already received his share of honour, he ought not to be offended at seeing the name of Alphonso at the head of the JERUSALEM DELIVERED. Tasso for three or four years suspended his determination : at length, being earnestly pressed by both the brothers to take up his residence in Ferrara, he suffered himself to be prevailed upon. The duke gave him an apartment in his palace, where he lived in peace and affluence, and pursued his design of compleating his JERUSALEM *, which he now resolved to dedicate to Alphonso. The duke, who was desirous of fixing Tasso near him, had thoughts of marrying him advantageously, but he always evaded any proposal of that kind : though he appeared peculiarly devoted to Alphonso, yet he neglected not to pay his court to the cardinal.

The name of Tasso now became famous through all Europe : and the caresses he received from Charles IX. in a journey he made to France † with cardinal Luigi, who went thither in quality of legate, shew that his reputation was not confined to his own country.

We cannot perhaps give a more striking instance of the regard that monarch had for him, than in the following story. A man of letters, and a poet of some repute, had un-

* Ann. æt. 23.   † Ann. æt. 27.

fortunately

fortunately been guilty of some enormous crime, for which he was condemned to suffer death: Tasso, touched with compassion, was resolved to petition the king for his pardon. He went to the palace, where he heard that orders had just been given to put the sentence immediately into execution. This did not discourage Tasso, who, presenting himself before the king, said: "I come to entreat your majesty that you would put to death a wretch, who has brought philosophy to shame, by shewing that she can make no stand against human depravity." The king, touched with the justness of this reflection, granted the criminal his life.

The king asked him one day, whom he judged superior to all others in happiness: he answered, God. The king then desired to know his opinion by what men resemble God in his happiness, whether by sovereign power, or by their capacity of doing good to others. A man more interested than Tasso might have said, that kings shew their greatness by dispensing their benefactions to others: but he eluded the discourse; and replied, "that men could resemble God only by their virtue."

Another time, in a conversation held before the king by several learned men, it was disputed what condition in life was the most unfortunate. "In my opinion" (said Tasso) "the most unfortunate condition is that of an impatient old man depressed with poverty; for," added he, "the state of that person is doubtless very deplorable, who has neither the gifts of fortune to preserve him from want, nor the principles of philosophy to support himself under affliction."

The cardinal's legation being finished, Tasso returned to Ferrara *, where he applied himself to finish his JERUSALEM, and in the mean time published his AMINTA, a pastoral comedy †, which was received with universal applause. This performance was looked upon as a master-piece in its kind, and is the original of the PASTOR FIDO and FILLI DI SCIRO.

It was not easy to imagine that Tasso could so well paint

* Ann. æt. 18.   † Ann. æt. 29.

the effects of Love, without having himself felt that passion: it began to be suspected that, like another Ovid, he had raised his desires too high, and it was thought that in many of his verses he gave hints of that kind; particularly in the following sonnet.

Se d'Icara leggesti, e di Fetonte
   Ben sai còme lu'n cadde in questo fiume
   Quando portar de l'Orientè il lume
   Volle, e di rai de sol cinger la fronte:
E l'altro in mar, che troppo ardite, e pronte
   A volo alzo le sue cerate piume,
   E così va chi di tentar presume
   Strade nel ciel per fama a pena conte.
Ma, chi dee paventare in alta impresa,
   S'avvien, ch'amor l'affide? e che non puote
   Amor, che non catena il cielo unisce?
Egli giù trahe de le celesti rote
   Di terrena belta Diana accesa
   E d'Ida il bel fanciullo al ciel rapisce.

Oft have we heard, in Po's imperial tide
   How hapless Phaëton was headlong thrown,
Who durst aspire the sun's bright steeds to guide,
   And wreathe his brows with splendors not his own!
Oft have we heard, how 'midst th' Icarian main
   Fell the rash youth who try'd too bold a flight;
Thus shall it fare with him, who seeks in vain
   On mortal wings to reach th' empyreal height.
But who, inspir'd by love, can dangers fear?
What cannot love that guides the rolling sphere;
   Whose powerful magic earth and heaven controls?
Love brought Diana from the starry sky,
Smit with the beauties of a mortal eye;
   Love snatch'd the Boy of Ida to the poles.

There were at the duke's court three Leonoras, equally witty and beautiful, though of different quality. The first

was

was Leonora of Estè, sister to the duke, who, having refused the most advantageous matches, lived unmarried with Lauretta, duchess of Urbino, her elder sister, who was separated from her husband, and resided at her brother's court. Tasso had a great attachment to this lady, who, on her side, honoured him with her esteem and protection. She was wise, generous, and not only well read in elegant literature, but even versed in the more abstruse sciences. All these perfections were undoubtedly observed by Tasso, who was one of the most assiduous of her courtiers: and it appearing by his verses that he was touched with the charms of a Leonora, they tell us that we need not seek any further for the object of his passion.

The second Leonora that was given him for a mistress was the countess of San Vitale, daughter of the count of Sala, who lived at that time at the court of Ferrara, and passed for one of the most accomplished persons in Italy. Those who imagined that Tasso would not presume to lift his eyes to his master's sister, supposed that he loved this lady. It is certain that he had frequent opportunities of discoursing with her, and that she had frequently been the subject of his verses.

The third Leonora was a lady in the service of the princess Leonora of Estè. This person was thought by some to be the most proper object of the poet's gallantry. Tasso, several times, employed his muse in her service: in one of his pieces he confesses that considering the princess as too high for his hope, he had fixed his affection upon her, as of a condition more suitable to his own. But if any thing can be justly drawn from this particular, it seems rather to strengthen the opinion, that his desires, at least at one time, had aspired to a greater height. The verses referred to above are as follow :

O con le Grazie eletta, e con gli Amori,
Fanciulla avventurosa :
A servir a colei, che Dia somiglia :
Poi che' l mio sguardo in lei mira, e non osa,

I' raggi e gli splendori,
    E' l bel seren de gli occhi, e de le ciglia,
Nè l'alta meraviglia,
Che ne discopre il lampeggiar del riso;
Nè quanto ha de celeste il petto, e'l volto;
Io gli occhi a te rivolto,
E nel tuo vezzosetto, e lieto viso
Dolcemente m' affiso.
Bruna sei tu, ma bella,
Qual virgine viola: e del tuo vago
Sembiante io si m' appago,
Che non disdegno Signoria d'Ancella.

O! by the Graces, by the Loves design'd,
    In happy hour t' enjoy an envy'd place:
Attendant on the fairest of her kind,
    Whose charms excel the charms of human race!

Fain would I view—but dare not lift my sight
    To mark the splendor of her piercing eyes;
Her heavenly smiles, her bosom's dazzling white,
    Her nameless graces that the soul surprise.

To thee I then direct my humbler gaze;
    To thee uncensur'd may my hopes aspire:
Less awful are the sweets thy look displays;
    I view, and, kindling as I view, desire.

Though brown thy hue, yet lovely is thy frame;
    (So blooms some violet, the virgin's care!)
I burn—yet blush not to confess my flame,
    Nor scorn the empire of a menial fair.

However, it appears difficult to determine with certainty
in relation to Tasso's passion; especially when we consider
the privilege allowed to poets: though M. Mirabaud [*]
makes no scruple to mention it as a circumstance almost cer-

* Abrégé de la Vie du Tasse.

tain, and fixes it without hesitation on the princess Leonora. Tasso, himself, in several of his poems, seems to endeavour to throw an obscurity over his passion, as in the following lines:

> Tre gran donne vid' io, ch'in esser belle
>   Monstran d'sparità, ma somigliante
>   Si che ne gli atti, e'n ogni lor sembiante
>   Scriver Natura par'; Noi siam sorelle.
> Ben ciascun' io lodai, pur una d'elle
>   Mi piacque sì, ch'io ne divenni Amante,
>   Et ancor fia, ch'io ne sospiri, e cante,
>   E'l mio foco, e'l suo nome alzi à le stelle
> Lei sol vagheggio; e se pur l'altre io miro,
>   Guardo nel vago altrui quel, ch'è in lei vago,
>   E ne gl' Idoli suoi vien ch'io l'adore:
> Ma contanto somiglia al ver l'imago
>   Ch'erro, e dolc' è l'error; pur ne sospiro,
>   Come d'ingiusta Idolatria d'Amore.

SONNET.

> Three courtly dames before my presence stood;
>   All lovely form'd, though differing in their grace:
> Yet each resembled each; for nature show'd
>   A sister's air in every mien and face.
>
> Each maid I prais'd; but one above the rest,
>   Soon kindled in my heart the lover's fire:
> For her these sighs still issue from my breast;
>   Her name, her beauties still my song inspire.
>
> Yet though to her alone my thoughts are due,
> Reflected in the rest her charms I view,
>   And in her semblance still the nymph adore:
> Delusion sweet! from this to that I rove;
> But, while I wander, sigh, and fear to prove
>   A traitor thus to Love's almighty power!

In the mean while Tasso proceeded with his JERUSALEM, which he completed in the thirtieth year of his age: but this

poem

poem was not published by his own authority; it was printed againſt his will, as ſoon as he had finiſhed the laſt book, and before he had time to give the reviſals and corrections that a work of ſuch a nature required. The public had already ſeen ſeveral parts, which had been ſent into the world by the authority of his patrons. The ſucceſs of this work was prodigious: it was tranſlated into the Latin, French, Spaniſh, and even the Oriental languages, almoſt as ſoon as it appeared; and it may be ſaid, that no ſuch performance ever before raiſed its reputation to ſuch a height in ſo ſmall a ſpace of time.

But the ſatisfaction which Taſſo muſt feel, in ſpite of all his philoſophy, at the applauſe of the public, was ſoon diſturbed by a melancholy event *. Bernardo Taſſo, who ſpent his old age in tranquillity at Oſtia upon the Po, the government of which place had been given him by the duke of Mantua, fell ſick. As ſoon as this news reached his ſon, he immediately went to him, attended him with the moſt filial regard, and ſcarce ever ſtirred from his bedſide during the whole time of his illneſs: but all theſe cares were ineffectual; Bernardo, oppreſſed with age, and overcome by the violence of his diſtemper, paid the unavoidable tribute to nature, to the great affliction of Torquato. The duke of Mantua, who had a ſincere eſteem for Bernardo, cauſed him to be interred, with much pomp, in the church of St. Egidius at Mantua, with this ſimple inſcription on his tomb.

OSSA BERNARDI TASSI.

This death ſeemed to forebode other misfortunes to Taſſo; for the remainder of his life proved almoſt one continued ſeries of vexation and affliction. About this time a ſwarm of critics began to attack his JERUSALEM, and the academy of Cruſca, in particular, publiſhed a criticiſm of his poem, in which they ſcrupled not to prefer the rhapſodies of Pulci and Boyardo to the JERUSALEM DELIVERED.

Ann. æt. 31.

During

During Tasso's residence in the duke's court, he had con-tracted an intimacy with a gentleman of Ferrara [*], and having entrusted him with some transactions of a very delicate nature, this person was so treacherous as to speak of them again.   Tasso reproached his friend with his indiscretion, who received his expostulation in such a manner, that Tasso was so far exasperated as to strike him : a challenge immediately ensued : the two opponents met at St. Leonard's gate, but, while they were engaged, three brothers of Tasso's antagonist came in and basely fell all at once upon Tasso, who defended himself so gallantly that he wounded two of them, and kept his ground against the others, till some people came in and separated them.   This affair made a great noise at Ferrara : nothing was talked of but the valour of Tasso ; and it became a sort of proverb, " That Tasso with his pen and his sword was superior to " all men [†]."

'The duke, being informed of the quarrel, expressed great resentment against the four brothers, banished them from his dominions, and confiscated their estates ; at the same time he caused Tasso to be put under arrest, declaring he did it to screen him from any future designs of his enemies. Tasso was extremely mortified to see himself thus confined ; he imputed his detention to a very different cause from what was pretended, and feared an ill use might be made of what had passed, to ruin him in the duke's opinion.

Though writers have left us very much in the dark with regard to the real motives that induced the duke to keep Tasso in confinement, yet, every thing being weighed, it seems highly probable that the affair of a delicate nature, said to have been divulged by his friend, must have related to the princess Leonora, the duke's sister : and indeed it will be extremely difficult, from any other consideration, to account for the harsh treatment he received from a prince

----

* Ann. Æt. 33.

† " Con la penna e con la spada
   " Nessun val quanto Torquato."

whe

who had before shewn him such peculiar marks of esteem
and friendship. However, Tasso himself had undoubtedly
secret apprehensions that increased upon him every day,
while the continual attacks, which were made upon his
credit as an author, not a little contributed to heighten his
melancholy. At length he resolved to take the first opportunity to fly from his prison, for so he esteemed it, which,
after about a year's detention, he effected, and retired to
Turin, where he endeavoured to remain concealed; but
notwithstanding all his precautions, he was soon known and
recommended to the duke of Savoy, who received him into
his palace, and shewed him every mark of esteem and affection. But Tasso's apprehensions still continued; he thought
that the duke of Savoy would not refuse to give him up to
the duke of Ferrara, or sacrifice the friendship of that prince
to the safety of a private person. Full of these imaginations
he set out for Rome *, alone and unprovided with necessa-
ries for such a journey. At his arrival there he went directly to his old friend Mauritio Cataneo, who received him
in such a manner as entirely to obliterate for some time the
remembrance of the fatigue and uneasiness he had under-
gone. He was not only welcomed by Cataneo, but the
whole city of Rome seemed to rejoice at the presence of so
extraordinary a person. He was visited by princes, cardinals, prelates, and by all the learned in general. But the
desire of revisiting his native country, and seeing his sister
Cornelia, soon made him uneasy in this situation. He left
his friend Mauritio Cataneo one evening, without giving
him notice, and, beginning his journey on foot, arrived by
night at the mountains of Veletri, where he took up his
lodging with some shepherds: the next morning, disguising himself in the habit of one of these people, he continued
his way, and in four days time reached Gaieta, almost spent
with fatigue; here he embarked on board a vessel bound for
Sorrento, at which place he arrived in safety the next day.
He entered the city and went directly to his sister's house:

Ann. æt. 34.

VOL. I.cshe

she was a widow, and the two sons she had by her husband being at that time absent, Tasso found her with only some of her female attendants. He advanced towards her, without discovering himself, and pretending he came with news from her brother, gave her a letter which he had prepared for that purpose. This letter informed her that her brother's life was in great danger, and that he begged her to make use of all the interest her tenderness might suggest to her, in order to procure letters of recommendation from some powerful person to avert the threatened misfortune. For further particulars of the affair, she was referred to the messenger who brought her this intelligence. The lady, terrified at the news, earnestly entreated him to give her a detail of her brother's misfortune. The feigned messenger then gave her so interesting an account of the pretended story, that, unable to contain her affliction, she fainted away. Tasso was sensibly touched at this convincing proof of his sister's affection, and repented that he had gone so far: he began to comfort her, and, removing her fears by little and little, at last discovered himself to her. Her joy at seeing a brother, whom she tenderly loved, was inexpressible: after the first salutations were over, she was very desirous to know the occasion of his disguising himself in that manner. Tasso acquainted her with his reasons, and, at the same time, giving her to understand, that he would willingly remain with her unknown to the world, Cornelia, who desired nothing further than to acquiesce in his pleasure, sent for her children and some of her nearest relations, whom she thought might be entrusted with the secret. They agreed that Tasso should pass for a relation of theirs, who came from Bergamo to Naples upon his private business, and from thence had come to Sorrento to pay them a visit. After this precaution, Tasso took up his residence at his sister's house, where he lived for some time in tranquillity, entertaining himself with his two nephews Antonio and Alessandro Sersale, children of great hopes. He continued not long in this repose before he received repeated letters from the princess Leonora of Este, who was ac-

quainted

quainted with the place of his retreat, to return to Ferrara: he resolved to obey the summons, and took leave of his sister, telling her he was going to return a voluntary prisoner. In his way he passed through Rome, where having been detained some time with a dangerous fever, he repaired from thence to Ferrara, in company with Gualingo, embassador from the duke to the pope.

Concerning the motive of Tasso's return to Ferrara, authors do not altogether agree: some declare that, soon wearied of living in obscurity, and growing impatient to retrieve the duke's favour, he had resolved, of his own accord, to throw himself on that prince's generosity: this opinion seems indeed drawn from Tasso's own words, in a letter written by him to the duke of Urbino, in which he declares "that he had endeavoured to make his peace with the duke, "and had for that purpose written severally to him, the "dutchess of Ferrara, the dutchess of Urbino, and the "princess Leonora; yet never received any answer but "from the last, who assured him it was not in her power to "render him any service." We see here that Tasso acknowledges himself the receipt of a letter from the princess; and in regard to what he says to be the purport of it, it is highly reasonable to suppose, that he would be very cautious of divulging the real contents to the duke of Urbino, when his affairs with that lady were so delicately circumstanced. This apparent care to conceal the nature of his correspondence with her, seems to corroborate the former suppositions of his uncommon attachment to her; and when all circumstances are considered, we believe it will appear more than probable that he returned to Ferrara at the particular injunction of Leonora.

The duke received Tasso with great seeming satisfaction, and gave him fresh marks of his esteem: but this was not all that Tasso expected; his great desire was to be master of his own works, and he was very earnest that his writings might be restored to him which were in the duke's possession; but this was what he could by no means obtain: his enemies had gained such an ascendency over the mind of

Alphonso

Alphonso, that they made him believe, or pretend to believe, that the poet had loft all his fire, and that in his prefent fituation he was incapable of producing any thing new, or of correcting his poems: he therefore exhorted him to think only of leading a quiet and eafy life for the future: but Taffo was fenfibly vexed at this proceeding, and believed the duke wanted him entirely to relinquifh his ftudies, and pafs the remainder of his days in idlenefs and obfcurity. " He would endeavour" (fays he, in his letter to the duke of Urbino) " to make me a fhameful deferter of Parnaffus for the gardens of Epicurus, for fcenes of pleafures unknown to Virgil, Catullus, Horace, and even Lucretius himfelf."

Taffo reiterated his entreaties to have his writings reftored to him, but the duke continued inflexible, and, to complete our poet's vexation, all accefs to the princeffes was denied him; fatigued at length with ufelefs remonftrances, he once more quitted Ferrara, and fled (as he expreffes it himfelf) like another Bias, leaving behind him even his books and manufcripts.

He then went to Mantua, where he found duke Guglielmo in a decrepid age, and little difpofed to protect him againft the duke of Ferrara: the prince Vincentio Gonzaga received him indeed with great careffes, but was too young to take him under his protection. From thence he went to Padua and Venice, but carrying with him in every part his fears of the duke of Ferrara, he at laft had recourfe to the duke of Urbino[a], who fhewed him great kindnefs, but perhaps was very little inclined to embroil himfelf with his brother-in-law, on fuch an account: he advifed Taffo rather to return to Ferrara, which counfel he took, refolving once more to try his fortune with the duke.

Alphonfo, it may be, exafperated at Taffo's flight, and pretending to believe that application to ftudy had entirely diforderd his underftanding, and that a ftrict regimen was neceffary to reftore him to his former ftate, caufed him to

* Ann. æt. 35.

be strictly confined in the hospital of St. Anne. Tasso tried every method to soften the duke and obtain his liberty; but the duke coldly answered those who applied to him, " that instead of concerning themselves with the complaints of a person in his condition, who was very little capable of judging for his own good, they ought rather to exhort him patiently to submit to such remedies, as were judged proper for his circumstances."

This confinement threw Tasso into the deepest despair; he abandoned himself to his misfortunes, and the methods that were made use of for the cure of his pretended madness had nearly thrown him into an absolute delirium. His imagination was so disturbed that he believed the cause of his distemper was not natural; he sometimes fancied himself haunted by a spirit, that continually disordered his books and papers; and these strange notions were perhaps strengthened by the tricks that were played him by his keeper. While Tasso continued in this melancholy situation, he is said to have written the following elegantly simple and affecting lines, which cannot well be translated into English verse :

> Tu che ne vai in Pindo
> Ivi pende mia cetra ad un cipresso,
> Salutala in mio nome, e dille poi
> Ch'io son dagl' anni e da fortuna oppresso *.

This second confinement of Tasso was much longer than the first. He applied in vain to the pope, the emperor, and all the powers of Italy, to obtain his liberty : till, at last, after seven years imprisonment, he gained what he so ardently wished for, in the following manner.

Cæsar of Estè having brought his new spouse, Virginia of Medicis, to Ferrara, all the relations of that illustrious house assembled together on this occasion, and nothing was seen in the whole city but festivals and rejoicings. Vin-

---

* Thou that goest to Pindus, where my harp hangs on a cypress, salute it in my name, and say that I am oppressed with years and misfortunes.

cento

cento Gonzaga, prince of Mantua, particularly diftinguifhed himfelf among the great perfonages then at the duke's
court. This nobleman interceded fo earneftly with Alphonfo for Taffo's liberty, that he at laft obtained it *, and
carried him with him to Mantua, where he lived with him,
fometime after the death of duke Guglielmo, highly fa-
voured.

It is faid that the young prince, who was naturally gay,
being defirous to authorife his pleafures by the example of a
philofopher, introduced one day into Taffo's company three
fifters, to fing and play upon inftruments; thefe ladies were
all very handfome, but not of the moft rigid virtue. After
fome fhort difcourfe, he told Taffo, that he fhould take two
of them away, and would leave one behind, and bade him
take his choice. Taffo anfwered; " that it coft Paris
very dear to give the preference to one of the Goddeffes,
and therefore, with his permiffion, he defigned to retain the
three." The prince took him at his word, and departed;
when Taffo, after a little converfation, difmiffed them all
handfomely with prefents.

At laft, weary of living in a continual ftate of dependence,
he refolved to retire to Naples and endeavour to recover his
mother's jointure, which had been feized upon by her relations when he went into exile with his father Bernardo.
This appeared the only means to place him in the condition
of life he fo much defired. He applied to his friends, and
having procured favourable letters to the viceroy, he took
leave of the duke of Mantua and repaired to Bergamo †,
where he ftayed fome time, and from thence went to Naples ‡.

While Taffo continued at Naples, dividing his time between his ftudies and the profecution of his law-fuit, the
young count of Palena, by whom he was highly efteemed,
perfuaded him to take up his refidence with him for fome
time : but in this affair he had not confulted the prince of
Conca, his father, who, though he had a value for Taffo,

<hr>

* Ann. Æt. 41.   † Ann. Æt. 43.   ‡ Ann. Æt. 44.

yet

yet could not approve of his son's receiving into his house
the only person that remained of a family once devoted to
the prince of Salerno.   A contention being likely to ensue,
on this account, betwixt the father and son, Tasso, with his
usual goodness of disposition, to remove all occasion of
dispute, withdrew from Naples, and retired to Bisaccio *,
with his friend Manso, in whose company he lived some time
with great tranquillity.

In this place Manso had an opportunity to examine the
singular effects of Tasso's melancholy; and often disputed
with him concerning a familiar spirit, which he pretended
to converse with.   Manso endeavoured in vain to persuade
his friend that the whole was the illusion of a disturbed imagination : but the latter was strenuous in maintaining the
reality of what he asserted; and, to convince Manso, desired him to be present at one of those mysterious conversa-
tions.   Manso had the complaisance to meet him next day,
and while they were engaged in discourse, on a sudden he
observed that Tasso kept his eyes fixed upon a window, and
remained in a manner immoveable : he called him by his
name several times, but received no answer : at last Tasso
cried out, " There is the friendly spirit who is come to
converse with me : look, and you will be convinced of the
truth of all that I have said."   Manso heard him with sur-
prise : he looked, but saw nothing except the sun-beams
darting through the window : he cast his eyes all over the
room, but could perceive nothing, and was just going to
ask where the pretended spirit was, when he heard Tasso
speak with great earnestness, sometimes putting questions
to the spirit, and sometimes giving answers, delivering the
whole in such a pleasing manner, and with such elevated
expressions, that he listened with admiration, and had not
the least inclination to interrupt him.   At last this uncommon conversation ended with the departure of the spirit, as
appeared by Tasso's words; who turning towards Manso,
asked him if his doubts were removed.   Manso was more

* Ann. Æt. 45.

c 4

amazed

amazed than ever; he scarce knew what to think of his
friend's situation, and waved any further conversation on
the subject.

At the approach of winter they returned to Naples, when
the prince of Palena again pressed Tasso to reside with him;
but Tasso, who judged it highly unadviseable to comply
with his request, resolved to retire to Rome, and wait there
the issue of his law-suit. He lived in that city about a
year in high esteem with pope Sextus V. when being invited to Florence by Ferdinando, grand duke of Tuscany,
who had been cardinal at Rome, when Tasso first resided
there, and who now employed the pope's interest to procure
a visit from him: he could not withstand such solicitations,
but went to Florence, where he met with a most gracious
reception *. Yet not all the caresses he received at the
duke's court, nor all the promises of that prince, could
overcome his love for his native country, or lessen the ardent desire he had to lead a retired and independent life.
He therefore took his leave of the grand duke, who would
have loaded him with presents; but Tasso, as usual, could
be prevailed upon to accept of no more than was necessary
for his present occasions. He returned to Naples by the
way of Rome †, and the old prince of Conca dying about
this time, the young count of Palena prevailed upon Tasso,
by the mediation of Manso, to accept of an apartment in
his palace. Here he applied himself to a correction of his
JERUSALEM, or rather to compose a new work entitled
JERUSALEM CONQUERED, which he had begun during his
first residence at Naples. The prince of Conca, being jealous left any one should deprive him of the poet and poem,
caused him to be so narrowly watched that Tasso observed
it, and being displeased at such a proceeding, left the
prince's palace and retired to his friend Manso's, where he
lived master of himself and his actions; yet he still continued upon good terms with the prince of Conca.

* Ann. Æt. 45.   † Ann. Æt. 47.

In

In a short time after he published his JERUSALEM CON-
QUERED, which poem, as a French writer observes *, "is
a sufficient proof of the injustice of the criticisms that have
been passed upon his JERUSALEM DELIVERED, since the
JERUSALEM CONQUERED, in which he endeavoured to
conform himself to the taste of his critics, was not received with the same approbation as the former poem,
where he had entirely given himself up to the enthu-
siasm of his genius." He had likewise designed a third
correction of the same poem, which, as we are informed,
was to have been partly compounded of the JERUSALEM
DELIVERED and CONQUERED; but this work was never
completed. The above-cited author remarks, " that in all
probality, this last performance would not have equalled
the first :" and indeed our poet seems to owe his fame to the
JERUSALEM DELIVERED, the second poem upon that subject being little known.

Manso's garden commanded a full prospect of the sea:
Tasso and his friend being one day in a summer-house with
Scipio Belprato, Manso's brother-in-law, observing the
waves agitated with a furious storm, Belprato said, " that
he was astonished at the rashness and folly of men, who
would expose themselves to the rage of so merciless an ele-
ment, when such numbers had suffered shipwreck." " And
yet" (said Tasso) " we every night go without fear to bed,
where so many die every hour. Believe me, death will find
us in all parts, and those places, that appear the least exposed, are not always the most secure from his attacks."

While Tasso lived with his friend Manso, cardinal Hip-
polito Aldobrandidi succeeded to the papacy by the name
of Clement VIII. His two nephews, Cynthio and Pietro
Aldobrandini, were created cardinals : the first, afterwards
called the cardinal of St. George, was the eldest, a great
patron of science, and a favourer of learned men : he had
known Tasso when he resided last at Rome, and had the
greatest esteem for him ; and now so earnestly invited him

* Vie de Tasse, à Amsterdam 1695.

to Rome, that he could not refuse, but once more abandoned his peaceful retreat at Naples.

The confines of the Ecclesiastical State being infested with banditti, travellers, for security, go together in large companies. Tasso joined himself to one of these; but when they came within sight of Mola, a little town near Gaieta, they received intelligence that Sciarra, a famous captain of robbers, was near at hand with a great body of men. Tasso was of opinion, that they should continue their journey, and endeavour to defend themselves, if attacked: however, this advice was over-ruled, and they threw themselves for safety into Mola, in which place they remained for some time in a manner blocked up by Sciarra. But this outlaw, hearing that Tasso was one of the company, sent a message to assure him that he might pass in safety, and offered himself to conduct him wherever he pleased. Tasso returned him thanks, but declined accepting the offer, not chusing, perhaps, to rely on the word of a person of such character. Sciarra, upon this, sent a second message, by which he informed Tasso, that, upon his account, he would withdraw his men, and leave the ways open. He accordingly did so, and Tasso, continuing his journey, arrived without any accident at Rome, where he was most graciously welcomed by the two cardinals and the pope himself. Tasso applied himself in a particular manner to cardinal Cynthio, who had been the means of his coming to Rome; yet he neglected not to make his court to cardinal Aldobrandini, and he very frequently conversed with both of them. One day the two cardinals held an assembly of several prelates, to consult, among other things, of some method to put a stop to the licenfe of the Pasquinades. One proposed that Pasquin's statue should be broken to pieces and cast into the river. But Tasso's opinion being asked, he said, " it would be much more prudent to let it remain where it was; for otherwise from the fragments of the statue would be bred an infinite number of frogs on the banks of the Tyber, that would never cease to croak day and night." The pope, to whom cardinal Aldobrandini

related

related what had paffed, interrogated Taffo upon the fubject. " It is true, holy father," (faid he) " fuch was my
opinion; and I fhall add moreover, that if your holinefs
would filence Pafquin, the only way is to put fuch people
into employments as may give no occafion to any libels or
difaffected difcourfe."

At laft, being again difgufted with the life of a courtier,
he obtained permiffion to retire to Naples to profecute his
law-fuit*. At his arrival there, he took up his lodging in the
convent of St. Severin, with the fathers of St. Benedict.

Thus was Taffo once more in a ftate of tranquillity and
retirement, fo highly agreeable to his difpofition, when cardinal Cynthio again found means to recal him, by prevailing
on the pope to give him the honour of being folemnly
crowned with laurel in the capitol. Though Taffo himfelf was not in the leaft defirous of fuch pomp, yet he
yielded to the perfuafion of others, particularly of his dear
friend Manfo, to whom he protefted that he went merely at
his earneft defire, not with any expectation of the promifed
triumph, which he had a fecret prefage would never be. He
was greatly affected at parting from Manfo, and took his
leave of him as of one he fhould never fee again.

In his way he paffed by Mount Caffino, to pay his devo-
tion to the relicks of St. Benedict, for whom he had a particular veneration. He fpent the feftival of Chriftmas in
that monaftery, and from thence repaired to Rome, where he
arrived in the beginning of the year 1595*. He was met at
the entrance of that city by many prelates and perfons of
diftinction, and was afterwards introduced, by the two cardinals, Cynthio and Pietro, to the prefence of the pope,
who was pleafed to tell him, " that his merit would add as
much honour to the laurel he was going to receive, as that
crown had formerly given to thofe on whom it had hitherto
been beftowed."

Nothing was now thought of but the approaching fo-
lemnity: orders were given to decorate not only the pope's

---

* Ann. Æt. 50.   † Ann. Æt. 51.

palace and the capitol, but all the principal ſtreets through
which the proceſſion was to paſs. Yet Taſſo appeared little
moved with theſe preparations, which he ſaid would be in
vain: and being ſhewn a ſonnet compoſed upon the occaſion by his relation, Hercole Taſſo, he anſwered by the following verſe of Seneca:

Magnifica verba mors propé admota excutit.

His preſages were but too true, for, while they waited for
fair weather to celebrate the ſolemnity, cardinal Cynthio
fell ill, and continued for ſome time indiſpoſed: and, as
ſoon as the cardinal began to recover, Taſſo himſelf was
ſeized with his laſt ſickneſs.

Though he had only completed his fifty-firſt year, his
ſtudies and misfortunes had brought on a premature old age.
Being perſuaded that his end was approaching, he reſolved
to ſpend the few days he had yet to live in the monaſtery of
St. Onuphrius. He was carried thither in cardinal Cynthio's coach, and received with the utmoſt tenderneſs by the
prior and brethren of that order. His diſtemper was now ſo
far increaſed and his ſtrength ſo exhauſted, that all kind
of medicine proved ineffectual. On the tenth of April he
was taken with a violent fever, occaſioned perhaps by having eat ſome milk, a kind of aliment he was particularly
fond of. His life now ſeemed in imminent danger, the moſt
famous phyſicians in Rome tried all their art, but in vain, to
relieve him: he grew worſe and worſe every day; Rinaldini,
the pope's phyſician and Taſſo's intimate friend, having informed him that his laſt hour was near at hand, Taſſo embraced him tenderly, and with a compoſed countenance returned him thanks for his tidings; then looking up to heaven, he " acknowledged the goodneſs of God, who was at
laſt pleaſed to bring him ſafe into port after ſo long a
ſtorm." From that time his mind ſeemed entirely diſen-
tangled from earthly affairs: he received the ſacrament in
the chapel of the monaſtery, being conducted thither by the
brethren. When he was brought back to his chamber, he
was aſked where he wiſhed to be interred; he anſwered in
the

the church of St. Onuphrius; and being defired to leave
fome memorial of his will in writing, and to dictate himfelf
the epitaph that fhould be engraven on his tomb; he fmiled
and faid, " that in regard to the firft, he had little worldly
goods to leave, and as to the fecond, a plain ftone would fuffice to cover him." He left cardinal Cynthio his heir, and
defired that his own picture might be given to Giovanni
Baptifta Manfo, which had been drawn by his direction.
At length having attained the fourteenth day of his illnefs,
he received the extreme unction. Cardinal Cynthio hearing that he was at the laft extremity, came to vifit him, and
brought him the pope's benediction, a grace never conferred
in this manner but on cardinals and perfons of the firft diftinction. Taffo acknowledged this honour with great de-
votion and humility, and faid, " that this was the crown he
came to receive at Rome." The cardinal having afked him,
"if he had any thing further to defire," he replied," the only
favour he had now to beg of him, was, that he would col-
lect together the copies of all his works (particularly his Jerusalem Delivered, which he efteemed moft imperfect)
and commit them to the flames: this tafk, he confefled,
might be found fomething difficult, as thofe pieces were dif-
perfed abroad in fo many different places, but yet he trufted
it would not be found altogether impracticable." He was
fo earneft in his requeft, that the cardinal, unwilling to dif-
compofe him by a refufal, gave him fuch a doubtful anfwer
as led him to believe that his defire would be complied with.
Taffo then requefting to be left alone, the cardinal took his
farewel of him with tears in his eyes, leaving with him his
confeffor and fome of the brethren of the monaftery. In
this condition he continued all night, and till the middle of
next day, the 25th of April, being the feftival of St. Mark,
when finding himfelf fainting, he embraced his crucifix, ut-
tering thefe words: *In manus tuas, Domine*—but expired before he could finifh the fentence.

Taffo was tall and well fhaped, his complexion fair, but
rather pale through ficknefs and ftudy; the hair of his head

was of a chefnut colour, but that of his beard fomewhat lighter, thick and bufhy; his forehead fquare and high, his head large, and the fore part of it, towards the end of his life, altogether bald; his eye-brows were dark; his eyes full, piercing, and of a clear blue; his nofe large, his lips thin, his teeth well fet and white; his neck well proportioned; his breaft full; his fhoulders broad, and all his limbs more finewy than flefhy. His voice was ftrong, clear, and folemn; he fpoke with deliberation, and generally reiterated his laft words: he feldom laughed, and never to excefs. He was very expert in the exercifes of the body. In his oratory, he ufed little action, and rather pleafed by the beauty and force of his expreffions, than by the graces of gefture and utterance, that compofe fo great a part of elocution. Such was the exterior of Taffo: as to his mental qualities, he appears to have been a great genius, and a foul elevated above the common rank of mankind. It is faid of him, that there never was a fcholar more humble, a wit more devout, or a man more amiable in fociety. Never fatisfied with his works, even when they rendered his name famous throughout the world; always fatisfied with his condition, even when he wanted every thing; entirely relying on Providence and his friends; without malevolence towards his greateft enemies; only wifhing for riches that he might be ferviceable to others, and making a fcruple to receive or keep any thing himfelf that was not abfolutely neceffary. So blamelefs and regular a life could not but be ended by a peaceable death, which carried him off Ann. 1595, in the fifty-fecond year of his age.

He was buried the fame evening, without pomp, according to his defire, in the church of St. Onuphrius, and his body was covered with a plain ftone. Cardinal Cynthio had purpofed to erect a magnificent monument to his memory, but this defign was fo long prevented by ficknefs and other accidents, that, ten years after, Manfo coming to Rome, went to vifit his friend's remains, and would have taken on himfelf the care of building a tomb to him; but this cardinal Cynthio would by no means permit, having determined him-

felf

felf to pay that duty to Taſſo.   However Manſo prevailed
ſo far as to have the following words engraved on the ſtone,

HIC IACET TORQVATVS TASSVS.

Cardinal Cynthio dying without putting his deſign in execution, cardinal Bonifacio Bevilacqua, of an illuſtrious family of Ferrara, cauſed a ſtately ſepulchre to be erected, in
the church of St. Onuphrius, over the remains of a Man
whoſe works had made all other monuments ſuperfluous.

THE

THE

FIRST BOOK

OF

JERUSALEM DELIVERED

Vol. I.   B

THE ARGUMENT.

The Christians, having assembled a vast army under different leaders, for the recovery of Jerusalem from the Saracens, after various successes, encamped in the plains of Tortosa. At this time the action of the Poem begins. God sends his angel to the camp, and commands Godfrey to summon a council of the chiefs. The assembly meets. Godfrey, with universal consent, is elected commander in chief of all the Christian forces. He reviews the army. The different nations described. The names and qualities of the leaders. The army begins its march towards Jerusalem. Aladine, king of Jerusalem, alarmed at the progress of the Christians, makes preparations for the defence of the city.

T H E

F I R S T   B O O K

O F

JERUSALEM DELIVERED.

ARMS, and the chief I fing, whofe righteous
    hands
Redeem'd the tomb of CHRIST from impious bands;
Who much in council, much in field fuftain'd,
Till juft fuccefs his glorious labours gain'd:
In vain the powers of hell oppos'd his courfe,   5
And Afia's arms, and Lybia's mingled force;
Heaven blefs'd his ftandards, and beneath his care
Reduc'd his wandering partners of the war.

   O facred Mufe! who ne'er, in Ida's fhade,
With fading laurels deck'ft thy radiant head;   10

But

Ver. 9. *O facred Mufe!*—] Some Italian commentatóre
fuppofe the poet intends the Virgin ·Mary; thus likewife
mentioned by Petrarch, *Coronata di ftelle,*—but it probably
means no more than a general appeal to fome celeftial being,
in oppofition to the Pagan theology.

Thus

B 2

But fit'ft enthron'd, with ftars immortal crown'd,
Where blifsful choirs their hallow'd ftrains refound;
Do thou inflame me with celeftial fire,   :
Affift my labours, and my fong infpire:
Forgive me, if with truth I fiction join,   15
And grace the verfe with other charms than thine.
Thou know'ft, the world with eager tranfport throng
Where fweet Parnaffus breathes the tuneful fong;
That truth can oft, in pleafing ftrains convey'd,
Allure the fancy, and the mind perfuade.   20
'Thus the fick infant's tafte difguis'd to meet,
We tinge the veffel's brim with juices fweet;
The bitter draught his willing lip receives;
He drinks deceiv'd, and fo deceiv'd he lives.

Thus Milton.
        Defcend from heaven, Urania, by that name
        If rightly thou art call'd, whofe voice divine
        Following, above th' Olympian hill I foar,
        Above the flight of Pegafean wing.
        The meaning, not the name I call: for thou
        Nor of the Mufes nine, nor on the top
        Of old Olympian dwell'ft——
                        PARADISE LOST, Book vii. v. 1.

 Ver. 21. *Thus the fick infant's tafte,*—] This admired
fimile is imitated from Lucretius.

    Sed veluti pueris abfynthia tetra medentes
    Cum dare conantur, prius oras pocula circum
    Contingunt dulci mellis, flavoque liquore, &c.
                                Lib. vi.
                                Thou

Thou, great Alphonso! who from Fortune's power
Haſt ſafely brought me to the peaceful ſhore;   26
When, like a wand'rer, o'er the ſeas I paſs'd
Amid the threatening rocks and watry waſte;
Vouchſafe, with ſmiles, my labours to ſurvey,
Theſe votive lines to thee the Muſes pay.   30
Some future time may teach my loftier lays
To ſing thy actions and record thy praiſe:
If e'er the Chriſtian powers their ſtrife forbear,
And join their forces for a nobler war;
With ſteeds and veſſels paſs to diſtant Thrace,   35
To gain their conqueſts from a barbarous race;
To thee the ſway of earth they muſt reſign,
Or, if thou rather chuſe, the ſea be thine:
Meanwhile, to rival Godfrey's glorious name,
Attend, and rouze thy ſoul to martial fame.   40

Five times his rolling courſe the year had run
Since firſt the Chriſtians had the war begun:
By fierce aſſault, already Nice they held;
And made, by ſtratagem, proud Antioch yield;

B 3   There,

Ver. 25. —*Alphonſo*—] Alphonſo of Eſte, duke of Ferrara.
Ver. 43. —*Nice*—] The city where Solyman, king of the Turks, a principal character in the poem, once held his ſeat of empire.
Ver. 44. —*by ſtratagem, proud Antioch yield;*—] This city having

There, with undaunted hearts, maintain'd their poft,
Againft the numbers of the Perfian hoft.   46
Tortofa won, the wintry months appear,
And clofe the conquefts of the glorious year.

  The feafon that oppos'd the victor's force,
Began to yield to fpring's benignant courfe;   50
When now th'Eternal, from his awful height,
Enthron'd in pureft rays of heavenly light,
(As far remov'd above the ftarry fpheres,
As Hell's foundations from the diftant ftars)
Caft on the fubject world his piercing eyes,   55
And view'd at once the feas, the earth, and fkies:
He turn'd his looks intent on Syria's lands,
And mark'd the leaders of the Chriftian bands;
No fecret from his fearching eye conceal'd
But all their bofoms to his view reveal'd.   60
Godfrey he fees, who burns with zeal to chace
From Sion's wall the Pagans' impious race;
And, while religious fires his breaft inflame,
Defpifes worldly empire, wealth, and fame.
Far other fchemes in Baldwin next he views,   65
Whofe reftlefs heart ambition's track purfues.

having been befieged eight months by the Chriftians, was
at laft taken by ftratagem, by means of one Pyrrhus, who
delivered a fort into the hands of Bœmond.

Tancred

Tancred he fees his life no longer prize,
Th' infenfate victim of a woman's eyes!
Bœmond he marks, intent to fix his reign
In Antioch's town, his new-acquir'd domain;   70
With laws and arts the people to improve,
And teach the worfhip of the powers above;
And while thefe thoughts alone his foul divide,
The prince is loft to every care befide.
He then beholds in young Rinaldo's breaft,   75
A warlike mind that fcorn'd ignoble reft;
Nor hopes of gold or power the youth inflame,
But facred thirft of never-dying fame;
From Guelpho's lips, with kindling warmth, he hears
The ancients' glory, and their deeds reveres.   80
    When now the Sovereign of the world had feen
The cares and aims below of mortal men;
He call'd on Gabriel, from th' angelic race,
Who held in glorious rank the fecond place;
A faithful nunciate from the throne above,   85
Divine interpreter of heavenly love!

Ver. 83. *He call'd on Gabriel, from th' angelic race,*
        Who held in glorious rank the fecond place;] " That
is, amongft the feven fpirits that are faid to ftand before the throne of God, Michael, Gabriel, Lamael, Raphael, Zachariel, Anael, and Oriphiel." GUSTAVINI.

B 4   He

He bears the mandate from the realms of light,
And wafts our prayers before th' Almighty's fight.

  To him th' Eternal :—Speed thy rapid way,
And thus to Godfrey's ear our words convey :   90
Why this neglect ? Why linger thus the bands
To free Jerusalem from impious hands ?
Let him to council bid the chiefs repair,
There rouze the tardy to purfue the war :
The power fupreme on him they fhall beftow,   95
I here elect him for my chief below :
The reft fhall to his fway fubmiffive yield,
Companions once, now fubjects in the field.

  He faid ; and ftrait with zealous ardour preft,
Gabriel prepares t'obey his Lord's beheft.   100
He clothes his heavenly form with ether light,
And makes it vifible to human fight ;
In fhape and limbs like one of earthly race,
But brightly fhining with celeftial grace :
A youth he feem'd, in manhood's ripening years, 105
On the fmooth cheek when firft the down appears ;
Refulgent rays his beauteous locks enfold ;
White are his nimble wings, and edg'd with gold :
With thefe through winds and clouds he cuts his way,
Flies o'er the land, and fkims along the fea.   110

Thus

Thus ſtood th' angelic power, prepar'd for flight,
Then inſtant darted from th' empyreal height;
Direct to Lebanon his courſe he bent,
There clos'd his plumes, and made his firſt deſcent;
Thence with new ſpeed his airy wings he ſteer'd, 115
Till now in ſight Tortoſa's plains appear'd.

The cheerful ſun his ruddy progreſs held,
Part rais'd above the waves, and part conceal'd:
Now Godfrey, as accuſtom'd, roſe to pay
His pure devotions with the dawning ray: 120
When the bright form appearing from the eaſt,
More fair than opening morn, the chief addreſs'd.

Again return'd the vernal ſeaſon view,
That bids the hoſt their martial toils renew:
What, Godfrey, now withholds the Chriſtians bands
To free Jeruſalem from impious hands?   126
Go, to the council every chief invite,
And to the pious taſk their ſouls incite.
Heaven makes thee general of his hoſt below,
The reſt ſubmiſſive to thy rule ſhall bow.   130
Diſpatch'd from God's eternal throne I came,
To bring theſe tidings in his awful name:
O think! what zeal, what glory now demands
From ſuch a hoſt committed to thy hands!

He

He ceas'd, and ceafing, vanifh'd from his fight
To the pure regions of his native light :   136
While, with his words and radiant looks amaz'd,
The pious Godfrey long in filence gaz'd.
But when, his firft furprize and wonder fled,
He ponder'd all the heavenly vifion faid ;   140
What ardour then poffefs'd his fwelling mind
To end the war, his glorious tafk affign'd !
Yet no ambitious thoughts his breaft inflame
(Though fingled thus from ev'ry earthly name)
But with his own, his Maker's will confpires,   145
And adds new fuel to his native fires.

Then ftrait the heralds round with fpeed he fends
To call the council of his warlike friends ;
Each word employs the fleeping zeal to raife,
And wake the foul to deeds of martial praife.   150
So well his reafons and his prayers were join'd,
As pleas'd at once, and won the vanquifh'd mind.

The leaders came, the fubject-troops obey'd,
And Bœmond only from the fummons ftay'd.
Part wait without encamp'd (a numerous band) 155
While part Tortofa in her walls detain'd.
And now the mighty chiefs in council fate,
(A glorious fynod !) at the grand debate ;

When,

When, rising in the midst, with awful look,
And pleasing voice, the pious Godfrey spoke.   160
   Ye sacred warriors! whom th' Almighty Power
Selects his pure religion to restore,
And safe has led, by his preserving hand,
Through storms at sea, and hostile wiles by land;
What rapid course our conquering arms have run!
What rebel lands to his subjection won!   166
How o'er the vanquish'd nations spread the fame
Of his dread ensigns, and his holy name!
Yet, not for this we left our natal seats;
And the dear pledges of domestic sweets;   170
On treacherous seas the rage of storms to dare,
And all the perils of a foreign war!
For this, an end unequal to your arms,
Nor bleeds the combat, nor the conquest charms:
Nor such reward your matchless labours claim, 175
Barbarian kingdoms, and ignoble fame!
Far other prize our pious toils must crown;
We fight to conquer Sion's hallow'd town;
To free from servile yoke the Christian train,
Oppress'd so long in slavery's galling chain,   180
To found in Palestine a regal seat,
Where piety may find a safe retreat,

                                        Where

Forbid it, Heaven! such favour should be lost,
And vainly lavish'd on a thankless host.
All great designs to one great period tend,
And every part alike respects its end.   210
Th' auspicious season bids the war proceed;
The country open, and the passes freed :
Why march we not with speed to reach the town,
The prize decreed our conquering arms to crown?
To what I now protest, ye chiefs! give ear,   215
(The present times, the future age shall hear,
The host of saints be witness from above)
The time is ripe the glorious task to prove.
The longer pause we make our hopes are less,
Delays may change our now assur'd success.   220
My mind foretels, if long our march is staid,
Sion will gain from Egypt powerful aid.

　　He ceas'd; a murmur at his words ensu'd :
When from his seat the hermit Peter stood;

Who

Ver. 224.—*the hermit Peter*—] Peter, commonly called
the hermit, was a native of Amiens, had made the pilgrim-
age to Jerusalem, and being affected with the dangers to
which the pilgrims were exposed since the infidels had
gained possession of the Holy Land, first entertained the
bold and to all appearance impracticable idea of estab-
lishing the Christians in Jerusalem. He went from province

Who fate with princes their debates to fhare ;   225
The holy author of this pious war.

What Godfrey fpeaks with ardor I approve,
Such obvious truth muft every bofom move;
'Tis yours, O chiefs ! to own its genuine power,
But let me add to his one counfel more.   230
When now, revolving in my careful mind,
I view our actions paft, by ftrife disjoin'd ;
Our jarring wills ; our difunited force ;
And many plans obftructed in their courfe ;
Methinks my judgment to their fpring can trace 235
The troubled motions that our caufe difgrace.
'Tis in that power, in many leaders join'd,
Of various tempers, and difcordant mind.
If o'er the reft no fovereign chief prefide,
To allot the feveral pofts, the tafks divide ;   240
To fcourge th' offender, or rewards beftow ;
What riot and mifrule the ftate o'erflow !

vince to province, with a crucifix in his hand, exciting the
princes and people to the holy war ; and we have the incredible account from contemporary authors, that fix millions
of perfons affumed the crofs, which was affixed to their right
fhoulder, and was the badge that diflinguifhed fuch as devoted themfelves to this holy warfare."

See Robertfon's Hiftory of Charles V. v. i.
and Hume's Hiftory of England, v. i.

Then

Then in one body join our focial band,
And truft the rule to one important hand;
To him refign the fceptre and the fway,   245
And him their king th' united hoft obey.

   Here ceas'd the reverend fage.   O zeal divine!
What bofoms can withftand a power like thine?
Thy facred breath the hermit's words infpir'd,
And with his words the liftening heroes fir'd;   250
Difpell'd their doubts, their paffions lull'd to reft,
And vain ambition chac'd from every breaft.
Then Guelpho firft and William (chiefs of fame)
Saluted Godfrey with a general's name,
Their chief elect: the reft approv'd the choice, 255
And gave the rule to him with public voice.
His equals once to his dominion yield,
Supreme in council, and fupreme in field!

   Th' affembly ended, fwift-wing'd Rumour fled,
And round from man to man the tidings fpread. 260
Meantime before the foldiers Godfrey came,
Who hail'd him as their chief with loud acclaim:
Sedate he heard th' applaufe on every fide,
And mildly to their duteous zeal reply'd;
Then on the morrow bade the troops prepare   265
To pafs before his fight in form of war.

                                      Now,

Now, to the eaft return'd, with purer ray
The glorious fun reveal'd the golden day;
When, early rifing with the morning light,
Appear'd each warrior fheath'd in armour bright. 270
Beneath their ftandards rang'd, the warlike train,
A goodly fight! were marfhall'd on the plain!
While on a height the pious Godfrey ftood,
And horfe and foot at once diftinctly view'd.

Say, Mufe! from whom no time can truth conceal,
Who canft thy knowledge to mankind reveal,   276
Oblivion's foe! thy poet's breaft inflame,
Teach him to tell each gallant leader's name;
Difclofe their ancient glories now to light,
Which rolling years have long obfcur'd in night:
Let eloquence like thine affift my tongue,   281
And future times attend my deathlefs fong!

Firft in the field the Franks their numbers bring,
Once led by Hugo, brother to the king:
From France they came, with verdant beauty crown'd,
Whofe fertile foil four running ftreams furround;
When death's relentlefs ftroke their chief fubdu'd,
Still the fame caufe the valiant band purfu'd:

Ver. 284. *Once led by Hugo*—] Hugo, or Hugh, count of
Vermandois, brother of Philip I. king of France.

Beneath

Beneath the brave Clotharius' care they came,
Who vaunts no honour of a regal name : 290
A thoufand, heavy arm'd, compos'd the train,
An equal number follow'd on the plain :
And like the firft their femblance and their mien,
Alike their arms and difcipline were feen :
Thefe brought from Normandy, by Robert led, 295
A rightful prince amid their nation bred.
William and Ademar to thefe fucceed,
(The people's paftors) and their fquadrons lead :
Far different once their tafk by Heaven affign'd,
Religious minifters to inftruct mankind ! 300
But now the helmet on their heads they bear,
And learn the deathful bufinefs of his war.

Ver. 295.—*by Robert led*—] " Robert, Duke of Normandy, had early enlifted himfelf in the crufade ; but being
unprovided with money, he refolved to mortgage or rather
fell his dominions, and offered them to his brother" (William Rufus, King of England) " for ten thoufand marks.
The bargain was concluded, and Robert fet out for the
Holy Land." See Hume's Hiftory of England, v. i.

Ver. 297. *William and Ademar*—] " William, archbifhop of Orange, and Ademaro, archbifhop of Poggio.
Thefe, according to Paolo Emilio, were the firft that on
their knees befought Pope Urban, at the council of Clar-
mont, to be fent on the crufade." GUASTAVINI.

This brings from Orange and the neighbouring land
Four hundred chosen warriors in his band,
And that conducts from Poggio to the field,   305
An equal troop, no less in battle skill'd.
Great Baldwin next o'er Boloign's force presides,
And, with his own, his brother's people guides,
Who to his conduct now resigns the post,
Himself the chief of chiefs, and lord of all the host.
Then came Carnuti's earl, not less renown'd   311
For martial prowess, than for counsel found,
Four hundred in his train : but Baldwin leads
Full thrice the number arm'd on generous steeds.

Ver. 311.—*Carnuti's earl*—] Stephano earl of Carnuti,
called afterwards earl of Chartres and Blois.

" There is extant a letter from Stephen the earl of Chartres and Blois, to Adela his wife, in which he gives her an
account of the progress of the crusaders. He describes the
crusaders as the chosen army of Christ, as the servants and
soldiers of God, as men who marched under the immediate
protection of the Almighty, being conducted by his hand to
victory and conquest.   He speaks of the Turks as accursed,
sacrilegious, and devoted by heaven to destruction ; and when
he mentions the soldiers in the Christian army which had
died, or were killed, he is confident that their souls were
admitted directly into the joys of Paradise."

See Robertson's History of Charles V. vol. i.

Near

Near thefe, the plain the noble Guelpho prefs'd, 315
By fortune equal to his merits blefs'd;
A chief, who by his Roman fire could trace
A long defcent from Efte's princely race;
But German by dominion and by name,
To Guelpho's name he join'd his priftine fame:
He rul'd Carynthia, and the lands poffefs'd   321
By Sueves and Rhethians once, his fway confefs'd:
O'er thefe the chief, by right maternal, reign'd,
To thefe his valour many conquefts gain'd:
From thence he brings his troop, a hardy race, 325
Still ready death in fighting fields to face;
Beneath their roofs fecur'd from wintry fkies,
The genial feaft each joyful day fupplies;
Five thoufand once; now fcarce a third remain'd,
Since Perfia's flight, of all the numerous band.   330
Next thofe, whofe lands the Franks and Germans ⎤
    bound,   ⎬
Where Rhine and Maes o'erflow the fruitful ground, ⎟
For countlefs herds and plenteous crops renown'd. ⎦
With thefe their aid the neighbouring ifles fupply'd,
Whofe banks defend them from th' encroaching tide:

Ver. 315. —*Guelpho*—] Son of Actius the fourth, marquis of Efte, and of Cunigunda.

Ver. 331. —*thofe whofe lands,*—] The Flemings.

                  All

All thefe a thoufand form'd, (a warlike band)   336
O'er whom another Robert held command.
More numerous was the Britifh fquadrons fhown,
By William led, the monarch's youngeft fon.
The Englifh in the bow and fhafts are fkill'd :   340
With them a northern nation feeks the field,
Whom Ireland from our world divided far,
From favage woods and mountains, fends to war.

    Tancred was next, than whom no greater name
(Except Rinaldo) fill'd the lift of fame ;   345
Of gentler manners, comelier to the fight,
Or more intrepid in the day of fight :
If aught of blame could fuch a foul reprove,
Or foil his glorious deeds, the fault was love :
A fudden love, that, born amidft alarms,   350
Was nurs'd with anguifh in the din of arms.
'Tis faid, that, on that great and glorious day,
When to the Franks the Perfian hoft gave way,

Ver. 339. *By William led, the monarch's youngeft fon.*]
William Rufus was then king, but he had no legitimate off-
fpring.

Ver. 344. *Tancred was next,—*] Son of a fifter of Boemond and of Rogero duke of Calabria : fhe married a marquis Guglielmo : Boemond and Rogero were born of Ro-
berto Guifcardo, of the Norman race.

Victorious

Victorious Tancred, eager to purfue
The fcatter'd remnants of the flying crew,   355
O'erfpent with labour, fought fome kind retreat
To quench his thirft and cool his burning heat ;
When, to his wifh, a cryftal ftream he found,
With bowery fhade and verdant herbage crown'd :
There fudden rufh'd before his wondering fight, 360
A Pagan damfel fheath'd in armour bright :
Her helm unlac'd her vifage bare difplay'd,
And tir'd with fight, fhe fought the cooling fhade.
Struck with her looks, he view'd the beauteous dame,
Admir'd her charms, and kindled at the flame. 365
O wonderous force of love's refiftlefs dart,
That pierc'd at once and rooted in his heart ! •
Her helm fhe clos'd, prepar'd t' affault the knight,
But numbers, drawing nigh, conftrain'd her flight ;
The lofty virgin fled, but left behind   370
Her lovely form deep imag'd in his mind ;
Still, in his thought, he views the confcious grove,
Eternal fuel to the flames of love !
Penfive he comes, his looks his foul declare,
With eyes caft downward and dejected air :   375
Eight hundred horfe from fertile feats he leads,
From hills of Tyrrhene and Campania's meads.

C 3   Two

Two hundred Grecians born, were next to fee,
Active in field, from weighty armour free :
Their crooked fabres at their fide they wear ;   380
Their backs the founding bows and quivers bear :
With matchlefs fwiftnefs were their fteeds indu'd,
Inur'd to toil, and fparing in their food :
Swift in attack they rufh, and fwift in flight,
In troops retreating and difpers'd they fight :   385
Tatinus led their force ¡ the only band
That join'd the Latian arms from Grecian land :
Yet near the fcene of war (O lafting fhame !
O foul difhonour to the Grecian name !)
Thou, Greece,. canft hear unmov'd the loud alarms,
A tame fpectator of the deeds of arms !   391
If foreign power opprefs thy fervile reign,
Thou well deferv'ft to wear the victor's chain.

A fquadron now, the laft in order, came,
In order laft, but firft in martial fame ;   395
Adventurers call'd, and heroes fam'd afar,
Terrors of Afia, thunderbolts of war !
Ceafe, Argo, ceafe to boaft thy warriors' might ;
And, Arthur, ceafe to vaunt each fabled knight ;

Ver. 386. *Tatinus led*—] Tatinus was fint with a
fquadron of horfe, by the emperor Alexas, from Conftanti-
nople, to join the Chriftians in their expedition.

Thefe

These all th' exploits of ancient times exceed :   400
What chief is worthy such a band to lead ?
By joint consent, to Dudon's sway they yield,
Of prudent age, experienc'd in the field ;
Who youthful vigour joins with hoary hairs,
His bosom mark'd with many manly scars.   405
Here stood Eustatius with the first in fame,
But more ennobled by his brother's * name,
Gernando here, the king of Norway's son,
Who vaunts his sceptred race and regal crown.
There Engerlan, and there Rogero shin'd ;   410
Two Gerrards with Rambaldo's dauntless mind ;
With gallant Ubald and Gentonio join'd.
Rosmondo with the bold must honour claim :
Nor must oblivion hide Obizo's name :
Nor Lombard's brethren three be left untold,   415
Achilles, Sforza, Palamedes bold ;
Nor Otho fierce, whose valour won the shield
That bears a child and serpent on its field :

* GODFREY.

Ver. 417. *Nor Otho fierce, whose valour won the shield*]
At the time of the crusade, Otho of the Visconti, over-
came one Volucius, a leader of the Saracens, who had de-
fied the Christians to single combat, and wore for his crest a
serpent and child, which device was ever after worn by
this Otho : this circumstance is mentioned by Ariosto.

   Nor

Nor Guasco, nor Ridolphus I forget,
Nor either Guido, both in combat great :   420
Nor must I Gernier pass, nor Eberard,
To rob their virtue of its due regard.
But why neglects my muse a wedded pair,
The gallant Edward and Gildippe fair?
O partners still in every battle try'd,   425
Not death your gentle union shall divide !
The school of love, which ev'n the fearful warms,
The dame instructed in the trade of arms :
Still by his side her watchful steps attend ;
Still on one fortune both their lives depend :   430
No wound in fight can either singly bear,
For both alike in every anguish share ;
And oft one faints to view the other's wound,
This shedding blood, and that in sorrow drown'd !

But lo ! o'er these, o'er all the host confest,   435
The young Rinaldo tower'd above the rest :

Ver. 424. —*Edward and Gildippe*—] Tasso, in one of his
letters, writes that Edward was an English baron, and that
his wife, by whom he was tenderly beloved, accompanied
him in this expedition, where they both perished.

Ver. 436. *The young Rinaldo*—] The poet by a poetical
anachronism feigns this Rinaldo to have been at the siege of
Jerusalem; for Rinaldo of Este, son of Bertoldo, was not
born till the year 1175, and Jerusalem was taken in 1097.

With

With martial grace his looks around he caſt,
And gazing crowds admir'd him as he pafs'd.
Mature beyond his years his virtues ſhoot,   439
As, mix'd with bloſſoms grows the budding fruit.
When clad in ſteel, he ſeems like Mars to move;
His face diſclos'd, he looks the God of Love!
This youth on Adige's far-winding ſhore,
To great Bertoldo fair Sophia bore.
The infant from the breaſt Matilda rears,   445
(The watchful guardian of his tender years)
And, while beneath her care the youth remains,
His ripening age to regal virtue trains;

Ver. 442.   *His face diſclos'd, he looks the God of Love!*]
Rinaldo, in many reſpects, is after the Achilles of Homer,
who is repreſented not only the braveſt, but the hand-
ſomeſt of all the Greeks, except Nireus, thus mentioned in
the catalogue of the forces.

> Nireus in faultleſs ſhape and blooming grace,
> The lovelieſt youth of all the Grecian race,
> Pelides only match'd his early charms ——
>   Pope's Il. vi. 817.

Ver. 445. —*Matilda rears,*] See the notes to Book xvii.
for an account of this extraordinary woman, here feigned to
have prefided over the education of Rinaldo.

Till

Till the loud trumpet, from the diftant eaft,
With early thirft of glory fir'd his breaft.   450
Then (fifteen fprings fcarce changing o'er his head)
Guidelefs, untaught, through ways unknown he fled;
Th' Egean fea he crofs'd and Grecian lands,
And reach'd, in climes remote, the Chriftian bands.
Three years the warrior in the camp had feen,   455
Yet fcarce the down began to fhade his chin.

   Now all the horfe were paft: in order led,
Next came the foot, and Raymond at their head:
Thouloufe he governs, and collects his train
Between the Pyreneans and the main: 460
Four thoufand, arm'd in proof, well us'd to bear
Th' inclement feafons, and the toils of war:
A band approv'd, in every battle try'd;
Nor could the band an abler leader guide.
Next Stephen of Amboife conducts his power: 465
From Tours and Blois he brings five thoufand more:
No hardy nation this, inur'd to fight,
Though fenc'd in fhining fteel, a martial fight!
Soft is their foil, and of a gentle kind,
And, like their foil, th' inhabitants inclin'd;   470

Ver. 45f.—*Raymond*—] Raymond count of Thouloufe, a
name well known in the hiftery of thofe times. .

Impetuous

Impetuous firſt they run to meet the foe,
But ſoon, repuls'd, their forces languid grow.
Alcaſtus was the third, with threatening mien;
(So Capeneus of old at Thebes was ſeen)
Six thouſand warriors, in Helvetia bred,   475
Plebeians fierce, from Alpine heights he led:
Their rural tools, that wont the earth to tear,
They turn'd to nobler inſtruments of war :
And with thoſe hands, accuſtom'd herds to guide,
They boldly now the might of kings defy'd.   480

   Lo ! rais'd in air the ſtandard proudly ſhown,
In which appear the keys and papal crown :
Sev'n thouſand foot there good Camillus leads,
In heavy arms that gleam acroſs the meads :
O'erjoy'd he ſeems, decreed his name to grace, 485
And add new honours to his ancient race;
Whate'er the Latian diſcipline may claim,
In glorious deeds to boaſt an equal fame.

   Now every ſquadron rang'd in order due,
Had paſs'd before the chief in fair review ;   490
When Godfrey ſtrait the peers aſſembled holds,
And thus the purport of his mind unfolds.

   Soon as the morning lifts her early head,
Let all the forces from the camp be led,

With

With speedy course to reach the sacred town,   495
Ere yet their purpose, or their march is known.
Prepare then for the way, for fight prepare,
Nor doubt, my friends! of conquest in the war!

These words, from such a chieftain's lips, inspire
Each kindling breast, and wake the slumbering fire:
Already for th' expected fight they burn,   501
And pant impatient for the day's return.
Yet still some fears their careful chief oppress'd,
But these he smother'd in his thoughtful breast:
By certain tidings brought, he lately heard,   505
That Egypt's king his course for Gaza steer'd:
(A frontier town that all the realm commands,
And a strong barrier to the Syrian lands)
Full well he knows the monarch's restless mind,
Nor doubts in him a cruel foe to find.   510
Aside the pious leader Henry took,
And thus his faithful messenger bespoke.

Attend my words, some speedy bark ascend,
And to the Grecian shore thy voyage bend:
A youth will there arrive of regal name,   515
Who comes to share our arms and share our fame;

Ver. 515. *A youth will there arrive of regal name,*] Sweno,
son to the king of Denmark. See note to Book VIII.

Prince

Prince of the Danes; who brings from diftant lands,
Beneath the frozen pole, his valiant bands :
The Grecian monarch, vers'd in fraud, may try
His arts on him, and every means employ   520
To ftop the youthful warrior in his courfe,
And rob our hopes of this auxiliar force.
My faithful nunciate thou, the Dane invite,
With every thought the gallant prince excite,
Both for his fame and mine, to fpeed his way,   525
Nor taint his glory with ill-tim'd delay.
Thou with the fovereign of the Greeks remain,
To claim the fuccours promis'd oft in vain.

  He faid; and having thus reveal'd his mind,
And due credentials to his charge confign'd,   530
The trufty meffenger his veffel fought,
And Godfrey calm'd awhile his troubled thought.

  Soon as the rifing morn, with fplendor dreft,
Unlocks the portals of the rofeate eaft,
The noife of drums and trumpets fills the air,   535
And bids the warriors for their march prepare.
Not half fo grateful to the longing fwain
The low'ring thunder that prefages rain,
As to thefe eager bands the fhrill alarms
Of martial clangors and the found of arms.   540

  At once they rofe, with generous ardour prefs'd,
At once their limbs in radiant armour drefs'd :

And

And rang'd in martial pomp (a dreadful band)
Beneath their numerous chiefs in order stand.
Now, man to man, the thick battalions join'd,   545
Unfurl their banners to the sportive wind;
And in th' imperial standard rais'd on high,
The Cross triumphant blazes to the sky.
Meantime the sun, above th' horizon gains
The rising circuit of th' ethereal plains :   550
The polish'd steel reflects the dazzling light;
And strikes with flashing rays the aking sight.
Thick and more thick the sparkling gleams aspire,
Till all the champaign seems to glow with fire;
While mingled clamours echo through the meads,
The clash of arms, the neigh of trampling steeds!   556

   A chosen troop of horse, dispatch'd before,
In armour light, the country round explore;
Lest foes in ambush should their march prevent;
While other bands the cautious leader sent   560
The dikes to level, clear the rugged way,
And free each pass that might their speed delay.
No troops of Pagans could withstand their force;
No walls of strength could stop their rapid course:
In vain oppos'd the craggy mountain stood,   565
The rapid torrent and perplexing wood.
So when the king of floods in angry pride,
With added waters swells his foamy tide,

I

With

With dreadful ruin o'er the banks he flows,
And nought appears that can his rage oppofe.   570
   The king of Tripoly had power alone,
(Well furnifh'd in a ftrongly guarded town,
With arms and men) to check the troops' advance,
But durft not meet in fight the hoft of France.
T' appeafe the Chriftian chief, the heralds bring 575
Pacific prefents from the Pagan king;
Who fuch conditions for the peace receives,
As pious Godfrey, in his wifdom, gives.
   There from mount Seir, that near toeaftward ftands,
And from above the fubject town commands,   580
The faithful pour in numbers to the plain;
(Each fex and every age, a various train!)
Their gifts before the Chriftian leader bear,
With joy they view him and with tranfport hear,
Gaze on the foreign garb with wondering eye,   585
And with unfailing guides the hoft fupply.
   Now Godfrey with the camp purfues his way,
Along the borders of the neighbouring fea:
For ftation'd there his friendly veffels ride,
From which the army's wants are well fupply'd: 590

Ver. 589. —*his friendly veffels ride,*] The poet means the
Genoefe, who had fupplied a great number of armed gallies,
under the direction of William Embraico.

For

For him alone each Grecian ifle is till'd,
For him their vintage Crete and Scios yield.
    The numerous fhips the fhaded ocean hide,
Loud groans beneath the weight the burthen'd tide.
The veffels thus their watchful poft maintain   595
And guard from Saracens the midland main.
Befide the fhips with ready numbers mann'd,
From wealthy Venice and Liguria's ftrand ;
England and Holland fend a naval pow'r,
And fertile Sicily and Gallia's fhore.   600
Thefe, all united, brought from every coaft
Provifions needful for the landed hoft ;
While on their march impatient they proceed,
(From all defence the hoftile frontiers freed)
And urge their hafte the hallow'd foil to gain   605
Where CHRIST endur'd the ftings of mortal pain.
But fame with winged fpeed before 'em flies
(Alike the meffenger of truth and lies)
She paints the camp in one united band,
Beneath one leader, moving o'er the land,   610
By none oppos'd : their nations, numbers tells ;
The name and actions of each chief reveals ;
Difplays their purpofe, fets the war to view,
And terrifies with doubts th' ufurping crew :

More

More dreadful to their anxious mind appears   615
The diftant profpect, and augments their fears :
To every light report their ears they bend,
Watch every rumour, every tale attend ;
From man to man the murmurs, fwelling ftill,
The country round and mournful city fill.   620
Their aged monarch, thus with danger preft,
Revolves dire fancies in his doubtful breaft :
His name was Aladine ; who fcarce maintain'd,
With fears befet, his feat fo lately gain'd :
By nature ftill to cruel deeds inclin'd,   625
Though years had fometime chang'd his favage mind.
When now he faw the Latian troops prepare,
Againft his city-walls to turn the war ;
Sufpicions, join'd with former fears, arofe ;
Alike he fear'd his fubjects and his foes,   630
Together in one town he faw refide
Two people, whom their different faiths divide.
While part the purer laws of CHRIST believe,
More numerous thofe who Macon's laws receive.
When firft the monarch conquer'd Sion's town, 635
And fought fecurely there to fix his throne ;

Ver. 623. *His name was Aladine*—] Taffo, with the licence of a poet, has made a king of Jerufalem ; but the city,
at that time, was in reality under the dominion of the Ca-
liph of Egypt, taken by him fome time before from the
Turks.

He freed his Pagans from the tax of ftate,
But on the Chriftians laid the heavier weight.
Thefe thoughts inflam'd and rouz'd his native rage,
(Now chill'd and tardy with the froft of age):   640
So turns in fummer's heat, the venom'd fnake,
That flept the winter harmlefs in the brake:
So the tame lion, urg'd to wrath again,
Refumes his fury, and erects his mane.

Then to himfelf: On every face I view   645
The marks of joy in that perfidious crew:
In general grief their jovial days they keep,
And laugh and revel when the public weep:
Ev'n now perhaps the dreadful fcheme is plann'd
Againft our life to lift a murderous hand;   650
Or to their monarch's foes betray the ftate,
And to their Chriftian friends unbar the gate.
But foon our juftice will their crimes prevent,
And fwift-wing'd vengeance on their heads be fent;
Example dreadful! death fhall feize on all: 655
Their infants at the mothers' breaft fhall fall:
The flames fhall o'er their domes and temples fpread,
Such be the funeral piles to grace their dead!
But midft their votive gifts, to fate our ire,
The priefts fhall firft upon the tomb expire.   660

So threats the tyrant; but his threats are vain;
Though pity moves not, coward fears reftrain;

5   Rage

Rage prompts his foul their guiltlefs blood to fpill,
But trembling doubts oppofe his favage will.
He fears the Chriftians, fhrinks at future harms, 665
Nor dares provoke too far the victor's arms:
This purpofe curb'd, to other parts he turns
The rage that in his reftlefs bofom burns:
With fire he waftes the fertile country round,
And lays the houfes level with the ground: 670
He leaves no place entire, that may receive
The Chriftian army, or their march relieve;
Pollutes the fprings and rivers in their beds,
And poifon in the wholefome water fheds;
Cautious with cruelty! meantime his care   675
Had reinforc'd Jerufalem for war.
Three parts for fiege were ftrongly fortify'd,
Though lefs fecurely fenc'd the northern fide.
But there, when firft the threaten'd ftorm was heard,
New ramparts, for defence, in hafte he rear'd; 680
Collecting in the town, from different lands,
Auxiliar forces to his fubject bands.

 END OF THE FIRST BOOK.

THE

SECOND BOOK

OF

JERUSALEM DELIVERED.

D 3

ALADINE transports an image of the Virgin from the temple
of the Christians, into the mosque, by the advice of Ifmeno, who proposes thereby to form a spell to secure the
city. In the night the image is secretly stolen away. The
king, unable to discover the author of the theft, and in-
censed against the Christians, prepares for a general maf-
sacre. Sophronia, a Christian virgin, accuses herself to
the king. Olindo, her lover, takes the fact upon himself.
Aladine, in a rage, orders both to be burned. Clorinda
arrives, intercedes for them, and obtains their pardon. In
the mean time Godfrey, with his army, reaches Emmaus.
He receives Argantes and Alethes, ambassadors from
Egypt. The latter, in an artful speech, endeavours to
dissuade Godfrey from attacking Jerusalem. His propo-
sals are rejected, and Argantes declares war in the name of
the king of Egypt.

WHILE thus the Pagan king prepar'd for fight,
   The fam'd Ifmeno came before his fight;
Ifmeno, he whofe power the tomb invades,
And calls again to life departed fhades:
Whofe magic verfe can pierce the world beneath,   5
And ftartle Pluto in the realms of death;
The fubject demons at his will reftrain,
And fafter bind or loofe their fervile chain.
Ifmeno once the Chriftian faith avow'd,
But now at Macon's impious worfhip bow'd: 10
Yet ftill his former rites the wretch retain'd,
And oft, with Pagan mix'd, their ufe prophan'd.
Now from the caverns, where, retir'd alone,
From vulgar eyes, he ftudied arts unknown,

D 4

He

He came affiftance to his lord to bring: 15
An ill advifer to a tyrant king!
  Then thus he fpoke : O king I behold at hand
That conquering hoft, the terror of the land !
But let us act as fits the noble mind :
The bold from earth and heaven will fuccour find. 20
As king and leader well thy cares prefide,
And with forefeeing thought for all provide.
If all, like thee, their feveral parts difpofe,
This land will prove the burial of thy foes.
Lo! here I come with thee the toils to bear,   25
To affift thy labours, and thy danger fhare.
Accept the counfel cautious years impart,
And join to this the powers of magic art :
Thofe angels, exil'd from th' ethereal plains,
My potent charms fhall force to fhare our pains. 30
Attend the fcheme, revolving in my breaft,
The firft enchantment that my thoughts fuggeft.
An altar by the Chriflians ftands immur'd
Deep under ground, from vulgar eyes fecur'd :
The ftatue of their goddefs there is fhow'd,   35
The mother of their human, buried God!
Before the image burns continual light ;
A flowing veil conceals her from the fight.

On

On every fide are tablets there difplay'd,
And votive gifts by fuperftition paid.   40
Hafte! fnatch their idol from that impious race,
And in thy mofque the boafted figure place.
Then will I raife fuch fpells of wondrous pow'r,
This fated pledge (while there detain'd fecure)
Shall prove the guardian of thy city's gate,   45
And walls of adamant fhall fence thy ftate.

    He faid, and ceas'd : his words perfuafion wrought,
And fwift the king the hidden temple fought:
Furious he drove the trembling priefts away,
And feiz'd, with daring hands, the hallow'd prey : 50
Then to the mofque in hafte the prize he bore,
(Where rites profane offend th' Almighty Power)
There, o'er the facred form, with impious zeal,
The foul magician mutter'd many a fpell.

    But foon as morning ftreak'd the eaft of heaven, 55
The watch, to whom the temple's guard was given,
No longer in its place the image found,
And fearch'd with fruitlefs care the dome around.
Then to the king the ftrange report he bears,
The king, inflam'd with wrath, the tidings hears : 60

    Ver. 45. —*the guardian of thy city's gate* ;] This paffage
is evidently borrowed from the ancient palladium, by which
the city of Troy was to be defended.

His

His thoughts fuggeft fome Chriftian's fecret hand
Has thence purloin'd the guardian of the land:
But whether Chriftian zeal from thence convey'd
The hallow'd form; or Heaven its power difplay'd,
To fnatch from impious fanes, and roofs unclean, 65
The glorious femblance of their virgin-queen,
Doubtful the fame; nor can we dare affign
The deed to human art, or hands divine.

   The king each temple fought and fecret place,
And vow'd with coftly gifts the man to grace,   70
Who brought the image, or the thief reveal'd,
But threaten'd thofe whofe lips the deed conceal'd.
The wily forc'rer every art apply'd
T' explore the truth: in vain his arts he try'd:
For whether wrought by Heaven, or earth alone, 75
Heaven kept it, fpite of all his charms, unknown.
But when the king perceiv'd his fearch was vain,
To find th' offender of the Chriftian train:
On all at once his fierce refentment turn'd,
On all at once his favage fury burn'd: 80
No bounds, no laws his purpofe could control,
But blood alone could fate his vengeful foul.
Our wrath fhall not be loft (aloud he cries)
The thief amidft the general flaughter dies.

                                        Guilty

Guilty and innocent, they perish all !   85
Let the juſt periſh, ſo the guilty fall.—
Yet wherefore juſt ? when none our pity claim ;
Not one but hates our rites, and hates our name.
Riſe, riſe, my friends ! the fire and ſword employ,
Lay waſte their dwellings, and their race deſtroy. 90
  So ſpoke the tyrant to the liſtening crew ;
Among the faithful ſoon the tidings flew.
With horror chill'd, the diſmal ſound they heard,
While ghaſtly death on every face appear'd.
None think of flight, or ſor defence prepare,   95
Or ſeek to deprecate their fate with prayer :
But lo ! when leaſt they hope, the timorous bands
Their ſafety owe to unexpected hands.

  A maid there was among the Chriſtian kind,
In prime of years, and of exalted mind :   100
Beauteous her form, but beauty ſhe deſpis'd,
Or beauty grac'd with virtue only priz'd.
From flattering tongues the modeſt fair withdrew,
And liv'd ſecluded from the public view :
But vain her cares to hide her beauty prov'd,   105
Her beauty worthy to be ſeen and lov'd.
Nor Love conſents, but ſoon reveals her charms,
And with their power a youthful lover warms ;

That

That Love who now conceals his piercing eyes,
And now, like Argus, every thing defcries;   110
Who brings to view each grace that fhuns the light,
And midft a thoufand guards directs the lover's fight!
    Sophronia fhe, Olindo was his name;
The fame their city, and their faith the fame.
The youth as modeft as the maid was fair,   115
But little hop'd, nor durft his love declare:
He knew not how, or fear'd to tell his pain,
She faw it not, or view'd it with difdain:
Thus to this hour in filent grief he mourn'd,
His thoughts unnoted, or his paffion fcorn'd.   120
    Meantime the tidings fpread from place to place,
Of death impending o'er the Chriftian race:
Soon in Sophronia's noble mind arofe
A generous plan to avert her people's woes:
Zeal firft infpir'd, but bafhful fhame enfu'd,   125
And modefty awhile the thought withftood:
Yet foon her fortitude each doubt fupprefs'd,
And arm'd with confidence her tender breaft.
Through gazing throngs alone the virgin goes,
Nor ftrives to hide her beauties, nor difclofe: 130
O'er her fair face a decent veil is feen,
Her eyes declin'd with modeft graceful mien:

An

An artless negligence compos'd her drefs,
And nature's genuine grace her charms confefs.
Admir'd by all, regardlefs went the dame,   135
Till to the prefence of the king fhe came :
While yet he rav'd, fhe dar'd to meet his view,
Nor from his threatening looks her fteps withdrew.
O king ! (fhe thus began) awhile contain
Thy anger, and thy people's rage reftrain :   140
I come to fhow, and to your vengeance yield
Th' offender from your fruitlefs fearch conceal'd.

    She faid, and ceas'd : the king in wonder gaz'd,
(Struck with her courage, with her looks amaz'd)
Her fudden charms at once his foul engage,   145
He calms his paffion, and forgets his rage.
If milder fhe, or he of fofter frame,
His heart had felt the power of beauty's flame :
But haughty charms can ne'er the haughty move ;
For fmiles and graces are the food of love.   150
Though love could not affect his favage mind,
He yet appear'd to gentle thoughts inclin'd.
Difclofe the truth at large (he thus reply'd)
No harm fhall to thy Chriftian friends betide.
Then fhe : Before thy fight the guilty ftands :   155
The theft, Q king ! committed by thefe hands.

                                        In

In me the thief who ſtole the image view;
To me the puniſhment decreed is due.

   Thus, fill'd with public zeal, the generous dame
A victim for her people's ranſom came.   160
O great deceit! O lye divinely fair!
What truth with ſuch a falſehood can compare?
In deep ſuſpence her words the tyrant heard,
No ſign of anger in his looks appear'd.
Declare (thus mildly to the maid he ſpoke)   165
Who gave thee counſel and the deed partook.
The deed alone was mine (reply'd the fair)
I ſuffer'd none with me the fame to ſhare:
Mine was the counſel, mine the firſt deſign,
And the laſt acting of the deed was mine.   170
Then only thou (he cry'd) muſt bear the pain
Our anger now and juſt revenge ordain.
'Tis juſt, ſince all the glory mine (ſhe cry'd)
That none with me the puniſhment divide.
With kindling ire the Pagan thus replies: 175
Say, where conceal'd the Chriſtian image lies.
'Tis not conceal'd (rejoin'd the dauntleſs dame)
I gave the hallow'd ſtatue to the flame;
So could no impious hands again profane
The ſacred image, and her beauty ſtain.   180

                                        Then

Then feek no more what never can be thine,
But lo! the thief I to thy hands refign;
If theft it may be call'd to feize our right,
Unjuftly torn away by lawlefs might.

   At this the king in threatening words return'd; 185
With wrath ungovern'd all his bofom burn'd:
Ah I hope no more thy pardon here to find,
O glorious virgin! O exalted mind!
In vain, againft the tyrant's fury held,
Love for defence oppofes beauty's fhield.   190

   Now doom'd to death, and fentenc'd to the flame,
With cruel hands they feize the beauteous dame.
Her veil and mantle rent beftrow the ground,
With rugged cords her tender arms are bound.
Silent fhe ftands, no marks of fear exprefs'd,   195
Yet foft commotions gently heave her breaft;
Her modeft cheeks a tranfient blufh difclofe;
Where lilies foon fucceed the fading rofe.
Meanwhile the people throng (the rumour fpread)
And with the reft Olindo there was led: 200
The tale he knew, but not the victim's name,
Till near the tragic fcene of fate he came:
Soon as the youth the prifoner's face furvey'd,
And faw, condemn'd to death, his lovely maid;

While

While the ftern guards their cruel tafk purfue,   205
Through the thick prefs with headlong fpeed he flew.
She's guiltlefs! (to the king aloud he cries)
She's guiltlefs of th' offence for which fhe dies!
She could not—durft not—fuch a work demands
Far other than a woman's feeble hands :   210
What arts to lull the keeper could fhe prove ?
And how the facred image thence remove ?
She fondly boafts the deed, unthinking maid !
'Twas I the ftatue from the mofque convey'd :
Where the high dome receives the air and light, 215
I found a paffage, favour'd by the night :
The glory mine, the death for me remains,
Nor let her thus ufurp my rightful pains :
The punifhment be mine, her chains I claim ;
Mine is the pile prepar'd, and mine the kindled
     flame !   220

    At this her head Sophronia gently rais'd,
And on the youth with looks of pity gaz'd.
Unhappy man ! what brings thee guiltlefs here ?
What frenzy guides thee, or what rafh defpair ?
Say, cannot I, without thy aid, engage   225
The utmoft threatening of a mortal's rage ?
This breaft undaunted can refign its breath,
Nor afks a partner in the hour of death.

She

She fpoke; but wrought not on her lover's mind,
Who, firm, retain'd his purpofe firft defign'd.   230
O glorious ftruggle for a fatal prize!
When love with fortitude for conqueft vies,
Where death is the reward the victor bears,
And fafety is the ill the vanquifh'd fears!
While thus they both contend the deed to claim, 235
The monarch's fury burns with fiercer flame:
He rag'd to find his power fo lightly priz'd,
And all the torments he prepar'd defpis'd.
Let both (he cry'd) their wifh'd defign obtain:
And both enjoy the prize they feek to gain!   240
The tyrant faid, and ftrait the fignal made
To bind the youth; the ready guards obey'd.
With face averted to one ftake confin'd,
With cruel cords the haplefs pair they bind.
Now round their limbs they place the rifing pyre; 245
And now with breath awake the flumbering fire;
When thus the lover, in a moving ftrain,
Befpeaks the lov'd companion of his pain.

Are thefe the bands with which I hop'd to join,
In happier times, my future days to thine?   250
And are we doom'd, alas! this fire to prove,
Inftead of kindly flames of mutual love?

Love promis'd gentler flames and fofter ties ;
But cruel fate far other now fupplies !
Too long from thee I mourn'd my life disjoin'd, 255
And now in death a haplefs meeting find !
Yet am I bleft, fince thou the pains muft bear,
If not thy bed, at leaft thy pile to fhare.
Thy death I mourn, but not my own lament,
Since dying by thy fide I die content.   260
Could yet my prayer one further blifs obtain,
How fweet, how envy'd then were every pain !
O could I prefs my faithful breaft to thine,
And on thy lips my fleeting foul refign !
So might we, fainting in the pangs of death,   265
Together mix our fighs and parting breath !
    In words like thefe unbleft Olindo mourn'd ;
To him her counfel thus the maid return'd :
    O youth ! far other thoughts, and pure defires,
Far other forrows now the time requires !   270
Doft thou forget thy fins ? nor call to mind
What God has for the righteous fouls affign'd ?
Endure for him, and fweet the pains will prove ;
Afpire with joy to happier feats above ;
Yon glittering fkies and golden fun furvey,   275
That call us hence to realms of endlefs day.

Here,

Here, mov'd with pity, loud the Pagans groan :
But more conceal'd the Chriſtians vent their moan.
The king himſelf, with thoughts unuſual preſs'd,
Felt his fierce heart ſuſpended in his breaſt :   280
But, ſcorning to relent, he turn'd his view
From the dire proſpeſt, and in haſte withdrew.
Yet thou, Sophronia, bear'ſt the general woe,
And, wept by all, thy tears diſdain to flow !

While thus they ſtand, behold a knight is ſeen, 285
(For ſuch he ſeem'd) of fierce and noble mien !
Whoſe foreign arms and ſtrange attire proclaim,
An alien from a diſtant land he came.
The ſculptur'd tigreſs on his helmet high,
(A well-known creſt !) attraſts each gazer's eye. 290
This ſign Clorinda in the field diſplay'd,
All ſee and own by this the warrior-maid.
She, from a child, beheld with ſcornful eyes
Her ſex's arts, deſpiſing female toys ;

Arachne's

Ver. 293.   *She, from a child—*] With reſpeſt to the cha-
raſter of a female warrior, however repugnant it may appear
to our preſent ideas, the example of Virgil, and the tradi-
tion of the Amazons, may be ſufficient authority for Taſſo
to introduce the beautiful variety in his poem, ariſing from
the characters of Clorinda and Gildippe. There is a ſingu-
lar

Arachne's labours ne'er her hours divide,   295
Her noble hands nor looms nor fpindle guide ;
From eafe inglorious and from floth fhe fled,
And mix'd in camps, a life unfully'd led :
With rigour pleas'd, her lovely face fhe arm'd
With haughty looks, yet ev'n in fiercenefs charm'd:
                                                  In

lar paffage in one of Petrarch's letters, defcribing particularly
an Amazonian woman, which it may not be here unpleaf-
ing to lay before the reader, from the Life of Petrarch, publifhed in 1776.

   " Of all the wonders I faw in my little journey, nothing
furprized me more than the prodigious ftrength and extraordinary courage of a young woman called Mary, whom we
faw at Puzzoli.   She paffed her life among foldiers, and it
was a common opinion that fhe was fo much feared, no one
dared attack her honour.   No warrior but envied her prowefs and fkill.   From the flower of her age fhe lived in camps,
and adopted the military rules and drefs.   Her body is that
of a hardy foldier, rather than a woman, and feamed all over
with the fcars of honour.   She is always at war with her
neighbours ; fometimes fhe attacks them with a little troop,
fometimes alone ; and feveral have died by her hand.   She is
perfect in all the ftratagems of the military art; and fuffers,
with incredible patience, hunger, thirft, cold, heat, and fatigue.   In fine, fhe lies on the bare ground ; her fhield ferves
for her pillow, and fhe fleeps armed in the open air.

   " I had feen her in my firft voyage to Naples, about three
years ago ; but as fhe was very much altered, I did not know
her again.   She came forward to falute me ; I returned it as
                                                  to

In early years her tender hand reftrain'd   301
The fiery courfer, and his courage rein'd :
She pois'd the fpear and fword : her growing force
She try'd in wreftling and the dufty courfe ;
Then through the mountain paths and lonely wood
The bear and fhaggy lion's tracks purfu'd :   306

to a perfon I was not acquainted with.   But by her laugh,
and the geflure of thofe about me, I fufpected fomething ;
and obferving her with more attention, I found under the
helmet the face of this formidable virgin.   Was I to inform
you of half the things they relate of her, you would take
them for fables.   I will therefore confine myfelf to a few
facts, to which I was witnefs. By accident feveral ftrangers
who came to Puzzoli to fee this wonder, were all affembled
at the citadel, to make trial of her ftrength.   We found her
alone, walking before the portico of the church, and not
furprized at the contourfe of the people.   We begged fhe
would give us a proof of her ftrength. She excufed herfelf at
firft, on having a wound in her arm ; but afterwards fhe took
up an enormous block of ftone, and a piece of wood loaded
with iron.   Upon thefe, faid fhe, you may try your ftrength
if you will.   After every one had attempted to move them,
with more or lefs fuccefs, fhe took and threw them with fo
much eafe over our heads, that we remained confounded, and
could hardly believe our eyes.   At firft fome deceit was fufpected, but there could be none.   This has rendered cre-
dible what the ancients relate of the Amazons, and Virgil
of the heroines of Italy, who were headed by Camilla."
See LIFE of PETRARCH, vol. i. p. 350.

E 3   In

In war, the dread of men the virgin shin'd :
In woods, the terror of the savage kind !
From Perfia, jealous of the Chriftian fame,
T' oppofe the victor-hoft Clorinda came :   310
And, oft before, in fight her daring hand
Had fatten'd with their blood the thirfty land.

When near the fatal place the virgin drew,
And the dire fcene appear'd before her view ;
She fpurr'd her fteed t' obferve the victims nigh, 315
And learn th' unhappy caufe for which they die.
The yielding crowd gave way : the curious maid
With fteadfaft eyes the pair in bonds furvey'd.
One mourn'd aloud, and one in filence ftood ;
The weaker fex the greater firmnefs fhow'd :   320
Yet feem'd Olindo like a man to moan
Who wept another's fufferings, not his own ;
While filent fhe, and fix'd on heaven her eyes,
Already feem'd to claim her kindred fkies.

Clorinda view'd their ftate with tender woe, 325
And down her cheeks the tears began to flow :
Yet moft fhe griev'd for her who grief difdain'd ;
And filence, more than plaints, her pity gain'd ;
Then to an aged fire who ftood befide,
Say, who are thofe to death devote (fhe cry'd ;) 330
Declare

Declare what brought them to this woeful ſtate,
Some ſecret crime, or blind decree of fate?
Thus ſhe: The reverend ſire in brief diſplay'd
Their mournful ſtory to the liſtening maid:
She heard, ſurpriz'd ſuch matchleſs worth to find,
And both acquitted in her equal mind.   336
Already now reſolv'd, by force or prayer,
To ſave from threaten'd death th' unhappy pair,
She ran, ſhe ſtopp'd the flame with eager haſte,
(Already kindling) and the guards addreſs'd: 340
    None in this cruel office dare to move,
Till to the monarch I my ſuit approve:
My power, believe me, ſhall protect your ſtay,
Nor ſhall your ſovereign chide your ſhort delay.
    She ſaid: th' attendants at her word obey'd, 345
Mov'd with the preſence of the royal maid:
Then, turning ſwift, ſhe met the king, who came
To welcome to his court the warrior dame.
To whom ſhe thus: Behold Clorinda here!
Clorinda's name, perchance, has reach'd your ear.
I come, O monarch! thus in arms, prepar'd   351
Thy kingdom and our common faith to guard:
Command me now what taſks I muſt ſuſtain,
Nor high attempts I fear, nor low diſdain:

E 4

Or

Or let my force in open field be shown;   355
Or here detain me to defend the town.

   To whom the king; What land so distant lies
From where the sun enlightens Asia's skies,
(O glorious virgin!) but resounds thy name,
Whose actions fill the sounding trump of fame? 360
Now to my aid thy conquering sword is join'd,
I give my fears and scruples to the wind;
Nor could I greater hopes of conquest boast,
Though join'd by numbers, succour'd by an host!
Methinks I seem to chide the lingering foe,   365
And Godfrey, to my wish, appears too slow!
Thou ask'st what labours I thy arm decree;
I deem the greatest only worthy thee:
To thee the rule of all our warrior-band
I here submit; be thine the high command.   370

   Thus said the king. The maid, with grateful look,
Her thanks return'd, and thus again she spoke:

   'Tis sure, O prince! a thing unusual heard,
Before the service done, to claim reward:
Yet (by thy goodness bold) I make my prayer, 375
And beg thy mercy yon condemn'd to spare;
Grant it for all my deeds in future time;
'Tis hard to suffer for a doubtful crime;

But

But this I wave, nor here the reasons plead
That speak them guiltless of th' imputed deed : 380
'Tis said some Christian hand the theft has wrought ;
But here I differ from the public thought :
The spell Ismeno fram'd t' assist our cause,
I deem an outrage on our sacred laws :
Nor fits it idols in our fanes to place,   385
Much less the idols of this impious race.
Methinks with joy the hand of Heaven I view,
To Macon's power the miracle is due ;
Who thus forbids his hallow'd rites to stain
With new religions in his awful fane.   390
Ismeno leave to spells and magic charms,
Since these to him supply the place of arms ;
While warriors we our foes in battle face,
Our swords our arts, in these our hopes we place.
  She ceas'd ; and, though the king could scarcely
        bend   395
His haughty soul, or ears to pity lend,
He yields his fury to the gentle maid ;
Her reasons move him, and her words persuade.
Let both have life and freedom (he reply'd)
To such a pleader nothing is deny'd !   400
If innocent, by justice let them live :
If criminal, I here their crime forgive.
                                    Thus

Thus were they freed: and lo! what blifsful fate,
What turns of fortune on Olindo wait!
His virtuous love at length awakes a flame   405
In the foft bofom of the generous dame.
Strait from the pile to Hymen's rites he goes,
Made of a wretch condemn'd, a joyful fpoufe:
Since death with her he fought, the grateful fair
Confents with him the gift of life to fhare.   410
The Pagan monarch, whofe fufpicious mind
Beheld with fear fuch wondrous virtue join'd,
Sent both in exile, by fevere command,
Beyond the limits of Judæa's land.
Then many others (as his fury fway'd)   415
Were banifh'd thence, or deep in dungeons laid.
But the fierce tyrant thofe remov'd alone,
Of ftrength approv'd, and daring fpirits known:
The tender fex and children he retain'd,
With helplefs age, as pledges in his hand.   420
Thus wretched wanderers, fome were doom'd to
          roam
From parents, children, wives, and native home:
Part rove from land to land with doubtful courfe;
And part againft him turn their vengeful force.
Thefe to the band of Franks unite their fate,   425
And meet their army entering Emmaüs' gate.

7   The

The town of Emmaüs near to Sion lay,
Not half the journey of an easy day.
The pleasing thought each Christian soul inspires,
And adds new ardour to their zealous fires !   430
But since the sun had past his middle race,
The leader there commands the tents to place.
The host were now encamp'd ; the setting sun
With milder lustre from the ocean shone,
When, drawing near, two mighty chiefs were seen,
In garb unknown, and of a foreign mien ,   436
Their acts pacific, and their looks, proclaim
That to the Christian chief as friends they came :
From Egypt's king dispatch'd, their way they bend,
And menial servants on their steps attend.   440

Alethes one : his birth obscure he ow'd
To the base refuse of th' ignoble crowd ,
Rais'd to the highest state the realm affords,
By plausive speech, and eloquence of words :
His subtle genius every taste could meet ;   445
In fiction prompt, and skilful in deceit :
Master of calumny such various ways,
He most accuses when he seems to praise.

The other chief from fair Circassia came
To Egypt's court, Argantes was his name :   450

Exalted

Exalted midſt the princes of the land,
And firſt in rank of all the martial band :
Impatient, fiery, and of rage unquell'd,
In arms unconquer'd, matchleſs in the field ;
Whoſe impious ſoul contempt of Heaven avow'd, 455
His ſword his law, his own right hand his God !

   Now theſe an audience of the leader ſought,
And now to Godfrey's awful ſight were brought.
There lowly ſeated, with his peers around,
In modeſt garb the glorious chief they found.   460
True valour, unadorn'd, attracts the ſight,
And ſhines conſpicuous by his native light.
To him a ſlight reſpect Argantes paid,
As one who little place or honours weigh'd.
But low Alethes bow'd in thought profound,   465
And fix'd his humble eyes upon the ground ;
His better hand his penſive boſom preſs'd,
With all the adoration of the eaſt :
And while attention on his accents hung,
Theſe words, like honey, melted from his tongue :

   O worthy thou alone ! to whoſe command   471
Submit the heroes of this glorious band !
To thee their laurels and their crowns they owe,
Thy conduct brings them victors from the foe :

Nor

Nor ſtops thy fame within Alcides' bounds,   475
To diſtant Egypt Godfrey's name reſounds!
Fame through our ſpacious realm thy glory bears,
And ſpeaks thy valour to our liſtening ears.
But on thy deeds our ſovereign chiefly dwells,
With pleaſure hears them, and with pleaſure tells:
In thee, what others fear or hate, he loves;·   481
Thy virtue fires him, and thy valour moves:
Fain would he join with thee in friendly bands,
And mutual peace and amity demands.
Since different faiths their ſanction here deny,   485
Let mutual virtue knit the ſacred tye.
But as he hears thy troops their marches bend
To expel from Sion's walls his ancient friend;
He now (to avoid thoſe evils yet behind)
By us unfolds the counſels of his mind.   490
Then thus he ſays: Thy firſt deſign forbear,
Content with what thou now haſt gain'd in war:
Nor on Judæa's realm thy forces bring,
Nor vex the lands protected by our king;
So will he, joiu'd with thee, thy power enſure,   495
And fix thy yet uncertain ſtate ſecure:
United both; their conqueſt to regain,
The Turks and Perſians ſhall attempt in vain.

Much

Much haſt thou done, O chief! in little ſpace,
Which length of ages never can deface.   500
What cities won! what armies overthrown!
What dangerous marches, and what ways unknown!
The neighbouring ſtates with terror own thy fame:
And diſtant regions tremble at thy name.

Your glory at the height, with heedful care   505
Avoid the chances of a doubtful war:
Increaſe of realm your further toils may crown,
But conqueſt ne'er can heighten your renown:
And ſhould your arms be now in battle croſt,
Loſt is your empire, and your glory loſt!   510
Infenſate he who riſks a certain ſtate,
For diſtant proſpects of uncertain fate.

Yet our advice perchance will lightly weigh,
And urge thy purpoſe, nor thy march delay;
While uncontrol'd ſucceſs thy ſoul inſpires,   515
While glows thy boſom with ambition's fires;
That glorious frailty of the noble mind,
To conquer nations, and ſubdue mankind!
For this you fly from proffer'd peace afar,
With more diſtaſte than others ſhun the war: 520
Theſe motives bid thee ſtill the path purſue,
Which fate has open'd largely to thy view:

Nor

Nor in the sheath return that dreaded sword,
(Of every conquest in the field assur'd)
Till in oblivion Macon's laws are laid,   525
And Asia, by thy arms, a desart made!
Alluring sounds, and grateful to the ear;
But O what dangers lurk beneath the snare!
Then, if no cloud of passion dims thy sight,
And casts a veil before thy reason's light;   530
Well may'st thou see what little hopes appear,
From every prospect of the lengthen'd war.
Reflect how soon the gifts of fortune turn;
Those who rejoice to-day, to-morrow mourn:
And he who soars an unexpected flight,   535
Oft falls as sudden from his towering height.
Say, to thy harm, should Egypt take the field
In arms, in treasure rich, in council skill'd;
And add to these (the war again begun)
The Turks, the Persians, and Cassano's son;   540
What forces could'st thou to their power oppose;
And how escape from such an host of foes!
Or do'st thou in the Grecian king confide,
By sacred union to thy cause ally'd?

 Ver. 540. —*Cassano's son*;] The son of the king of
Antioch.

To

To whom is not the Grecian faith difplay'd ?   545
What fnares for thee the guileful race have laid !
Will thofe, who once your common march withftood,
Now rifk for you their lives in fields of blood ?
But thou perhaps (fecure amidft thy foes)
Do'ft in thefe fquadrons all thy hopes repofe ;   550
And deem'ft the fcatter'd bands thy force o'erthrew
As eafy, when united, to fubdue ;
Though toilfome marches have your troops annoy'd,
Your ftrength enfeebled, and your men deftroy'd ;
Though unexpected nations fhould combine,   555
And Egypt with the Turks and Perfians join.
Yet grant that fate fo ftrongly arms thy band,
No fword can conquer, and no foe withftand :
Lo ! Famine comes, with all her ghaftly train ;
What further fubterfuge, what hopes remain ?   560
Then draw the falchion, and the javelin wield ;
Then dream of conqueft in the boafted field.
Behold th' inhabitants have wafted wide
The fertile country, and the fields deftroy'd ;
And fafely lodg'd in towers their ripen'd grain : 565
What hopes are left thy numbers to fuftain ?
Thy fhips, thou fay'ft, will due provifion fend :
Does then thy fafety on the winds depend ?

Perhaps

Perhaps thy fortune can the winds reſtrain;
Thy voice appeaſe the roaring of the main.   570
Yet think; ſhould once our nation riſe in fight,
And with the Perſians and the Turks unite,
Could we not then oppoſe a numerous fleet,
On equal terms, thy naval power to meet?
If here, O chief! thou ſeek'ſt to gain renown,   575
A double conqueſt muſt thy labours crown :
One loſs may ſully every former deed ;
One loſs may unexpeſted dangers breed :
Before our veſſels ſhould thy navy fly,
Thy forces here, oppreſt by famine, die :   580
Or ſhould'ſt thou loſe the battle here, in vain
Thy fleet would ride victorious on the main.
Then if thy ſoul reject the peace we bring,
And ſcorn the friendſhip of th' Egyptian king :
This conduct (undiſguis'd the truth I tell)   585
Nor ſuits thy·virtue, nor thy wiſdom well.
But if thy purpoſe ſeem to war inclin'd,
Heaven change, to gentle peace, thy better mind :
So Aſia may at length from troubles ceaſe,
And thou enjoy thy conquer'd lands in peace.   590
And you, ye leaders, who his dangers ſhare,
Fellows in arms, and partners of the war !

Ah, let not fortune's smiles your souls excite,
To tempt again the doubtful chance of fight.
But as the pilot, 'scap'd the treacherous deep,   595
Rests in the welcome port his weary ship :
Now surl your sails with pleasure near the shore,
And trust the perils of the sea no more.

  Here ceas'd Alethes ; and the heroes round,
With looks displeas'd, return'd a murmuring sound:
With deep disdain the terms propos'd they heard, 601
While discontent in every face appear'd.
Then thrice the chief his eyes around him threw,
And cast on every one his piercing view ;
Next to Alethes turn'd his careful look,   605
Who waited his reply, and thus he spoke.

  Ambassador ! with threats and praises join'd,
Full wisely hast thou told thy sovereign's mind :
If he esteem us, and our worth approve,
With grateful pleasure we receive his love.   610
But where thy words a threaten'd storm disclose
Of Pagan armies, and confederate foes ;
To this I speak ; to this my answer hear ;
An open purpose cloath'd in words sincere.
Know first the cause for which we have sustain'd 615
Such various hazards both by sea and land ;

By day and night such pious toils have known: —
To free the passage to yon' hallow'd town;
To merit favour from the King of heaven,
By freedom to the suffering Christians given.   620
Nor shall we fear, for such a glorious end,
Our kingdom, lives, and worldly fame to spend.
No thirst of riches has our bosoms fir'd;
No lust of empire our attempt inspir'd:
If any thoughts like these our souls infest,   625
Th' Eternal drive such poison from the breast!
Still may his mercy o'er our steps preside,
His hand defend us, and his wisdom guide!
His breath inspir'd; his pow'r has brought us far
Through every danger of the various war: 630
By this are mountains past, and rivers crost;
This tempers summer's heat, and winter's frost:
This can the rage of furious tempests bind,
And loosen or restrain th' obedient wind:
Hence lofty walls are burnt and tumbled down; 635
Hence martial bands are slain and overthrown:
Hence springs the hope and confidence we boast;
Not from the forces of a mortal host:
Not from our vessels; nor from Grecian lands
With numbers swarming; nor the Gallic bands. 640

F 2   And

And if we ſtill th' Almighty's care partake,
Let nations, at their will, our cauſe forſake !
Who knows the ſuccour of his powerful hands,
No other aid, in time of need, demands.
But ſhould he, for our ſins, his help withdraw, 645
(As who can fathom Heaven's eternal law !)
Lives there a man who would not find his tomb,
Where hallow'd earth did once his God inhume ?
So ſhall we die, nor envy thoſe who live ;
Nor unreveng'd ſhall we our death receive ;   650
Nor Aſia ſhall rejoice to view our ſtate ;
Nor we ſubmit with ſorrow to our fate !
Yet think not that our wayward minds prefer,
To gentle peace, the horrid ſcenes of war :
Nor think we ill your monarch's love return ;   655
Or with contempt his friendly union ſcorn.
But wherefore do his cares on Sion bend ?
And wherefore thus another's realms defend ?
Then let him not require our arms to ceaſe ;
So may he rule his native lands in peace !   660
    Thus anſwer'd Godfrey : and with fury ſwell'd
The fierce Argantes, nor his wrath repell'd :
The boiling paſſion from his boſom broke ;
Before the chief he ſtood, and thus he ſpoke :

Let

Let him, who will not proffer'd peace receive, 665
Be fated with the plagues that war can give !
And well thy hatred of the peace is known,
If now thy foul reject our friendfhip fhown.

This faid, his mantle in his hand he took,
And folding round before th' affembly fhook, 670
Then thus again with threatening accent fpoke :

O thou ! who every peril would'ft defpife,
Lo ! peace or war within this mantle lies !
See here th' election offer'd to thy voice ;
No more delay—but now declare thy choice !   675

His fpeech and haughty mien each leader fir'd,
And with a noble rage their fouls infpir'd :
War ! war ! aloud with general voice they cry'd ;
Nor waited till their god-like chief reply'd.
At this the Pagan fhook his veft in air—   680
Then take defiance, death, and mortal war !
So fierce he fpoke, he feem'd to burft the gates
Of Janus' temple, and difclofe the fates :

Ver. 669. *This faid, his mantle in his hand he took,—*] Thus
Livy relates of the Roman ambaffador before the Cartha-
ginian fenate. " Tum Romanus, finu ex toga facto ; his,
inquit, vobis bellum et pacem portamus, utrum placet,
fumite. Sub hanc vocem haud minus ferociter daret utrum
vellet fic clamatum eft. Et cum is, finu iterum effufo, bellum
dixiffet ; accipere fe omnes refponderunt, &c." Lib. xxi.

While from his mantle, which aſide he threw,
Infenſate rage and horrid diſcord flew :   685
Alecto's torch ſupply'd her helliſh flame,
And from his eyes the flaſhing ſparkles came.
So look'd the chief of old, whoſe impious pride,
With mortal works, the King of heaven defy'd ;
So ſtood, when Babel rear'd her front on high,   690
To threaten battle 'gainſt the ſtarry ſky.

   Then Godſrey—To thy king the tidings bear ;
And tell him we accept the threaten'd war ;
Go, bid him haſten here to prove our might,
Or on the banks of Nile expect the fight.   695

   This ſaid ; the leader honour'd either gueſt,
And due reſpect, by different gifts, expreſs'd.
Alethes firſt he gave a helm of price ;
A prize among the ſpoils of conquer'd Nice.
A coſtly ſword Argantes next obtain'd,   700
Well wrought and faſhion'd by the workman's hand :
Matchleſs the work, and glorious to behold,
The hilt with jewels blaz'd, and flam'd with gold.
With joy the Pagan chief the gift ſurvey'd,
Admir'd the rich deſign and temper'd blade :   705

   Ver. 688. *So look'd the chief of old,—*] Nimrod, who built
the tower of Babel.

Then

Then thus to Godfrey: When we meet in field,
Behold how well our hands thy prefent wield!
    Now, parting from the camp, their leave they
        took,
And thus Argantes to Alethes fpoke.
    Lo! to Jerufalem my courfe I take;   710
To Egypt thou thy purpos'd journey make:
Thou with the early rays of morning light;
But I impatient with the friendly night.
Well may th' Egyptian court my prefence fpare:
Suffice that thou the Chriftian's anfwer bear;   715
Be mine to mingle in the lov'd alarms
Of noble conflict, and the found of arms.
    Thus he, ambaffador of peace who came,
Departs a foe in action and in name:
Nor heeds the warrior, in his haughty mind,   720
The ancient laws of nations and mankind:
Nor for Alethes' anfwer deign'd to ftay,
But through furrounding fhades purfu'd his way,
And fought the town, impatient of delay.   724

    Ver. 720. *Nor heeds the warrior,—*] By the law of na-
tions, no perfon, exercifing the office of meffenger or ambaffador, fhould take an active hoftile part, till his office is
completely expired.

.F 4

Now

Now had the night her drowfy pinions fpread !
The winds were hufh'd ; the weary waves were dead !
The fifh repos'd in feas and cryftal floods ;
The beafts retir'd in covert of the woods ;
The painted birds in grateful filence flept ;
And o'er the world a fweet oblivion crept.   730
But not the faithful hoft, with thought opprefs'd,
Nor could their leader tafte the gift of reft ;
Such ardent wifhes in their bofoms burn ;
So eager were they for the day's return ;
To lead their forces to the hallow'd town,   735
The foldier's triumph, and the victor's crown !
With longing eyes they wait the morning light,
To chace with early beams the dufk of night,

END OF THE SECOND BOOK.

THE THIRD BOOK

OF

JERUSALEM DELIVERED.

THE ARGUMENT.

The Christian army arrives before Jerusalem. The alarm is given to the Saracens, who prepare for the reception of the enemy. Clorinda makes the first sally; she encounters and kills Gardo; she meets and engages with Tancred; a short interview ensues between them. In the mean time, Argantes, falling on the Christians with a great slaughter, the action becomes more general. Erminia, from the walls, shows and describes to the king the several commanders of the Christian army. Rinaldo and Tancred perform great actions. Dudon, having signalized himself, is killed by Argantes. The Pagans, being closely pressed, are at last compelled to retreat to the city. Godfrey causes Dudon to be interred with funeral honours; and sends his workmen to fell timber for making engines to carry on the siege.

THIRD BOOK

OF

JERUSALEM DELIVERED.

NOW from the golden eaſt the Zephyrs borne,
    Proclaim'd with balmy gales th' approach of
        morn;
And fair Aurora deck'd her radiant head
With roſes cropt from Eden's flowery bed;
When from the ſounding camp was heard afar   5
The noiſe of troops preparing for the war:
To this ſucceed the trumpet's loud alarms,
And rouze, with ſhriller notes, the hoſt to arms.
The ſage commander o'er their zeal preſides,
And with a gentle rein their ardour guides.   10
Yet eaſier ſeem'd it, near Charybdis' caves,
To ſtay the current of the boiling waves;
Or ſtop the north, that ſhakes the mountain's brow,
And whelms the veſſels in the ſeas below.

He

He rules their order, marshals every band :   15
Rapid they move, but rapid with command.
With holy zeal their swelling hearts abound ;
And their wing'd footsteps scarcely print the ground.
When now the sun ascends th' ethereal way,
And strikes the dusty field with warmer ray ;   20
Behold Jerusalem in prospect lies !
Behold Jerusalem salutes their eyes !
At once a thousand tongues repeat the name,
And hail Jerusalem with loud acclaim !

    To sailors thus, who, wandering o'er the main, 25
Have long explor'd some distant coast in vain,
In seas unknown and foreign regions lost,
By stormy winds and faithless billows tost,
If chance at length th' expected land appear,
With joyful shouts they hail it from afar ;   30
They point, with rapture, to the wish'd-for shore,
And dream of former toils and fears no more.

    At first, transported with the pleasing sight,
Each Christian bosom glow'd with full delight ;

Ver. 21. *Behold Jerusalem*—] The emphatical repetition
of the name Jerusalem, is adopted from Virgil, and has a fine
effect in this book, which opens with wonderful solemnity.

    Italiam, Italiam primus conclamat Achates ! Æn. III.

                                     But

But deep contrition foon their joy fuppreſs'd,　35
And holy forrow fadden'd every breaſt :
Scarce dare their eyes the city walls furvey,
Where, cloth'd in fleſh, their dear Redeemer lay :
Whoſe facred earth did once their Lord encloſe,
And where triumphant from the grave he roſe !　40
Each faltering tongue imperfect fpeech fupplies ;
Each labouring boſom heaves with frequent fighs ;
At once their mingled joys and griefs appear,
And undiſtinguiſh'd murmurs fill the air.
So when the grove the fanning wind receives,　45
A whiſpering noiſe is heard among the leaves :
So, near the craggy rocks or winding ſhore,
In hollow founds the broken billows roar.
Each took th' example as their chieftans led,
With naked feet the hallow'd foil they tread :　50
Each throws his martial ornaments afide,
The creſted helmets, with their plumy pride :
To humble thoughts their lofty hearts they bend,
And down their cheeks the pious tears defcend :
Yet each, as if his breaſt no forrow mov'd,　55
In words like theſe his tardy grief reprov'd :

Ver. 50.　*With naked feet—*]　This circumſtance is recorded in the hiſtory of the crufaders

Here,

Here, where thy wounds, O Lord! diftill'd a flood,
And dy'd the hallow'd foil with ftreaming blood,
Shall not thefe eyes their grateful tribute fhower,
In fad memorial of that awful hour ?   60
Ah ! wherefore frozen thus my heart appears,
Nor melts in fountains of perpetual tears !
Why does my harden'd heart this temper keep ?
Now mourn thy fins, thy Saviour's fufferings weep !

    Meantime the watch that in the city ftood,   65
And from a lofty tower the country view'd,
Saw midft the fields a rifing duft appear,
That like a thickening cloud obfcur'd the air ;
From whence, by fits, a flafhing fplendor came,
And fudden gleams of momentary flame :   70
Refulgent arms and armour next were feen,
And fteeds diftinguifh'd, and embattled men :
Then thus aloud—What mift obfcures the day !
What fplendors in yon dufty whirlwind play !
Rife, rife, ye citizens ! your gates defend :   75
Hafte, fnatch your weapons, and the walls afcend !
Behold the foe at hand !—he faid, and ceas'd :
The Pagans heard, and fnatch'd their arms in hafte.
The helplefs children, and the female train,
With feeble age that could not arms fuftain,   80

                                        Pale

Pale and affrighted to the mofques repair,
And humbly fupplicate the powers with prayer.
But thofe of limbs robuft, and firm of foul,
Already arm'd, impatient of control,
Part line the gates, and part afcend the wall :   85
The king with care provides, and orders all :
From place to place he marfhall'd every crew,
Then to the fummit of a tower withdrew,
From whence in profpect lay the fubject-lands, '
From whence he could with eafe direct the bands. 90
And there Erminia by his fide he plac'd,
The fair Erminia, who his palace grac'd,
Since Antioch fell before the Chriftian hoft,
And her dear fire the haplefs virgin loft.

   Now had Clorinda with impatient fpeed,   95
T' attack the Franks, a chofen fquadron led :
But, in a different part, Circaffia's knight *
Stood at a fecret gate prepar'd for fight.
The generous maid with looks intrepid fir'd
Her brave companions, and with words infpir'd. 100
'Tis ours to found the glorious work, (fhe cries)
The hope of Afia in our courage lies !
While thus fhe fpeaks, fhe fees a Chriftian band
With rural fpoils advancing o'er the land ;

         * ARGANTES.

                            Who

Who fent, as wont, to forage round the plain,   105
Now feek with flocks and herds the camp again.
Sudden on thefe fhe turn'd ; their chief beheld
Her threatening force, and met her in the field :
Gardo his name, a man approv'd in fight,
But weak his ftrength t' oppofe Clorinda's might. 110
Slain in the dreadful fhock, on earth he lies,
O'erthrown before the Franks' and Syrians' eyes.
Loud, at the fight, exclaim the Pagan train,
And hail this omen, but their hopes were vain !
Fierce on the reft the warlike virgin flew,   115
And pierc'd their battle, and their ranks o'erthrew ;
And, where her flaughtering fword a paffage hew'd,
Her following troops the glorious path purfu'd.
Soon from the fpoilers' hands their fpoil they take :
The Franks, by flow degrees, the field forfake ; 120
At length the fummit of a hill they gain,
And, aided by the height, the foes fuftain.

    Now, like a whirlwind rufhing from the fkies,
Or fwift as lightening through the ether flies,
At Godfrey's fignal, noble Tancred near   125
His fquadron moves, and fhakes his beamy fpear.
So firm his hands the ponderous javelin wield,
So fierce the youthful warrior fcours the field ;

The

The king, who view'd him from his towery height,
Esteem'd him sure some chief renown'd in fight: 130
Then to the maid beside him thus he spoke,
(Whose gentle soul with soft emotions shook)
Thou canst, by use, each Christian's name reveal,
Though here disguis'd, and cas'd in shining steel:
Say, who is he, so fierce in combat seen,   135
Of dauntless semblance, and erected mien?
At this the virgin heav'd a tender sigh,
The silent drops stood trembling in her eye:
But, all she could, the fair her tears suppress'd,
And stopp'd the murmurs of her troubled breast: 140
Yet on her cheeks the trickling dews appear'd,
And from her lips a broken sigh was heard.
Then artful to the king she thus reply'd;
(And strove with angry words her thoughts to hide)
Ah me! I know him sure, have cause too well, 145
Among a thousand, that dire chief to tell:
Oft have I seen him strow the purple plain,
And glut his fury with my people slain!

Ver. 133. *Thou canst, by use, each Christian's name reveal,*]
The following passages, where Erminia describes the leaders
of the Christian army, are closely copied from Homer,
where Helen, in like manner, shows the Grecian commanders to Priam from the walls of Troy. ILIAD, iii.

VOL. I.   G   Alas!

Alas! how fure his blows! the wounds they give,
Nor herbs can heal, nor magic arts relieve :   150
Tancred his name — O! grant fome happier hour
May yield him, living, prifoner to my pow'r!
So might my foul fome fecret comfort find,
And fweet revenge appeafe my reftlefs mind!

  She faid, and ceas'd; the king the damfel heard,
But to a diff'erent fenfe her fpeech referr'd;   156
While, mingled with thefe artful words fhe fpoke,
A figh fpontaneous from her bofom broke.

  Meanwhile, her lance in reft, the warrior-dame
With eager hafte t' encounter Tancred came.   160
Their vizors ftruck, the fpears in fhivers flew;
The virgin's face was left expos'd to view;
The thongs that held her helmet burft in twain;
Hurl'd from her head, it bounded on the plain:
Loofe in the wind her golden treffes flow'd,   165
And now a maid, confefs'd to all fhe ftood;
Keen flafh her eyes, her look with fury glows;
Yet ev'n in rage, each feature lovely fhows:
What charms muft then her winning fmiles dif-
      clofe ?
What thoughts, O Tancred! have thy bofom mov'd?
Do'ft thou not fee and know that face belov'd ? 171
                                             Lo !

Lo! there the face that caus'd thy amorous pains;
Afk thy fond heart, for there her form remains:
Behold the features of the lovely dame,
Who for refreſhment to the fountain came!   175
  The knight, who mark'd not firſt her creſt and
      ſhield,
Aſtoniſh'd now her well-known face beheld.
She, o'er her head diſarm'd, the buckler threw,
And on her ſenſeleſs foe with fury flew:
The foe retir'd; on other parts he turn'd   180
His vengeful ſteel: yet ſtill her anger burn'd;
And with a threatening voice aloud ſhe cry'd;
And with a two-fold death the chief defy'd.
Th' enamour'd warrior ne'er returns a blow,
Nor heeds the weapon of his lovely foe;   185
But views, with eager gaze, her charming eyes,
From whence the ſhaft of love unerring flies:
Then to himſelf — In vain the ſtroke deſcends;
In vain her angry ſword the wound intends;

Ver. 175. *Who for refreſhment to the fountain came!*] . See Book i. ver. 352, where the firſt account is given of Tan-cred's love to Clorinda, and the adventure here referred to.

Ver. 183. *And with a two-fold death —*] Con doppia morte — The Italian commentator explains this to mean, a natural death, and the death of love, *una amoroſa* ALTRA CORPORALE.

G 2

While

While from her face unarm'd she sends the dart,   190
That rives, with surer aim, my bleeding heart!

    At length resolv'd, though hopeless of relief,
No more in silence to suppress his grief,
And that the dame might know her rage pursu'd
A suppliant captive by her charms subdu'd,   195
O thou! (he cry'd) whose hostile fury glows
On me alone amid this host of foes,
Together let us from the field remove,
And, hand to hand, our mutual valour prove.

    The maid his challenge heard, and, void of fear,
With head unarm'd rush'd furious to the war: 201
Her trembling lover's steps in haste pursu'd,
And now, prepar'd, in act of combat stood,
Already aim'd a stroke, when loud he cry'd;
First make conditions ere the strife be try'd.   205

    Awhile her lifted arm the virgin staid,
And thus the youth, by love embolden'd, said.

    Ah! since on terms of peace thou wilt not join,
Transfix this heart, this heart no longer mine:
For thee with pleasure I resign my breath;   210
Receive my life, and triumph in my death.
See unresisting in thy sight I stand;
Then say what cause detains thy lingering hand?

                                        Or

Or shall I from my breast the corslet tear,
And to the stroke my naked bosom bare ?   215
    Thus wretched Tancred spoke, and more had said
T' unfold his sorrows to the wondering maid;
But sudden now his troops appear'd at hand,
Who closely press'd the Pagan's yielding band :
Or fear or art impell'd the Syrian race;   220
One seem'd to fly, while t'other held the chace.
When lo ! a soldier, who his foes pursu'd,
And, part expos'd, the fair Clorinda view'd,
Aim'd, as he pass'd behind th' unwary maid,
A sudden stroke at her defenceless head.   225
Tancred, who sees, exclaims with eager cries,
And with his sword to meet the weapon flies.
Yet not in vain was urg'd the hostile steel,
On her fair neck, beneath her head, it fell :
Slight was the wound; the crimson drops appear, 230
And tinge the ringlets of her golden hair.
So shines the gold, which skilful artists frame,
And, mix'd with rubies, darts a ruddy flame.

    Ver. 229. *On her fair neck,—*] This circumstance of
Clorinda being wounded, is very similar to the passage in
Boyardo, adopted by Ariosto, where Bradamant is in like
manner wounded in the head by a Pagan, while she is par-
leying with Rogero.

G 3

Fir'd

Fir'd at the deed, the prince in anger burn'd,
And, with his falchion, on th' offender turn'd.   235
This flies, and that purfues with vengeful mind,
Swift as an arrow on the wings of wind!
The mufing virgin view'd their courfe from far,
Then join'd her flying partners of the war.
By turns fhe flies; by turns fhe makes a ftand;   240
And boldly oft attacks the Chriftian band.
So fares a bull, with mighty ftrength indu'd,
In fome wide field by troops of dogs purfu'd;
Oft as he fhows his horns, the fearful train
Stop fhort, but follow when he flies again.   245
And ftill Clorinda as fhe fled the field,
Her head defended with her lifted fhield.
Now thefe the battle fly, and thofe purfue,
Till near the lofty walls appear in view;
When, with a dreadful fhout that fills the air,   250
The Pagans, turning fwift, renew the war;
Around the plain in circuit wide they bend,
And flank the Chriftians, and their rear offend.
Then bold Argantes, from the city's height,
Pours, with his fquadron, on the front of fight.   255
Impatient of delay, before his crew,
With furious hafte, the fierce Circaffian flew.

2

The

The firſt he met his thundering javelin found,
And horſe and horſeman tumbled to the ground :
And ere the truſty ſpear in ſhivers broke,   260
What numbers more an equal fate partook !
His falchion next he drew, and every blow,
Or ſlays, or wounds, or overturns the foe !
Clorinda ſaw, and kindled at the view,
And old Ardelius, fierce in battle, ſlew :   265
Robuſt in age ! two ſons their father guard ;
But nought can now the deadly weapon ward.
Alcander, eldeſt born, her fury found,
His ſire deſerting with a ghaſtly wound ;
And Poliphernes, next his place in fight,   270
Scarce ſav'd his life from brave Clorinda's might.

　　But Tancred, weary'd with the fruitleſs chace
Of him whoſe courſer fled with ſwiſter pace,
Now turn'd his eyes, and ſaw his troops from far
Engag'd too boldly in unequal war :   275
He view'd them by ſurrouding Pagans preſs'd,
And ſpurr'd his courſer to their aid in haſte.
Nor he alone, but to their reſcue came
The band, the firſt in dangers as in fame ;
The band by Dudon led, the hero's boaſt,   280
The ſtrength and bulwark of the Chriſtian hoſt.

G 4

Rinaldo,

Rinaldo, braveſt of the brave confeſs'd,
Like flaſhing lightening ſhone before the reſt!
Erminia ſoon the gallant prince beheld,
Known by the eagle in an azure field.   285
Then to the king, who thither turn'd his eyes :
Behold a chief, unmatch'd in arms ! (ſhe cries)
No ſword like his in yonder camp is ſeen,
Yet ſcarce appears the down to ſhade his chin.
Six champions more, his equals in the field,   290
Had made already conquer'd Syria yield :
The furtheſt regions had confeſs'd their ſway,
The diſtant realms beneath the riſing day !
And ev'n the Nile, perhaps, his head unknown
Had vainly then conceal'd, the yoke to ſhun !   295
Such is the youth ! his name Rinaldo call—
Whoſe hand with terror ſhakes the threaten'd wall !
Now turn your eyes, and yonder chief behold,
Array'd in verdant arms and ſhining gold :
Dudon his name, (the gallant band he leads,   300
Adventurers call'd, and firſt in martial deeds)

Ver. 285. *Known by the eagle* —] The white eagle in the
azure ſhield was the enſign of the houſe of Eſtè : much is
ſaid of this device by Arioſto, who gives it to Mandricardo
and Rogero, and feigns it to have been borne by Hector of
Troy.

OF

Of noble lineage, with experience crown'd,
In age fuperior, as in worth renown'd.
See where yon leader clad in fable ftands,
(Whofe brother holds the rule of Norway's lands)
Gernando fierce, of no unwarlike name,   306
But with his pride he fullies all his fame.
The friendly couple, who, in vefture white,
So clofe together fhare the tafk of fight,
Are Edward and Gildippe, (blamelefs pair!)   310
In love unequall'd, and renown'd in war!

    While thus fhe fpoke; upon the plain below,
They faw more deep the dreadful carnage grow:
There Tancred and Rinaldo's furious hands
Pierc'd the thick ranks, and broke th' oppofing bands.
Next, with his fquadron, Dudon rufh'd along,   316
And pour'd impetuous on the hoftile throng.
Ev'n fierce Argantes, tumbled to the ground
By brave Rinaldo, fcarce his fafety found:
Nor had the haughty chief efcap'd fo well,   320
But lo! Rinaldo's horfe that inftant fell,
And chancing on his mafter's foot to light,
Detain'd awhile the champion from the fight.
The routed Pagans, now opprefs'd with dread,
Forfook their ranks, and to the city fled.   325

Alone

Alone Clorinda and Argantes bear
The raging storm that thunders on the rear.
Intrepid these maintain their dangerous post,
And break the fury of the conquering host :
Their daring hands the foremost battle meet,   330
Bid slaughter pause, and cover the retreat.
Impetuous Dudon chac'd the flying crew,
And fierce Tigranes, with a shock, o'erthrew ;
Then through his neck the sword a passage found,
And left the carcase headless on the ground.   335
In vain his cuirass steel'd Algazor wore ;
Corbano's temper'd casque avail'd no more !
This through the nape and face the weapon press'd ;
That, through the back, and issu'd at his breast.
Then Amurath and Mahomet he slew ;   340
Their souls reluctant from their bodies flew.
The stern Almanzor next his valour prov'd ;
And scarce secure the great Circassian mov'd.
Argantes rav'd, his breast with fury burn'd,
And oft, retreating, on the foe he turn'd ;   345
Till with a sudden stroke the chief he found,
And in his flank impress'd a mortal wound.
Prone falls the leader, stretch'd on earth he lies,
An iron sleep invades his swimming eyes :

And

And thrice he strives to view the light in vain,   350
And on his arm his sinking bulk sustain ;
Thrice backward falls, and sickens at the sight,
And shuts at length his eyes in endless night :
A chilly sweat o'er all his body streams ;
A mortal coldness numbs his stiffening limbs.   355
The fierce Argantes stay'd not o'er the dead,
But, turning to the Franks, aloud he said :

  Warriors, attend ! survey this bloody sword,
But yester's sun the present of your lord !
Mark how this hand has try'd its use to-day :   360
Haste ! to his ears the glad report convey :
What secret pleasure must your leader feel,
To find his glorious gift approv'd so well !
Bid him, to nobler purpose soon address'd,
Expect this weapon bury'd in his breast ;   365
And should he long delay our force to meet,
This hand shall tear him from his dark retreat.

  Boastful he spoke ; enrag'd the Christians hear,
And furious round him drive the thickening war ;
But he already, with the flying crew,   370
Safe in the shelter of the town withdrew.

  Now from the wall the close defenders pour
Their stones, like storms of hail, a missile show'r :

Unnumber'd

Unnumber'd quivers shafts for bows supply;
And clouds of arrows from the ramparts fly !   375
Awhile they force th' advancing Franks to stand,
Till in the gates retreat the Pagan band;
When lo ! Rinaldo came, (who now had freed
His foot encumber'd by his fallen steed)
Eager he rush'd, on proud Argantes' head   380
To take revenge for haplefs Dudon dead :
Through all the ranks, inspiring rage, he flies :
Why stand we lingering here ? (the warrior cries)
Lost is the chief who rul'd our band of late,
Why haste we not t' avenge the leader's fate ?   385
When such a cause our vengeful force demands,
Shall these weak ramparts stop our conquering hands ?
Did walls of triple steel the town enclose,
Or adamantine bulwarks guard the foes,
Yet vainly there should hope to lurk secure   390
The fierce Argantes from your wrathful power.—
Haste ! let us storm the gates.—He said, and flew
With foremost speed before the warring crew ,
Dauntlefs he goes, nor falling stones he fears,
Nor storms of arrows, hissing round his ears :   395
So fierce he nods his crest, so towers on high,
Such lightening flashes from his angry eye ;

The

The Pagans · on   the   walls,   with   doubts op-
        prefs'd,
Feel fudden terrors rife in every breaft.

While thus Rinaldo to the battle moves,   400
And thefe encourages, and thofe reproves ;
Behold, difpatch'd by Godfrey's high commands,
The good Sigero ftopp'd th' advancing bands :
He, in the leader's name, reprefs'd their heat,
And bade the Chriftians from the field retreat. 405
Return, ye warriors ! (thus aloud he cry'd)
Till fitter feafon lay your arms afide :
This Godfrey wills, and be his will obey'd.—
He faid : Rinaldo then his ardor ftaid,
And ftern obedience to the fummons paid.   410
He turn'd ; but his difdainful looks reveal'd
The fury in his breaft but ill conceal'd.

Now from the walls th' unwilling fquadrons go,
Retiring, unmolefted by the foe ;
Yet leave not Dudon's corfe, in battle flain,   415
Depriv'd of rites, neglected on the plain :
Supported in their arms, with pious care,
His faithful friends their honour'd burthen bear.
Meantime aloft their leader Godfrey ftood,
And from a rifing ground the city view'd.   420

On

On two unequal hills the city stands,
A vale between divides the higher lands.
Three sides without impervious to the foes:
The northern side an easy passage shows,
With smooth ascent; but well they guard the part
With lofty walls, and labour'd works of art.   425
The city lakes and living springs contains;
And cisterns to receive the falling rains:
But bare of herbage is the country round;
Nor springs nor streams refresh the barren ground.
No tender flower exalts its cheerful head: 431
No stately trees at noon their shelter spread,
Save where two leagues remote a wood appears,
Embrown'd with noxious shade, the growth of years!

   Where morning gilds the city's eastern side,   435
The sacred Jordan pours its gentle tide.
Extended lie, against the setting day,
The sandy borders of the midland sea:
Samaria to the north, and Bethel's wood,
Where to the golden calf the altar stood: 440

Ver. 421. *On two unequal hills* —] Ariosto, in like manner, particularly describes the situation of the city of Paris, before the attack made by the Pagan army.
           ORLANDO FURIOSO, Book xiv. ver. 772:

                       And

And on the miny south, the hallow'd earth
Of Bethl'em, where the Lord receiv'd his birth.
    While Godfrey thus, above the subject field,
The lofty walls and Sion's strength beheld ;
And ponder'd where t' encamp his martial pow'rs, 445
And where he best might storm the hostile tow'rs ; .
Full on the chief Erminia cast a look,
Then show'd him to the king, and thus she spoke.
    There Godfrey stands, in purple vesture seen,
Of reg-l presence, and exalted mien.   450
He seems by nature born to kingly sway,
Vers'd in each art to make mankind obey :
Well skill'd alike in every task of fight ;
In whom the soldier and the chief unite :   .
Nor can the troops of yonder numerous host, 455
A wiser head or steadier courage boast.
Raymond alone with him the praise can share
Of wisdom in the cool debates of war ;.
Tancred alone, and great Rinaldo claim
An equal glory in the field of fame.   460
    All tongues (reply'd the king) his worth report ;
I saw and knew him at the Gallic court,
When Egypt sent me envoy into France :
Oft in the lists I saw him wield the lance ;

A stripling

A ſtripling then, for ſcarce the down began   465
To clothe his cheeks, the promiſe of a man !
Yet did his words and early deeds preſage,
Too ſure, alas ! his fame in riper age !
  Sighing he ſpoke, and hung his penſive head,
Then rais'd his eyes again, and thus he ſaid.   470
  Say, what is he who ſtands by Godfrey's ſide,
His upper garments with vermilion dy'd ?
How near his air, his looks how much the ſame ;
Though ſhort his ſtature, leſs erect his frame !
'Tis Baldwin, brother to the prince (ſhe cry'd) 475
In feature like, but more by deeds ally'd.
Now turn thy eyes where, with a reverend mien,
In act to council yonder chief is ſeen :
Raymond is he, in every conduct ſage,
Mature in wiſdom of experienc'd age :   480
None better warlike ſtratagems can frame,
Of all the Gallic or the Latian name.
Beyond, the Britiſh monarch's ſon behold,
The noble William with the caſque of gold.
Next Guelpho, whom his birth and actions raiſe, 485
Among the foremoſt names to equal praiſe :
Full well I know the chief, to ſight confeſs'd,
By his broad ſhoulders and his ample cheſt.

                                              But

But still, amidst yon numerous troops below,
My eyes explore in vain their deadliest foe :   490
Bœmond, whose fury all my race purfu'd,
The stern destroyer of my royal blood !

    Thus commune they : while from the hill descends
The Christian chief, and joins his warlike friends.
The city view'd; he deems th' attempt were vain; 495
O'er craggy rocks the steepy pass to gain.
Then on the ground, that rose with smooth ascent,
Against the northern gate, he pitch'd his tent ;
And thence, proceeding to the corner tower,
Encamp'd in length the remnant of his power ; 500
But could not half the city's wall enclose,
So wide around the spacious bulwarks rose.

    But Godfrey well secures each several way
That might assistance to the town convey :
To seize on every pass his care he bends,   505
And round with trenches deep the camp defends.

    These works perform'd ; his steps the hero turn'd,
Where lay the breathless corse of Dudon mourn'd :
Arriv'd, the lifeless leader prone he found,
With many weeping friends encompass'd round : 510
High on a stately bier the dead was plac'd,
With funeral pomp and friendly honours grac'd.

When Godfrey enter'd, foon the mournful crowd
Indulg'd their fecret woes and wept aloud :
While, with a face compos'd, the pious chief   515
Beheld in filence, and fupprefs'd his grief :
Till, having view'd awhile the warrior dead,
With thoughtful looks intent, at length he faid.

   Nor plaints nor forrow to thy death we owe,
Though call'd fo fudden from our world below : 520
In heaven thou liv'ft again ; thy mortal name
Has left behind thee glorious tracks of fame.
Well haft thou kept on earth the Chriftian laws ;
Well haft thou dy'd a warrior in their caufe !
Now, happy fhade ! enjoy thy Maker's fight,   525
Unfading laurels now thy toils requite !
Hail and be blefs'd ! we mourn not here thy fate,
But weep the chance of our deferted ftate.
With thee, fo bravely parting from our hoft,
How ftrong a finew of the camp is loft !   530

   Ver. 513. *When Godfrey enter'd, —*] The following paffage is taken from Virgil's account of the behaviour of
Æneas at the death of Pallas, Æn. xi. and from Ariofto's
funeral of Brandimart, Book xliii. where Orlando is introduced making a noble and pathetic oration over his de-
ceafed friend.

                                        But

But though the fate, which fnatch'd thee from our
      eyes,
Thy earthly fuccour to our caufe denies;
Thy foul can yet celeftial aids obtain,
Elected one of Heaven's immortal train.
Oft have we feen thee in th' embattled field,   535
A mortal then, thy mortal weapons wield:
So hope we ftill to fee thee wield in fight
The fatal arms of Heaven's refiftlefs might.
O! hear our prayers; our pious vows receive;
With pity all our earthly toils relieve: 540
Procure us conqueft, and our hoft fhall pay
Their thanks to thee, on that triumphant day.

   Thus fpoke the chief: and now the fable night
Had banifh'd every beam of chearful light;
And, with oblivion fweet of irkfome cares,   545
Impos'd a truce on mortal plaints and tears.

   But fleeplefs Godfrey lay, who faw 'twere vain
T' attempt, without machines, the walls to gain:
What foreft might the ample planks provide,
And how to frame the piles his thoughts employ'd.

   Up with the fun he rofe, and left his bed   551
T' attend the funeral rites of Dudon dead.
Near to the camp, beneath a hillock, ftood
The ftately tomb, compos'd of cyprefs-wood:

H 2

Above

Above a palm-tree fpread its verdant fhade.   555
To this the mourning troop the corfe convey'd :
With thefe the holy priefts (a reverend train !)
A requiem chanted to the warrior flain.
High on the boughs were hung, difplay'd to fight,
The various arms and enfigns worn in fight ;   560
In happier times the trophies of his hands,
Gain'd from the Syrian and the Perfian bands.
The mighty trunk his fhining cuirafs bore,
And all thofe arms which once the hero wore.
Then on the fculptur'd tomb thefe words appear : 565
" Here Dudon lies—the glorious chief revere !"
    Soon as the prince thefe pious rites had paid,
(The laft fad office to the worthy dead)
He fent his workmen to the woods, prepar'd,
And well fupported with a numerous guard.   570
Conceal'd in lowly vales the foreft ftands,
A Syrian fhew'd it to the Chriftian bands.
To this they march to hew the timbers down,
To fhake the ramparts of the hallow'd town.
To fell the trees each other they provoke ;   575
Th' infulted foreft groans at ev'ry ftroke.

Ver. 571. *Conceal'd in lowly vales* —] This foreft was fix
miles diftant from the city, and, agreeable to what the poet
here fays, was firft pointed out to them by a Syrian.

Cut by the biting axe, on earth are laid
The pliant ash, the beech's spreading shade,
The sacred palm, the funeral cypress fall;
The broad-leav'd sycamore, the plantane tall.   580
The married elm his nodding head declines,
Around whose trunk the vine her tendril twines.
Some fell'd the pine; the oak while others hew'd,
Whose leaves a thousand changing springs renew'd;
Whose stately bulk a thousand winters stood,   585
And scorn'd the winds that rend the lofty wood.
Some, on the creaking wheels, with labour, stow'd
The unctuous fir, and cedar's fragrant load.
Scar'd at the sounding axe, and cries of men,
Birds quit the nest, and beasts forsake the den l   590

END OF THE THIRD BOOK.

H 3

THE

FOURTH BOOK

OF

JERUSALEM DELIVERED.

THE ARGUMENT.

PLUTO calls a council of the infernal powers. His speech to urge them to employ their machinations against the Chriſtians. Hidraotes, king of Damaſcus, incited by a demon, ſends his niece Armida to the Chriſtian camp. She is introduced to Godfrey; and endeavours, by a feigned ſtory of her misfortunes, to raiſe his compaſſion. Many of the chiefs, touched with her pretended ſorrows, and enflamed with her beauty, are very preſſing with Godfrey to permit them to engage in her cauſe. He at length yields to their requeſt. Armida, during her reſidence in the camp, captivates, by her arts, almoſt all the principal commanders.

THE

FOURTH BOOK

OF

JERUSALEM DELIVERED.

WHILE thefe intent their vaft machines prepare
    T' affail the city with decifive war;
The foe of man, whofe malice ever burns,
His livid eyes upon the Chriftians turns:
He fees what mighty works their care engage,   5
And grinds his teeth, and foams with inward rage;
And, like a wounded bull with pain opprefs'd,
Deep groans rebellow from his hideous breaft.
Then bending every thought his fchemes to frame,
For fwift deftruction on their hated name;   10
He fummon'd in his court, to deep debate,
A horrid council of th' infernal ftate:
Infenfate wretch! as if th' attempt were light
T' oppofe JEHOVAH's will, and dare his might:

Ah!

Ah ! too forgetful how the vengeful hand   15
Of Heaven's Eternal hurls the forked brand !
   The trumpet now, with hoarfe-refounding breath,
Convenes the fpirits in the fhades of death :
The hollow caverns tremble at the found ;
The air re-echoes to the noife around !   20
Not louder terrors fhake the diftant pole,
When through the fkies the rattling thunders roll :
Not greater tremors heave the labouring earth,
When vapours, pent within, contend for birth !
The Gods of hell the awful fignal heard,   25
And, thronging round the lofty gates, appear'd
In various fhapes ; tremendous to the view !
What terror from their threatening eyes they threw !

Ver. 25. *The Gods of hell the awful fignal heard,*] There
can be little doubt but Milton made ufe of this paffage in
his account of the fallen angels, and in particular of the
fpeech which Taffo here puts into the mouth of Pluto (as
he injudicioufly calls him) which is very characteriftic of
his infernal difpofition.   The poet has with fingular judgment made him ufe a phrafe only fuitable to the Supreme
Being, " Let what I will be fate !" But how infinitely fuperior is our great countryman in his firft and fecond books
of PARADISE LOST, without any mixture of the Italian's
puerile and difgufting imagery !

Some,

Some, cloven feet with human faces wear,
And curling fnakes compofe their dreadful hair;   30
And from behind is feen, in circles. caft,
A ferpent's tail voluminous and vaft!
A thoufand Harpies foul and Centaurs here,
And Gorgons pale, and Sphinxes dire, appear,
Unnumber'd Scyllas barking rend the air,   35
Unnumber'd Pythons hifs, and Hydras glare!
Chimeras here are found ejecting flame;
Huge Polypheme and Geryon's triple frame:
And many more, of mingled kind were feen,
All monftrous forms, unknown to mortal men!   40
    In order feated now, th' infernal band
Enclos'd their grifly king on either hand.
Full in the midft imperial Pluto fate;
His arm fuftain'd the maffy fceptre's weight.
Nor rock, nor mountain lifts its head fo high;   45
Ev'n towering Atlas, that fupports the fky,
A hillock, if compar'd with him appears,
When his large front and ample horns he rears!
A horrid majefty his looks exprefs'd,
Which fcatter'd terror, and his pride increas'd: 50
His fanguine eyes with baleful venom ftare,
And, like a comet, caft a difmal glare:

A length of beard defcending o'er his breaſt,
In rugged curls conceals his hairy cheſt;
And, like a whirlpool in the roaring flood,   55
Wide gapes his mouth obfcene with clotted blood,
As fmoky fires from burning Ætna rife,
And fteaming fulphur that infeſts the ſkies:
So from his throat the cloudy fparkles came,
With peſtilential breath and ruddy flame: 60
And, while he fpoke, fierce Cerberus forbore
His triple bark, and Hydra ceas'd to roar:
Cocytus ſtay'd his courſe; th' abyſſes fhook;
When from his lips thefe thundering accents broke.

    Tartarean powers! more worthy of a place   65
Above the fun, whence fprung your glorious race;
Who loſt with me, in one difaſtrous fight,
Yon blifsful feats, and realms of endlefs light!
Too well our former injuries are known;
Our bold attempt againſt th' Almighty's throne: 70
See now he rules at will the cryſtal fphere,
And we the name of rebel angels bear:
And (fad reverfe!) exil'd from cloudlefs days,
The golden fun above, and ſtarry rays;
He fhuts us here in dreary glooms immur'd,   75
Our purpofe thwarted, and our fame obfcur'd,

And

And now elects (a thought that stings me more
Than all the pains I e'er endur'd before)
To fill our station, man of abject birth,
A creature fashion'd of the dust of earth!   80
Nor this suffic'd; his only Son he gave
(T' oppress us more) a victim to the grave:
Who came, and burst th' infernal gates in twain,
And boldly enter'd Pluto's fated reign;
And thence releas'd the souls, by lot our due,   85
And with his spoils to heaven victorious flew,
Triumphant there, our dire disgrace to tell,
He spreads the banners wide of conquer'd hell!
But wherefore should I thus renew our woe;
And who are those but must our sufferings know? 90
Was there a time that e'er our foe we saw
The purpose, which his wrath pursu'd, withdraw?
Then cast each thought of former wrongs behind,
And let the present outrage fill the mind:
See now what arts he practises to gain   95
The nations round to worship in his fane!
And shall we lie neglectful of our name,
Nor just revenge our kindling breasts enflame?
And tamely thus behold, in Asia's lands,
New vigour added to his faithful bands?   100

Beneath

Beneath his yoke shall Sion's city bend,
And further still his envy'd fame extend?
Shall other tongues be taught to sound his praise;
For him shall others tune their grateful lays?
Shall other monuments his laws proclaim?   105
New sculptur'd brass, and marble bear his name?
Our broken idols cast to earth, and scorn'd?
Our altars to his hated worship turn'd?
To him shall gifts of myrrh and gold be made?
To him alone be vows and incense paid?   110
Where every temple once ador'd our power,
Their gates be open to our arts no more?
Such numerous souls no longer tribute pay,
And Pluto here an empty kingdom sway?
Ah! no—our former courage still we boast;   115
That dauntless spirit which inspir'd our host,
When, girt with flames and steel, in dire alarms
We durst oppose the King of Heaven in arms!
'Tis true we lost the day (so fate ordain'd)
But still the glory of th' attempt remain'd: 120
To him was given the conquest of the field;
To us; superior minds that scorn'd to yield.—
But wherefore thus your well-known zeal detain?
Go, faithful peers and partners of my reign,

My

My pride and strength! our hated foes oppress,   125
And crush their empire ere its power increase :
Haste (ere destruction end Judæa's name)
And quench the fury of this growing flame ;
Mix in their councils, fraud and force employ,
With every art industrious to destroy :   130
Let what I will be fate; let some be slain,
Some wander exiles from their social train ;
Some, sunk the slaves of love's lascivious pow'r,
An amorous eye or dimpled smile adore.
Against its master turn th' infensate steel,   135
And teach discordant legions to rebel.
Perish the camp, in final ruin lost,
And perish all remembrance of the host !
  Scarce had the tyrant ceas'd, when sudden rose
The raging band of God's rebellious foes ;   140
And, eager to review the chearful light,
They rush'd impatient from the shades of night.
As sounding tempests, with impetuous force,
Burst from their native caves, with furious course,
To blot the lustre of the gladsome day,   145
And pour their vengeance on the land and sea :
So these from realm to realm their pinions spread,
And o'er the world their baneful venom shed ;

And

And all their hellish arts and frauds apply'd,
In various shapes and forms before untry'd.   150
Say, muse! from whence, and how the fiends began
To vent their fury on the Christian train;
For well to thee each secret work is known,
Which Fame to us transmits but faintly down.

  O'er wide Damascus and the neighbouring land,
A fam'd magician Hidraotes reign'd;   156
Who, from his youth, his early studies bent
T' explore the seeds of every dark event:
But fruitless still! not all his arts declare
The secret issue of the dubious war: 160
Nor fix'd nor wandering stars by aspects tell,
Nor truth he finds from oracles of hell.
And yet (O knowledge of presuming man
Of thought fallacious and of judgment vain!)
He deem'd that Heaven would sure destruction
     shower,   165
To crush the Christians' still unconquer'd power;
His fancy view'd at length their army lost,
And palms and laurels for th' Egyptian host;
Hence sprung a wish his subject-bands might share,
With these, the spoils and glory of the war: 170
But, since the valour of the Franks was known,
He fear'd the conquest would be dearly won.

                          Now

Now various fchemes his wily thoughts employ'd
To fow diffention, and their force divide :
So might his troops, with Egypt's numbers join'd,
An eafier field againft the Chriftians find.   176
While thus he thought, th' apoftate angel came,
And added fuel to his impious flame ;
And fudden with infernal counfels fir'd
His reftlefs bofom, and his foul infpir'd.   180

    A damfel for his niece the monarch own'd,
Whofe matchlefs charms were through the eaft re-
          nown'd ;
To her was every art of magic known,
And all the wiles of womankind her own.
To her the king th' important tafk affign'd ;   185
And thus reveal'd the purpofe of his mind.

    O ! thou, my beft belov'd ! whofe youthful charms,
(Sweet fmiles and graces, Love's refiftlefs arms !)
A manly mind and thoughts mature conceal ;
Whofe arts in magic even my own excel ;   190
Great fchemes I frame, nor fhall thofe fchemes be vain,
Affift but thou the labours of my brain.
Then heed my counfel, in the tafk engage,
And execute the plan of cautious age.
Go, feek the hoftile camp : and there improve   195
Each female artifice that kindles love :

With fpeaking forrows bathe thy powerful eyes;
And mix thy tender plaints with broken fighs:
For beauty, by misfortune's hand opprefs'd,
Can fafhion to her will the hardeft breaft.   200
With bafhful mien relate the plaufive tale;
With fhew of truth the fecret falfehood veil.
Ufe every art of words and winning fmiles
'T' allure the leader Godfrey to thy toils:
That thus, a flave to love and beauty won,   205
His foul may loath his enterprize begun.
But if the Fates this fnare fhall render vain,
Inflame the boldeft of the warrior-train;
And lead them diftant from the camp afar,
Ne'er to return and mingle in the war.   210
All ways are juft to guard religion's laws,
All means are lawful in our country's caufe!

　　The great attempt Armida's bofom warms,
(Proud of her bloom and more than mortal charms):
She thence, at evening's clofe, departs alone   215
Through folitary paths and ways unknown;
And trufts in female vefts, and beauty bright,
To conquer armies unfubdu'd in fight.
But various rumours of her flight, diffus'd
With purpos'd art, the vulgar-crowd amus'd.   220

Few

Few days were paſt, when near the damſel drew
To where the Chriſtian tents appear'd In view.
Her matchleſs charms the wondering bands ſurpriſe,
Provoke their whiſpers and attract their eyes.
So mortals, through the midnight fields of air, 225
Obſerve the blaze of ſome unuſual ſtar.
Sudden they throng to view th' approaching dame,
Eager to learn her meſſage and her name.
Not Argos, Cyprus, or the Delian coaſt
Could e'er a form or mien ſo lovely boaſt,   230
Now through her ſnowy veil, half hid from ſight,
Her golden locks diffuſe a doubtful light ;
And now, unveil'd, in open view they flow'd ;
So Phœbus glimmers through a fleecy cloud,
So from the cloud again redeems his ray,   235
And ſheds freſh glory on the face of day.
In wavy ringlets falls her beauteous hair,
That catch new graces from the ſportive air ;
Declin'd on earth, her modeſt look denies
To ſhow the ſtarry luſtre of her eyes: 240
O'er her fair face a roſy bloom is ſpread,
And ſtains her ivory ſkin with lovely red :
Soft-breathing ſweets her opening lips diſcloſe ;
The native odours of the budding roſe !

I 2

Her

Her bofom bare difplays its fnowy charms,   245
Where Cupid frames and points his fiery arms:
Her fmooth and fwelling breafts are part reveal'd,
And part beneath her envious veft conceal'd;
Her robes oppofe the curious fight in vain,
No robes oppos'd can amorous thoughts reftrain: 250
The gazer, fir'd with charms already fhown,
Explores the wonders of the charms unknown.
As through the limpid ftream, or cryftal, bright,
The rays of Phœbus dart their piercing light;
So through her veft can daring fancy glide,   255
And view what modefty attempts to hide;
Thence paints a thoufand loves and foft defires,
And adds frefh fuel to the lover's fires!

   Thus pafs'd Armida through th' admiring crowd,
(With fecret joy her heart exulting glow'd)   260
She read their thoughts, and various wiles defign'd,
And fchemes of future conqueft fill'd her mind.
While in fufpenfe her cautious eyes explor'd
Some guide to lead her to the Chriftian lord,
Before her fight the young Euftatius ftands,   265
Great Godfrey's brother, who the hoft commands;
Her beauty's blaze the warrior's breaft alarms,
He ftays, and, wondering, gazes on her charms:

                                                At

At once the flames of love his foul infpire;
As o'er the ſtubble runs the blazing fire.   270
Then bold through youth, by amorous paſſion preſs'd,
He thus, with courtly words, the dame addreſs'd.

   Say, damſel! (if thou bear'ſt a mortal name,
For ſure thou ſeem'ſt not of terreſtrial frame!
Since Heaven ne'er gave to one of Adam's race 275
So large a portion of celeſtial grace!)
What fortune bids thee to our camp repair?
What fortune ſends to us a form ſo fair?
What art thou? If of heavenly lineage ſay,
So let me, proſtrate, rightful homage pay.   280
   Too far thy praiſe extends, (ſhe made reply)
My merits ne'er attain'd a flight ſo high.
Thy eyes, O chief! a mortal wretch ſurvey,
To pleaſure dead, to grief a living prey!
Unhappy fate my footſteps hither led,   285
A fugitive forlorn, a wandering maid!
Godfrey I ſeek, on him my hopes depend,
Oppreſſion's ſcourge, and injur'd virtue's friend!
Then, generous as thou ſeem'ſt, indulge my grief,
And grant me audience of thy godlike chief.   290
   Then he: A brother ſure may gain his ear,
May lead thee to him, and thy ſuit prefer:

I 3

Thou

Thou haſt not choſen ill, O lovely dame!
Some intereſt in the leader's breaſt I claim.
Uſe as thou wilt (nor deem in vain my word)   295
His powerful ſceptre and his brother's ſword.

  He ceas'd, and brought her where, retir'd in ſtate,
Encircled by his chiefs, the Hero ſate.
With awful reverence at his ſight ſhe bow'd,
Then ſeem'd abaſh'd with ſhame, and ſilent ſtood. 300
With gentle words the leader ſtrove to chear
Her drooping ſpirits, and diſpel her fear ;
Till thus ſhe fram'd her tale with fraudful art,
In accents ſweet, that won the yielding heart.

  Unconquer'd prince ! whoſe far-reſounding name
With every virtue fills the mouth of fame !   306
Whom kings themſelves, ſubdu'd, with pride obey,
While vanquiſh'd nations glory in thy ſway !
Known is thy valour, and thy worth approv'd,
By all eſteem'd, and by thy foes belov'd !   310
Ev'n thoſe confide in him they fear'd before,
And, when diſtreſs'd, thy ſaving hand implore.
I, who a different faith from thine profeſs ;
A faith obnoxious, which thy arms oppreſs ;
Yet hope, by thee, t' aſcend my rightful throne, 315
Where once my ſires, in regal luſtre, ſhone.

If,

If, from their kindred, others aid demand,
T' oppofe the fury of a foreign band ;
I, fince my friends no ties of pity feel,
Againft my blood invoke the hoftile fteel.   320
On thee I call ; in thee my hopes I place :
'Tis thine alone my abject ftate to raife.
No lefs a glory fhall thy labours crown,
T' exalt the low, than pull the mighty down :
An equal praife the name of mercy yields   325
With routed fquadrons in triumphant fields.
Oft haft thou fnatch'd from kings the fovereign power :
Win now a like renown, and mine reftore.
O ! may thy pitying grace my caufe fuftain,
Nor let me on thy help rely in vain !   330
Witnefs that Power, to all an equal God !
Thy aid was ne'er in jufter caufe beftow'd.
But hear me firft my haplefs fortune fhow,
And fpeak the treachery of a kindred-foe.

In me the child of Arbilan furvey,   335
Who o'er Damafcus once maintain'd the fway :
He, fprung of humbler race, in marriage gain'd
Fair Chariclea, and the crown obtain'd.
But fhe, who rais'd him to the fovereign ftate,
Ere I was born, receiv'd the ftroke of fate.   340

I 4

One

One fatal day my mother fnatch'd from earth;
The fame, alas! beheld my haplefs birth!
Five annual funs had fcarce their influence fhed,
Since from the world my deareft parent fled,
When, yielding to the fate of all mankind,   345
My fire in Heaven his faithful confort join'd.
The monarch, to a brother's guardian care,
Confign'd his fceptre and his infant-heir:
In whom he deem'd he juftly might confide,
If ever virtue did in man refide.   350
The kingdom's rule he feiz'd, but ftill he fhow'd
A zeal for me, and for my country's good;
While all his actions feem'd th' effects to prove
Of faith untainted and paternal love.
But thus perchance, with fhows of anxious zeal, 355
He fought his traitorous purpofe to conceal:
Or elfe, fincere, t' effect his deep defign,
My hand in marriage with his fon to join.
I grew in years, and with me grew his fon;
In whom no knightly virtues ever fhone: 360
Rude was his afpect, ruder was his foul,
Rapacious, proud, impatient of control;
Such was the man my guardian had decreed
To fhare my kingdom and my nuptial bed.

In

In vain to win me to his will he try'd,   365
I heard in silence, or his suit deny'd.
One day he left me, when his looks confess'd
Some fatal treason lurking in his breast;
Alas! methought I then could clearly trace
My future fortune in the tyrant's face: 370
From thence what visions did my soul affright,
Distract my sleep, and skim before my sight!
O'er all my spirits hung a mournful gloom,
A sure presage of every woe to come!
Oft to my view appear'd my mother's ghost,   375
A bloodless form, in tears and sorrows lost!
Ah me! far distant from her former look!
Fly, fly, my daughter! (thus the phantom spoke)
For thee the murderous steel the tyrant bears:
For thee his rage th'envenom'd bowl prepares! 380
   But what avail'd these bodings of my mind?
Why was I warn'd to shun the ills design'd?
Could I, an helpless maid, resolve to roam,
A willing exile from my native home?
A milder choice it seem'd to close my sight   385
In that dear place where first I saw the light.
Yet death I fear'd, and fear'd from death to fly;
Nor knew on whom for counsel to rely.

                                              To

To none I durſt my ſecret thoughts relate,
But liv'd in dread ſuſpenſe, uncertain of my fate! 390
Like one, who, every moment, thinks to feel
On his defenceleſs head th' impending ſteeL
But (whether fortune now was kinder grown,
Or Heaven reſerv'd me yet for woes unknown)
A faithful courtier, who, with anxious cares,   395
Had bred my father from his infant years,
Touch'd with compaſſion for my death decreed,
Reveal'd the tyrant's meditated deed;
And own'd himſelf th' elected miniſter
That day the poiſon to my hand to bear.   400
He bade me fly, if ſtill I wiſh'd to live,
And proffer'd every aid his power could give :
With ſoothing words againſt my fears he wrought ;
And ſoon confirm'd my undetermin'd thought :
With him I then reſolv'd, at parting light,   405
To fly, and truſt my ſafety to my flight.

   'Twas now the hour that ſilence reign'd around,
And welcome darkneſs hover'd o'er the ground ;
When, unperceiv'd, I paſs'd the palace-gate ;
(Two faithful maids companions of my fate)   410
Yet, with a tearful eye, and heavy mind,
I left my dear paternal ſeat behind ;

While, as my tardy feet their courfe purfu'd,
With longing looks, my lov'd, loft home I view'd.
So feems a fhip by fudden tempefts toft,   415
And torn, unwilling, from its friendly coaft.
All night, and all th' enfuing day, we pafs'd
Through pathlefs deferts, and a dreary wafte :
Till, feated on the borders of the land,
A caftle's fafe retreat at length we gain'd.   420
Here dwelt Arontes, who, with pious truth,
Preferv'd my life, the guardian of my youth.

  But when the traitor faw his treafon vain,
And found me thus efcap'd his deathful train,
He, with inveterate rage and fraudful mind,   425
Accus'd us of a crime himfelf defign'd.
My bribes (he faid) had falfe Arontes wrought.
To mingle deadly poifon in his draught ;
That, when he could no more my will reftrain,
To loofe defires my foul might give the rein.   430
Ah ! firft let lightening on my head defcend,
Ere, facred virtue ! I thy laws offend !
With grief the tyrant on my throne I view'd,
And faw him thirfting ftill to fhed my blood ;
But, more than all, I mourn'd my virgin-name 435
Traduc'd, difhonour'd, made the fport of fame !

The

The wretch, who fear'd the vulgar herd enrag'd,
With plaufive tales the public ear engag'd ; .
That, dubious of the truth, in deep fufpenfe,
The city rofe not in their queen's defence.   440
Thus, while he feigns a zeal t' efface the fhame
My crimes have brought upon the regal name,
He feeks my ruin, which he knows alone
Can fix the bafis of his tottering throne. '
And, ah, the wretch too fure fuccefs will find   445
In the dire purpofe of his ruthlefs mind !
Since tears are vain, my blood muft quench his rage,
Unlefs thy mercy in my caufe engage.
To thee, O mighty chief! I fly for aid,
An ill-ftarr'd orphan, and an helplefs maid !   450
O ! let thefe tears, that have thy feet bedew'd,
Prevent th' effufion of my guiltlefs blood !
O ! by thofe feet that tread the proud in duft ! ·
By that right-hand that ever helps the juft !
By all the laurels that thy arms have won !   455
By every temple in yon hallow'd town !
In pity grant what thou alone canft give ;
Reftore my crown, in fafety bid me live !—
But what from pity can I hope to prove,
If piety and juftice fail to move !   · · · ··   460

S

Thou,

Thou, to whom Heaven and fate decree to will
Whate'er is juſt, and what thou will'ſt, fulfil ;
O ! ſtretch thy hand, my threaten'd life retrieve,
And, in return, my kingdom's crown receive.
Among the numbers that thy arms attend,   465
Let ten ſelected chiefs my cauſe befriend ;
Theſe, with my people and paternal train,
May well ſuffice my ancient ſeat to gain.
For he, to whom is given the portal's care,
Will, at my word, by night the gates unbar ;   470
By his advice t' implore thy aid I came :
Thy leaſt of ſuccours will his hopes inflame ;
So much his ſoul reveres thy arms and name.

   She ſaid ; and ceaſing, waited his reply
With ſilent eloquence and downcaſt eye.   475
But various thoughts revolv'd in Godfrey's mind,
Now here, now there, his dubious heart inclin'd :
He fear'd the hoſtile guiles ; for well he knew
How little truſt to Pagan faith was due :
But tender pity ſtill his ſoul confeſs'd,   480
Pity, that ſleeps not in a noble breaſt :
Nor this alone within his boſom wrought ;
The common good employ'd his careful thought :
He ſaw th' advantage that his arms might gain,
Should fair Armida o'er Damaſcus reign :   485
                            Who

Who thence, her state dependent on his hands, ⎫
Might furnish every aid the time demands, ⎬
Against th' Egyptians and auxiliar bands. ⎭
While thus he paus'd, the dame attentive stood,
Dwelt on his face, and every gesture view'd ;   490
But when she found his speech so long delay'd,
Her frequent sighs her doubts and fears betray'd.
At length the leader her request denies ;
Yet thus with mild and gracious words replies.

　　If God, whose holy service arms our band,   495
Did not, ev'n now, our pious swords demand ;
Well might thy hopes expect the wish'd success,
Nor find our pity only, but redress.
But, while yon city walls and chosen flock
We seek to free from proud oppression's yoke ;   500
It ill befits to turn aside our force,
And stop our conquests in the middle course.
Yet here to thee my solemn faith I give,
And in that pledge do thou securely live ;
If e'er, indulgent to our arms, 'tis given   505
To free those holy walls, belov'd of Heaven !
Then will we place thee in thy native lands,
As justice bids, and piety commands :
But piety, like this, must impious show,
If first we pay not what to God we owe.   510

At

At this unwelcome speech the damsel turn'd
Her eyes awhile to earth, and silent mourn'd ;
Then rais'd them slow, with pearly drops bedew'd,
And thus, with pleading looks, her plaint renew'd.

Ah, wretch ! did ever Heaven on one bestow   515
A life so fix'd in never-ending woe ;
That others even their nature shall forget,
Ere I subdue the rigour of my fate !
Why should I weep, since hopes no more remain,
And prayers assail the human breast in vain ?   520
Or will my savage foe his ears incline
To griefs, that fail to move a mind like thine ?
Yet think not that my words thy heart accuse,
Whose firm resolves so small an aid refuse :
Heaven I accuse ; from thence my sorrows flow ! 525
Heaven steels thy heart against a virgin's woe !
Not thou, O chief ! but Fate this aid denies.—
Then let me view no more the hated skies.—
Suffic'd it not (by unrelenting doom)
To lose my parents in their early bloom !   530
But, exil'd, must I lead a wandering life,
Or fall a victim to the murderer's knife ?
Since the chaste laws, by which our sex is ty'd,
Amidst your camp forbid me to reside,

Where

Where shall I fly ? what friendly powers engage ? 535
How save my person from the tyrant's rage ?
No forts but open to his fury lie——
Then wherefore hesitates my soul to die ?
And, since 'tis vain with fortune to contend,
This hand at once my life and woes shall end. 540
    She ceas'd ; and turn'd aside with regal grace ;
A generous anger kindling in her face ;
Disdain and sorrow seem her breast to rend,
While from her eyes the copious tears descend,
And, trickling, down her lovely visage run,   545
Like lucid pearls transparent to the sun !
O'er her fair cheeks the crystal moisture flows,
Where lilies mingle with the neighbouring rose.
So, wet with dew, the flowers at dawning day,
To balmy gales their opening sweets display :   550
Aurora views, and gathers from the mead
A vary'd garland for her radiant head.
    Thus sweet in woe appears the weeping dame,
Her falling tears a thousand hearts enflame.
O ! wondrous force of Love's mysterious fire,   555
That lights in tears the flames of soft desire !
Almighty Love the world in triumph leads,
But now, by her inspir'd, himself exceeds !

Her

Her feeming grief bids real forrows flow,
And melts the heart with fympathetic woe ;   560
While each apart, with indignation, cries :
" If Godfrey ftill his pitying ear denies,
" His infant years fome hungry tigrefs fed,
" Some horrid rock on Alpine mountains bred ; 564
" Or waves produc'd him 'midft the howling main,
" Who fees fuch beauty mourn, and mourn in vain !"
But young Euftatius, by his zeal infpir'd,
Whom moft tho torch of love and pity fir'd,
(When others murmur'd, or their words reprefs'd)
Stood forth, and boldly thus the chief addrefs'd. 570

   O prince and brother ! whofe unfhaken mind
Too firmly holds its purpofe firft defign'd,
If ftill unpitying thou refufe to hear
The fenfe of all, their univerfal prayer,
I afk not that the chiefs whofe care prefides   575
O'er fubject kingdoms, and their actions guides,
Should from the hallow'd city's walls recede,
Neglectful of their tafk, by Heaven decreed ;
But from our band, that independent came,
Adventurous warriors to the field of fame,   580
Ten champions yield, felected from the reft,
To cherifh virtue, and relieve th' opprefs'd :

Nor does the man forsake the cause of Heaven
Whose succour to a helpless maid is given :
For sure I deem a tyrant's death must prove   585
A grateful tribute to the powers above.
And should I wave th' advantage here in view,
That must undoubted to our cause ensue;
Yet duty would alone my arms excite;
By knighthood sworn to guard a virgin's right.   590
Forbid it, Heaven! that ever France should hear,
Or any land where courteous acts are dear;
That dangers or fatigues our souls dismay'd,
When piety and justice claim'd our aid.
No longer let me then this helmet wear,   595
No longer wield the sword, or corslet bear;
No more in steed, or glittering arms, delight;
No more usurp the honour'd name of knight!
   Thus spoke the youth: his brave companions,
      mov'd
To open murmurs, all his words approv'd;   600

Ver. 599. *Thus spoke the youth :*—] In this episode of
Armida, Tasso seems to have had his eye upon a passage in
the beginning of Boyardo's poem, where Angelica is sent
by her father Galaphron to the camp of Charlemain, on
like design with Armida, and captivates all the Christian
commanders. See ORLANDO INNAMORATO, B. I. c. i.

With

With earneſt ſuit around their leader preſs'd,
And urg'd the juſtneſs of the knight's requeſt.
   Then Godfrey thus : Be what ye aſk fulfill'd :
To ſuch united prayers my will I yield :
Her aid requeſted let the dame receive;   605
Whom not my counſels, but your own relieve.
Yet, if my words can ſuch deſires control,
Subdue theſe warm emotions of the ſoul.
   No more he ſaid : nor needed more reply,
All heard his grant, and heard with eager joy. 610
What cannot beauty, join'd with ſorrow, move,
And tender accents from the lips of love ?
Each roſy mouth ſupplies a golden chain
To bind the fancy, and the heart conſtrain !
   Euſtatius then the weeping fair addreſs'd :   615
O lovely maid ! be now thy grief ſuppreſs'd :
Soon ſhalt thou find the ſuccour from our hands,
Such as thy merit, or thy fear demands.
   At this Armida clears her clouded brow ;
With riſing joy her blooming features glow ;   620
While, with her veil, ſhe wipes the tears away,
And adds new luſtre to the ſace of day !
Then thus—For what your pitying grace beſtows,
Accept the thanks a grateful virgin owes ;

K 2

The

The world due honour to your worth fhall give, 625
And in my heart your name's fhall ever live !
    She faid ; and what it feem'd her tongue deny'd,
Her looks, with fofter eloquence, fupply'd !
While outward fmiles conceal'd, with fraudful art,
The mighty mifchief lurking in her heart.   630
    Soon as fhe faw how far her power had won,
And fortune favouring what her wiles begun,
She feiz'd th' occafion, and her fchemes revolv'd,
To finifh all her impious thoughts refolv'd,
With female beauty every breaft to quell,   635
And Circe or Medæa's charms excel ;
And, like a Syren, with her foothing ftrain,
To lull the firmeft of the warrior-train.
Each vary'd art to win the foul fhe tries :
To this, to that a different mien applies ;   640
Now fcarcely dares her modeft eyes advance,
And now fhe rolls them with a wanton glance :
She thefe repels, and thofe incites to love,
As various paffions various bofoms move.
And when fome youth appears, who doubts to name
His hidden thoughts, or ftruggles with his flame ; 646
Soon on his face a chearful fmile fhe bends,
And from her eye a melting fweetnefs fends ;

Revives

Revives his hopes, inflames his flow desire,
And thaws the frost of fear with amorous fire. 650
From him, who, urg'd by fiercer passion, roves
Beyond the bound that modesty approves,
The wily fair her gentle look withdraws,
And with rebukes and frowns his rashness awes:
Yet, midst the anger rising in her face, 655
A ray of pity blends the softening grace:
The lover, while he fears, pursues the dame,
And in her pride finds fuel to his flame.

With arts like these a thousand souls she gains,
From every eye the tender tear constrains: 660
In pity's flame she tempers Cupid's dart,
To pierce the warrior's unresisting heart.

Ah! cruel love! thou bane of every joy,
Whose pains or sweets alike our peace destroy:
Still equal woes from thee mankind endure, 665
Fatal thy wounds, and fatal is the cure!

While thus she gives alternate frost and fires,
And joy, and grief, and hope, and fear inspires,
With cruel pleasure she their state surveys,
Exulting in those ills her power could raise. 670
Oft when some lover trembling wooes the fair,
She seems to lend an unexperienc'd ear;

K 3

Or,

Or, while a crimson blush her visage dyes,
With coyness feign'd, she downward bends her eyes ;
While shame and wrath, with mingled grace, adorn
Her glowing cheeks, like beams of early morn ! 676
But when she sees a youth prepare to tell
The secret thoughts that in his bosom dwell ;
Now sudden from his sight the damsel flies ;
Now gives an audience to his plaints and sighs !   680
Thus holds from morn till eve his heart in play,
Then slips, delusive, from his hope away ;
And leaves him like a hunter in the chace,
When night conceals the beast's uncertain trace !

   With arms like these she made a thousand yield, 685
A thousand chiefs unconquer'd in the field.
What wonder then, if love Achilles mov'd ;
His power if Hercules or Theseus prov'd ;
When those, who drew the sword in Jesus' cause,
Submissive bent beneath his impious laws ?   690

END OF THE FOURTH BOOK.

THE

FIFTH BOOK

OF

JERUSALEM DELIVERED.

K 4

THE ARGUMENT.

GERNANDO, afpiring to the command of the adventurers, is
jealous left Rinaldo fhould fucceed to that honour. By
his calumnies, he draws on himfelf the indignation of that
hero, who kills him in the face of the whole army. Godfrey, incenfed at this action of Rinaldo, refolves to bring
him to a public trial : the latter, difdaining to fubmit to
this, quits the camp, and goes into voluntary exile. Armida preffes Godfrey for the promifed fuccours : ten warriors are chofen by lot, with whom fhe leaves the camp.
In the night, many others depart by ftealth to accompany
her. Godfrey receives ill advices from the fleet.

WHILE thus her snares the false Armida
    spread,
And in the guileful toils the warriors led;
Nor hop'd alone the promis'd aid to gain,
But other chiefs, by further arts, obtain;
The careful Godfrey ponder'd in his mind,   5
To whom the doubtful charge should be consign'd:
The worth and number of th' adventurer-band,
Their various hopes his wavering thoughts detain'd.
At length, by caution urg'd, the chief decreed
Themselves should fix on one their band to lead, 10
Whose merit well might Dudon's loss supply;
On whom th' election of the ten should lie:
Thus, while to them he left th' important choice,
No knight, displeas'd, could blame his partial voice.

The

The wariors then he call'd, and thus addrefs'd: 15
Full well ye know the counfels of my breaft:
I would not fuccours to the dame deny;
But at a fitter time our aid fupply.
What once I fpoke, I now propofe anew;
Still may your better thoughts th' advice purfue: 20
For here, in this unftable world, we find
We oft muft change our purpofe firft defign'd.
Yet if your fouls, with generous ardor prefs'd,
Difdain the judgments of a cooler breaft;
I would not here unwilling arms detain,   25
Nor, what I gave fo lately, render vain.
Still let me mildly rule each faithful band,
And fway the fceptre with a gentle hand.
Then go, or ftay; no longer I contend;
And on your pleafure let the choice depend.   30
But firft elect, amid your martial train,
A chief who may fucceed to Dudon flain:
To name the damfel's champions be his care;
Ten warriors only fhall th' adventure fhare:
In this the fovereign power I ftill retain;   35
In this alone his conduct I reftrain!

    Thus Godfrey fpoke; nor long his brother ftay'd,
But, with his friends' confent, this anfwer made.

With

With thee full well, O prudent chief! agrees
The cooler thought that each event forefees: 40
But ftrength of hand, and hearts of martial fire,
Are due from us, and what our years require:
And that which bears in others wifdom's name,
In us were bafenefs and reproachful fhame.
Then fince fo light the rifk we may fuftain,   45
When juftly weigh'd againft th' expected gain,
Th' elected ten fhall go (by thee difmifs'd)
And in this righteous caufe a helplefs maid affift.

He faid; and thus with fhow of public zeal,
His words th' emotions of his heart conceal,   50
While all profefs in honour's name to move,
And with that fpecious title veil their love.

But young Euftatius, by his paffion fway'd,
With jealous eyes Sophia's fon furvey'd,
His envious mind thofe virtues could not bear   55
That fhone more brightly in a form fo fair.
He fear'd with him Rinaldo fhould be join'd,
And 'gainft his fears a cautious fcheme defign'd.
The rival warrior then afide he took,
And plaufive thus, with wily words befpoke.   60

O thou, ftill greater than thy glorious fire,
Whom, yet a youth in arms, the world admire!

Say,

Say, who shall now our valiant squadron lead ?
Who next to slaughter'd Dudon can succeed ?
I scarcely could the hero's rule obey,   65
And to his years alone resign'd the sway.
Who now o'er Godfrey's brother shall command ?
Thou, thou alone of all our martial band :
Thy glorious race can match the noblest line ;
Thy warlike deeds superior far to mine.   70
Ev'n Godfrey's self would own inferior might,
And yield to thee in arduous fields of fight.
Thee, mighty warrior ! thee our chief I claim,
Whose soul disdains t' attend the Syrian dame ,
And slights the trivial honour which proceeds   75
From dark atchievements and infidious deeds.
Here will thy valour find an ampler field ;
This camp to thee a nobler prospect yield.
Accept, brave youth ! to guide th' adventurer-band ,
Myself will frame their minds to thy command. 80
Thou, in return, attend my sole request ;
(Since doubtful thoughts as yet divide my breast)
Whate'er I purpose, let my will be free,
T' assist Armida, or remain with thee.

    He ceas'd ; and as these artful words he said, 85
A sudden blush his conscious cheeks o'erspread.

                                        Rinaldo,

Rinaldo, fmiling, faw, with heedful eyes,
His fecret paffion thro' the thin difguife.
But he, whom lefs the darts of love had found,
Whofe bofom fcarcely felt the gentle wound,   90
With unconcern regards a rival's name,
Nor frames a wifh t' attend the Pagan dame.
On Dudon's haplefs fate his thoughts he turn'd;
For Dudon's death the generous hero mourn'd.
He deem'd his former glories would be loft   95
If long Argantes liv'd the deed to boaft:
With pleafure yet Euftatius' words he heard,
That to the rank deferv'd his youth preferr'd:
His confcious heart exulted in the praife;
Pleas'd with the tribute truth to virtue pays.   100

   Far rather would I chufe (he thus replies)
To merit honours, than to honours rife.
Let virtuous actions dignify my name,
I envy not the great, nor fceptres claim.
Yet if thou think'ft fo far my merits weigh,   105
I fhall not then reject the proffer'd fway;
But prize (with gratitude and pleafure mov'd)
So fair a token of my worth approv'd.
I feek not, nor refufe the chief command;
But fhould the power be yielded to my hand, 110
Thou fhalt be one amongft th' elected band.

Thus

Thus he: Euſtatius ſpeeds his peers to find,
And faſhion to his will each warrior's mind.
But that pre-eminence Gernando claims;
And though at him her darts Armida aims,   115
Yet not the power of beauty can control
The thirſt of honour in his haughty ſoul.
From Norway's powerful kings this chief deſcends,
Whoſe rule o'er many a province wide extends:
The crowns and ſceptres which his fathers held 120
From ancient times, with pride his boſom ſwell'd.
Rinaldo in himſelf his glory plac'd,
More than in diſtant deeds of ages paſt;
Though long his fires with every fame were crown'd,
In war illuſtrious, and in peace renown'd.   125
    The barbarous prince, whoſe pride no worth al-
        lows,
Save what from treaſure or dominion flows;
And every virtue deems an empty name,
Unleſs ennobled by a regal claim;
Indignant ſees a private warrior dare   130
With him in merit and in praiſe compare:
No bound, no law, his fiery temper knows;
With rage he kindles, and with ſhame he glows.
    The fiend of hell, who ſees his tortur'd mind
Expos'd to what her ſubtle arts deſign'd,   135
                              Unſeen

Unseen through all his troubled bosom glides,
There rules at will, and o'er his thoughts presides;
His hate increases, and enflames his ire,
And rouzes in his heart infernal fire;
While every moment, from within, he hears   140
This hollow voice refounding in his ears.

  Shall thus, oppos'd to thee, Rinaldo dare
His boasted anceftors with thine compare?
First let him count, whofe pride thy equal ftands,
His fubject realms and tributary lands;   145
His fceptres fhow, and (whence his glory fprings)
Mate his dead heroes with thy living kings.
Shall fuch a chief exalt his worthlefs head,
A fervile warrior in Italia bred?
To him let fortune lofs or gain decree,   150
He gains a conqueft who contends with thee;
The world fhall fay (and great the fame will prove)
" Lo! this is he, who with Gernando ftrove."
The place that once experienc'd Dudon fill'd,
New honours to thy former ftate may yield.   155
But he no lefs with thee in glory vies,
Who boldly dares demand fo vaft a prize.
If human paffions touch the bleft above,
What holy wrath muft aged Dudon move,

                                        When,

When, from his heaven, he sees this haughty knight,
(A stripling-warrior in the field of fight)   161
Aspire so high; while some his counsels join,
And (shame eternal!) second his design.
If Godfrey such injustice tamely view,
And suffer him t' usurp thy honours due,   165
It rests on thee t' assert thy rightful claim,
Declare thy power, and vindicate thy name.

   Fir'd at these words, more fell his fury grows,
Within his heart the torch of discord glows:
His raging passion, now to madness stung,   170
Flames in his eye, and points his haughty tongue.
Whate'er his envious speech can turn to blame,
He boldly charges on Rinaldo's fame:
And every virtue that the youth adorns,
To foul reproach, with artful malice, turns: 175
He paints him proud and turbulent of mind,
And calls his valour headstrong, rash, and blind.
He scatters falshood in the public ears,
Till even the rival knight the rumour hears.
But still th' insensate wretch pursues his hate,   180
Nor curbs the rage that hurries on his fate:
While the dire demon all his soul possess'd,
Rav'd from his lips, and madden'd in his breast.

Amid

Amid the camp appear'd a level fpace,
And warriors oft reforted to the place,   185
In tournaments, in wreftling, and the courfe,
Their limbs to fupple, and improve their force.
Here, midft the throng (for fo his doom requir'd)
He vented all his vengeful fpleen infpir'd,
And 'gainft Rinaldo turn'd his impious tongue, 190
On which the venom of Avernus hung.

His contumelious fpeech Rinaldo hears,
And now no more his dreadful wrath forbears,
At once the bafe infulter he defies,
Unfheaths his falchion, and to vengeance flies: 195
His voice like thunder echoes from afar,
His threatning fteel like lightening gleams in air.
Gernando fees, nor hopes t' efcape by flight,
For inftant death appears before his fight.
Meanwhile, to all the wondering army's view, 200
A fhow of valour o'er his fears he threw:
He grafps his fword, he waits his mighty foe,
And ftands prepar'd to meet the coming blow.

Now fudden, drawn from many warriors' thighs,
A thoufand weapons flafh againft the fkies.   205
In throngs around the gathering people prefs;
The tumult thickens, and the crowds encreafe:

Difcordant murmurs rife, and echo round,
And mingled clamours to the clouds refound.
So, near the ocean on the rocky fhore,   210
With broken noife the wind and billows roar.

But not their cries, nor murmurs could detain
Th' offended warrior, or his wrath reftrain:
He fcorns the force that dares his fury ftay;
He whirls his fword with unrefifting fway: 215
The throng divides; alone his arm prevails,
And, midft a thoufand friends, the prince affails.
Then from his hand, that well his rage obey'd,
A thoufand blows th' aftonifh'd foe invade.
Now here, now there the rapid weapon flies,   220
Confounds his fenfes, and diftraĉls his eyes.
At length the cruel fteel, with ftrength imprefs'd,
Rinaldo buries in his panting breaft.

Prone fell the wretch, and finking on the ground,
His blood and fpirit iffu'd through the wound. 225
The victor o'er the dead no longer ftay'd,
But in the fheath return'd the reeking blade:
And, thence departing, to his tent retir'd,
His vengeance fated, and his wrath expir'd.

Now near the tumult pious Godfrey drew,   230
When the dire feene was open to his view.

Gernando

Gernando pale with lifeless looks appear'd,
His hair and veft with fordid blood befmear'd.
He faw the tears his friends in pity fhed,   234
And heard their plaints and forrows o'er the dead :
Surpris'd, he afk'd what hand had wrought the deed,
And whence could fuch deftructive rage proceed.

  Arnaldo, deareft to the flaughter'd prince,
The tale relates, and aggravates th' offence ;
That, urg'd by flender caufe to impious ftrife,   240
Rinaldo's hand had robb'd the chief of life ;
And turn'd that weapon, which for CHRIST he bore,
Againft the champions of the Chriftian power;
And fhow'd how little he his leader priz'd,
How much his mandates, and his fway defpis'd: 245
That public juftice to th' offence was due,
And death the bold offender fhould purfue.
Such acts muft hateful be at every time,
But, doubly here, the place enhanc'd the crime.
That fhould he pafs abfolv'd, the fatal deed   250
A dire example through the hoft might fpread ;
And all that own'd the murder'd warrior's fide,
Would take that vengeance which the law deny'd :
From whence might conteft fpring and mutual rage,
As would the camp in civil broils engage.   255

L 2

He

He call'd to mind the merits of the slain,
All that could waken wrath or pity gain.

   T' acquit his friend the noble Tancred tries,
And fearless for the knight accus'd replies :
While Godfrey hears, and with a brow severe,   260
But little gives to hope, and much to fear.

   Then Tancred thus: O prudent leader! view
What to Rinaldo and his worth is due :
Think from himself what honours he may claim,
What from his glorious race and Guelpho's name.
Not those who rule exalted o'er mankind,   266
Should equal punishment for errors find :
In different stations crimes are different found,
By vulgar laws the great can ne'er be bound.

   To him the leader thus : In every state,   270
The vulgar learn obedience from the great :
Ill, Tancred, doft thou judge, and ill conceive,
That we the mighty should unpunish'd leave :
What is our empire and our vain command,
If only ruler o'er th' ignoble band ?   275
If such my sceptre and imperfect reign,
I here resign the worthless gift again.
But freely, from your choice, the power I hold,
Nor shall the privilege be now control'd :

And.

And well I know to vary from my hand   280
Rewards and punishments, as times demand;
And when, preserving all in equal state,
T' include alike the vulgar and the great.

  Thus Godfrey said; and Tancred nought reply'd,
But, struck with awe, stood silent at his side.   285
  Raymond, a lover of the laws severe
Of ancient times, exults his speech to hear.
While thus (he cries) a ruler holds the sway,
With reverence due the subjects will obey.
In government what discipline is found,   290
Where pardons more than punishments abound?
Ev'n clemency destructive must appear,
And kingdoms fall, unless maintain'd by fear.

  Thus they; while Tancred every sentence
    weigh'd,
Then, swift departing, seiz'd his rapid steed,   295
And with impatience to Rinaldo fled:
Him in his tent he finds, and there relates
The words of Godfrey, and the past debates.
Then thus pursues: Though outward looks we find
Uncertain tokens of the secret mind!   300
Since far too deep, conceal'd from prying eyes,
Within the breast the thought of mortals lies;

L. 3

Thus

Thus far methinks the chief's design I see;
(In this his speeches and his looks agree)
Thou must submit, and by the laws be try'd,   305
When public justice shall thy cause decide.

  At this a scornful smile Rinaldo show'd,
Where noble pride and indignation glow'd.

  Let those (he cry'd) in bonds their cause maintain,
By nature slaves, and worthy of the chain: 310
Free was I born, in freedom will I live,
And sooner die than shameful bonds receive.
This hand is us'd the glorious sword to wield,
To palms of conquest, and disdains to yield
To base constraint: if thus we meet regard,   315
If Godfrey thus our merits would reward;
And thinks to drag me hence, a wretch confin'd
To common prisons, like th' ignoble kind:
Then let him come—I here shall firm abide,
And arms and fate between us shall decide: 320
Soon shall our strife in sanguine torrents flow,
A prospect grateful to the gazing foe!

  This said, he call'd for arms; and soon around
His manly limbs the temper'd harness bound:
Then to his arm the ponderous shield apply'd,   325
And hung the fatal falchion at his side:

                                        Now

Now sheath'd in polish'd mail (a martial sight)
He shone terrific in a blaze of light.
He seem'd like Mars, descending from his sphere,
When rage and terror by his side appear!   330.
   Tancred, meanwhile, essays each soothing art
To calm the passions in his swelling heart.
Unconquer'd youth! (he cries) thy worth is known,
And victory in every field thy own:
Secure from ill, thy godlike virtue goes   335
Through toils and dangers midst embattled foes:
But Heaven forbid that e'er thy friends should feel
The cruel fury of thy vengeful steel!
What would'st thou do? Say, what thy rage demands,
In civil war to stain thy glorious hands?   340
Thus, with the slaughter of the Christian name,
Transfixing CHRIST, in whom a part I claim.
Shall worldly glory (impotent and vain,
That fluctuates like the billows of the main!)
Shall this with more respect thy bosom move   345
Than zeal for crowns, that never fade, above?
Avert it, Heaven! be here thy rage resign'd,
Religion claims this conquest o'er thy mind.
If early youth, like mine, may plead the right
To bring examples past before thy sight: 350

L 4

I once

I once was injur'd, yet my wrath fupprefs'd,
Nor with the faithful would the caufe conteft.
My arms a conqueft of Cilicia made,
And there the banner'd fign of CHRIST difplay'd ;
When Baldwin came, and feiz'd, with covert wiles,
My rightful prize, and triumph'd in my fpoils. 356
His feeming friendfhip won my artlefs mind,
Nor faw I what his greedy thoughts defign'd.
Yet not with arms I ftrove my right to gain,
Though haply arms had not been try'd in vain. 360
But if thy foul difdains a prifoner's name,
And fears th' ignoble breath of vulgar fame :
Be mine the friendly care thy caufe to plead,
To Antioch thou, and ftrait to Bœmond fpeed :
Thou muft not now before the chief appear,   365
And the firft impulfe of his anger bear.
But fhould th' Egyptian arms our force oppofe,
Or other fquadrons of the Pagan foes,

Ver. 353. *My arms a conqueft of Cilicia made,*] Hiftory
relates, that Tancred with his forces made a conqueft of
Cilicia, to which Baldwin claimed a right; and that Tancred having likewife fixed his ftandard at Tarfus, Baldwin
claimed the victory in the fame manner; in both which
inftances Tancred fubmitted.

Then

Then will thy valour fhine with double fame,
And abfence add new luftre to thy name :   370
Th' united camp fhall mourn thy virtues loft,
A mangled body and a lifelefs hoft !

    Here Guelpho came, and, joining his requeft,
With fpeed to leave the camp Rinaldo prefs'd.
And now the noble youth his ear inclin'd,   375
And to their purpofe bent his lofty mind.
A crowd of friends around the hero wait ;
All feek alike t' attend and fhare his fate :
Their zeal he thanks : and now his fteed he takes,
And, with two faithful fquires, the camp forfakes.
A thirft of virtuous fame his foul infpires,   381
That fills the noble heart with great defires :
He mighty actions in his mind revolves,
And deeds, unheard before, in thought refolves ;
T' affail the foe, and death or laurels gain,   385
While ftill his arms the Chriftian faith maintain ;
Egypt t' o'er-run ; and bend his daring courfe
To where the Nile forfakes his hidden fource,

    Rinaldo parting thence ; without delay,
To Godfrey's prefence Guelpho took his way ; 390
Him drawing near the pious chief efpy'd :
Thou com'ft in happy time (aloud he cry'd)

                                        Ev'n

Ev'n now the heralds through the camp I fent,
To feek, and bring thee, Guelpho, to our tent.
    Then having firft difmifs'd th' attending train, 395
He thus, with low and awful words, began :
    Too far, O Guelpho ! does thy nephew ftray,
As paffion o'er his heart ufurps the fway :
And ill, I deem, his reafon can fuffice
To clear the ftain that on his honour lies :   400
Yet happy fhall I prove if this befall :
For Godfrey is an equal judge of all.
The right he will defend, and guard the laws, . .
And with impartial voice award the caufe.
But if, as fome allege, Rinaldo's hand,   405
Unwilling, err'd againft our high command ;
Then let the fiery youth, fubmiffive, bend
To our decifion, and the deed defend :
Free let him come ; no chains he fhall receive ;
(Lo ! what I can I to his merits give.)   410
But if his lofty fpirit fcorn to bow,
(As well his high unconquer'd pride we know)
The care be thine to teach him to obey,
Nor dare provoke too far our lenient fway ;
And force our hand, with rigour, to maintain   415
Our flighted laws, and violated reign.

                                        Thus

Thus faid the chief; and Guelpho made reply :
A generous foul, difdaining infamy,
Can ne'er endure, without a brave return,
The lies of envy, and the taunts of fcorn :   420
And fhould th' offender in his wrath be flain,
What man can juft revenge in bounds reftrain ?
What mind fo govern'd, while refentment glows,
To meafure what th' offence to juftice owes !
'Tis thy command the youth fhall humbly come, 425
And yield himfelf beneath thy fovereign doom ;
But this (with grief I fpeak) his flight denies :
A willing exile from the camp he flies.
Yet with this fword I offer to maintain,
'Gainft him who dares my nephew's honour ftain, 430
That juftly punifh'd fierce Gernando dy'd,
A victim due to calumny and pride.
In this alone (with forrow I agree)
He rafhly err'd, to break thy late decree.

   Thus he ; when Godfrey—Let him wander far, 435
And ftrife and rage to other regions bear ;
But vex not thou with new debates the peace ;
Here end contention, here let anger ceafe.

   Meantime, Armida, midft the warrior-train,
Us'd all her power th' expected aid to gain :   440

In

In tears and moving prayers the day employ'd,
And every charm of wit and beauty try'd.
But when the night had fpread her fable veſt,
And clos'd the finking day-light in the weſt,
Betwixt two knights and dames, from public view,
The damfel to her lofty tent withdrew.   446

Though well the fair was vers'd in every art
By words and looks to ſteal th' unguarded heart;
Though in her form celeſtial beauty ſhin'd,
And left the faireſt of her ſex behind;   450
Though in her ſtrong, yet pleaſing, charms compell'd,
The greateſt heroes of the camp ſhe held,
In vain ſhe ſtrove, with ſoft bewitching care,
To lure the pious Godfrey to her ſnare:
In vain ſhe fought his zealous breaſt to move,   455
With earthly pleaſures, and delights of love:
For, fated with the world, his thoughts deſpiſe
Theſe empty joys, and ſoar above the ſkies.
His ſteadfaſt foul, defended from her charms,
Contemns love's weak eſſays, and all his feeble arms.
No mortal bait can turn his ſteps aſide,   461
His ſacred faith his guard, and GOD his guide.
A thouſand forms the falſe Armida tries,
And proves, like Proteus, every new difguife.

                              Her

Her looks and actions every heart might move,   465
And warm the coldest bosom to her love :
But here, so Heaven and grace divine ordain,
Her schemes, her labours, and her wiles were vain.

  Not less impervious to her fraudful art,
The gallant Tancred kept his youthful heart :   470
His earlier passion every thought possess'd,
Nor gave another entrance to his breast.
As poison oft the force of poison quells,
So former love the second love repels.
Her charms these two alone beheld secure ;   475
While others own'd resistless beauty's pow'r.
Sore was she troubled in her guileful mind,
That all succeeded not her wiles design'd :
Yet, 'midst her grief, the dame, exulting, view'd
The numerous warriors whom her smiles subdu'd :
Now, with her prey, she purpos'd to depart,   481
Ere chance disclos'd her deep-designing art ;
Far from the camp her captives to detain,
In other bonds than love's too gentle chain.

  'Twas now the time appointed by the chief   485
To give th' afflicted damsel his relief :
Him she approach'd, and lowly thus begun :
The day prefix'd, O prince ! its course has run :

I

And should the tyrant learn (by doubtful fame,
Or certain spies) that to the camp I came   490
T' implore thy succour, his preventive care
Would all his forces for defence prepare.
But ere such tidings shall his ears attain,
O! let my prayer some friendly succours gain:
If Heaven beholds not with regardless eyes   495
The deeds of men, or hears the orphan's cries,
My realms I shall retrieve, whose subject-sway
To thee, in peace or war, shall tribute pay.

　　She said; the leader to her suit agreed,
(Nor could he from his former grant recede)   500
Yet since her swift departure thence she press'd,
He saw th' election on himself would rest:
While all, with emulative zeal, demand
To fill the number of th' elected band.

　　Th' insidious damsel fans the rivals' fires,   505
And envious fear and jealous doubt inspires,
To rouze the soul; for love, full well she knows,
Without these aids remiss and languid grows:
So runs the courser with a slacken'd pace,
When none contend, his partners in the race.   510
Now this, now that, the soothing fair beguiles
With gentle speech, soft looks, and winning smiles;

That

That each his fellow views with envious eyes,
Till mingled paffions ev'n to frenzy rife :
Around their chief they prefs, unaw'd by fhame,   515
And Godfrey would in vain their rage reclaim.

   The leader gladly, in his equal mind,
Would all content, alike to all inclin'd ;
(Yet oft was fill'd with juft difdain, to view
Th' ungovern'd rafhnefs of the headlong crew)   520
At length his better thoughts the means fupply'd,
To ftay contention, and the ftrife decide.

   To chance (he cry'd) your feveral names commend;
Let lots decide it, and the conteft end.

   Sudden the rival knights their names difpos'd,   525
And in a flender urn the lots enclos'd :
The vafe then fhaken ; firft to view, the name
Of Pembroke's earl, Artemidorus, came :
Then Gerrard; Vincilaüs next was found,
An aged chief for counfel once renown'd,   530
A hoary lover now, in beauty's fetters bound !

   Thefe happy three with fudden joys were fill'd ;
The reft, by figns, their anxious fears reveal'd,
And hung upon his lips, with fix'd regard,
Who, drawing forth the lots, the names declar'd.   535
The fourth was Guafco ; then Ridolphus' name ;
And next Ridolphus, Olderico came.

                              Roufillon

Rousillon then was read; and next appear'd
Henry the Frank; Bavarian Eberard:
Rambaldo laſt, who left the Chriſtian laws,   540
And girt his weapon in the Pagan cauſe:
So far the tyrant love his vaſſal draws !

    But thoſe, excluded from the liſt, exclaim
On fickle fortune as a partial dame ;
Love they accuſe, who ſuffer'd her to guide   545
His ſacred empire, and his laws decide ;
Yet many purpos'd to purſue the maid,
When parting light ſhould yield to ſable ſhade ;
In fortune's ſpight, her perſon to attend,
And, with their lives, from every chance defend. 550
With gentle ſighs and ſpeeches half diſclos'd,
Their willing minds to this ſhe more diſpos'd :
To every knight alike ſhe fram'd her art,
And ſeem'd to leave him with dejected heart.

    Now, clad in ſhining arms, th' allotted band 555
Diſmiſſion from their prudent chief demand.
The hero then admoniſh'd each aſide,
How ill they could in Pagan faith confide ;

    Ver. 540. *Rambaldo laſt, who left the Chriſtian laws,*] The
hiſtory makes mention of a ſoldier who abjured Chriſtianity
and went over to the Infidels, but his name was Rainaldo,
not Rambaldo; he was a native of Holland.

So

So frail a pledge enjoin'd 'em to beware,
And guard their souls from every hidden fnare. 560
But all his words were loft in empty wind ;
Love takes not counfel from a wholefome mind.

   The knights difmifs'd, the dame no longer ftay'd,
Nor till th' enfning morn her courfe delay'd.
Elate with conqueft, from the camp fhe pafs'd, 565
('The rival knights, like flaves, her triumph grac'd)
While rack'd with jealoufy's tormenting pain,
She left the remnant of the fuitor-train.
But foon as night with filent wings arofe;
The minifter of dreams and foft repofe ;   570
In fecret many more her fteps purfue :
But firft Euftatius from the tents withdrew ;
Scarce rofe the friendly fhade, when fwift he fled,
Through darknefs blind; by blind affection led:
He roves uncertain all the dewy night,   575 ⎤
But foon as morning ftreaks the fkies with light,   ⎬
Armida's camp falutes his eager fight.   ⎦

   Fir'd at the view, th' impatient lover flies ;
Him, by his arms, Rambaldo knows, and cries—
What feek'ft thou here, or whither doft thou bend ?
I come (he faid) Armida to defend :   581
In me, no lefs than others, fhall fhe find
A ready fuccour and a conftant mind.

Who dares (the knight replies) that choice approve,
And make such honour thine ? He answer'd—Love.
From fortune thou, from love my right I claim :   586
Say, whose the greatest boast and noblest name ?
Rambaldo then—Thy empty titles fail,
Such fond delusive arts shall ne'er prevail.
Think not to join with us thy lawless aid,   590
With us the champions of the royal maid.
Who shall oppose my will ? (the youth reply'd)
In me behold the man ! (Rambaldo cry'd)
Swift at the word he rush'd ; with equal rage
Eustatius sprung his rival to engage.   595
But here the lovely tyrant of their breast
Advanc'd between them, and their rage suppress'd.
Ah ! cease, (to that she cry'd) nor more complain,
That thou a partner, I a champion gain :
Canst thou my welfare or my safety prize,   600
Yet thus deprive me of my new allies ?
In happy time (to this began the dame)
Thou com'st, defender of my life and fame :
Reason forbids, that e'er it shall be said,
Armida scorn'd so fair an offer'd aid.   605
    Thus she ; while some new champion every hour
Pursu'd her standard, and increas'd her power.

Some

Some wandering here, some there, the damsel join'd,
Though each concealing what his thoughts design'd,
Now scowl'd with jealous looks his rivals there to
    find.   610
She seem'd on all to cast a gracious eye,
And every one receiv'd with equal joy.

   Scarce had the day dispell'd the shades of night,
When heedful Godfrey knew his warriors' flight ;
And while his mind revolv'd their shameful doom, 615
He seem'd to mourn some threaten'd ills to come.
As thus he mus'd, a messenger appear'd,
Breathless and pale, with dust and sweat besmear'd.
His brow was deep imprefs'd with careful thought,
And seem'd to speak th' unwelcome news he brought.

   Then thus—O chief! th' Egyptians soon will hide
Beneath their numerous fleet the briny tide ;
William, whose rule Liguria's ships obey,
By me dispatch'd these tidings from the sea.
To this he adds ; that, sending from the shore   625
The due provisions for the landed power,
The steeds and camels, bending with their load,
Were intercepted in the midmost road ;
Affail'd with dreadful rage on every hand,
Deep in a valley, by th' Arabian band :   630

M 2

Nor

Nor guards nor drivers could their posts maintain,
The stores were pillag'd, and the men were slain.
To such a height was grown the Arabs' force,
As ask'd some power t' obstruct their daring course;
To guard the coast, and keep the passage free,   635
Betwixt the Christian camp and Syrian sea.

  At once from man to man the rumour fled,
And growing fears among the soldiers spread :
The threatening evils fill'd them with affright,
And ghastly famine rose before their sight.   640
The chief, who saw the terrors of the host,
Their former courage sunk, their firmness lost ;
With looks serene, and chearful speeches strove
To raise their ardor and their fears remove.

  O friends ! with me in various regions thrown, 645
Amidst a thousand woes and dangers known ;
God's sacred champions ! born t' assert his cause,
And cleanse from stain the holy Christian laws !
Who wintry climes and stormy seas have view'd,
And Persian arms and Grecian frauds subdu'd ; 650

  Ver. 650.—*and Grecian frauds subdu'd,*] Alexas, emperor
of Constantinople, though in the first book he appears to
have sent a squadron of horse to the Christians, is said to
have used many stratagems to frustrate the expedition, and
had once made Hugo the great prisoner, who was afterwards delivered by Godfrey.

Who

Who could the rage of thirst and hunger bear—
Will you refign your fouls to abject fear ?
Shall not th' Eternal Power (our fovereign guide,
And oft in more difaftrous fortunes try'd)
Revive our hopes ?—deem not his favour loft,   655
Or pitying ear averted from our hoft :
A day will come with pleafure to difclofe
Thefe forrows paft, and pay to God your vows.
Endure and conquer then your prefent ftate ;
Live, and referve yourfelves for happier fate.   660
    He faid, but yet a thoufand cares, fupprefs'd,
The hero bury'd in his thoughtful breaft :
What means to nourifh fuch a numerous train,
And midft defeat or famine to fuftain :
How on the feas t' oppofe th' Egyptian force ;   665
And ftop the plundering Arabs in their courfe.

END OF THE FIFTH BOOK.

THE ARGUMENT.

ARGANTES sends a challenge to the Christians. Tancred
is chosen to oppose him; but while he is upon the point
of entering the list, is detained by the appearance of Clorinda. Otho, in the mean time, meets Argantes, is van-
quished, and made prisoner. Tancred and Argantes then
engage: they are parted by the heralds. Erminia, dif-
tressed with her fears for Tancred, resolves to visit that
hero. She disguises herself in Clorinda's armour, and
leaves the city by night; but, falling in with an advanced
guard of the Christians, is assaulted, and flies.

THE

SIXTH BOOK

OF

JERUSALEM DELIVERED.

BUT, in the town befieg'd, the Pagan crew
    With better thoughts their cheerful hopes
      renew:
Befides provifions which their roofs contain'd,
Supplies, of various kinds, by night they gain'd:
They raife new fences for the northern fide,   5
And warlike engines for the walls provide.
With ftrength increas'd the lofty bulwarks fhow,
And feem to fcorn the battering-rams below.
Now here, now there, the king directs his powers,
The walls to thicken, or to raife the towers: 10
By day, or fable eve, the works they ply,
Or when the moon enlightens all the fky.
Th' artificers, with fweat and ceafelefs care,
New arms and armour for the field prepare:
Meanwhile,

Meanwhile, impatient of inglorious reft,   15
Argantes came and thus the king addrefs'd.

     How long, inactive, muft we here remain
Coop'd in thefe gates, a bafe and heartlefs train ?
From anvils huge I hear the ftrokes rebound,
I hear the helm, the fhield, the cuirafs found :   20
Say, to what ufe, while yon rapacious bands
O'er-run the plains, and ravage all the lands ?
And not a chief fhall meet thefe haughty foes,
And not a trumpet break their foft repofe ?
In genial feafts the cheerful days they wafte,   25
And undifturb'd enjoy each calm repaft :
By day at eafe, by night at reft they lie ,
Alike fecurely all their moments fly.
But you, at length, with pining want diftrefs'd,
Muft fink beneath the victor's force opprefs'd ;   30
Or bafely fall to death an eafy prey,
If Egypt fhould her fuccours long delay.
For me, no fhameful fate fhall end my days,
And with oblivion veil my former praife :
Nor fhall the morning fun, to fight expos'd,   35
Behold me longer in thefe walls enclos'd.
I ftand prepar'd my lot unknown to prove,
Decreed already by the Fates above.

                                        Ne'er

Ne'er be it said, the trusty sword untry'd,
Inglorious, unreveng'd, Argantes dy'd.   40
Yet if the seeds of valour, once confess'd,
Are not extinguish'd in thy generous breast :
Not only hope in fight to fall with praise,
But your high thoughts to life and conquest raise.
Then rush we forth united from the gate,   45
Attack the foe, and prove our utmost fate !
Beset with dangers, and with toils oppress'd,
The boldest counsels oft are prov'd the best.
But if thy prudence now refuse to yield,
To hazard all thy force in open field ;   50
At least procure two champions to decide
Th' important strife, in single combat try'd :
And that the leader of the Christian race
With readier mind our challenge may embrace,
Th' advantage all be his the arms to name,   55
And at his will the full conditions frame.
For were the foe endu'd with twofold might,
With heart undaunted in the day of fight;
Think no misfortune can thy cause attend,
Which I have sworn in combat to defend.   60
This better hand can fate itself supply ;
This hand can give thee ample victory :

Behold

Behold I give it as a pledge fecure;
In this confide, I here thy reign enfure.

He ceas'd: Intrepid chief! (the king reply'd) 65
Though creeping age has damp'd my youthful pride,
Deem not this hand fo flow the fword to wield,
Nor deem this foul fo bafely fears the field,
That rather would I tamely lofe my breath,
Than fall ennobled by a glorious death;   70
If aught I fear'd, if aught my thoughts foretold
Of want or famine which thy words unfold;
Forbid it, Heaven!—Then hear me now reveal
What from the reft, with caution, I conceal.
Lo! Solyman of Nice, whofe reftlefs mind   75
Has vengeance for his former wrongs defign'd,
Collects, beneath his care, from different lands,
The fcatter'd numbers of Arabia's bands;
With thefe will foon by night the foes invade,
And hopes to give the town fupplies and aid.   80
Then grieve not thou to fee our realms o'er-run,
Nor heed our plunder'd towns, and caftles won;
While here the fceptre ftill remains my own;
While here I hold my ftate and regal throne.
But thou, meantime, thy forward zeal affuage,   85
And calm awhile the heat of youthful rage;

5   With

With patience yet attend the hour of fate,
Due to thy glory, and my injur'd state.
  Now swell'd with high disdain Argantes' breast,
A rival long to Solyman profess'd :   90
Inly he griev'd, and saw, with jealous eye,
The king so firmly on his aid rely.
  'Tis thine, (he cry'd) O monarch ! to declare
(Thine is th' undoubted power) or peace or war ;
I urge no more—here Solyman attend,   95
Let him, who lost his own, thy realm defend !
Let him, a welcome messenger from Heaven,
To free the Pagans from their fears be given :
I safety from myself alone require ;
And freedom only from this arm desire.   100
Now, while these walls the rest in sloth detain,
Let me descend to combat on the plain :
Give me to dare the Franks to single fight,
Not as thy champion, but a private knight.
  The king reply'd : Though future times demand
Thy nobler courage, and more needful hand ;   106
Yet to thy wish I shall not this deny :
Then, at thy will, some hostile chief defy.
  Thus he.   Th' impatient youth no longer stay'd,
But, turning to the herald, thus he said.   110
Haste

Halte to the leader of the Franks, and there,
Before th' united hoft, this meffage bear :
Say, that a champion, whofe fuperior mind
Scorns in thefe narrow walls to be confin'd,
Defires to prove, in either army's fight,   115
With fpear and fhield his utmoft force in fight;
And comes prepar'd his challenge to maintain,
Betwixt the tents and city, on the plain ;
A gallant proof of arms ! and now defies
The boldeft Frank that on his ftrength relies.   120
Nor one alone amid the hoftile band ;
The boldeft five that dare his force withftand,
Of noble lineage, or of vulgar race,
Unterrify'd be ftands in field to face :
The vanquifh'd to the victor's power fhall yield, 125
So wills the law of arms and cuftom of the field.

Argantes thus.   The herald ftrait withdrew,
His vary'd furcoat o'er his fhoulders threw,
And thence to Godfrey's regal prefence went,
By mighty chiefs furrounded in his tent.   130
O prince ! (he cry'd) may here a herald dare,
Without offence, his embaffy declare ?
To him the chief : Without conftraint or fear,
In freedom fpeak, what we as freely hear.

The

The herald then the challenge fierce diſclos'd,   135
In boaſtful words and haughty terms compos'd.
Fir'd at his ſpeech the martial bands appear'd,
And with diſdain the ſtern defiance heard.
Then thus in anſwer pious Godfrey ſpeaks :
A mighty taſk your warrior undertakes :   140
And well I truſt, whate'er his boaſted might,
One champion may ſuffice his arms in fight.
But let him come ; I to his will agree ;
I give him open field, and conduct free :
And ſwear ſome warrior, from our Chriſtian band,
On equal terms ſhall meet him hand to hand.   146
   He ceas'd ; the king at arms without delay,
Impatient, meaſur'd back his former way ;
From thence, with haſty ſteps, the city ſought,
And to the Pagan knight their anſwer brought.   150
Arm ! valiant chief ! (he cry'd) for fight prepare,
The Chriſtian powers accept thy proffer'd war :
Not leaders fam'd alone demand the fight,
The meaneſt warriors burn to prove their might.
I ſaw a thouſand threatening looks appear,   155
A thouſand hands prepar'd the ſword to rear :
The chief to thee a liſt ſecure will yield.
He ended : When, impatient for the field,

3   Argantes

Argantes call'd for arms with furious hafte,
And round his limbs the fteely burthen caft.   160
   The wary king Clorinda then enjoin'd:
While he departs, remain not thou behind;
But, with a thoufand arm'd, attend the knight;
Yet foremoft let him march to equal fight,
The care be thine to keep thy troops in fight.   165
   The monarch fpoke; and now the martial-train
Forfook the walls and iffu'd to the plain.
Advanc'd before the band, Argantes prefs'd
His foaming fteed, in radiant armour drefs'd.
Between the city and the camp was found   170
An ample fpace of level champaign ground;
That feem'd a lift felected, by defign,
For valiant chiefs in deeds of arms to join.
To this the bold Argantes fingly goes,
And there, defcending, ftands before the foes: 175
Proud in his might, with giant-ftrength indu'd,
With threatening looks the diftant camp he view'd:
So fierce Enceladus in Phlegra fhow'd;
So in the vale the huge Philiftine ftood.
Yet many, void of fear, the knight beheld,   180
Nor knew how far his force in arms excell'd.
   Still Godfrey doubted, midft his valiant hoft,
What knight fhould quell the Pagan's haughty boaft.
                                        To

To Tancred's arm (the braveſt of the brave)
The great attempt the public favour gave.   185
With looks, with whiſpers, all declar'd their choice ;
The chief, by ſigns, approv'd the general voice.
Each warrior now his rival claim withdrew ;
When each the will of mighty Godfrey knew.
The field is thine ! (to Tancred then he cry'd) 190
Go ! meet yon Pagan, and chaſtiſe his pride.
The glorious charge with joy the champion heard,
A dauntleſs ardour in his looks appear'd :
His ſhield and helmet from his ſquire he took,
And, follow'd by a crowd, the vale forſook.   195
But ere he reach'd th' appointed liſt of fight,
The martial damſel met his eager fight :
A flowing veſt was o'er her armour ſpread,
White as the ſnows that veil the mountain's head :
Her beaver rear'd her lovely face diſclos'd,   200
And on a hill ſhe ſtood at full expos'd.

  No longer Tancred now the foe eſpies,
(Who rears his haughty viſage to the ſkies)
But ſlowly moves his ſteed, and bends his ſight
Where ſtands the virgin on a neighbouring height :
The lover to a lifeleſs ſtatue turns ;   206
With cold he freezes, and with heat he burns :

  Vol. I.   N   Fix'd

Fix'd in a ftupid gaze, unmov'd he ftands,
And now no more the promis'd fight demands!
 Meantime Argantes looks around in vain,   210
No chief appears the combat to maintain.
Behold I come (he cry'd) to prove my might,
Who dares approach and meet my arms in fight ?
 While Tancred loft in deepeft thought appear'd,
Nor faw the Pagan, nor his challenge heard,   215
Impetuous Otho fpurr'd his foaming horfe,
And enter'd firft the lift with eager courfe.
This knight, before, by thirft of glory fir'd,
With other warriors, to the fight afpir'd :
And yielding then to Tancred's nobler claim,   220
Mix'd with the throng that to attend him came ;
But when he thus th' enamour'd youth beheld
All motionlefs, neglectful of the field,
Eager he ftarts t' attempt the glorious deed ;
Lefs fwift the tiger's or the panther's fpeed !   225
Againft the mighty Saracen he prefs'd,
Who fudden plac'd his ponderous fpear in reft.
 But Tancred now, recovering from his trance,
Saw fearlefs Otho to the fight advance :
Forbear ! the field is mine ! (aloud he cries)— 230
In vain he calls, the knight regardlefs flies.

Th'

Th' indignant prince beheld, with rage and shame ;
He blush'd another should defraud his name,
And reap th' expected harvest of his fame.

    And now Argantes, from his valiant foe,   235
Full on his helm receiv'd the mighty blow.
With greater force the Pagan's javelin struck ;
The pointed steel thro' shield and corslet broke :
Prone fell the Christian thundering on the sand ;
Unmov'd the Saracen his seat maintain'd ;   240
And, from on high, inflam'd with lofty pride,
Thus to the prostrate knight insulting cry'd :
Yield to my arms ! suffice the glory thine
To dare with me in equal combat join.
Not so (cry'd Otho) are we fram'd to yield,   245
Nor is so soon the Christian courage quell'd :
Let others, with excuses, hide my shame,
'Tis mine to perish, or avenge my fame !

    Then like Alecto, terrible to view,
Or like Medusa, the Circassian grew,   250
While from his eyes the flashing lightening flew !
Now prove our utmost force (enrag'd he cries)
Since thus thou dar'st our offer'd grace despise.
This said ; he spurr'd his steed, nor heeded more
Th' establish'd laws of arms and knightly lore.   255

N 2

The

The Frank, retiring, disappoints the foe,
And, as Argantes pass'd, directs a blow,
That to the right descending pierc'd his side;
The smoking steel returns with crimson dy'd:
But what avails it, when the wound inspires   260
New force and fury to the Pagan's fires?
Argantes, wheeling round with sudden speed,
Direct on Otho urg'd his fiery steed:
Th' unguarded foe the dreadful shock receiv'd;
All pale he fell, at once of sense bereav'd: 265
Stretch'd on the earth his quivering limbs were
          spread,
And clouds of darkness hover'd o'er his head!
   With brutal wrath the haughty victor glow'd,
And o'er the vanquish'd knight in triumph rode.
Thus every insolent shall fall (he cries)   270
As he who now beneath my courser lies!
   But valiant Tancred now no longer stay'd,
Who with disdain the cruel act survey'd;
Resolv'd to veil the fallen warrior's shame,
And with his arms retrieve the Christian name; 275
He flew, and cry'd—O thou! of impious kind,
In conquest base, and infamous of mind!
From deeds like these what glory canst thou gain?
What praises from the courteous heart obtain?

Thy

Thy manners sure were fram'd in savage lands, 280
Among th' Arabian thieves, or barbarous bands!
Hence, shun the light; to woods and wilds confin'd,
Among thy brethren of the brutal kind!.

   He ceas'd: Impatience swell'd the Pagan's breast,
But eager rage his struggling words suppress'd: 285
He foam'd like beasts that haunt the gloomy wood;
At length, releas'd, his anger roar'd aloud,
Like thunder bursting from a distant cloud.

   Now for the field th' impetuous chiefs prepare,
And wheel around their coursers for the war. 290
O sacred muse! inflame my voice with fire,
And ardor equal to the fight inspire:
So may my verse be worthy of th' alarms,
And catch new vigour from the din of arms!

   The warriors place their beamy spears in rest; 295
Each points his weapon at the adverse crest.
Less swiftly to the goal a racer flies;
Less swift a bird on pinions cleaves the skies.
No chiefs for fury could with these compare;
Here Tancred pour'd along, Argantes there! 300
The spears against the helms in shivers broke;
A thousand sparks flew diverse from the stroke.
The mighty conflict shook the solid ground,
The distant hills re-echo'd to the sound;

N 3

But

But firmly feated, moveless as a rock,   305
Each hardy champion bore the dreadful fhock :
While either courfer tumbled on the plain,
Nor from the field with fpeed arofe again.
The warriors then unfheath'd their falchions bright,
And left their fteeds, on foot to wage the fight. 310
Now every pafs with wary hands they prove ;
With watchful eyes and nimble feet they move.
In every form their pliant limbs they fhow ;
Now wheel, now prefs, now feem to fhun the foe :
Now here, now there, the glancing fteel they bend ;
And where they threaten leaft the ftrokes defcend. 316
Sometimes they offer fome defencelefs part,
Attempting thus to baffle art with art.
Tancred, unguarded by his fword or fhield,
His naked fide before the Pagan held :   320
To feize th' advantage fwift Argantes clos'd,
And left himfelf to Tancred's fword expos'd ;
The Chriftian dafh'd the hoftile fteel afide,
And deep in Pagan gore his weapon dy'd ;
Then fudden on his guard collected ftood :   325
The foe, who found his limbs bedew'd with blood,
Groan'd with unwonted rage, and rais'd on high
His weighty falchion, with a dreadful cry :

But,

But, ere he strikes, another wound alights
Where to the shoulder-bone the arm unites.   330
As the wild boar that haunts the woods and hills,
When in his side the biting spear he feels,
To fury rouz'd, against the hunter flies,
And every peril scorns, and death defies:
So fares the Saracen, with wrath on flame;   335
Wound follows wound, and shame succeeds to shame:
And, burning for revenge, without regard,
He scorns his danger, and forgets to ward.
He raves, he rushes headlong on the foe,
With all his strength impelling every blow.   340
Scarce has the Christian time his sword to wield,
Or breathe awhile, or lift his fencing shield;
And all his art can scarce the knight secure
From the dire thunder of Argantes' power.

  Tancred, who waits to see the tempest cease,   345
And the first fury of his foe decrease,
Now wards the blows, now circles o'er the plain;
But when he sees the Pagan's force remain
Untir'd with toil, he gives his wrath the rein:
He whirls his falchion; art and judgment yield, 350
And now to rage alone resign the field.
No strokes, enforc'd from either champion, fail:
The weapons pierce or sever plate and mail.

N 4 With

With arms and blood the earth is cover'd o'er,
And streaming sweat is mixt with purple gore ; 355
The swords, like lightening, dart quick flashes round,
And fall, like thunderbolts, with horrid found,
On either hand the gazing people wait,
And watch the dreadful fight's uncertain fate :
No motion in th' attentive host appear'd,   360
No voice, no whisper from the troops was heard :
'Twixt hope and fear they stand, and nicely weigh
The various turns, and fortune of the day.

    Thus stood the war ; and now each weary knight
Had undetermin'd left the chance of fight ;   365
When rising eve her sable veil display'd,
And wrapt each object in surrounding shade.
From either side a herald bent his way,
To part the warriors and suspend the fray.
The one a Frank, Arideus was his name ;   370
Pindorus one, rever'd for wisdom's fame,
Who with the challenge to the Christians came.
Intrepid these before the chiefs appear'd,
And 'twixt their swords their peaceful sceptres rear'd ;
Secur'd by all the privilege they find   375
From ancient rights and customs of mankind.
Ye warriors brave ! (Pindorus thus begun)
Whose deeds of valour equal praise have won ;

Here

Here ceafe, nor with untimely ftrife profane
The facred laws of night's all-peaceful reign.   380
The fun our labour claims; with toil oppref's'd,
Each creature gives the night to needful reft;
And generous fouls difdain the conquefts made
In fullen filence, and nocturnal fhade.

  To him Argantes: With regret I yield   385
To quit th' unfinifh'd conteft of the field;
Yet would I chufe the day our deeds might view:
Then fwear, my foe, the combat to renew.

  To whom the Chriftian: Thou thy promife plight
Here to return, and bring thy captive * knight;   390
Elfe fhall no caufe induce me to delay
Our prefent conflict to a future day.
This faid, they fwore.   The heralds then decreed
The day that fhould decide th' important deed;
And, time allow'd to heal each wounded knight,   395
Nam'd the fixth morning to renew the fight.

  The dreadful combat long remain'd imprefs'd
In every Saracen and Chriftian breaft:
Each tongue the fkill of either warrior tells;
Each thought, with wonder, on their valour dwells.
Yet who the prize fhould gain, on either fide   401
The vulgar vary and in parts divide:

* OTHO.

If

If fury shall from virtue win the field,
Or brutal rage to manly courage yield.

But fair Erminia, mov'd above the rest,   405
With growing fears torments her tender breast ;
She sees the dearest object of her care
Expos'd to hazards of uncertain war.
Of princely lineage came this haplefs maid,
From him who Antioch's powerful fceptre fway'd :
But, when her state by chance of war was loft,   411
She fell a captive to the Chriftian hoft.
Then gallant Tancred gave her woes relief,
And, midft her country's ruin, calm'd her grief:
He gave her freedom, gave her all the ftore   415
Of regal treafure fhe poffefs'd before,
And claim'd no tribute of a victor's power.
The grateful fair the hero's worth confefs'd ;
Love found admittance in her gentle breaft :
His early virtues rais'd her firft defire ;   420
His manly beauty fann'd the blamelefs fire.
In vain her outward liberty fhe gain'd,
When, loft in fervitude, her foul remain'd !
She quits her conqueror with a heavy mind,
And with regret her prifon leaves behind.   425
But honour chides her ftay, (for fpotlefs fame
Is ever dear to every virtuous dame)

And

And, with her aged mother, thence conftrain'd
Her banifh'd fteps to feek a friendly land ;
Till at Jerufalem her courfe fhe ftay'd,   430
Where Aladine receiv'd the wandering maid.
Here foon again, by adverfe fortune croft,
With tears the virgin mourn'd a mother loft.
Yet not the forrow for her parent's fate,
Nor all the troubles of her exil'd ftate,   435
Could from her heart her amorous pains remove,
Or quench the fmalleft fpark of mighty love:
She loves, and burns !—Alas, unhappy maid !
No foothing hopes afford her torments aid :
She bears, within, the flames of fond defire ; 440
Vain fruitlefs wifhes all her thoughts infpire,
And, while fhe ftrives to hide, fhe feeds the ftifled
    fire.
Now Tancred near the walls of Sion drew,
And, by his prefence, rais'd her hopes anew.
The reft with terror fee the numerous train   445
Of foes unconquer'd on the dufty plain :
She clears her brow, her dewy forrow dries,
And views the warlike bands with cheerful eyes:
From rank to rank her looks inceffant rove,
And oft fhe feeks in vain her warrior love ;   450

And

And oft, diftinguifh'd midft the field of fight,
She fingles Tancred to her eager fight.

Join'd with the palace, to the ramparts nigh,
A ftately caftle rifes in the fky,
Whofe lofty head the profpect wide commands, 455
The plain, the mountain, and the Chriftian bands:
There, from the early beams of morning light,
Till deepening fhades obfcure the world in night,
She fits, and, fixing on the camp her eyes, 459
She communes with her thoughts, and vents her fighs.
From thence fhe view'd the fight with beating heart,
And faw expos'd her foul's far dearer part;
There, fill'd with terror and diftracting care,
She watch'd the various progrefs of the war;
And, when the Pagan rais'd aloft his fteel, 465
She feem'd herfelf the threatening ftroke to feel.

When now the virgin heard fome future day
Was deftin'd to decide th' unfinifh'd fray,
Cold fear in all her veins congeal'd the blood,
Sighs heav'd her breaft, her eyes with forrow flow'd,
And o'er her face a pallid hue was fpread, 471
While every fenfe was loft in anxious dread.
A thoufand horrid thoughts her foul divin'd;
In fleep a thoufand phantoms fill'd her mind:

Oft,

Oft, in her dreams, the much-lov'd warrior lies 475
All gaſh'd and bleeding; oft, with feeble cries,
Invokes her aid; then, ſtarting from her reſt,
Tears bathe her cheeks, and trickle down her breaſt.
Nor fears alone of future evils fill
Her careful heart, ſhe fears the preſent ill.   480
The wounds her Tancred late receiv'd in fight
Diſtract her mind with anguiſh and affright.
Fallacious rumours, that around are blown,
Increaſe with added lies the truth unknown.

   Taught by her mother's ſkill, the virgin knew 485
The ſecret power of every herb that grew:
She knew the force of every myſtic ſtrain,
To cloſe the wound, and eaſe the throbbing pain;
(In ſuch repute the healing arts were held,
In theſe the daughters of the kings excell'd.)   490
Fain would ſhe now her cares to Tancred ſhow;
But fate condemns her to relieve his foe.
Now was ſhe tempted noxious plants to chuſe,
And poiſon in Argantes' wounds infuſe:
But ſoon her pious thoughts the deed diſclaim, 495
And ſcorn with treachery to pollute her fame.
Yet oft ſhe wiſh'd that every herb apply'd
Might loſe its wonted power, and virtue try'd.

She

She fear'd not (by such various troubles tost)
Alone to travel through the adverse host;   500
Accustom'd wars and slaughter to survey,
And all the perils of the wanderer's way:
Thus use to daring had inur'd her mind
Beyond the nature of the softer kind:
But mighty love, superior to the rest,   505
Had quell'd each female terror in her breast:
Thus arm'd, she durst the sands of Afric trace,
Amidst the fury of the savage race.
Though danger still and death her soul despis'd,
Her virtue, and her better fame she priz'd.   510
And now her heart conflicting passions rend;
There love and honour (powerful foes!) contend.
Thus honour seem'd to say: O thou! whose mind
Has still been pure, within my laws confin'd;
Whom, when a captive midst yon hostile train,   515
I kept in thought and person clear from stain;
Wilt thou, now freed, the virgin boast forego,
So well preserv'd when prisoner to the foe?
Ah! what can raise such fancies in thy breast?
Say, what thy purpose, what thy hopes suggest,   520
Alone to wander midst a foreign race,
And with nocturnal love thy sex disgrace?

3   Justly

Juſtly the victor ſhall reproach thy name,
And deem thee loſt to virtue, as to ſhame;
With ſcorn ſhall bid thee from his ſight remove, 525
And bear to vulgar ſouls thy proffer'd love.

But gentler counſels, on a different part,
Thus ſeem'd to whiſper to her wavering heart.

Thou wert not ſurely of a ſavage born,
Nor from a mountain's frozen entrails torn; 530
No adamant and ſteel compoſe thy frame;
Deſpiſe not then love's pleaſing dart and flame,
And bluſh not to confeſs a lover's name.
Go, and obey the dictates of thy mind—
But wherefore ſhould'ſt thou feign thy knight un-
        kind?   535
Like thine his ſighs may heave, his tears may flow;
And wilt not thou thy tender aid beſtow?
Lo! Tancred's life (ungrateful!) runs to waſte,
While on another all thy cares are plac'd!
To cure Argantes then thy ſkill apply,   540
So by his arm may thy deliverer die!
Is this the ſervice to his merits due,
And canſt thou ſuch a hateful taſk purſue?
O! think what tranſports muſt thy boſom feel
Thy Tancred's wounds, with lenient hand, to heal.

                                        Think,

Think, when thy pious care his health retrieves, 546
Life's welcome gift from thee the youth receives!
Thou shalt with him in every virtue share,
With him divide his future fame in war:
Then shall he clasp thee to his grateful breast, 550
And nuptial ties shall make thee ever blest:
Thou shalt be shown to all, and happy nam'd,
Among the Latian wives and matrons fam'd;
In that fair land where martial valour reigns,
And where religion her pure seat maintains. 555
  With hopes like these deceiv'd, th'unthinking maid
A flattering scene of future bliss had laid:
But still a thousand doubts perplexing rise,
What means for her departure to devise.
The guards, incessant, near the palace stand, 560
And watch the portals, and the walls command,
Nor dare, amid the hazards of the war,
Without some weighty cause the gates unbar.
  Full oft Erminia, to beguile her cares,
The time in converse with Clorinda shares: 565
With her each western sun beheld the maid,
Each rising morn the friendly pair survey'd:
And when in gloomy shade the day was clos'd,
Both in one bed their weary limbs repos'd.

S

One

One fecret only, treafur'd in her breaft,   570
The fond Erminia from her friend fupprefs'd ;
With cautious fear her love fhe ftill conceal'd ;
But when her plaints her inward pains reveal'd,
She to a different caufe affign'd her woe,
And for her ruin'd ftate her forrows feem'd to flow.

   Through every chamber of the martial maid,   576
By friendfhip privileg'd, Erminia ftray'd.
One day it chanc'd, intent on many a thought,
The royal fair her friend's apartment fought ;
Clorinda abfent, there her anxious mind   580
Revolv'd the means t' effect the flight defign'd.
While various doubts, by turns, the dame diftrefs'd,
Aloft fhe mark'd Clorinda's arms and veft :
Then to herfelf, with heavy fighs, fhe faid :
How bleft above her fex the warrior maid !   585
How does het ftate, alas ! my envy raife !
Yet not for female boaft, or beauty's praife.
No length of fweeping veft her ftep reftrains ;
No envious cell her dauntlefs foul detains ;
But, cloth'd in fhining fteel, at will fhe roves ;   590
Nor fear with-holds, nor confcious fhame reproves.
Why did not Heaven with equal vigour frame
My fofter limbs, and fire my heart to fame ?

   VOL. I.   O   So

So might I turn the female robe and veil
To the bright helmet and the jointed mail :   595
My love would change of heat and cold defpife,
And all the feafons of inclement fkies,
In arms alone, or with my martial train,
By day or night to range on yonder plain.
Thy will, Argantes, then thou hadft not gain'd, 600
And with my lord the combat firft maintain'd :
This hand had met, and ah ! that happy hour
Perchance had made him prifoner to my power :
So from his loving foe he fhould fuftain
A gentle fervitude and eafy chain :   605
So might my foul awhile forget to grieve,
And Tancred's bonds Erminia's bonds relieve.
Elfe had his hand this panting bofom gor'd,
And through my heart impell'd the ruthlefs fword
Thus had my deareft foe my peace reftor'd !   610
Then had thefe eyes in lafting fleep been laid,
While the dear victor o'er the fenfelefs dead,
Perchance, with pitying tears, had mourn'd my doom,
And given thefe limbs the honours of a tomb !
But ah ! I wander, loft in fond defire,   615
And fruitlefs wifhes fruitlefs thoughts infpire ;
Then fhall I ftill refide with anguifh here,
In abject ftate, the flave of female fear ?

O no !

O no!—confide, my foul, refolve and dare :
Can I not once the warrior's armour bear ?   620
Yes—Love fhall give the ftrength th' attempt re-
          quires ;
Love, that the weakeft with his force infpires ;
'That ev'n to dare impels the timorous hind—
But 'tis no martial thought that fills my mind :
I feek, beneath Clorinda's arms conceal'd,   625
To pafs the gates unqueftion'd to the field.
O love ! the fraud, thyfelf infpir'd, attend !
And fortune with propitious fmiles befriend !
'Tis now the hour for flight—(what then detains ?)
While with the king Clorinda ftill remains.   630

    Thus fix'd in her refolves, th' impatient maid,
By amorous paffion led, no longer ftay'd ;
But to her near apartment thence repairs,
And with her all the fhining armour bears.
No prying eyes were there her deeds to view ;   635
For when fhe came the menial train withdrew ;
While night, that theft and love alike befriends,
T' affift the deed her fable veil extends.

    Soon as the virgin faw the ftars arife,
That faintly glimmer'd through the dufky fkies, 640
She call'd, in fecret, her defign to aid,
A fquire of faith approv'd, and favour'd maid :

O 2

To

To thefe in part her purpofe fhe reveal'd,
But, with feign'd tales, the caufe of flight con-
    ceal'd,
The trufty fquire prepar'd, with ready care,   645
Whate'er was needful for the wandering fair.
Meantime Erminia had her robes unbound,
That, to her feet defcending, fwept the ground.
Now, in her veft, the lovely damfel fhin'd
With charms fuperior to the female kind.   650
In ftubborn fteel her tender limbs fhe drefs'd,
The maffy helm her golden ringlets prefs'd:
Next in her feeble hand fhe grafp'd the fhield,
A weight too mighty for her ftrength to wield.
Thus, clad in arms, fhe darts a radiant light   655
With all the dire magnificence of fight!
Love prefent laugh'd, as when he view'd of old
The female weeds Alcides' bulk enfold.
Heavy and flow, fhe moves along with pain;
And fcarce her feet th' unwonted load fuftain.   660
The faithful damfel by her fide attends,
And with affifting arm her ftep befriends.
But love her fpirits and her hopes renews,
And every trembling limb with ftrength indues.
Till, having reach'd the fquire, without delay   665
They mount their ready fteeds, and take their way.

S   Difguis'd

Difguis'd they pafs'd amid the gloomy night,
And fought the filent paths obfcur'd from fight ;
Yet fcatter'd foldiers here and there they fpy'd,
And faw the gleam of arms on every fide.   670
But none attempt the virgin to moleft ;
All know her armour, ev'n by night confefs'd,
The fnow-white mantle and the dreadful creft.

   Erminia, though her doubts were partly eas'd,
Yet found not all her troubled thoughts appeas'd ;
She fear'd difcovery, but her fears fupprefs'd,   676
And reach'd the gates, and thus the guard addrefs'd:
Set wide the portal, nor my fteps detain,
Commiffion'd by the king, I feek the plain.
Her martial garb deceiv'd the foldiers' eyes ;   680
Her female accents favour'd the difguife.
The guards obey'd ; and through the gate, in hafte,
The princefs, with her two attendants, pafs'd ;
Thence from the city-walls, with caution, went
Obliquely winding down the hill's defcent.   685

   Now fafe at diftance in a lonely place,
Erminia check'd awhile her courfer's pace,
Efcap'd the former perils of the night,
No guards, no ramparts now t' obftruct her flight ;
With thought mature fhe ran her purpofe o'er,   690
And weigh'd the dangers lightly weigh'd before.

O 3

More

More arduous far fhe faw th' attempt would prove
Than firft appear'd to her defiring love :
Too rafh it feem'd, amidft a warlike foe,
In fearch of peace, with hoftile arms to go :   695
For ftill fhe purpos'd to conceal her name,
Till to the prefence of her knight fhe came.
To him fhe wifh'd to ftand reveal'd alone,
A fecret lover, and a friend unknown !
Then ftopp'd the fair, and now, more heedful made,
Thus to her fquire, with better counfel, faid.   701
    'Tis thou, my friend ! who muft, with fpeed and
        care,
To yonder tents my deftin'd way prepare.
Go—let fome guide direct thy doubtful eyes,
And bring thee where the wounded Tancred lies.
To him declare, there comes a friendly maid,   706
Who peace demands, and brings him healing aid ;
Peace—(for the war of love now fills my mind)
Whence he may health, and I may comfort find.
Say, that, with him fecure from fcorn or fhame, 710
A virgin to his faith commits her fame.
In fecret this—If more the knight require,
Relate no further, but with fpeed retire.
Here will I fafely wait.—So fpoke the maid ;
Her meffenger at once the charge obey'd ;   715

                                    He

He fpurr'd his courfer, and the trenches gain'd,
And friendly entrance from the guard obtain'd.
Conducted then, the wounded chief he fought,
Who heard, with joy, the pleafing meffage brought.
  The fquire now leaves the knight to doubts re-
      fign'd,   720
(A thoufand thoughts revolving in his mind)
To bring the welcome tidings to the fair,
That fhe, conceal'd, may to the camp repair.
  Meanwhile the dame, impatient of his ftay,
Whofe eager wifhes fear the leaft delay,   725
Counts every ftep, and meafures oft in vain
The fancy'd diftance 'twixt the camp and plain :
And oft her thoughts the meffenger reprove,
Too flow for the defires of ardent love !
At length, advancing to a neighbouring height, 730
The foremoft tents falute her longing fight.
  Now was the night in ftarry luftre feen,
And not a cloud obfcur'd the blue ferene :
The rifing morn her filver beams difplay'd,
And deck'd with pearly dew the dufky glade.   735
With anxious foul, th' enamour'd virgin ftrays
From thought to thought, in love's perplexing maze ;
And vents her tender plaints, and breathes her fighs
To all the filent fields and confcious fkies.

O 4

Then,

Then, fondly gazing on the camp, she said : 740
Ye Latian tents, by me with joy survey'd !
From you, methinks, the gales more gently blow,
And seem already to relieve my woe !
So may kind Heaven afford a milder state
To this unhappy life, the sport of fate ! 745
As 'tis from you I seek t' assuage my care,
And hope alone for peace in scenes of war !
Receive me then !—and may my wishes find
That bliss, which love has promis'd to my mind ;
Which ev'n my worst of fortune could afford, 750
When made the captive of my dearest lord !
I seek not now, inspir'd with fancies vain,
By you my regal honours to regain :
Ah no !—Be this my happiness and pride,
Within your shelter humbly to reside ! 755

So spoke the hapless fair, who little knew
How near her sudden change of fortune drew ;
For, pensive while she stood, the cloudless moon
Full on th' unheedful maid with splendor shone ;
Her snow-white vesture caught the silver beam ; 760
Her polish'd arms return'd a trembling gleam ;
And on her lofty crest, the tigress rais'd,
With all the terrors of Clorinda blaz'd,

When

When lo ! (fo will'd her fate) a numerous band
Of Chriftian fcouts were ambufh'd near at hand; 765
Difpatch'd t' impede the paffage, o'er the plain,
Of fheep and oxen to the Pagan train.
Thefe Polyphernes and Alcander guide,
Two Latian brethren, who the tafk divide.

Young Polyphernes, who had feen his fire   770
Beneath Clorinda's thundering arm expire,
Soon as his eyes the dazzling veft furvey'd,
Confefs'd the femblance of the martial maid ;
He fir'd his crew ; and heedlefs of control,
Gave loofe to all the fury of his foul ;   775
Take this ! and perifh, by my weapon flain—
He faid ; and hurl'd his lance, but hurl'd in vain.

As when a hind, opprefs'd with toil and heat,
To fome clear fpring directs her weary feet ;
If, as fhe thinks to eafe her fainting limbs   780
In the cool fhade, and drink the cryftal ftreams,
The fatal hounds arrive ; fhe takes her flight,
And all her thirft is loft in wild affright.

Thus fhe, who hop'd fome kind relief to prove,
And fought t' allay the burning thirft of love, 785
Soon as the warriors, clad in fteel, appear,
Forgets her former thoughts in fudden fear :

She

She flies, nor dares th' approaching danger meet;
The plain re-echoes with her courser's feet.
With her th' attendant flies; the raging knight, 790
First of the band, pursues the virgin's flight.
Now from the tents the faithful squire repairs,
And to the dame his tardy tidings bears;
Struck with like fear, he gives his steed the rein,
And all are scatter'd diverse o'er the plain.   795
Alcander still, by cooler prudence sway'd,
Fix'd at his station, all the field survey'd:
A message to the camp he sent with speed,
That not the lowing ox, nor woolly breed,
Nor prey like these was seen; but, smit with fear,
The fierce Clorinda fled his brother's spear.   801
Nor could he think that she, no private knight,
But one who bore the chief command in fight;
At such a time would issue from the gate,
Without some public weighty cause of state: 805
But Godfrey's wisdom must th' adventure weigh,
And what he bade Alcander should obey.

Soon to the camp the flying tidings came,
But first the Latian tents receiv'd the same.
Tancred, whose soul the former message mov'd, 810
Now felt new terrors for the maid he lov'd.

To

To me (he cry'd) she came, with pious care,
Alas ! for me this danger threats the fair !
Then of his heavy arms a part he takes,
He mounts his courser, and the tent forsakes   815
With silent haste ; and, where the track he 'spies,
With furious course along the champaign flies.

THE END OF THE SIXTH BOOK.

THE

SEVENTH BOOK

OF

JERUSALEM DELIVERED.

THE ARGUMENT.

ERMINIA, flying from the Christian guard, is received by
a shepherd. Tancred, who pursued her, supposing her to
be Clorinda, falls into Armida's snare, and is made prisoner in her castle. In the mean time Argantes, on the
appointed day, enters the list to finish the combat with
Tancred. Tancred being absent, none of the warriors
have the courage to supply his place. Godfrey reproaches
their pusillanimity, and resolves himself to meet Argantes.
Raymond dissuades him. Many others then, filled with
emulation, are desirous to engage. They cast lots; and
the lot falls on Raymond. He enters the list, and, assisted
by his guardian angel, has the advantage of Argantes;
when Beelzebub incites Oradine to wound Raymond, and
thus breaks off the combat. A general battle ensues.
The Pagans are almost defeated; but the infernal powers
raising a storm, the fortune of the day is changed. Godfrey, with his army, retires to his entrenchments.

THE

SEVENTH BOOK

OF

JERUSALEM DELIVERED.

MEANWHILE the courser with Erminia
    ſtray'd
Through the thick covert of a woodland ſhade:
Her trembling hand the rein no longer guides,
And through her veins a chilling terror glides.

By

Ver. 1. *Meanwhile the courſer with Erminia ſtray'd*] In
my notes to Arioſto, Book i. I have pointed out that this
flight of Erminia is cloſely copied from the flight of Angelica, and that both the Italian poets were afterwards
followed by Spenſer in his account of Florimel. The beginning of this book exhibits one of the moſt beautiful
paſtoral ſcenes in any language. Milton was not inſen-
ſible

I

By winding paths her steed pursu'd his flight,   5
And bore at length the virgin far from sight.

  As, after long and toilsome chace in vain,
The panting dogs unwilling quit the plain,
If chance the game their eager search elude,
Conceal'd in shelter of the favouring wood :   10
So to the camp the Christian knights return,
While rage and shame in every visage burn.
Still flies the damsel, to her fears resign'd,
Nor dares to cast a transient look behind.

sible to such poetry, and, in the following verses, may
be thought to transfuse some ideas from the Italian.

> Now morn her rosy steps in th' eastern clime
> Advancing, sow'd the earth with orient pearl,
> When Adam wak'd, so custom'd, for his sleep
> Was airy light from pure digestion bred,
> And temperate vapours bland, which th' only sound
> Of leaves and fuming rills, Aurora's fan,
> Lightly dispers'd, and the shrill matin song
> Of birds on every bough ———
>
>   PARAD. LOST. B. v. ver. 1.

> Non si desto fin che garrir gli augelli
>   Non senti lieti e salutar gli albori,
>   E mormorar il fiume, e gli arboscelli,
>   E con l'onda scherzar l'aura e co i fiori ;
>   Apre i languidi occhi ———
>
>   Stanza v. ver. 29 of the Translation.

All

All night she fled, and all th' enfuing day,   15
Her tears and fighs companions of her way :
But when bright Phœbus from his golden wain
Had loos'd his fteeds, and funk beneath the main,
To facred Jordan's cryftal flood fhe came ;
There ftay'd her courfe, and refted near his ftream. 20
No nourifhment her fainting ftrength renew'd,
Her woes and tears fupply'd the place of food.
But fleep, who with oblivious hand can clofe
Unhappy mortals' eyes in foft repofe,
To eafe her grief, his gentle tribute brings,   25
And o'er the virgin fpreads his downy wings :
Yet love ftill breaks her peace with mournful themes,
And haunts her flumbers with diftracting dreams.
She fleeps, till, joyful at the day's return,
The feather'd choirs falute the break of morn ;   30
Till rifing zephyrs whifper through the bowers,
Sport with the ruffled ftream and painted flowers ;
Then opes her languid eyes, and views around
The fhepherds' cots amid the fylvan ground :
When, 'twixt the river and the wood, fhe hears 35
A found, that calls again her fighs and tears.
But foon her plaints are ftopp'd by vocal ftrains,
Mix'd with the rural pipes of village fwains :

Vol. I.   P   She

She rose, and saw, beneath the shady grove,
An aged sire that ozier baskets wove :   40
His flocks around him graz'd the meads along,
Three boys, beside him, tun'd their rustic song.

Scar'd at th' unusual gleam of armour bright,
The harmless band were seiz'd with sudden fright,
But fair Erminia soon dispels their fears ;   45
From her bright face the shining helm she rears,
And undisguis'd her golden hair appears.
Pursue your gentle tasks with dread unmov'd,
O happy race ! (she cry'd) of Heav'n belov'd !
Not to disturb your peace these arms I bear,   50
Or check your tuneful notes with sounds of war.
Then thus—O father ! 'midst these rude alarms,
When all the country burns with horrid arms,
What power can here your blissful seats insure,
And keep you from the soldiers' rage secure ?   55

To whom the swain : No dangers here, my son,
As yet my kindred or my flock have known :
And these abodes, remov'd to distance far,
I have ne'er been startled with the din of war.
Or whether Heaven, with more peculiar grace,   60
Defends the shepherds' inoffensive race :
Or, as the thunder scorns the vale below,
And spends its fury on the mountain's brow ;

So

So falls alone the rage of foreign swords
On scepter'd princes and on mighty lords.   65
No greedy soldiers here for plunder wait,
Lur'd by our poverty and abject state:
To others abject; but to me so dear,
Nor regal power, nor wealth is worth my care.
No vain ambitious thoughts my soul molest,   70
No av'rice harbours in my quiet breast.
From limpid streams my draught is well supply'd;
I fear no poison in the wholesome tide.
My little garden and my flock afford
Salubrious viands for my homely board.   75
How little, justly weigh'd, our life requires!
For simple nature owns but few desires.
Lo! there my sons (no menial slaves I keep)
The faithful guardians of their father's sheep.
Thus in the groves I pass my hours away,   80
And see the goats and stags around me play;
The fishes through the crystal waters glide,
And the plum'd race the yielding air divide.
There was a time (when early youth inspires
The mind of erring man with vain desires)   85
I scorn'd in lowly vales my flock to feed,
And from my native soil and country fled.

At Memphis once I liv'd; and, highly grac'd,
Among the monarch's houfhold train was plac'd:
And, though the gardens claim'd my cares alone, 90
To me the wicked arts of courts were known.
There long I ftay'd, and irkfome life endur'd,
Still by ambition's empty hopes allur'd:
But when, with flowery prime, thofe hopes were fled,
And all my paffions with my youth were dead, 95
Once more I wifh'd to live an humble fwain,
And figh'd for my forfaken peace again;
Then bade adieu to courts; and, free from ftrife,
Have fince in woods enjoy'd a blifsful life.

While thus he fpoke, Erminia filent hung 100
In fix'd attention on his pleafing tongue:
His fage difcourfes, on her heart imprefs'd,
Affuag'd the tempeft of her troubled breaft:
'Till, after various thoughts, the princely maid
Refolv'd to dwell beneath the lonely fhade; 105
At leaft, fo long fequefter'd to refide,
Till fortune fhould for her return provide.

Then to the hoary fwain her fpeech fhe mov'd:
O happy man! in fortune's frowns approv'd;
If Heaven unenvying view thy peaceful ftate, 110
Let pity touch thee for my haplefs fate:

Ah!

Ah ! deign to take me to your pleaſing ſeat ;
To me how grateful were this kind retreat !
Perhaps theſe lonely groves may eaſe in part
The mournful burthen of my ſwelling heart.   115
If gold or jewels can allure thy mind,
(Thoſe idols ſo ador'd by human kind !)
From me thy ſoul may all its wiſhes find.

Then, while her lovely eyes with ſorrows flow,
She half reveals the ſtory of her woe :   120
The gentle ſwain her tale with pity hears,
Sighs back her grief, and anſwers tears with tears ;
With kindly words confoles th' afflicted fair,
At once receives her with a father's care,
And' thence conducts her to his ancient wife,   125
The faithful partner of his humble life.

And now (her mail unbrac'd) the royal maid
In ruſtic weeds her graceful limbs array'd ;
But, in her courtly looks and beauteous mien,
Appear'd no tenant of the ſylvan ſcene.   130
No dreſs could veil the luſtre of her eyes,
No outward form her princely air diſguiſe :
A ſecret charm, and dignity innate
Each act exalted of her lowly ſtate.
She drives the flock to paſture on the plain.   135
And, with her crook, conducts to fold again :

P 3

From

From the rough teat she drew the milky stream,
And prest in circling vats the curdled cream.

  Oft, when beneath some shady grove's retreat
The flocks are shelter'd from meridian heat,   140
On the smooth beechen rind the pensive dame
Carves in a thousand forms her Tancred's name ;
Oft on a thousand plants inscribes her state,
Her dire distress, and love's disasterous fate :
And, while her eyes her own sad lines peruse,   145
A shower of tears her lovely face bedews.
Then thus she cries—Ye friendly trees! retain
My story'd sorrows, and declare my pain ;
Should e'er, beneath your grateful shade, reside
Some love-sick youth in true affection try'd ;   150
His heart may learn with friendly grief to glow,
Touch'd by my sad variety of woe ;
So may he love and Fortune's rigour blame,
That thus reward a virgin's constant flame.
If e'er indulgent Heaven vouchsafe to hear   155
The tender wishes of a lover's prayer :

  Ver. 137. *From the rough teat*—] The Italian commentator justly observes, that the poet has very happily expressed the simple employment of making cheeses.

      ——da l'irsute mamme il latte preme,
      E'n giro accolto poi lo stringe insieme.

                                        Ev'n

Ev'n he may haply to thefe dwellings rove,
Who heeds not now forlorn Erminia's love;
And, cafting on the ground his pitying eyes,
Where clos'd in earth this breathlefs body lies;   160
May to my fufferings yield a late return,
And with a pious tear my fortune mourn.
Thus, if my life was never doom'd to reft,
At leaft in death my fpirit fhall be bleft;
And my cold afhes fhall the blifs receive,   165
Which here relentlefs Fate refus'd to give !

   Thus to the fenfelefs trunks her pains fhe told,
While down her cheek the copious forrows roll'd.

   Tancred, meantime, the damfel's flight purfu'd,
And, guided by the track, had reach'd the wood: 170
But there the trees fo thick a gloom difplay'd,
He rov'd uncertain through the dufky fhade.
And now he liftens with attentive ear,
The noife of fteeds or found of arms to hear.
Each bird or beaft that ruftles in the brakes,   175
Each whifpering breeze his amorous hope awakes.
At length he leaves the wood; the favouring moon
Directs his wandering fteps through paths unknown.
A fudden noife at diftance feems to rife,
And thither ftrait th' impatient warrior flies.   180

And now he comes where, from a rock diftils
A plenteous ftream that falls in lucid rills;
Then down the fteep th' united waters flow,
And murmur in the verdant banks below.
Here Tancred call'd aloud: in vain he cry'd;   185
No found, fave echo, to his voice reply'd.
Meanwhile he faw the gay Aurora rife,
And rofy blufhes kindling in the fkies:
Inly he groan'd, accufing Heaven, that held
The flying damfel from his fearch conceal'd;   190
And vow'd his vengeance on the head to bend
Whofe rafhnefs fhould the much-lov'd maid offend.

At length the knight, though doubtful of the way,
Refolv'd to feek the camp without delay;
For near at hand the deftin'd morning drew,   195
That with Argantes muft his fight renew.
When, iffuing from a narrow vale, he fpy'd   ⎫
A meffenger, that feem'd on fpeed to ride,   ⎬
His crooked horn depending at his fide.   ⎭
Tancred from him demands the ready way   200
To where encamp'd the Chriftian army lay.
Then he—Thou foon from me the path may'ft know,
Difpatch'd by Bœmond to the camp I go.
Th' unwary knight the guileful words believ'd,
And follow'd, by his uncle's name deceiv'd,   205

And

And now they came to where, amidſt a flood
Obſcene with filth, a ſtately caſtle ſtood;
What time the ſun withdrew his cheerful light,
And ſought the ſable caverns of the night.
At once the courier blew a ſounding blaſt,   210
And ſudden o'er the moat the bridge was caſt.
Here, if a Latian (ſaid the wily guide) . ...
Thou may'ſt at eaſe till morning dawn reſide:
Three days are paſt ſince from the Pagan band
Coſenza's valiant earl this caſtle gain'd.   215

He ceas'd : The warrior all the fort ſurvey'd,
Impregnable by art and nature made;
Awhile he paus'd, ſuſpecting in his mind
In ſuch a place ſome ſecret fraud to find ;
But, long to dangers and to toils inur'd,   220
He ſtood undaunted, in himſelf ſecur'd;
Reſolv'd, whate'er or choice or chance procure,
His own right arm his ſafety ſhould inſure.
But now another taſk his ſword demands,
And from each new attempt reſtrains his hands. 225
Before the caſtle, cloſe beſide the flood,
In deep ſuſpenſe awhile the hero ſtood;

Ver. 207—*a ſtately caſtle ſtood*;] The following paſſage
bears a nearer reſemblance to the romances of chivalry than
any part of the poem, and is much in the ſpirit of Arioſto.

Nor

Nor o'er the ſtream the doubtful paſſage try'd,
Though oft invited by his treacherous guide.
When ſudden on the bridge a knight was ſeen   230
All ſheath'd in arms, of fierce and haughty mien;
His naked falchion, held aloft, he ſhook,
And thus in loud and threatening accents ſpoke.

  O thou! who thus haſt reach'd Armida's land,
Or led by choice, or by thy fate conſtrain'd,   235
Hope not to fly—be here thy ſword reſign'd,
And let thy hands ignoble fetters bind,
This caſtle enter, and the laws receive,
The laws our ſovereign miſtreſs deigns to give :
And ne'er expect, for length of rolling years,   240
To view the light of heaven or golden ſtars,
Unleſs thou ſwear, with her aſſociate-train,
To war on all that Jesus' faith maintain.

  He ſaid; and, while his voice betray'd the knight,
On the known armour Tancred fix'd his ſight.   245
Rambaldo this, who with Armida came,
Who, for her ſake, embrac'd the Pagan name;
And now was ſeen in arms t' aſſert her cauſe,
The bold defender of her impious laws.
With holy zeal th' indignant warrior burn'd,   250
And to the foe this anſwer ſoon return'd.

I.o!

Lo ! impious wretch ! that Tancred now appears,
Who still for CHRIST his faithful weapon wears ;
His champion ! taught by him the foes to quell,
That dare against his sacred word rebel.   255
Soon shalt thou find in me thy scourge is given,
And own this hand the minister of Heaven.

Confounded at his name th' apostate stood ;
Swift vanish'd from his cheek the frighted blood :
Yet thus, with courage feign'd, he made reply : 260
Why com'st thou, wretch ! predestin'd here to die ?
Here shall thy lifeless limbs on earth be spread,
And, sever'd from the trunk, thy worthless head
Soon to the leader of the Franks I'll send,
If fortune, as of old, my arms befriend.   265

While thus he spoke, the day its beams withdrew,
And deeper shades obscur'd the doubtful view :
When strait a thousand lamps resplendent blaze,
And all the castle shines with starry rays.
Armida plac'd aloft (herself conceal'd)   270
Heard all the contest, and the knights beheld.
Th' undaunted hero for the fight prepares,
Collects his courage and his falchion bares ;
Nor kept his steed, but leaping from his seat,
Approach'd on equal terms the foe to meet.   275
                                            The

The foe advanc'd on foot, and held before
His fencing shield ; his head the helmet wore ;
In act to strike the naked steel he bore.
To him with dauntlefs pace the prince drew nigh,
Rage in his voice, and lightening in his eye.   280
The wary Pagan wheels his steps afar,
Now feems to strike, and now to shun the war.
Tancred, though weak with many a former wound,
Though lately spent with toil, maintain'd his ground ;
And, where Rambaldo shrunk, his steps he prefs'd,
And oft the sword before his face addrefs'd   286
With threatening point ; but chiefly bent his art,
To aim the wounds at every vital part.
His dreadful voice he rais'd at every blow,
And pour'd a furious tempeft on the foe :   290
Now here, now there, the foe deceives his eyes,
With sword and shield to ward the danger tries,
And from th' impending steel elufive flies,
Yet not fo swift the Pagan can defend,
But swifter far the Christian's strokes defcend.   295
Rambaldo's arms were now with blood bedew'd,
His shield was broken, and his helmet hew'd :
While in his heart contending paffions strove,
Remorfe, and fear, and shame, revenge and love,

At

At length, impell'd by fury and defpair,   300
To prove the utmoſt fortune of the war,
His buckler caſt afide, with either hand
He grafp'd his falchion, yet with blood unftain'd;
Then, inftant clofing, urg'd the vengeful fteel:
On Tancred's thigh the furious weapon fell,   305
And through the mail infix'd a ghaftly wound; }
His helmet next the Pagan's falchion found,   }
The helmet, ftruck, return'd a ringing found. }
The cafque fuftain'd the ftroke, with temper fteel'd,
Beneath the force the ftaggering warrior reel'd ; 310
But, foon recovering, gnafh'd his teeth with ire,
While from his eye-balls flafh'd avenging fire !

    And now Rambaldo durft no longer wage
The doubtful fight with Tancred's rifing rage :
His ftartled ear the hiffing fword confefs'd ;   315
He deem'd the point already in his breaft :
He fees, he flies the blow : th' impetuous fteel
With erring force againſt a column fell
Befide the flood ; beneath the furious ftroke
The marble in a thoufand fhivers broke.   320
Swift to the bridge th' affrighted traitor flies ;
In fwiftnefs all his hope of fafety lies :
Him Tancred chac'd, and ftep by ftep impell'd ;
Now o'er his back the threatening fword he held :
                                        When

When lo ! (the trembling Pagan's flight to shield)
A sudden darkness cover'd all the field :   326
At once the lamps were vanish'd from the sight ;
At once the moon and stars withdrew their light.
No more the victor could his foe pursue,
In gloom of friendly night conceal'd from view. 330
His eyes in vain explor'd the magic shade,
While unsecure with doubtful feet he stray'd.
Unconscious where he pass'd, with luckless tread
He enter'd at a gate, as fortune led ;
But sudden heard the portal clos'd behind,   335
And found himself in prison drear confin'd.
So the mute race from troubled waves retreat,
To seek in peaceful bays a milder seat,
And heedless enter in the fatal snare,
Where fishers place their nets with guileful care. 340
   The gallant Tancred prisoner thus remain'd,
By strange enchantment in the fort detain'd,
In vain to force the gate his strength he try'd,
The stronger gate his utmost pains defy'd :
And soon a voice was heard—" Attempt no more,
" Armida's captive now, t' escape her pow'r ? 346
" Here live ; nor fear that death should prove thy
        doom,
" Here living sentenc'd to a doleful tomb !"
            3   Th'

Th' indignant knight his rifing grief fupprefs'd,
Yet groan'd full deeply from his inmoft breaft ; 350
Accufing love, from whence his errors rofe,
Himfelf, his fortune, and his treacherous foes.
Thus oft in whifpers to himfelf he mourns :
To me no more the cheerful fun returns !
Yet that were little—thefe unhappy eyes   355
Muft view no more the fun of beauty rife !
No more behold Clorinda's charms again,
Whofe power alone can eafe a lover's pain !
The deftin'd combat then his mind affail'd ;
Too much (he cry'd) my honour here has fail'd :
Well may Argantes now defpife my name ;   361
O ftain to glory ! O eternal fhame !

While thoughts like thefe diftracted Tancred's
          breaft,
Argantes fcorn'd the downy plumes of reft :
Difcord and ftrife his cruel foul employ ;   365
Fame all his wifh, and flaughter all his joy :
And ere his wounds are heal'd, he burns to view
Th' appointed day, the combat to renew.
The night before the morn for fight defign'd,
The Pagan fcarce to fleep his eyes inclin'd :   370
While yet the fkies their fable mantle fpread,
Ere yet a beam difclos'd the mountain's head,

He

He rofe, and call'd for arms; his 'fquire prepares,
And to his lord the radiant armour bears;
Not that he wont to wear; a nobler load,   375
A coftly gift, the monarch this beftow'd.
Eager he feiz'd, nor gaz'd the prefent o'er,
His limbs, with eafe, the maffy burthen bore.
He girt the trufty falchion to his fide;
Full well in many a dangerous combat try'd.   380
As fhaking terrors from his blazing hair,
A fanguine comet gleams through dufky air,
To ruin ftates, and dire difeafes fpread,
And baleful light on purple tyrants fhed:
So flam'd the chief in arms, and fparkling ire,   385
He roll'd his eyes fuffus'd with blood and fire:
His dreadful threats the firmeft hearts control'd,
And with a look he wither'd all the bold:
With horrid fhout he fhook his naked blade,
And fmote th' impaffive air and empty fhade.   390
   Soon fhall the Chriftian thief (aloud he cries)
Who dares with me in fight difpute the prize,
Vanquifh'd and bleeding, prefs th' enfanguin'd land,
And foil his flowing treffes in the fand!
Spite of his God, he living fhall furvey   395
This hand, unpitying, rend his fpoils away.

Then

Then shall his prayers in vain a grave implore,
The dogs his mangled carcafe shall devour !

  So fares a bull whom jealous fires engage,
Loudly he roars, and calls up all his rage ;   400
Againft a tree his fharpen'd horns he tries,
To battle vain the paffing wind defies,
He fpurns the yellow fands, and from afar
His mortal rival dares to deadly war.
Thefe paffions fwelling in Argantes' breaft,   405
The herald ftraight he call'd, and thus addrefs'd :
Hafte to the camp, and there the fight proclaim
With yonder champion of the Chriftian name.

  This faid, he feiz'd his fteed, nor longer ftay'd,
But from the walls the captive knight * convey'd. 410
He left the city, and impetuous went
With eager fpeed along the hill's defcent.
Impatient then his founding horn he blew,
And wide around the horrid echo flew ;
The noife, like thunder, ftruck th' aftonifh'd ears,
And every heart was fill'd with fudden fears.   416

  The Chriftian princes, now conven'd, enclofe
Their prudent chief ; to thefe the herald goes,
And Tancred firft to combat due demands,
Then dares each leader of the faithful bands.   420

* OTHO.

Now Godfrey casts around his heedful sight, ·
No champion offers equal to the fight.
The flower of all his warlike train is lost ;.
No news of Tancred yet has reach'd the host :
Bœmond afar ; and exil'd from the field   425
Th' unconquer'd * youth who proud Gernando kill'd..
Beside the ten, by lot of fortune nam'd,
The heroes of the camp, for. valour fam'd,
Pursu'd the falfe Armida's guileful flight,
Conceal'd in covert of the friendly night.   430
The rest, less firm of foul or brave of hand,
Around their chief unmov'd and filent stand ;
Not one in such a rifk would feek for fame ;.
In fear of ill was lost the fenfe of fhame.

    Well, by their filence and their looks difplay'd, 435
Their fecret fears the general foon furvey'd,
And, fill'd with noble warmth and high difdain,
He started from his feat, and thus began.

    Ah l how unworthy were this breast of life,
If now I' fhun t' attempt the glorious strife ;   440
Or let yon Pagan foe our name difgrace,
And tread in dust the glory of our race.
Here let my camp fecure, inactive, lie,
And view my danger with a diftant eye :.

                * RINALDO..

                                      Hafte,

Hafte, bring my arms !—Then, fwift as winged
      thought,   445
His ponderous armour to the chief was brought.
But Raymond (in experienc'd wifdom known,
Whofe courage with the firft in peril fhone ;
Whofe vigorous age the fire of youth confefs'd)
Turn'd to the leader, and thefe words addrefs'd. 450
  Forbid it, Heaven ! that e'er the Chriftian ftate,
Thus in their chief fhould hazard all their fate !
On thee our empire and our faith depend,
By thee muft Babel's impious kingdom bend.
'Tis thine to rule debates, the fceptre wield ;   455
Let others boldly prove the fword in field.
Ev'n I, though bending with the weight of age,
Refufe not here the danger to engage.
Let others fhun the force of yonder knight,
No thoughts fhall keep me from fo brave a fight. 460
O ! could I boaft an equal ftrength of years
With you who ftand difmay'd with heartlefs fears,
(Whom neither fhame nor indignation moves,
While yonder foe your daftard train reproves)
Such as I was, when all Germania view'd   465
Stern Leopold beneath my arms fubdu'd !
At mighty Conrade's court my weapon tore
The warrior's breaft, and drank his vital gore.
Q 2   Such

Such was the deed ! more noble far to bear
The fpoils of fuch a chief renown'd in war,   470
Than fingly here, unarm'd, in flight to chace
A numerous band of this inglorious race.
Had I the vigour now I then poffefs'd,
This arm had foon the Pagan's pride fupprefs'd.
But, as I am, this heart undaunted glows,   475
No coward fear this aged bofom knows ;
And, fhould I breathlefs prefs the hoftile plain,
No eafy conqueft fhall the foe obtain.
Behold, I arm !——this day, with added praife,
Shall crown the luftre of my former days.   480
    So fpoke the hoary chief ; his words infpir'd
Each kindling foul, and fleeping virtue fir'd.
And thofe whofe filence firft their fear confefs'd,
With voice embolden'd to the combat prefs'd.
No more a knight is fought ; a generous band, 485
By emulation urg'd, the fight demand.
That tafk Rogero, Guelpho, Baldwin fam'd,
Stephen, Gernier, and either Guido claim'd ;
Pyrrhus, whofe art the walls of Antioch won,
And gave to Bœmond's hand the conquer'd town. 490
Brave Eberard the glorious trial warms ;
Ridolphus and Rofmondo, known in arms :

And,

And, with like thirst to gain a deathless name,
The conflict Edward and Gildippe claim.
But first the venerable warrior stands,   495
And with superior zeal the fight demands.
Already arm'd he darts resplendent fires,
And now his burnish'd helm alone requires:
Him Godfrey thus bespoke—O glorious sage!
Thou lively mirror of a warlike age!   500
From thee our leaders catch the god-like flame,
Thine is the art of war and martial fame!
O! could I now in youthful prowess find
Ten champions more to match thy dauntless mind,
Soon should I conquer Babel's haughty towers, 505
And spread the Cross from Ind to Thule's shores.
But here forbear: reserve for counsel sage
The nobler glory of thy virtuous age.
And let the rest their rival names enclose
Within a vase, and chance the lots dispose,   510
Or rather God dispose, whose sovereign will,
Fortune and Fate, his ministers, fulfil.

He said; but Raymond still asserts his claim,
And fearless with the rest includes his name.
Then pious Godfrey in his helmet threw   515
The lots, and, shaking round, the first he drew,
Thouloufe's valiant earl appear'd in view.

Q 3

With

With cheerful shouts the Christians hail the name,
Nor dares a tongue the lot of Fortune blame.
The hero's looks a sudden vigour warms,   520
And a new youth his stiffen'd limbs informs.
So the fierce snake, with spoils renew'd, appears,
And to the sun his golden circles rears.
But Godfrey most extoll'd the hoary knight,
And promis'd fame and conquest in the fight ;   525
Then from his side his trusty falchion took,
To Raymond this he gave, and thus he spoke:

See here the sword which, drawn in many a field,
The rebel Saxon once was wont to wield ;
This from his hand I won in glorious strife,   530
And forc'd a passage for his hated life :
This sword, that ever did my arm befriend,
Receive, and equal fortune thine attend !

Thus they : The haughty foe impatient stay'd,
And with loud threats provok'd the strife delay'd :

Unconquer'd nations ! Europe's martial bands !
Behold a single chief the war demands !   537
Why comes not Tancred, once so fam'd in fight,
If still he dare to trust his boasted might ?

Ver. 529. *The rebel Saxon*—] The Saxons rebelled in Germany, and made Count Ridolphus their king, who was afterwards overcome and slain by Godfrey.

                                    Or,

Or, does he chuse, in downy flumber laid,   540
To wait again the night's auxiliar fhade ?
If thus he fears, let others prove their force ;
Come all, united powers of foot and horfe !
Since not your thoufands can a warrior yield
Who dares oppofe my might in fingle field.   545
Lo ! there the fepulchre of Mary's fon—
Approach, and pay your offering at the ftone.
Behold the way ! what caufe detains your band ?
Or does fome greater deed your fwords demand ?

    Thefe bitter taunts each Chriftian's rage provoke,
But chiefly Raymond kindled as he fpoke :   551
Indignant fhame his fwelling breaft infpires.
And noble wrath his dauntlefs courage fires.
He vaults on Aquiline, of matchlefs fpeed ;
The banks of Tagus bred this generous fteed :   555
There the fair mother of the warrior-brood
(Soon as the kindly fpring had fir'd her blood)
With open mouth, againft the breezes held,
Receiv'd the gales with warmth prolific fill'd :
And (ftrange to tell !) infpir'd with genial feed, 560
Her fwelling womb produc'd this wondrous fteed.
Along the fand with rapid feet he flies,
No eye his traces in the duft defcries ;

Q 4

To

To right, to left, obedient to the rein,
He winds the mazes of th' embattled plain.   565
On this the valiant earl to combat prefs'd,
And thus to Heaven his pious prayer addrefs'd :
   O thou ! that 'gainft Goliath's Impious head
The youthful arms in Terebinthus fped,
When the proud foe, who fcoff'd at Ifrael's band,
Fell by the weapon of a ftripling's hand :   571
With like example now thy caufe maintain,
And ftretch yon Pagan breathlefs on the plain :
Let feeble age fubdue the mighty's pride,
Which feeble childhood once fo well defy'd !   575
   So pray'd the earl; and ftraight his zealous prayers
Flew, wing'd with faith, to reach the heavenly fpheres,
As flames afcend. Th' Eternal Father heard,
And call'd an angel from th' ethereal guard,
Whofe watchful aid the aged chief might fhield, 580
And fafe return him from the glorious field.
Th' angelic power, to whom, decreed by Heaven,
The care of Raymond from his birth was given,
Soon as he heard anew his Lord's command,
Obey'd the charge entrufted to his hand :   585
Ile mounts the facred tower, where, rang'd on high,
The arms of all th' immortal legions lie.

                                        There

There fhines the fpear, by which the ferpent driven
Lies pierc'd with wounds ; the fiery bolts of heaven ;
The viewlefs arrows that in tainted air   590
Difeafe and plagues to frighted mortals bear.
There, hung aloft, the trident huge is feen,
The deadlieft terror to the race of men,
What time the folid earth's foundations move,
And tottering cities tremble from above.   595
But o'er the reft, on piles of armour, flam'd
A fhield immenfe, of blazing di'mond fram'd,
Whofe orb could all the realms and lands contain
That reach, from Caucafus, th' Atlantic main !
This buckler guards the righteous prince's head ;
O'er holy kingdoms this defence is fpread :   601
With this the angel from his feat defcends,
And near his Raymond, unperceiv'd, attends.
    Meantime the walls with various throngs were
        fill'd ;
And now Clorinda (fo the tyrant will'd)   605
Led from the city's gate an armed band,
And halted on the hill ; the Chriftians ftand
In rank of battle on a different hand.
Before the camp, in either army's fight,
An ample lift lay open for the fight.   610

Argantes

Argantes feeks his foe, but feeks in vain ;
A knight unknown appears upon the plain.
Then Raymond thus—The chief thy eyes would find,
Thy better fate has from our hoft disjoin'd.
Yet let not this thy empty pride excite,   615
Behold me here prepar'd to prove thy might.
For him I dare with thee the war maintain :
Nor think me meaneft of the Chriftian train.

   The Pagan fmil'd, and fcornful thus reply'd :
Say, in what part does Tancred then refide ?   620
He firft with boaftful threats all Heaven defies,
Then trembling on his coward feet relies !
But let him fly, and veil his fears in vain
Beneath the central earth, or boundlefs main :
Not earth profound, nor ocean's whelming wave, 625
Shall from my hand the recreant warrior fave !

   Falfely thou fay'ft (the Chriftian thus replies)
That he, thy better far, the combat flies.

   To whom the foe incens'd—Then fwift prepare,
I fhall not here refufe thy proffer'd war :   630
Soon fhall we prove, on this contended plain,
How well thy deeds thy fenfelefs boaft maintain.

   This faid, the champions to the combat prefs'd,
And 'gainft the helm their threatening fpears ad-
    drefs'd,

True

True to his aim, good Raymond reach'd the foe, 635
Who, in his feat unmov'd, fuſtain'd the blow.
No leſs in vain was fierce Argantes' might;
The heavenly guardian, watchful o'er the fight,
The ſtroke averted from the Chriſtian knight.
The Pagan gnaw'd his lips, with rage he ſhook, 640
And 'gainſt the plain his lance, blaſpheming, broke;
Then drew his ſword, and ſwift at Raymond flew,
On cloſer terms the combat to renew.
Againſt him full he drove his furious ſteed;
So butting rams encounter head to head :   645
But Raymond to the right eludes the ſhock;
And on his front the paſſing Pagan ſtruck.
Again the ſtern Circaſſian ſeeks the foe :
Again the Chriſtian diſappoints the blow;
And every turn obſerv'd with heedful eyes;   650
He fear'd Argantes' ſtrength and giant ſize;
By fits he ſeem'd to fight, by fits to yield,
And round the liſt in flying circles wheel'd.
As when ſome chief a tower beleaguers round,
With fens encloſ'd, or on a hilly ground;   655
A thouſand ways, a thouſand arts he proves :
Thus o'er the field the wary Chriſtian moves.
In vain he ſtrives the Pagan's ſcales to rend,
That well his ample breaſt and head defend;   659

But

But where the jointed plates an entrance show'd,
Thrice with his sword he drew the purple flood,
And stain'd the hostile arms with streaming blood.
His own, secure, the adverse weapon brav'd;
Untouch'd the plumage o'er his helmet wav'd.
At length, amidst a thousand vainly spent,   665
A well-aim'd stroke the raging Pagan sent;
Then, Aquiline! thy speed had prov'd in vain,
The fatal blow had aged Raymond slain;
But here he fail'd not heavenly aid to prove;
The guard invisible, from realms above,   670
To meet the steel th' ethereal buckler held,
Whose blazing orb the powerful stroke repell'd.
The sword broke short, nor could the force withstand;
(No earthly temper of a mortal hand
Could arms divine, infrangible, sustain)   675
The brittle weapon shiver'd on the plain.
The Pagan scarce believes; with wondering eye,
He sees on earth the glittering fragments lie:
And still he deem'd against the Christian's shield
His falchion broken strew'd the dusty field: 680
Good Raymond deem'd no less; nor knew, from heaven
      heaven
What powerful guardian to his life was given.

But

But when difarm'd the hoftile band he view'd,
Awhile fufpended in himfelf he ftood;
He fear'd fuch palms would little fame beftow, 685
With fuch advantage ravifh'd from the foe.
Go, feek a fword!—the chief begins to fay,
But different thoughts his generous purpofe ftay.
He fears alike to win the fhield with fhame;
He fears alike to rifk the general fame.   690
While doubtful thus he ftands, with rage anew
The hilt Argantes at his helmet threw;
Then fpurr'd his fteed to grapple with his foe:
The earl, unmov'd, receives the Pagan's blow,
And wounds his arm, that came with threatening
        fway,   695
Fierce as a vulture rufhing on its prey!
At every turn his fword Argantes found,
And pierc'd his limbs with many a ghaftly wound.
Whate'er his art or vigour could confpire,
His former wrath, his now redoubled ire,   700
At once againft the proud Circaffian join,
And Heaven and fortune in the caufe combine.
But ftill the foe, with dauntlefs foul fecure,
Refifts, unterrify'd, the Chriftian's power.
So feems a ftately fhip, in billows toft,   705
Her tackle torn, her mafts and canvafs loft;

With

With strong ribb'd sides the rushing storm she braves,
Nor yet despairs amidst the roaring waves.
Ev'n such, Argantes, was thy dangerous state,
When Beelzebub prepar'd to ward thy fate :   710
From hollow clouds he fram'd an empty shade,
(Wondrous to speak !) in human form array'd :
To this Clorinda's warlike looks he join'd ;
Like her the form in radiant armour shin'd :
He gave it speech and accents like the dame ;   715
The same the motion, and the mien the same.
To Oradine its course the phantom took,
And him, renown'd for archery, bespoke :
O Oradine ! whose never-failing art
To every mark directs the distant dart,   720
Think what a loss Judea must sustain,
Should thus the guardian of her walls be slain ;
Should his rich spoils the haughty foe adorn,
And he in safety to his train return.
On yonder robber let thy skill be try'd,   725
Deep in his blood be now thy arrows dy'd.
What endless praise were thine ! nor praise alone,
The king with vast rewards the deed shall crown.
   The spectre ceas'd ; nor long the warrior stay'd ;
The hopes of gain his greedy soul persuade :   730

From

From the full quiver, deftin'd for the deed,
To the tough yew he fits the feather'd reed :
He bends the bow, loud twangs the trembling ftring,
The fhaft impatient hiffes on the wing ;
Swift to the mark the airy paffage finds,   735
Juft where the belt the golden buckle binds ;
The corflet piercing, through the fkin it goes ;
But fcarce the wound with purple moifture flows ;
The guard celeftial ftops its further courfe,
And robs the arrow of its threatening force.   740
The earl the weapon from his corflet drew,
And faw the fprinkling drops of fanguine hue ;
Then on the Pagan turn'd, with fury mov'd,
And, with loud threats, his breach of faith reprov'd.

    The pious Godfrey now, whofe careful look   745
Was fix'd on Raymond, found the truce was broke :
With fears he faw his lov'd affociate bleed,
And urg'd his troops t' avenge the treacherous deed.
Then might you fee their ready beavers clos'd,
Their courfers rein'd, their fpears in reft difpos'd.
At once the fquadrons, plac'd on either hand,   751
Move in their ranks, and thicken o'er the land :
The field is vanifh'd ; clouds of duft arife,
And roll in fable volumes to the fkies.

                                        They

They meet, they fhock; the clamours echo round;
And helms and fhields and fhiver'd fpears refound.
Here lies a fteed, and there (his rider flain)
Another runs at random o'er the plain.
Here lies a warrior dead; in pangs of death,
There one, with groans, reluctant yields his breath.
Dire was the conflict; deep the tumult grows; 761
And now with all its rage the battle glows;
Argantes midft them flew with eager pace,
And from a foldier fnatch'd an iron mace;
This whirl'd around, with unrefifted fway,   765
Through the thick prefs he forc'd an ample way:
Raymond he feeks, on him his arms he turns,
On him alone his dreadful fury burns;
And, like a wolf, with favage wrath endu'd,
He thirfts infatiate for the Chriftian's blood.   770
But now, on every fide, the numbers clos'd,
And thronging warriors his attempts oppos'd:
Ormano and Rogero (names renown'd!)
Guido, with either Gerrard, there he found.
Yet more impetuous ftill his anger fwell'd,   775
The more thefe gallant chiefs his force repell'd.
So, pent in narrow fpace, more dreadful grows
The blazing fire, and round deftruction throws.

Guido

Guido he wounded,; brave Ormano flew;
And midft the flain to earth Rogero threw,   780
Stunn'd with the fall. While here the martial train
On either hand an equal fight maintain;
Thus to his brother Godfrey gave command:
Now to the fight conduct thy warlike band;
And where the battle rages in its force,   785
There to the left direct thy fpeedy courfe.
He faid; the warrior at his word obey'd,
And on their flank a fudden onfet made.
Languid and fpent the Afian troops appear,
Nor can the Franks' impetuous vigour bear: 790
Their ranks are broke, their ftandards fcatter'd
      round,
And men and fteeds lie mingled on the ground.
The fquadrons, on the right, now fled the plain;
Alone Argantes dares the fhock fuftain;
Alone he turns, alone the torrent ftands: 795
Not he who brandifh'd in his hundred hands
His fifty fwords and fifty fhields in fight,
Could have furpafs'd the fierce Argantes' might!
The mace's fweepy way, the clafhing fpears,
Th' impetuous fhock of charging fteeds he bears.
Alone he feems for all an equal force: 801
Now here, now there, by turns he fhifts his courfe:

His limbs are bruis'd, his shatter'd arms resound; ⎫
The blood and sweat in mingled streams abound, ⎬
Yet whole he seems, and fearless of a wound. 805 ⎭
But now so closely press'd the flying crew,
That in their flight th' unwilling chief they drew :
Constrain'd he turn'd, nor longer could abide
Th' o'erbearing fury of the rapid tide.
Yet seems he not to fly, his looks declare   810
His dauntless soul, and still maintain the war ;
Still in his eyes the glancing terrors glow ;
And still with threatening voice he dares the foe.
With every art he tries, but tries in vain,
To stop the panic of the routed train :   815
No art, no rein, can rule the vulgar fear ;
Nor earnest prayers, nor loud commands they hear.
    The pious Godfrey, who, with zeal inspir'd,
Saw fortune favouring all his soul desir'd,
Pursu'd with joy the battle's glorious course,   820
And to the victors sent auxiliar force.
And, but the fatal hour not yet was come,
Prefix'd by God in his eternal doom,
This day, perchance, their arms success had found,
This day had all their sacred labours crown'd. 825
But hell's dire crew, who saw the conquering host,
And in the combat fear'd their empire lost,

(By

(By Heaven permitted) fpread the changing fkies
With clouds condens'd, and gave the winds to rife.
Infernal horrors darken all the air,   830
Pale livid lightenings thro' the æther glare;
The thunder roars; the mingled hail and rain
With rattling torrents deluge all the plain:
The trees are rent; nor yield the trees alone,
The rocks and mountains to the tempeft groan. 835
The wind and rain with force united ftrove,
And on the Chriftians' face impetuous drove:
The fudden ftorm their eager courfe reprefs'd,
And fatal terrors daunted many a breaft:
While, round their banners, fome maintain'd the
        field,   840
Nor yet the fortune of the day beheld.
But this Clorinda, from afar, defcries,
And fwift to feize the wifh'd occafion flies.

   She fpurs her fteed, and thus her fquadron warmst
See! Heaven, my friends! affifts our righteous arms?
His tempeft lights not on our favour'd bands, 846
But leaves to action free our valiant hands:
Againft th' aftonifh'd foe his wrath he bends,
Full in their face his vengeful ftorm defcends:
They lofe the ufe of arms and light of day: 850
Hafte, let us go where fortune points the way.
R 2   She

She said, and rouz'd her ardent troops to war,
And while behind th' infernal storm they bear,
With dreadful fury on the Franks they turn,
And mock their vigour, and their weapons scorn :
Meanwhile Argantes on their forces flew,   856
(So lately victors) and with rage o'erthrew :
These, swift retreating from the field, oppose
Their backs against the storm and hostile blows.
Fierce on the rear the Pagan weapons pour :   860
Fierce on the rear their wrath the furies shower.
The mingled blood in streaming torrents swell'd,
And purple rivers delug'd all the field.
There, midst the dying and the vulgar slain,
Pyrrhus and good Ridolphus press'd the plain : 865
The fierce Circassian this of life depriv'd ;
From that Clorinda noble palms deriv'd.

Thus fled the Franks ; while still th' infernal crew
And Syrian bands their eager flight pursue.
Godfrey alone the hostile arms defies,   870
The roaring storm and thunder of the skies ;
With dauntless front amid the tumult moves,
And loud each leader's coward fear reproves.
Against Argantes twice he urg'd his horse,
And bravely twice repell'd the Pagan's course : 875

As

As oft on high his naked fword he rear'd
Where, thickeſt join'd, the hoſtile troops appear'd :
Till, with the reſt conſtrain'd the day to yield,
He gain'd the trenches, and forſook the field.
Back to the walls return'd the Pagan band ;   880
The weary Chriſtians in the vale remain'd ;
Nor then could ſcarce th' increaſing tempeſt bear,
And the wild rage of elemental war.
Now here, now there, the fires more faintly ſhow ;
Loud roar the winds ; the ruſhing waters flow : 885
The tents are ſhatter'd, ſtakes in pieces torn ;
And whole pavilions far to diftance borne.
The thunder, rain, and wind, and human cries,
With deafening clamours rend the vaulted ſkies !

END OF THE SEVENTH BOOK.

THE

EIGHTH BOOK

OF

JERUSALEM DELIVERED.

R 4

THE ARGUMENT.

A Dane arrives at the Chriſtian camp, and informs Godfrey that the band, conducted by Sweno, was attacked in
the night, near Paleſtine, by a numerous army of Arabs
commanded by Solyman: that the Danes were cut in
pieces, and Sweno killed; and that himſelf only eſcaped
the general ſlaughter: to this he adds, that he had received an injunction to preſent Sweno's ſword to Rinaldo.
The Chriſtian army, deceived by appearances, ſuſpect
Rinaldo to have been aſſaſſinated. Argillan, inſtigated
in a dream by Alecto, incites the Italians to revolt; and
throws the odium of Rinaldo's ſuppoſed murder upon
Godfrey. The diſaffection ſpreads through the troops.
Godfrey goes himſelf to quell the tumult; he cauſes Argillan to be arreſted, and reſtores tranquillity to the
camp.

EIGHTH BOOK

OF

JERUSALEM DELIVERED.

NOW ceas'd the thunder's noise, the storm was
     o'er,
And every blustering wind forgot to roar;
When the fair morning, from her radiant seat,
Appear'd with rosy front and golden feet:
But those, whose power the raging tempest brew'd, 5
Still with new wiles their ruthless hate pursu'd;
While one (Astagoras the fiend was nam'd)
Her partner, dire Alecto, thus inflam'd.

  Behold yon knight, Alecto! on his way,
(Nor can our arts his destin'd purpose stay)   10
Who 'scap'd with life, on yonder fatal plain,
The great * defender of th' infernal reign.
         * SOLYMAN.

                              He

He to the Franks his comrades' fate shall tell,
And how in fight their daring leader fell.
This great event among the Christians known,   15
May to the camp recall Bertoldo's son.
Thou know'st too well if this our care may claim,
And challenge every scheme our power can frame.
Then mingle with the Franks to work their woes,
And each adventure to their harms dispose: 20
Go—shed thy venom in their veins, inflame
The Larian, British, and Helvætian name;
Be every means, be every fraud apply'd,
And all the camp in civil broils divide.
This task were worthy thee, would crown thy word,
So nobly plighted to our sovereign lord.   26

   She spoke; nor needed more her speech employ;
The fiend embrac'd th' attempt with horrid joy.

   Meantime the knight, whose presence thus they
     fear'd,
Arriving, in the Christian camp appear'd: 30
Conducted, soon the leader's tent he sought;
(All thronging round to hear the news he brought)
Lowly he bow'd, and kiss'd the glorious hand
That shook the lofty towers of Babel's land.

   O chief! (he cry'd) whose wide-extended fame   35
Alone the ocean bounds and starry frame;

9

Would

Would Heaven I here with happier tidings ftood!—
This faid, he figh'd, and thus his fpeech purfu'd.
  Sweno, the Danifh monarch's only fon,
(Pride of his age, and glory of his throne)   40
Impatient burn'd his name with theirs to join,
Who, led by thee, in Jesus' caufe combine;
Nor toils nor dangers could his thought reftrain,
Nor all th' allurements of his future reign;
Not filial duty to his aged fire   45
Could in his bofom quench the glorious fire.
By thy example, and beneath thy care,
He long'd to learn the labours of the war;
Already had he heard Rinaldo's name,
In bloom of youth, refound with deeds of fame: 50
But, far above an earthly frail renown,
His foul afpir'd to heaven's eternal crown.
Refolv'd to meet in arms the Pagan foes,
. The prince a faithful daring fquadron chofe;
Direct for Thrace, with thefe, his way purfu'd, 55
Till now the Greeks' imperial feat he view'd.
The Grecian king the gallant youth carefs'd,
And in his court detain'd the royal gueft.
There from the camp thy trufty envoy came,
Who told the triumphs of the Chriftian name: 60
                        How

How firſt you conquer'd Antioch's ſtately town,
Then 'gainſt the foe maintain'd the conqueſt won,
When Perſia brought her numerous ſons from far,
And ſeem'd t' exhauſt her ſpacious realms for war.
On thine, on every leader's deeds he dwells,   65
And laſt the praiſe of brave Rinaldo tells:
How the bold youth forſook his native land;
What early glory ſince his arms had gain'd.
To this he adds, that now the Chriſtian powers
Had laid the ſiege to Sion's lofty towers;   70
And urg'd the prince with thee at leaſt to ſhare
The laſt great conqueſt of the ſacred war.
Theſe ſpeeches gave new force to Sweno's zeal;
He thirſts in Pagan blood to drench his ſteel.
Each warrior's trophy ſeems his ſloth to blame,   75
Each valiant deed upbraids his tardy fame,
One thought alone his dauntleſs ſoul alarms;
He fears to join too late the victors' arms.
Impell'd by fate, he ſcarcely deigns to ſtay
'Till the firſt bluſh of dawn renew'd the day.   80
We march'd, intrepid, o'er a length of land
Beſet with various foes on every hand:
Now rugged ways we prove; now famine bear;
To ambuſh now expos'd, or open war:

But

But every labour, fearless, we fuſtain ;   85
Our foes were vanquiſh'd, or in battle ſlain.

　Succeſs in danger every doubt ſuppreſs'd,
Preſumptuous hope each ſwelling heart poſſeſs'd.
At length we pitch'd our tents one fatal day,
As near the bounds of Paleſtine we lay ;   90
Our ſcouts were there ſurpriz'd with loud alarms
Of barbarous clamours and the din of arms :
And countleſs banners they deſcry'd from far,
The ſtreaming ſignals of approaching war.

　Our matchleſs chief unmov'd the tidings heard ; 95
Firm was his voice, unchang'd his looks appear'd ;
Though the dire peril ſtartled many a breaſt,
And many a changing cheek its fears confeſs'd.
Then thus he cry'd : Prepare for ſure renown,
The victor's laurel, or the martyr's crown !   100
The firſt I hope, nor leſs the laſt I prize,
Whence greater merits, equal glories riſe !
This field, O friends ! ſhall future honours claim,
A temple ſacred to immortal fame ;
Where diſtant ages ſhall our trophies tell,   105
Or ſhow the ſpot on which we greatly fell !

　Thus ſaid the chief, and ſtrait the guard prepares,
Divides the taſks, and every labour ſhares.

　3   He

He wills the troops in arms to pass the night,
Nor from his breast removes his corslet bright, 110
But sheath'd in mail expects the threaten'd fight.

When now the silent night her veil extends,
The peaceful hour that balmy sleep befriends;
The sky with dreadful howling echoes round,
And every cave returns the barbarous sound.   115
To arms, to arms! (each startled soldier cries)
Before the rest impetuous Sweno flies.
He darts his eyes that glow with martial flame;
His looks the ardor of his soul proclaim.
And soon th' invading troops our camp enclose: 120
'Thick and more thick the steely circle grows;
Javelins and swords around us form a wood,
And o'er our heads descends an iron cloud.

In this unequal field the war we wag'd,
Where every Christian twenty foes engag'd;   125
Of these were many wounded midst the gloom:
By random shafts full many met their doom.
But none, amidst the dusky shades, could tell
The wounded warriors, or what numbers fell.
Night o'er our loss her sable mantle threw,   130
And, with our loss, conceal'd our deeds from view.
Yet fierce in arms, and towering o'er the rest,
The gallant Sweno stood to all confess'd;

Ev'n

Ev'n through the dusk they mark his daring course,
And count the actions of his matchless force.   135
His thirsty sword the purple slaughter spread,
And round him rais'd a bulwark of the dead :
Where'er he turns he scatters, through the band,
Fear from his looks and slaughter from his hand.

  Thus stood the fight : but when th' ethereal ray 140
With ruddy streaks proclaim'd the dawning day,
The morn reveal'd the fatal scenes of night,
And death's dire horrors open'd to our sight.
We saw a field with mangled bodies strown,
And in one combat all our force o'erthrown !   145
A thousand first compos'd our martial band,
And scarce an hundred now alive remain'd !
But when the chief beheld the dreadful plain,
The mangled troops, the dying and the slain,
'Twas doubtful how his soul sustain'd his part, 150
Or what emotions touch'd his mighty heart ;
Yet thus aloud he fir'd his fainting crew :
Haste, let us now our slaughter'd friends pursue,
Who, far from Styx and black Avernus' flood,
Have mark'd our happy paths to heaven in blood.

  He said ; and, fix'd his glorious fate to close, 156
Undaunted rush'd amidst the thickest foes :

He

He rives the helmet, and he hews the shield;
The strongest arms before his falchion yield:
With streams of hostile gore he dies the ground, 160
While all his form is one continu'd wound.
His life decays, his courage still remains;
Th' unconquer'd soul its noble pride retains:
With equal force his martial ardor burns;
He wounds for blows, and death for wounds returns.
When thundering near a dreadful warrior came, 166
Of stern demeanour and gigantic frame;
Who, join'd by many, on the hèro flew,
And, after long and painful battle, flew.
Prone fell the generous youth, (ah ! haplefs death !)
Nor one had power t' avenge his parting breath. 171
Be witnefs yet, and bear me juft record,
Ye laft dear relicks of my much-lov'd lord !
I fought not then to fave my worthlefs life,
Nor fhunn'd a weapon in the dreadful ftrife.　　175
Had Heaven vouchfaf'd to end my mortal ftate,
I fure by actions well deferv'd my fate !
Alive I fell, and fenfelefs prefs'd the plain,
Alone preferv'd amidft my comrades flain ;
Nor can I further of the Pagans tell,　　　　180
So deep a trance o'er all my fenfes fell.

But

But when again I rais'd my feeble fight,
The fkies were cover'd o'er with fhades of night,
And from afar I faw a glimmering light:
I faw like one who half in flumber lies,   185
And opes and fhuts by fits his languid eyes.
But now my limbs a deeper anguifh found,
The pains increas'd in every gaping wound,
While on the earth I lay, expos'd and bare
To damps unwholefome and nocturnal air.   190
Meanwhile advancing nearer drew the light,
By flow degrees, and gain'd upon my fight.
Low whifpers then and human founds I heard;
Again, with pain, my feeble eyes I rear'd ;
And faw two fhapes in facred robes array'd ;   195
Each in his hand a lighted torch difplay'd,
And thus an awful voice diftinctly faid :
O fon ! confide in him whofe mercy fpares,
Whofe pitying grace prevents our pious prayers.
Then, with uplifted hands, my wounds he blefs'd,
And many a holy vow to Heaven addrefs'd.   201
He bade me rife—and fudden from the ground
I rofe ; my limbs their former vigour found;
Fled were my pains, and clos'd was every wound !
Stupid I ftood, all fpeechlefs and amaz'd,   205
And doubtful on the reverend ftranger gaz'd.

O thou of little faith! (the hermit cry'd)
What thought has led thy troubled sense aside?
Thou see'st two bodies of terrestrial frame,
Two servants dedicate to Jesus' name.   210
From the vain world and all its follies fled,
In wilds and deserts here our lives are led.
Lo! I am sent thy safety to enfure,
By him who rules o'er all with sovereign power;
Who ne'er disdains by humble means to show   215
His wondrous works of providence below;
Nor here will suffer on the naked plains
To lie expos'd those honour'd lov'd remains,
'That must again th' exalted mind receive,
And, join'd above, in bliss eternal live.   220
To Sweno's corse he wills a tomb to raise,
A tomb as lasting as his deathless praise;
Which future times with wonder shall survey,
Where future times shall every honour pay.
But lift thy eyes, yon friendly moon behold   225
Through fleecy clouds her silver face unfold,
To guide thy devious footsteps o'er the plain,
To find the body of thy leader slain.

   Then from the peaceful region of the night
I saw defcend a ray of slanting light: 230

Where

Where on the field the breathlefs corfe was laid,
There full the lunar beam refplendent play'd ;
And fhow'd each limb deform'd with many a wound,
Midft all the mingled fcene of carnage round.
He lay not prone, but, as his zealous mind   235
Still foar'd beyond the views of human kind,
In death he fought above the world to rife,
And claim'd, with upward looks, his kindred fkies.
One hand was clos'd, and feem'd the fword to rear ;
One prefs'd his bofom with a fuppliant air,   240
As if to Heaven he breath'd his humble prayer.

    While o'er his wounds the copious tears I fhed,
And, loft in fruitlefs grief, deplor'd the dead,
His lifelefs hand the holy hermit feiz'd,
And from his grafp the fatal fteel releas'd ;   245
To me then turning : View this fword, (he faid)
Whofe edge to-day fuch copious ftreams has fhed,
Still dy'd in gore ; thou know'ft its virtue well,
No temper'd weapon can its force excel !
But fince its lord, in glorious conflict flain,   250
No more fhall grafp the mortal fword again,
It muft not here be loft ; decreed by Heaven,
To noble hands the mighty prize is given ;
To hands that longer fhall the weapon wield
With equal valour in a happier field :   255

S 2

From

From thofe the world expects the vengeance due
On him whofe fury gallant Sweno flew.
By Solyman has Sweno prefs'd the plain ;
By Sweno's fword muft Solyman be flain.
Go then, with this, and feek the tented ground 260
Where Chriftian powers the hallow'd walls furround ;
Nor fear, left wandering o'er a foreign land,
The foe again thy purpos'd courfe withftand.
That Power, who fends thee, fhall thy toils furvey,
His hand fhall guide thee on the dangerous way : 265
He wills that thou (from every peril freed)
Should'ft tell the virtues of the hero dead :
So, fir'd by him, may others learn to dare,
And on their arms the Crofs triumphant bear :
That every breaft may pant for righteous fame,   270
And diftant ages catch the glorious flame !
It now remains the champion's name to hear,
Whofe arm muft next the fatal weapon rear :
Rinaldo he, a youth approv'd in fight,
In valour firft of every Chriftian knight ;   275
Prefent him this ; inflame his generous ire ;
Say, heaven and earth (let this his foul infpire)
From him alone the great revenge require !

  While thus intent the fage's words I heard,
Where Sweno lay a fepulchre appear'd,   280

That,

That, rifing flow, by miracle difpos'd,
Within its marble womb the corfe enclos'd :
Grav'd on the monumental ftone were read
The name and merits of the warrior dead.
Struck with the fight, I ftood, with looks amaz'd, 285
And on the words and tomb alternate gaz'd.

   Then thus the fage : Befide his followers flain
Thy leader's corfe fhall here infhrin'd remain ;
While, in the manfions of the bleft above,
Their happy fouls enjoy celeftial love.   290
But thou enough haft mourn'd the noble dead,
To nature now her dues of reft be paid ;
With me refide, till, in the eaftern fkies,
Propitious to thy courfe, the morn arife.

   He ceas'd ; and led me thence through rugged
     ways,   295
Now high, now low, in many a winding maze ;
Till underneath the mountain's pendant fhade,
Befide a hollow cave, our fteps we ftay'd.
Here dwelt the fage, amidft the favage brood
Of wolves and bears (the terrors of the wood !) 300
Here, with his pupil, liv'd fecure from harms :   ⎫
More ftrong than fhield or corflet, virtue arms   ⎬
And guards the naked breaft in all alarms.   ⎭

S 3

My

My hunger firſt ſuffic'd with ſylvan food,
A homely couch my ſtrength with ſleep renew'd. 305
But when, rekindled with the riſing day,
The radiant morn reveal'd her golden ray;
Each wakeful hermit to his prayers aroſe,
And, rouz'd with them, I left my ſoft repoſe:
Then to the holy ſage I bade adieu,   310
And turn'd the courſe directed to purſue.

Here ceas'd the Dane. Then thus the pious chief:
Thou com'ſt a mournful meſſenger of grief:
Thy words, O knight! with pain our camp ſhall
        know,
Thy tale ſhall ſadden every breaſt with woe.   315
Such gallant friends, by hoſtile fury croſt,
From all our hopes, alas ! ſo ſudden loſt !
Where thy dear leader, like a flaſhing light,
But juſt appear'd, and vaniſh'd from the ſight;

Ver. 312. *Here ceas'd the Dane.*] This admirable and
affecting epiſode is founded on hiſtorical fact, though en-
larged and beautified by the poet with many poetical and
intereſting circumſtances. Paolo Emilio, the writer of
the hiſtory, gives the following account of this Sweno :
" Lætas triſtibus (ut res humanæ ſunt) miſcebantur :
Sueno Dani regis filius cum mille quingentis equitibus
cruce inſignitis, tranſmiſſo ad Conſtantinopolim Boſphoro
inter Antiochiam ad reliquos Latinos iter faciebat; Inſidiis
Turcorum ad unum omnes cum regio juvene cæſi."

Yet

Yet bleft a death like this, and nobler far   320
Than conquer'd towns and ample fpoils of war :
Nor can the capitol examples yield
Of wreaths fo glorious, or fo brave a field.
In heaven's high temple now, with honours crown'd,
Immortal laurels every brow furround ;   325
Each hero there with confcious tranfport glows,
And every happy wound exulting fhows.
But thou, efcap'd from peril, ftill to know
The toil and warfare of the world below ;
This gloom of forrow from thy brow remove,   330
And learn to triumph in their blifs above.
Seek'ft thou Bertoldo's fon ? in exile loft,
Unknown he wanders from th' abandon'd hoft :
Nor think to trace his flight with doubtful feet,
Till certain tidings tell the youth's retreat.   335

   Thefe fpeeches heard, and young Rinaldo's name,
With former love each kindling mind enflame.
" Alas ! (they cry) amid the Pagan bands
" The blooming warrior roves in diftant lands !"
Each tongue with pleafure on his glory dwells; 340
Each to the wondering Dane his valour tells,
And all his battles, all his deeds reveals.

   While thoughts, like thefe, in every bofom raife
The dear remembrance of their hero's praife ;

S 4

A band

A band of foldiers, fent to fcour the plain,   345
With plenteous pillage feek the camp again ;
With lowing oxen, and the woolly breed,
And generous corn to cheer the hungry fteed :
And, join'd with thefe, a mournful load they bore,
The good Rinaldo's arms, the veft he wore,   350
The armour pierc'd, the vefture ftain'd with gore.
The doubtful chance the vulgar herd alarms,
With grief they throng to view the warrior's arms.
They fee and know too well the dazzling fight,
The ponderous cuirafs, with its beamy light;   355
The creft, where high the towering eagle fhone,
That proves his offspring in the mid-day fun.
Oft were they wont, amid th' embattled fray,
To fee them foremoft rule the bloody day ;
And now with mingled grief and rage beheld   360
Thofe glorious trophies broken on the field.

   While whifpers fill the camp, and every breath
Relates by various means the hero's death,
The pious Godfrey bade the chief be fought
Who led the fquadron that the pillage brought. 365
Brave Aliprando was the leader nam'd,
For truth of fpeech and noble franknefs fam'd.
Declare (cry'd Godfrey) whence thefe arms ye bear,
Nor hide a fecret from your general's ear.

As

As far remov'd from hence (he thus reply'd) 370
As in two days a trufty fcout may ride,
Near Gaza's walls a little plain is found,
From public ways with hills encompafs'd round,
A riv'let murmurs down the mountain's fides,
And through the fhade with gentle current glides;
Thick wood and brambles form a horrid fhade; 376
(A place by nature well for ambufh made)
Here, while we fought for flocks and herds that came
To crop the mead befide the cryftal ftream,
Surpriz'd we faw the grafs diftain'd with blood, 380
And on the banks a murder'd warrior view'd:
The arms and veft we knew (oft feen before)
Though now deform'd with duft, and foul with gore.
Then near I drew, the features to furvey,
But found the fword had lopt the head away; 385
The right hand fever'd; and the body round
From back to breaft was pierc'd with many a wound.
Not far from thence the empty helm was laid,
Where the white eagle ftood with wings difplay'd.
While fome we fought from whom the truth to
    hear,   390
We faw a village fwain approaching near;
Who, having fpy'd us, fled with fudden fear.

Him

Him following soon we seize; he trembling stands,
And gives a full reply to our demands.
That he, the former day, conceal'd, had view'd 395
A band of warriors issue from the wood,
Whose mien and arms the Christians' likeness show'd.
One by the golden locks sustain'd a head,
That newly sever'd seem'd, and freshly bled:
The face appear'd a youth's of semblance fair, 400
The cheeks unconscious of a manly hair.
Soon o'er the head his scarf the soldier flung,
And at the saddle-bow the trophy hung.
This heard, I stripp'd the corse with pitying tears,
My anxious mind perplex'd with secret fears, 405
And hither brought these arms, and orders gave
To yield the limbs the honours of a grave:
But if this trunk is what my thoughts declare,
It claims far other pomp, far other care.

Here Aliprando ceas'd: the leader heard 410
His tale with sighs; he doubted and he fear'd;
By certain signs he wish'd the corse to know,
And learn the hand that gave the murderous blow.

Meantime the night, with sable pinions spread,
O'er fields of air her brooding darkness shed; 415
And sleep, the soul's relief, the balm of woes,
Lull'd every mortal sense in sweet repose.

Thou,

Thou, Argillan! alone, with cares oppreſt,
Revolv'ſt dire fancies in thy troubled breaſt!
No quiet power can cloſe thy wakeful eyes,⠀⠀⠀420
But from thy couch the downy ſlumber flies.
This man was bold, of licence unconfin'd,
Haughty of ſpeech, and turbulent of mind:
Born on the banks of Trent, his early years
Were nurs'd in troubles and domeſtic jars:⠀⠀⠀425
Till exil'd thence, he fill'd the hills and ſtrand
With blood, and ravag'd all the neighbouring land;
When now to war on Aſia's plains he came,
And there in battle gain'd a nobler fame.
At length, when morning's dawn began to peep,⠀430
He clos'd his eyes, but not in peaceful ſleep;
Alecto o'er him ſheds her venom'd breath,
And chains his ſenſes like the hand of death:
In horrid ſhapes ſhe chills him with affright,
And brings dire viſions to his ſtartled ſight:⠀⠀⠀435
A headleſs trunk before him ſeem'd to ſtand,
All pierc'd with wounds, and lopt the better hand:
Alecto's hand the ſever'd viſage bore,
The features grim in death, and ſoil'd with gore;
The lips yet ſeem'd to breathe, and breathing ſpoke,
Whence, mix'd with ſobs, theſe dreadful accents
⠀⠀⠀⠀broke.⠀⠀⠀⠀⠀⠀⠀⠀⠀⠀⠀⠀⠀⠀⠀⠀⠀⠀⠀441

⠀⠀⠀⠀⠀⠀⠀⠀⠀⠀⠀⠀⠀⠀⠀⠀⠀⠀⠀⠀⠀⠀⠀⠀⠀Fly,

Fly, Argillan ! behold the morning nigh—
Fly thefe dire tents, the impious leader fly !
Who fhall my friends from Godfrey's rage defend,
And all the frauds that wrought my haplefs end ? 445
Ev'n now thy tyrant burns with canker'd hate,
And plans, alas ! like mine, thy threaten'd fate :
Yet if thy foul afpires to fame fo high,
And dares fo firmly on its ftrength rely,
Then fly not hence ; but let thy reeking blade   450
Glut with his ftreaming blood my mournful fhade :
Lo ! I will prefent rife your force to arm,
To ftring each nerve, and every bofom warm.

    The vifion faid ; with hellifh rage infpir'd,
His furious breaft a fudden madnefs fir'd :   455
He ftarts from fleep ; he gazes wild with fear ;
With wrath and venom fill'd his eyes appear ;
Already arm'd, with eager hafte he flew,
And round him foon th' Italian warriors drew :
High o'er the brave Rinaldo's arms he ftood,   460
And with thefe words inflam'd the liftening crowd.

    Shall then a favage race, whofe barbarous mind
No reafon governs and no laws can bind,
Shall thefe, infatiate ftill of wealth and blood,
Lay on our willing necks the fervile load ?   465

Such

Such are the fufferings and th' infulting fcorn,
Which feven long years our paffive train has borne,
That diftant Rome may blufh to hear our fhame,
And future times reproach th' Italian name :
Why fhould I here of generous Tancred tell,   470
When by his gallant arms Cilicia fell ;
How the bafe Frank by treafon feiz'd the land,
And fraud ufurp'd the prize which valour gain'd ?
Nor need I tell, when dangerous deeds require
The boldeft hands and claim the warrior's fire, 475
Firft in the field the flames and fword we bear,
And midft a thoufand deaths provoke the war :
The battle o'er, when bloody tumults ceafe,
And fpoils and laurels crown the foldiers' peace ;
In vain our merits equal fhare may claim ;   480
Their's are the lands, the triumphs, wealth, and fame.
Thefe infults once might well our thoughts engage,
Thefe fufferings juftly might demand our rage :
But now I name thofe lighter wrongs no more,
This laft dire act furpaffes all before.   485
In vain divine and human laws withftand,
Behold Rinaldo murder'd by their hand !
But Heaven's dread thunders feal not yet their doom,
Nor earth receives them in her opening womb !

Rinaldo

Rinaldo have they slain, the soldiers' boast,   490
Guard of our faith and buckler of our host !
And lies he unreveng'd ?—to changing skies
All pale, neglected, unreveng'd he lies !
Ask ye who'e barbarous sword the deed has wrought ?
The deed must open lie to every thought.   495
All know, that, jealous of our growing fame,
Godfrey and Baldwin hate the Latian name.
But wherefore this ?—Be Heaven my witness here,
(That heaven who hears with wrath the perjur'd swear)
What time this morn her early beams display'd, 500
I saw confess'd his wretched wandering shade.
Ah me ! too plain his warning voice reveal'd
The snares for us in Godfrey's breast conceal'd.
I saw—'twas not a dream—before my eyes,
Where'er I turn, the phantom seems to rise !   505
What course for us remains ? Shall he, whose hand
Is stain'd with murder, rule our noble band ?
Or shall we hence conduct our social train
Where, distant far, Euphrates laves the plain ?
Where, midst a harmless race, in fields of peace, 510
He glads such numerous towns with large increase.
There may we dwell, and happier fate betide,
Nor shall the Franks with us those realms divide.

Then

Then let us leave, if such the general mind,
These honour'd relicks unreveng'd behind!— 515
But ah! if virtue still may claim a part,
(That frozen seems in every Latian heart)
This hateful pest, whose poisonous rage devours
The grace and glory of th' Italian powers,
Cut off from life, should pay the forfeit due, 520
A great example to the tyrant crew!
Then thus I swear, be now your force display'd,
Let each that hears me lend his glorious aid,
This arm to-day shall drive th' avenging sword
In that fell breast with every treason stor'd! 525
    In words like these his fiery soul express'd,
With dread commotion fill'd each hearer's breast.
To arms, to arms! (th' insensate warrior cry'd)
To arms, to arms! each furious youth reply'd.
Alecto 'round the torch of discord whirl'd, 530
And o'er the field her flames infernal hurl'd;
Disdain and madness rag'd without control,
And thirst of slaughter fill'd each vengeful soul.
The growing mischief flew from place to place,
And soon was spread beyond th' Italian race: 535
Among th' Helvætians then it rais'd a flame,
And next diffus'd among the English name.

Nor

Nor public forrow for Rinaldo flain
Alone to frenzy fir'd the warrior-train;
But former quarrels, now reviv'd, confpire,   540
And add new fuel to their prefent fire.
Againft the Franks they vent their threats aloud;
No more can reafon rule the madding crowd.
So in a brazen vafe the boiling ftream
Impetuous foams and bubbles to the brim;   545
Till, fwelling o'er the brinks, the frothy tide
Now pours with fury down the veffel's fide.
Nor can thofe few, who ftill their fenfe retain,
The folly of the vulgar herd reftrain:
Camillus, Tancred, William, thence remov'd,   550
And every other in command approv'd.
Confus'd and wild th' unthinking foldiers fwarm;
Through all the camp they run, they hafte to arm.
Already warlike clangors echo round;
Seditious trumpets give the warning found.   555
And now a thoufand tongues the tidings bear,
And bid the pious chief for arms prepare.
Then Baldwin firft in fhining fteel appear'd,
And ftood by Godfrey's fide, a faithful guard!
The chief, accus'd, to Heaven directs his eyes,   560
And on his God, with wonted faith relies:

2

O Thou,

O Thou, who know'ft my foul with zealous care
Shuns the dire horrors of a civil war ;
From thefe the veil that dims their fight remove ;
Reprefs their errors, and their rage reprove :   565
To thee reveal'd my innocence is known,
O let it now before the world be fhown !

He ceas'd ; and felt his foul new firmnefs prove,
With warmth unufual kindled from above :
A fudden confidence infpir'd his mind,   570
While on his vifage hope embolden'd fhin'd.
Then, with his friends, he went, in awful ftate,
'Gainft thofe who fought t' avenge Rinaldo's fate.
Not loudeft clafh of arms his courfe delay'd,
Nor impious threats his fteps intrepid ftay'd.   575
His back the cuirafs arm'd, a coftly veft
The hero wore, in pomp unufual dreft ;
Bare were his hands, his face reveal'd to fight,
His form majeftic beam'd celeftial light.
The golden fceptre (enfign of command)   580
He fhook, to ftill the loud rebellious band :
Such were his arms : while thus the chief appear'd,
Sounds more than mortal from his lips were heard.

What ftrange tumultuous clamours fill my ears ?
Who dares difturb the peaceful camp with fears ?   585

Thus am I grac'd? Is thus your leader known,
After such various toils and labours shown?
Is there who now with treason blots my name?
Or shall suspicion sully Godfrey's fame?
Ye hope, perchance, to see me humbly bend, 590
And with base prayers your servile doom attend:
Shall then that earth, which witness'd my renown,
Behold such insults on my glory thrown?
This sceptre be my guard, fair truth my shield,
And all my deeds in council and in field!   595
But justice shall her ear to mercy lend,
Nor on th' offender's head the stroke descend.
Lo! for your merits I your crime forgive,
And bid you for your lov'd Rinaldo live.
Let Argillan alone the victim fall,   600
And with his blood atone th' offence of all.
Who, urg'd by light suspicion, rais'd th' alarms,
And fir'd your erring bands to rebel arms.

  While thus he spoke, his looks with glory beam'd,
And from his eye the flashing lightening stream'd;
Ev'n Argillan himself, surpris'd and quell'd, 606
With awe the terrors of his face beheld.
The vulgar throng, so late by madness led,
Who pour'd their threats and curses on his head;

Who

Who grafp'd, as rage fupply'd, with ready hand 610
The fword, the javelin, or the flaming brand;
Soon as they heard his voice with fear were ftruck,
Nor longer durft fuftain their fovereign's look;
But tamely, while their arms begirt him round,
Saw Argillan in fudden fetters bound.   615

   So when his fhaggy mane a lion fhakes,
And with loud roar his flumbering fury wakes;
If chance he views the man, whofe foothing art
Firft tam'd the fiercenefs of his lofty heart,
His pride confents th' ignoble yoke to wear;   620
He fears the well-known voice and rule fevere:
Vain are his claws, his dreadful teeth are vain,
He yields fubmiffive to his keeper's chain.

   'Tis faid, that, darting from the fkies, was feen,
With louring afpect and terrific mien,   625
A winged warrior with his guardian fhield,
Which full before the pious chief he held;
While, gleaming lightening, in his dreadful hand
He fhook a fword with gory crimfon ftain'd:
Perchance the blood of towns and kingdoms, given
By frequent crimes to feel the wrath of Heaven. 631

   The tumult thus appeas'd, and peace reftor'd,
Each warrior fheaths again the wrathful fword.

T 2

Now,

Now, various ſchemes revolving in his thought,
His tent again the careful Godfrey ſought ;   635
Reſolv'd by ſtorm the city walls t' aſſail,
Ere the third evening ſpreads her ſable veil ;
And thence he went the timbers hewn to view,
Where towering high to huge machines they grew.

END OF THE EIGHTH BOOK.

THE ARGUMENT.

SOLYMAN, incited by Alecto, attacks, with his Arabs, the
Christian camp by night, and makes a great slaughter; till
Godfrey, encouraging his troops, opposes the sudden in-
cursion. In the mean time Argantes and Clorinda march
with their forces from the city, and join the Arabs. GOD
sends the angel Michael to drive away the demons that af-
sisted the Pagans. The battle is continued with great fury.
Clorinda particularly distinguishes herself. Argillan, at
day-break, escaping from his prison, rushes amongst the
enemy and kills many, till he himself falls by the hand of
Solyman: the fortune of the day still remains doubtful:
at length the Christians, receiving an unexpected aid, the
victory declares in their favour: the Pagans are defeated,
and Solyman himself is obliged to retreat.

BUT hell's dire fiend, who faw the tumults ceafe,
   And every vengeful bofom calm'd to peace,
Still unreftrain'd, by Stygian rancour driven,
Oppos'd the laws of fate and will of Heaven:
She flies, and where fhe takes her loathfome flight, 5
The fields are parch'd, the fun withdraws his light.
For new attempts fhe plies her rapid wings,
And other plagues and other furies brings!
She knew her comrades, with induftrious care,
Had driven the braveft champions from the war; 10
That Tancred and Bertoldo's greater fon,
Remov'd afar, no more in battle fhone.
Then wherefore this delay? (the fury cries)
Let Solyman th' unguarded foes furprife;

T 4

Fierce

Fierce on their camp with dread incurfion pour,   15
And crufh their forces in the midnight hour.
   This faid, fhe flew where Solyman commands
The roving numbers of Arabia's bands ;
That Solyman, than whom none fiercer rofe
Among the race of Heaven's rebellious foes :   20
Nor could a greater rife, though teeming earth,
Again provok'd, had given her giants birth.
O'er Turkey's kingdom late the monarch reign'd,
And then at Nice th' imperial feat maintain'd.
Oppos'd to Greece, the nations own'd his fway,   25
That 'twixt Meander's flood and Sangar lay ,
Where Myfians once, and Phrygians held their place,
With Lydia, Pontus, and Bithynia's race.
But, 'gainft the Turks and every faithlefs crew,
Since foreign ftates their arms to Afia drew,   30
His lands were wafted, and he twice beheld
His numerous army routed in the field ;
'Till, every chance of war effay'd in vain,
Expell'd a wanderer from his native reign,
To Egypt's court he fled ; nor fail'd to meet   35
A royal welcome, and fecure retreat.
With joy the king his valiant gueft furvey'd ;
With greater joy receiv'd his proffer'd aid :

Refolv'd

Refolv'd in thought to guard the Syrian lands,
And ftop the progrefs of the Chriftian bands.   40
    But ere the king would open war declare,
He gives to Solyman th' important care,
With fums of gold to raife th' Arabian bands,
And teach them to obey a chief's commands.
Thus while from Afia and the Moorifh reign,   45
Th' Egyptian monarch calls his numerous train,
To Solyman the greedy Arabs throng,
The lawlefs fons of violence and wrong.
Elected now their chief, Judæa's plains
He fcours around, and various plunder gains: 50
The country wide he waftes, and blocks the way
Between the Latian army and the fea:
And, not forgetful of his antient hate
And the vaft ruins of his falling ftate,
He mighty vengeance in his breaft revolves,   55
And greater fchemes, as yet unform'd, refolves.
    To him Alecto comes, but firft fhe wears
A warrior's femblance bent with weight of years;
All wrinkled feem'd her face; her chin was bare;
Her upper lip difplay'd a tuft of hair;   60
Thick linen folds her hoary head enclofe;
Beneath her knees a length of vefture flows;
      6   The

The fabre at her fide ; and, ftooping low,
Her back the quiver bears, her hand the bow.
Then thus fhe.fpoke : While here our wandering
     bands   65
Rove o'er the defert plains and barren fands ;
Where.nothing worthy can reward our toils,
Where conqueft yields us but ignoble fpoils ;
See ! Godfrey on th' imperial city falls,
He fhakes the towers, he faps the lofty walls !   70
And yet we linger (O eternal fhame !)
Till there he brings his arms and vengeful flame.
Are cots deftroy'd, or fheep and oxen gain'd,
The boafted trophies of the fuldan's hand ?
Will this thy realm reftore, retrieve thy name,   75
And on the Franks avenge thy injur'd fame ?
Then rouze thy foul ! againft the Chriftian go,
Now funk in fleep, and crufh the hated foe :
Thy old Arafpes fpeaks, his counfel hear,
In peace or exile faithful to thy ear.   80
No fear the unfufpecting chief alarms,
He fcorns the Arabs and their feeble arms ;
Nor deems their timorous bands fo far can dare, .
In flight and plunder bred, to mix in war :
Hafte, with thy courage rouze thy kindling hoft,   85
And triumph o'er their camp, in flumber loft !
                               Thus

Thus said the fiend ; and, breathing in his mind
Her venom'd rage, dissolves to empty wind.
The warrior lifts his hands, and loud exclaims :
O thou ! whose fury thus my heart inflames !   90
Whose hidden power a human form bely'd ;
Behold I follow thee, my potent guide :
A mound shall rise, where now appears a plain,
A dreadful mound of Christian heroes slain :
The field shall float with blood : O grant thy aid, 95
And lead my squadron through the dusky shade.

He said, and instant bids the troops appear ;
The weak he heartens, and dispels their fear :
His warlike transports every breast excite,
Eager they burn, and hope the promis'd fight. 100
Alecto sounds the trump ; her hand unbinds
The mighty standard to the sportive winds :
Swift march the bands like rapid floods of flame,
And leave behind the tardy wings of fame.

The fury then resumes her airy flight,   105
And seems a hasty messenger to fight ;
And when the world a dubious light invades,
Between the setting day and rising shades,
She seeks Jerusalem, and, midst a ring
Of timid citizens, accosts the king ;   110

Displays

Difplays the purpofe of th' Arabian power,
The fignal for th' attack, and fatal hour.
  Now had the night her fable curtain fpread,
And o'er the earth unwholefome vapours fhed;
The ground no cool refrefhing moifture knew, 115
But horrid drops of warm and fanguine dew:
Monfters and prodigies in heaven were feen;
Dire fpeƈtres, fhrieking, fkim'd along the green:
A deeper gloom exulting Pluto made,
With added terrors from th'infernal fhade.   120
    Through this dread darknefs tow'rds the tented
        foes,
Secure from fear, the fiery foldan goes:
And, when the night had gain'd her middle throne,
From whence with rapid fpeed fhe courfes down;
He came, where near the Chriftian army lay,   125
Forgetful of the cares and toils of day.
Here firft the chief refrefh'd his troops with food,
Then thus inflam'd their cruel thirft of blood.
  Survey yon camp, an impious band of thieves,
That more from fortune than defert receives;   130
That, like a fea, within its ample breaft
Abforbs the fhining riches of the eaft:
The fates for you thefe glorious fpoils ordain:
(How fmall the peril, and how vaft the gain!)
Your

Your unconteſted plunder there behold;   135
Their glittering arms, and courſers deck'd with gold!
Not this the force that could the Perſians quell,
By whom the powers of Nice in battle fell:
What numbers from their native country far,
Have fall'n the victims of a tedious war !   140
Were now their ſtrength the ſame they once could
          boaſt,
Thus ſunk in ſleep, an unreſiſting hoſt,
With eaſe they muſt reſign their forfeit breath,
For ſhort the path that leads from ſleep to death !
On then, my friends ! this falchion firſt ſhall gain 145
Your entrance to the camp o'er piles of ſlain.
From mine each ſword ſhall learn to aim the blow;
From mine the ſtern demands of vengeance know !
This happy day the reign of CHRIST ſhall end,
And liberty o'er Aſia's climes extend !   150

     He ſaid, and rouz'd their ſouls to martial deeds;
Then ſlow and ſilent on his march proceeds.
     Now through the miſty ſhades a gleam of light
Diſplays the heedful centry to his ſight:
By this his hopes are loſt to ſeize ſecure   155
The cautious leader of the Chriſtian power.
Soon as the watch their numerous foes eſpy,
They take their flight, and raiſe a fearful cry:

The

The neareſt guards awake; they catch th' alarms,
And, rouzing at the tumult, ſnatch their arms. 160
  Th' Arabian troops no longer ſilent paſs,
But barbarous clangors pour through breathing
     braſs:
To heaven's high arch the mingled noiſe proceeds
Of ſhouting ſoldiers and of neighing ſteeds:
The ſteepy hills, the hollow vales around, 165
The winding caverns echo to the ſound.
Alecto ſhakes on high th' infernal brand,
And gives the ſignal from her lofty ſtand.
  Firſt flies the ſoldan, and attacks the guard,
As yet confus'd, and ill for fight prepar'd. 170
Rapid he moves; far leſs impetuous raves
A tempeſt burſting from the mountain caves:
A foaming flood, that trees and cots o'erturns;
The lightening's flaſh, that towers and cities burns;
Earthquakes, that fill with horror every age; 175
Are but a faint reſemblance of his rage:
True to his aim the fatal ſword deſcends;
A wound the ſtroke, and death the wound attends.
Dauntleſs he bears the ſtorm of hoſtile blows,
And mocks the falchions of the ruſhing foes: 180
His helm reſounded as the weapons fell,
And fire flaſh'd dreadful from the batter'd ſteel.
                    Now

Now had his arm compell'd, with fingle might,
The foremoft fquadrons of the Franks to flight:
When, like a flood with numerous rivers fwell'd, 185
The nimble Arabs pour along the field:
The Franks no longer can th'attack fuftain,
But backward turn, and fly with loofen'd rein.
Purfuers and purfu'd, with equal hafte,
Together mingled, o'er the trenches pafs'd: 190
Then with unbounded wrath the victor ftorm'd,
And rage and woe and death the camp deform'd.

A dragon on his cafque the foldan wore,
That, ftretching, bends his arching neck before;
High on his feet he ftands with fpreading wings, 195
And wreaths his forky tail in fpiry rings:
Three brandifh'd tongues the fculptur'd monfter
    fhows;
He feems to kindle as the combat glows:
His gaping jaws appear to hifs with ire,
And vomit mingled fmoke and ruddy fire!   200
Th'affrighted Chriftians through the gloomy light
The foldan view'd: fo mariners by night,
When ocean's face a driving tempeft fweeps,
By flafhing flames behold the troubled deeps.
Some, by their fears impell'd, for fafety fly;   205
And fome, intrepid, on their fwords rely:

3   The

The night's black fhade adds tumult to the prefs,
And, by concealing, makes their woes increafe.
   Amongft the chiefs, whofe hearts undaunted
     glow'd,
Latinus, born by Tiber's yellow flood,   210
Confpicuous o'er the reft in combat fhin'd ;
Nor length of years had damp'd his vigorous mind ı
Five fons he told ı and equal by his fide
They mov'd, in war his ornament and pride :
To deeds of early fame their youth he warms,   215
And fheaths their tender limbs in ponderous arms.
Thefe, while they ftrive to emulate their fire,
And glut with blood their fteel and vengeful ire,
The chief befpeaks : Now prove your valiant hands
Where yon proud foe infults our fhrinking bands ;
Nor let the bloody famples of his force   221
Abate your ardour, or detain your courfe :
For, O my fons ı the noble mind difdains
All praife but that which glorious danger gains ı
   So leads the favage lionefs her young,   225
Ere yet their necks with fhaggy manes are hung ;
When fcarce their paws the fharpen'd nails difclofe,
Nor teeth have arm'd their mouths in dreadful rows ı
She brings them fearlefs to the dangerous chace,
And points their fury on the hunters' race ;   230
                     That

That oft were wont to pierce their native wood,
And oft in flight the weaker prey purfu'd.
  Now with the daring band the father goes ;
Thefe fix affail, and Solyman enclofe.
At once, directed by one heart and mind,   235
Six mighty fpears againft the chief combin'd :
But, ah ! too bold ! (his javelin caft afide)
The eldeft born a clofer conflict try'd ;
And with his falchion vainly aim'd a blow
To flay the bounding courfer of the foe.   240
But as a rock, whofe foot the ocean laves,
Exalts its ftately front above the waves,
Firm in itfelf, the winds and feas defies,
Nor fears the threats and thunder of the fkies :
The fiery foldan thus unmov'd appears   245
Amidft the threatening fwords and miffive fpears.
Furious he turns on him who ftruck the fteed,
And 'twixt the cheeks and eyebrows parts his head.
Swift Aramantes haftes to his relief,
And in his pious arms fupports the chief :   250
Vain, unavailing piety is fhown,
That to his brother's ruin adds his own !
Full on his arm the Pagan drove the fteel ;
Down the fupported and fupporter fell ;

Together fainting in the pangs of death, 255
They mix their ftreaming bloxd and parting breath.
Then with a ftroke he cuts Sabinus' fpear,
With which the youth had gall'd him from afar;
And rufhing on the fteed with fudden force,
Th' ill-fated ftripling fell beneath his horfe. 260
Now trampled on the ground the warrior lies,
The mournful fpirit from its manfion flies;
Unwilling leaves the light of life behind,
And blooming youth with early pleafures join'd!

But Picus and Laurentes ftill remain'd; 265
(The fole furvivors of the filial band)
One day firft gave this haplefs pair to light,
Whofe likenefs oft deceiv'd their parents' fight:
But thefe no more with doubt the friends furvey'd;
A dire diftinction hoftile fury made: 270
From this, the head divided rolls in duft;
That, in his panting breaft receives the thruft.

The wretched father (father now no more!
His fons all flaughter'd in one deathful hour!)
View'd, in his offspring breathlefs on the place, 275
His fate approaching, and his ruin'd race!
What power, O mufe! fuch ftrength in age could give,
That midft thefe woes he ftill endures to live,

Still

Still lives and fights ? Perchance the friendly night
Conceal'd the horrors from a father's fight.   280
Wild thro' the ranks his raging course he breaks,
With equal ardor death and conqueſt ſeeks :
Scarce knows he which his wiſhes would attain,
To ſlaughter others, or himſelf be ſlain.

Then, ruſhing on the foe, aloud he cries :   285
Doſt thou ſo far this feeble hand deſpiſe,
Not all its force can urge thy cruel rage
To cope with waſting grief and wretched age ?

He ceas'd ; and, ceaſing, aim'd a dreadful ſtroke ;
Through ſteel and jointed mail the falchion broke :
The weapon pierc'd th' unwary Pagan's ſide,   291
And ſtreaming blood his ſhining armour dy'd.
Rouz'd at the call and wound, at once he turns
With brandiſh'd ſteel, more fell his fury burns :
Firſt through his ſhield he drives, which, ſeven times
        roll'd,   295
A tough bull-hide ſecur'd with winding fold,
A paſſage next the corſlet's plates afford,
Then, in his bowels plung'd, he ſheaths the ſword.
Unbleſt Latinus ſobs, and, ſtaggering round,   ⎫
Alternate from his mouth and gaping wound 300 ⎬
A purple vomit flows, and ſtains the ground.   ⎭

U 2

As

As falls a mountain oak, that, ages paft,
Has borne the weftern wind and northern blaft,
When, rooted from the place where once it ftood,
It crufhes in its fall the neighbouring wood :   305
So funk the chief, and more than one he drew
To grace his fate, and ev'n in dying flew :
Glorious he fell, and in his lateft breath
With dreadful ruin fcatter'd fear and death.

While thus his inward hate the foldan fed,   310
And glutted his revenge with hills of dead ;
The Arabs pour impetuous o'er the field :
The fainting Chriftians to their fury yield.
Then Englifh Henry, Holiphernes, flain
By thee, O fierce Dragutes ! prefs'd the plain.   315
Gilbert with Philip Ariadenus flew,
Who on the banks of Rhine their being drew.
Beneath Albazar's mace Ernefto fell,
And Engerlan by Algazelles' fteel.
But who the various kinds of death can name,   320
And multitudes that funk unknown to fame ?

Meantime the tumults Godfrey's flumber broke ;
Alarm'd he ftarted, and his couch forfook :
Now, clad in arms, he call'd a band with fpeed,
And forth he mov'd intrepid at their head.   325
But

But nearer foon th' increafing clamours drew,
And all the tumult open'd to the view.
He knew the Arabs fcour'd the country far,
Yet never deem'd their infolence would dare
To ftorm his trenches with offenfive war.   330

   Thus while he marches, from the adverfe fide,
To arms ! to arms ! a thoufand voices cry'd :
At once a barbarous fhout was rais'd on high,
And dreadful howlings echo'd to the fky.
Thefe were the troops of Aladine, who came   335
Led by Argantes and the * warrior-dame.
To noble Guelpho, who his ftation took
The next in arms, the Chriftian leader fpoke.

   Hark ! what new din of battle, labouring on,
Swells from the hills and thickens from the town ;
This claims thy courage, this thy fkill demands, 341
To meet the onfet of th' approaching bands.
Go then, yon quarter from their rage fecure ;
But firft divide with me my martial power ;
Myfelf will on a different hand engage   345
The daring foe, and check their impious rage.

   This having faid ; the chiefs divide their force,
And take, with equal cares, a vary'd courfe ;
Guelpho to reach the hill ; while Godfrey drew
To where, refiftlefs, rag'd th' Arabian crew :   350

       * CLORINDA.

U 3

While

While as he march'd the diftant fight to gain,
Supplies were added to his eager train;
Till now a powerful numerous band he led,
And faw where Solyman the flaughter fpread.
So where the Po firft leaves his native hills,   355
His river fcarce the fcanty channel fills;
But as new ftreams he gathers in his courfe,
He fwells his waves, and rifes in his force;
Above the banks his horned front he fhows,
And o'er the level meads triumphant flows;   360
Through many currents makes his rapid way,
And carries war, not tribute, to the fea.

  Where Godfrey fees his timorous band's retreat,
He thus upbraids them with a generous heat.

  What fear is this, and whither bends your pace?
Oh! turn and view the foes that give you chace! 366
A bafe degenerate throng, that neither know
To give, nor take, in fight a manly blow:
O turn again! your trufty weapons rear;
Your looks will freeze their coward fouls with fear.

  This faid; he fpurr'd his fteed, and eager flew 371
Where murderous Solyman appear'd in view.
Through ftreaming blood and clouds of duft he
      goes,
Through wounds and death amidft furrounding foes:
                                        Through

Through breaking ranks his furious courfe he guides,
And the clofe Phalanx with his fword divides : 376
No foes, on either hand, the fhock fuftain ;
Arms, fteeds, and warriors tumble to the plain :
High o'er the flaughter'd heaps, with bounding courfe,
The glorious leader drives his foaming horfe.   380
Th' intrepid foldan fees the ftorm from far,
Nor turns afide, nor fhuns the proffer'd war ;
But, eager for the ftrife, his foe defies,
Whirls his broad fword and to the combat flies.
In thefe what matchlefs warriors fortune fends   385
To prove their force from earth's remoteft ends ?
With virtue fury now the conflict tries
In little fpace, the Afian world the prize !
What tongue the horrors of the fight can tell,
How gleam'd their falchions and how fwift they fell !
I pafs the dreadful deeds their arms difplay'd,   391
Which envious night conceal'd in gloomy fhade ;
Deeds that might claim the fun and cheerful fkies
And all the world to view with wondering eyes !
Their courage foon the Chriftian bands renew, 395
And their brave leader's daring courfe purfue :
Their choiceft warriors Solyman enclofe,
And round him thick the fteely circle grows.

U 4

Not

Not lefs the Faithful, than the Pagan band,
With ftreaming blood diftain the thirfty land ;   400
By turns the victors and the vanquifh'd mourn,
And wound for wound, and death for death return.
As when, with equal force, and equal rage,
The north and fouth in mighty ftrife engage ;
Nor this, nor that, can rule the feas or fkies,   405
But clouds on clouds and waves on waves arife :
So far'd the battle in the doubtful field ;
Nor here nor there the firm battalions yield ;
With horrid clangor fwords to fwords oppos'd,
Shields clafh'd with fhields, with helmets helmets
    clos'd.   410
   No lefs in other parts the battle rag'd,
Nor lefs the throng of warring chiefs engag'd ;
High o'er the hofts the Stygian fiends repair,
And hell's black myriads fill the fields of air.
Thefe vigour to the Pagan troops fupply ;   415
None harbour fear, or turn their fteps to fly :
The torch of hell Argantes' foul infpires,
And adds new fury to his native fires !
He fcatters foon in flight the guards around,
And leaps the trenches with an eager bound ;   420
With mangled limbs he ftrows the fanguine plain,
And fills th' oppofing foffe with heaps of flain:
                        Him

Him o'er the level fpace his troops purfue,
And dye the foremoft tents with purple hue.
Clofe at his fide appears the martial dame,   425
Whofe foul difdains the fecond place in fame.
Now fled the Franks; when fudden drew at hand
The noble Guelpho with his welcome band:
He ftopp'd, with generous zeal, their fearful courfe,
And turn'd them back to face the Pagan force. 430
   While thus on either fide the combat ftood,
And ftreaming gore in equal rivers flow'd,
The Heavenly Monarch from his awful height
Declin'd his eyes and view'd the dreadful fight.
There, plac'd aloft, prefides th' Omnifcient CAUSE,
And orders all with juft and equal laws,   436
Above the confines of this earthly fcene,
By ways unfearchable to mortal men.
There, on eternity's unbounded throne,
With triple light he blazes, Three in One!   440
Beneath his footftep Fate and Nature ftand;
And Time and Motion wait his dread command.
There power and riches no diftinction find;
Nor the frail honours that allure mankind:
Like duft and fmoke they fleet before his eyes; 445
He mocks the valiant, and confounds the wife!

There

There from the blaze of his effulgent light
The pureſt ſaints withdraw their dazzled ſight,
Around th' unnumber'd bleſt for ever live,
And, though unequal, equal bliſs receive :   450
The tuneful choirs repeat their Maker's praiſe :
The heavenly realms reſound the ſacred lays.

　　Then thus to Michael ſpoke the WORD DIVINE ;
(Michael whoſe arms with lucid di'mond ſhine)
See'ſt thou not yonder from th' infernal coaſt   455
What impious bands diſtreſs my favour'd hoſt ?
Go——bid them ſwift forſake the deathful ſcene,
And leave the buſineſs of the war to men ;
Nor longer dare amongſt the living riſe,
To blot the luſtre of the purer ſkies ;   460
But ſeek the ſhades of Acheron beneath,
Th' allotted realms of puniſhment and death !
There on the ſouls accurs'd employ their hate ;
Thus have I will'd ; and what I will is fate.

　　Ver. 455. *See'ſt thou not yonder* —] Very ſimilar to this,
is the addreſs of God to Raphael on ſeeing Satan's entrance
into Paradiſe.

　　Raphael (ſaid he) thou hear'ſt what ſtir on earth
　　Satan from hell, 'ſcap'd through the darkſome gulph,
　　Hath rais'd in Paradiſe——
　　　　　　　　　　　　　PARAD. LOST, B. v. ver. 224.

He

He ceas'd: With reverence at the high command
Low bow'd the leader of the winged band: 466
His golden pinions he difplays, and fpeeds
With rapid flight, that mortal thought exceeds.
The fiery region paft; the feats of reft
He leaves (eternal manfions of the bleft!)   470
From thence he paffes through the cryftal fphere
That whirls around with every fhining ftar;
Thence to the left, before his piercing eyes,
With different afpects, Jove and Saturn rife;
And every ftar that mortals wandering call,   475
Though God's high power alike directs them all.
Then from the fields that flame with endlefs day,
To where the ftorms are bred, he bends his way;
Where elements in mix'd confufion jar,
And order fprings from univerfal war.   480
The bright archangel gilds the face of night,
His heavenly features dart refplendent light:
So fhines the beamy fun through fhowery fkies,
And paints the fleecy clouds with various dies:
So through the liquid regions of the air,   485
With rapid radiance, fhoots a falling ftar.
But now arriv'd, where hell's infernal crew
Their venom'd rage amongft the Pagans threw,

Hovering

Hovering in air on pinions strong he stay'd,
And shook his lance, and awful thus he said.   490
   Your force has prov'd the Sovereign of the World,
What thunders from his dreadful hand are hurl'd:
O blind in ill! that no remorse can know,
In torture proud, and obstinate in woe!
The sacred Cross shall conquer Sion's wall;   495
Her gates must open, and her bulwarks fall:
And who shall Fate's resistless will withstand,
Or dare the terrors of th' Almighty hand?
Hence then, ye curfed! to your realms beneath,
The realms of torment and eternal death!   500
There on devoted souls employ your rage,
Be there your triumphs, there the wars ye wage:
There, midst the founding whips, the din of chains,
And gnashing teeth, laments and endless pains!
   He said; and those that lingering seem'd to move
Resistless with his fatal lance he drove.   506
With sighs, reluctant, from the field they fly,
And leave the golden stars and upper sky,
And spread their pinions to the realms of woe,
To wreak their fury on the damn'd below.   510
Not o'er the seas in equal numbers fly
The feather'd race, to seek a warmer sky:

Not,

Not, when the wood the wintry blaft receives,
In equal number Autumn ftrows her leaves.
Freed from th' infernal train and Stygian glooms,
Serene the night her wonted face refumes.   516
    But not the lefs Argantes' fury glows,
Though hell no more her venom'd fire beftows :
He whirls his fword with unrefifted rage,
Where, clofely preft, the Chriftian bands engage :
The high and low his equal prowefs feel ;   521
The braveft warriors fink beneath his fteel.
Alike the carnage fierce Clorinda fpread,
And ftrow'd the field with heaps of mangled dead.
Through Berlinger the fatal fword fhe guides,   525
And rives his heart where panting life refides ;
The pointed fteel its furious paffage tore,
And iffu'd at his back befmear'd with gore.
Albine fhe wounds, where firft the child receives
His food ; and Gallus' head afunder cleaves,   530
Then Gernier's better hand, that aim'd a blow,
She fends divided to the plain below ;

Ver. 515. *Freed from th' infernal train —*] So Milton,
when the rebellious fpirits are driven out of heaven.

    Difburthen'd heaven rejoic'd ——
            PARAD. LOST, B. vi. ver. 878.

                                        Yet

Yet still the parted nerves some life retain,
The trembling fingers still the falchion strain:
Dissever'd thus a serpent's tail is seen   535
To seek the part divided on the green.
The foe thus maim'd, the dame no longer stay'd,
But 'gainst Achilles ran with trenchant blade:
Between the neck and nape the weapon flew;
The neck it cleft, and cut the nerves in two: 540
First tumbled on the plain the parted head,
With dust obscene the pallid face was spread,
While in the saddle by the steed sustain'd,
(Dreadful to view !) the headless trunk remain'd;
But soon th' ungovern'd courser with a bound   545
Shook the sad burthen to th' ensanguin'd ground.
    While thus th' unconquer'd maid such numbers
        flew,
And the thick squadrons of the west o'erthrew;
No less Gildippe fair the slaughter led,
And on the Saracens her fury fed.   550
The same her sex, her dauntless mind the same,
And equal valour shone in either dame.
But these to meet in battle fate withstands;
Both doom'd to prove the force of greater hands.
Now this, now that essays to pierce the tide,   555
In vain ; the throng of troops the pass deny'd.
                                            The

The noble Guelpho's fword Clorinda found,
And in her tender fide imprefs'd a wound,
That ting'd the fteel : the maid on vengeance bent,
Betwixt his ribs her cruel anfwer fent.   560
Guelpho his ftroke renew'd, but mifs'd the foe,
Ofmida, as he pafs'd, receiv'd the blow :
Deep in his front the deadly fteel he found,
And perifh'd by another's deftin'd wound.
The numerous troops by Guelpho led enclofe   565
Their valiant chief; more thick the tumult grows;
While various bands from diftant parts unite,
And fwell the fury of the mingled fight.
    Aurora now, in radiant purple dreft,
Shone from the portals of the golden eaft :   570
When, midft the horrid clang and mingled cries,
Intrepid Argillan from prifon flies :
The readieft arms he fnatch'd with eager hafte,
And foon his limbs in fhining fteel were cas'd :
Eager he comes, t' efface his former fhame   575
With glorious actions in the field of fame.
As when, to battle bred, the courfer, freed
From plenteous ftalls, regains the wonted mead,
There unreftrain'd amid the herds he roves,
Bathes in the ftream, and wantons in the groves;

His

A fudden darkneſs ſhades his ſwimming eyes; 605
Through every vein a chilling tremor flies:
Headlong he falls, and breathes his lateſt breath,
And bites the hated ſoil in pangs of death.
With fury next on Saladine he flew,
And Agricaltes and Mulaſſes ſlew: 610
Then Aldiazelles' ſide his falchion found;
And cleft him through with one continu'd wound:
Through Ariadenus' breaſt the ſteel he guides,
And the fall'n chief with bitter taunts derides;
The dying warrior lifts his languid eyes, 615
And to th' inſulting victor thus replies.

Not thou, whoe'er thou art, with vaunting breath
Shalt long enjoy the triumph of my death:
Like fate attends thee; by a mightier hand
Thou too muſt fall, and preſs with me the ſand. 620
    Then Argillan, ſeverely ſmiling, cry'd:
Let Heaven's high will my future fate decide;
Die thou! to ravenous dogs and fowls a prey—
Then with his foot he preſs'd him as he lay,
And rent at once the ſteel and life away. 625
    Meanwhile a ſtripling of the ſoldan's train
Mix'd in the ſhock of arms and fighting men:
In his fair cheeks the flower of youth was ſeen,
Nor yet the down had fledg'd his tender chin:

The fweat that trickled on his blooming face,   630
Like orient pearls, improv'd the blufhing grace :
The duft gave beauty to his flowing hair,
And wrath was pleafing in a form fo fair.
He rode a courfer white as new-fall'n fnow
On hoary Apennine's afpiring brow :   635
Nor winds nor flames his fwiftnefs could exceed,
Practis'd to turn, and matchlefs in his fpeed :
Grafp'd in the midft, the youth a javelin bore ;
A crooked fabre at his fide he wore :
With barbarous pomp (refplendent to behold !) 640
He fhone in purple veftments wrought with gold.

  While thus the boy (whom martial fires inflame,
Pleas'd with the din of arms, and new to fame)
Now here, now there, o'erthrew the warring band,
And met with none his fury to withftand ;   645
Fierce Argillan, advancing, near him drew,
Then with a fudden ftroke his fteed he flew,
And on the tender foe impetuous flew.
In vain with moving prayers he fues for grace,
In vain he begs with fupplicating face ;   650
The fword is rais'd againft the blooming boy,
The faireft work of nature to deftroy :
Yet pity feem'd to touch the fenfelefs fteel ;
The edge turn'd, harmlefs, as the weapon fell :

9

But

But what avail'd it ? when the cruel foe,   655
With the sharp point, retriev'd his erring blow.

   Fierce Solyman, who, thence not diftant far,
By Godfrey prefs'd, maintain'd a doubtful war ;
Soon as his favourite's dangerous ftate he fpies,
Forfakes the fight, and to his refcue flies :   660
Now with his thundering fword the ways are freed :
He comes t' avenge, but not prevent the deed.
He fees, alas ! his dear Lefbinus flain,
Like a young flower that withers on the plain.
His dying eyes a trembling luftre fhed ;   665
On his fair neck declin'd his drooping head ;
His languid face in mortal palenefs charm'd,
And every breaft to foft compaffion warm'd :
Untouch'd before, now melts the marble heart,
And, midft his wrath, the gufhing forrows ftart. 670
And weep'ft thou, Solyman ! at pity's call,
Who, tearlefs, faw thy mighty kingdom's fall ?
But when his eyes the hoftile weapon view'd,
Still warm and reeking in the ftripling's blood,
Th' indignant fury boiling in his breaft,   675
Awhile his pity and his tears fupprefs'd :
On Argillan the rapid fteel he drives,
At once th' oppofing fhield and helmet rives,

X 2

And

And cleaves his head beneath the weighty blow:
A wound well worthy of so great a foe !   680
His wrath still unappeas'd, he quits his steed,
And wreaks his vengeance on the warrior dead.
So with the stone, that gall'd him from afar,
The mastiff wages unavailing war.
O ! vain attempt his sorrows to allay,   685
By rage infensate on the breathless clay !

Meantime the leader of the Christian train,
Nor spends his anger, nor his blows in vain.
A thousand Turks against him held the field,
Arm'd with the jointed mail, the helm, and shield:
Their limbs robust to hardy toils were bred ;   691
And, skill'd in fight, their souls no danger dread.
These oft with Solyman in battle stood,
And midst the deserts late his steps pursu'd ;
In Araby partook his wandering state,   695
The faithful partners of his adverse fate :
These, close collected in one daring band,
The pressing valour of the Franks withstand.

Here noble Godfrey well his falchion ply'd,
And pierc'd Corcutes' brow, Rosteno's side ;   700
Then from the shoulders sever'd Selim's head,
And lopp'd Rosano's arms with trenchant blade.

Nor

Nor thefe alone, but numbers more he kill'd,
And mangled trunks and limbs beftrow'd the field.

   While thus he fought againft the Turkifh band,
And with intrepid force their rage fuftain'd ;   706
While fortune ftill with equal pinions flew,
Nor hopes of conqueft left the Pagan crew ;
Behold a cloud of rifing duft appear,
Teeming with threatening arms, and big with war ;
And hence a fudden flafh of armour bright   711
Fill'd all the Pagan hoft with panic fright.
Of purple hue there fifty warriors held
A Crofs triumphant in an argent field.
Had I an hundred mouths, a hundred tongues,   715
A voice of iron breath'd from iron lungs,
I could not all the Pagan numbers tell
That by this troop's impetuous onfet fell :
The fearful Arab finks ; the Turk in vain
Refifts the ftorm, and fights but to be flain.   720
Around the field in various forms appear,
Rage, horror, cruelty, and abject fear :
On every fide, exulting, death is found,
And purple torrents deluge all the ground.

   Now with a fquadron, iffuing from the gate, 725
(Unconfcious of the Pagan's woeful ftate)

X 3

King

King Aladine appear'd, and from his height
Beheld the subject plain and doubtful fight:
Full soon his eyes the scene of slaughter meet,
And strait he gives command to sound retreat : 730
And oft the monarch calls, but calls in vain,
Clorinda and Argantes from the plain :
The furious couple still reject his prayer,
With carnage drunk, infatiable of war !
At length they yield : yet every means they try'd 735
Their troops in order from the field to guide.
But who with laws can coward souls reftrain ?
The rout is general 'mongft th' affrighted train :
This cafts afide his fhield, and that his fword ;
Thefe ufelefs burthens no defence afford.   740
A vale between the camp and city lies,
Stretch'd from the weftern to the fouthern fkies ;
There fled the timorous bands, with many a groan,
And clouds of duft roll'd onward to the town.
The Chriftian powers purfue their eager chace, 745
With dreadful flaughter of the Pagan race :
But when, afcending, near the walls they drew,
Where, with his aid, the king appear'd in view,
His victor-force the cautious Guelpho ftay'd,
Nor would the dangerous rocky height invade : 750

While

While Aladine collects his men with care,
The scatter'd remnants of successless war.

  The soldan's waining strength can now no more,
(The utmost stretch essay'd of human power)
His breath in shorter pantings comes and goes, 755
And blood with sweat from every member flows.
His arm grows weak beneath the weighty shield;
His weary hand can scarce the falchion wield:
Feebly he strikes, and scarce can reach the foe,
While the blunt weapon aims a fruitless blow. 760
And now he paus'd awhile, immers'd in thought,
A labouring doubt within his bosom wrought:
If by his own illustrious hand to bleed,
Nor leave the foes the glory of the deed;
Or if, survivor in the fatal strife,   765
To quit the field, and save his threaten'd life.
Fate has subdu'd (at length the leader cry'd)
My shame shall swell the haughty victor's pride:
Again th' insulting foe my flight shall view,
Again my exile with their scorn pursue;   770
But soon behold me turn in arms again,
To blast their peace, and shake their tottering
    reign.

X 4

Nor .

Nor yield I now—my rage ſhall burn the ſame ;
Eternal wrongs eternal vengeance claim :
Still will I riſe a more inveterate foe,   775
And, dead, purſue them from the ſhades below !

END OF THE NINTH BOOK.

THE

TENTH BOOK

OF

JERUSALEM DELIVERED.

THE ARGUMENT.

SOLYMAN, in his journey to Gaza, is accosted by Ismeno,
who persuades him to return; and conveys him in an
enchanted chariot to Jerusalem. The magician conducts the soldan through a subterraneous cave into the
city, and brings him to the council-hall, where he stands,
concealed in a cloud, and hears the debates. The speeches
of Argantes and Orcanes. Solyman at last discovers himself, and is received with the greatest joy by the king.
In the mean time it is known to Godfrey, that the warriors who came to his assistance were those who had followed Armida. One of them relates to the general their
adventures. Peter foretells the return and future glory
of Rinaldo.

THE

TENTH BOOK

OF

JERUSALEM DELIVERED.

WHILE thus the foldan fpoke, a fteed he fpy'd,
That wander'd near, unburthen'd of his guide ;
Then inftant, fpent with toil and faint with heat,
He feiz'd the reins and prefs'd the welcome feat :
Fall'n is his creft, that late fo dreadful rofe,   5
His helm difgrac'd no more its fplendor fhows ;
His regal vefture ftrows the dufty plains,
And not a trace of all his pomp remains !
  As, from the nightly fold, the wolf purfu'd,
Flies to the fhelter of the friendly wood ;   10
Though fill'd with carnage, ftill he thirfts for more,
And licks his ravenous jaws impure with gore :

So fled the foldan, from the field compell'd,
Still bent on flaughter, still his rage unquell'd :
Safe from furrounding fpears he took his flight,   15
And all the deathful weapons of the fight :
Alone, unfeen, the warrior journey'd on,
Through folitary paths, and ways unknown :
His future courfe revolving in his mind ;
Now here, now there, his doubtful thoughts inclin'd.
At length he fix'd to feek the friendly coaft   21
Where Egypt's king collects his powerful hoft,
And join with him his fortune in the field,
To prove what arms another day would yield.
And, thus refolv'd, the well-known courfe he bore 25
That led to ancient Gaza's fandy fhore.
Though now his weary limbs require repofe,
And every wound with keener anguifh glows ;
Yet all the day he fled with eager hafte,
Nor left his courfer, nor his mail unbrac'd.   30
But when the dufky gloom perplex'd the fight,
And objects loft their colour by the night,
He fwath'd his wounds ; a palm-tree near him ftood,
From this he fhook the fruit (his homely food !)
His hunger thus appeas'd, the ground he prefs'd, 35
And fought to eafe his limbs with needful reft :

On

On his hard shield his pensive head reclin'd,
He strove to calm the tumult of his mind.
Disdain and grief his heart alternate rend,
And like two vultures in his breast contend.   40
At length when night had gain'd her midmost way,
And all the world in peaceful silence lay,
O'ercome with labour, sleep his eyes oppress'd,
And steep'd his troubles in Lethean rest.
While thus on earth he lay, a voice severe,   45
With these upbraidings, thunder'd in his ear.

  O ! Solyman ! regardless chief, awake !—
In happier hours thy grateful slumber take.
Beneath a foreign yoke thy subjects bend,
And strangers o'er thy land their rule extend.   50
Here dost thou sleep ? here close thy careless eyes,
While uninterr'd each lov'd associate lies ?
Here, where thy fame has felt the hostile scorn,
Canst thou, unthinking, wait the rising morn ?

  The soldan wak'd, then rais'd his sight, and view'd
A sire, of reverend mien, who near him stood :   56
Feeble he seem'd with age, his steps to guide
A friendly staff its needful aid supply'd.
Say, what art thou, who dar'st (the monarch cries)
Dispel soft slumber from the traveller's eyes ?   60

What

What part canſt thou in all our glory claim,
And what to thee our vengeance or our ſhame ?
  In me behold a friend, (the ſtranger ſaid)
To whom in part thy purpoſe ſtands diſplay'd :
And here I proffer, with auxiliar care,   65
In all thy labours and deſigns to ſhare.
Forgive my zeal; reproaches oft inſpire
The noble mind, and raiſe the hero's fire.
Thou ſeek'ſt th' Egyptian king—ſuch thoughts re-
       ſtrain !
Nor tempt a long and toilſome tract in vain;   70
Ev'n now the monarch calls his numerous bands,
And moves his camp t'aſſiſt Judæa's lands.
Think not thy worth at Gaza can be ſhown,
Nor 'gainſt our foes can there thy force be known;
But follow where I lead, and, ſafe from harms,   75
Within yon wall, begirt by Latian arms,
To place thee, ev'n at noon of day, I ſwear,
Without the brandiſh'd ſword or lifted ſpear.
New toils, new dangers there thy arms attend;
There ſhall thy force the town beſieg'd defend, 80
Till Egypt's hoſt, arriv'd, their ſuccour yield,
And call thy courage to a nobler field.
  Thus while he ſpoke, the liſtening Turk amaz'd,
Full on the hoary ſire in ſilence gaz'd :

His

His haughty looks no more their fierceneſs boaſt, 85
And all his anger is in wonder loſt.
   Then thus : O father ! ready to obey,
Behold I follow where thou point'ſt the way :
But ever beſt that counſel ſhall I prize,
Where moſt of toil, where moſt of danger lies. 90
   The ſire his words approv'd ; then ſearch'd, with
      care,
Each recent wound, annoy'd by chilling air ;
With powerful juice, inſtill'd, his ſtrength renew'd,
And eas'd the pain, and ſtanch'd the flowing blood.
Aurora now her roſy wreaths diſplays,   95
And Phœbus gilds them with his orient rays.
Time calls (he cries) the ſun directs our way,
That ſummons mortals to the toils of day.
Then to a car, that near him ready ſtood,
He paſs'd ; the chief of Nice his ſteps purſu'd : 100
They mount the ſeat ; the ſtranger takes the reins,
Before the laſh the courſers ſcour the plains ;
They foam, they neigh, their ſmoking noſtrils blow,
And the champ'd bits are white with frothy ſnow.
Then (ſtrange to tell) the air, condens'd in clouds,
With thickeſt veil the rolling chariot ſhrouds ; 106
Yet not a mortal ſight the miſt eſpy'd,
Nor could an engine's force the cloud divide ;
               While

While from its secret womb, with piercing eyes,
They view'd around the plains, the hills, and skies.
Struck with the sight his brows the soldan rais'd, 111
And steadfast on the cloud and chariot gaz'd;
While on their course with ceaseless speed they flew
Well by his looks the sire his wonder knew;
And, calling on his name, the chief he shook; 115
When, rouzing from his trance, the warrior spoke.

O thou! whoe'er thou art, whose wondrous skill
Can force the laws of nature to thy will,
Who, at thy pleasure, view'st with searching eyes
The human breast, where every secret lies: 120
If yet thy knowledge (which so far transcends
All human thought) to future time extends,
O say! what rest or woe is doom'd by fate
To all the toils of Asia's broken state?
But first declare thy name; what hidden art 125
Can power to work such miracles impart?
This wild amazement from my soul remove,
Or vain will all thy future speeches prove.

To whom, with smiles, the ancient sire reply'd:
In part thy wishes may be satisfy'd: 130
Behold Ismeno! (no ignoble name)
In magic lore all Syria owns my fame.

But

But that my tongue should distant times relate,
And trace the annals of mysterious fate,
A greater power denies; thy thoughts exceed   135
The narrow bounds to mortal man decreed.
Let each his valour and his wisdom show,
To stem the tide of human ills below;
For oft 'tis seen, that with the brave and wise,
The power to make their prosperous fortune lies. 140
Thy conquering arms may prove a happier field;
Thy force may teach the boastful Franks to yield:
Think not alone the city to defend,
On which the Latian foes their fury bend;
Confide! be bold! for fire and sword prepare; 145
A happy issue still may crown the war.
Yet to my words attend, while I recite
What, as through clouds, I view with doubtful light,
I see! or seem to see, ere many a year
Th' eternal planet gild the rolling sphere,   150
A chief whose rule shall fertile Egypt bless,
Whose mighty actions Asia shall confess.

Ver. 151. *A chief whose rule —*] He means Saladine, for
his valour made soldan of Egypt, who took Jerusalem from
the Christians, after they had been eighty years in possession of it, and had there established a seat of kingly government.

Let this fuffice; not only in the field,
Beneath his force the Chriftian powers fhall yield;
But from their race his arms fhall rend the fway,   155
And all their ftate ufurp'd in ruin lay :
Till, fenc'd by feas, within a narrow land
Groan the fad relicks of the wretched band.
He from thy blood fhall fpring.—Ifmeno faid :
And thus the king his generous anfwer made;   160
(His bofom kindling at the hero's fame)
O happy chief l whofe deeds fuch glory claim !
For me, let good or ill my life betide,
And fortune, as prefcrib'd above, provide :
No power fhall e'er my vigorous mind control,   165
Or bend th' unconquer'd temper of my foul :
Firft fhall the moon and ftars their courfe forfake,
Ere I my foot remove from glory's track.
He faid ; and, while he fpoke, with martial ire
His eyeballs flafh'd, his vifage feem'd on fire.   170
    Thus commun'd they, till near the chariot drew
To where the Chriftian tents appear'd in view :

Ver. 158. *Groan the fad relicks —*] The poet is here
thought to mean Cyprus, which was given by Lufignan to
Enrico count of Campagna, and which continued in poffeffion of fome of the Chriftians after the eftablifhment of
Saladine in the holy land.

A fcene

A fcene of carnage here their eyes furvey'd,
Where death appear'd in various forms difplay'd.
Touch'd at the fight, the foldan's tears o'erflow, 175
And all his face is fpread with generous woe:
He fees, inflam'd with anger and difdain,
His mighty ftandards fcatter'd on the plain :
He fees the Franks exulting o'er the dead,
And on his deareft friends in triumph tread :   180
While from the breathlefs corfe the arms they tear,
And from the field the glorious trophies bear.
There fome he views, whofe funeral care attends
Th' unbury'd relicks of their Chriftian friends:
And others here prepare the blazing pyre,   185
Where Turks and Arabs feed one common fire.
    Deeply he figh'd, and ftrait his falchion drew,
And from the lofty car impetuous flew :
But foon Ifmeno check'd his eager hafte,
And in the feat again the warrior plac'd;   190
Then fought the hill, while diftant on the plain,
Behind their courfe the Chriftian tents remain.
    Then from the car they 'light (at once from view,
Diffolv'd in air, the wondrous car withdrew)
Still with the cloud infhrin'd, on foot they fare, 195
And down the mountain to the vale repair;

Y 2

Where

Where Sion's hill, that here begins to rife,
Turns its broad back againft the weftern fkies.
Th' enchanter ftay'd ; and now, advancing nigh,
Explor'd the fteepy fide with heedful eye :   200
A hollow cavern open'd, in the ftone,
A darkfome pafs, in former ages known,
But now with weeds and brambles overgrown :
Through this the forcerer foon the paffage try'd,
And held his better hand the prince to guide.   205
    Then thus the foldan : Through what darkfome
        way
Muft here my fteps by ftealth inglorious ftray ?
O ! rather grant that, with this trufty blade,
Through fcatter'd foes a nobler path be made.
Let not thy feet difdain (Ifmeno faid)   210
To tread the path which Herod wont to tread,
Whofe fame in arms o'er many regions fpread.
This monarch firft the hollow cavern fram'd,
What time his fubjects to the yoke he tam'd :
By this he could with eafe the tower afcend,   215
(Then call'd Antonia from his deareft friend)

    Ver. 216. *Then call'd Antonia* —] Jofephus relates that
Herod gave this name to the tower from Mare Antony the-
triumvir.

Thence

Thence with his troops could leave the town unseen,
Or there re-enter with supplies of men.
But now to me reveal'd, to me alone
Of all mankind, this secret path is known.   220
This way shall lead us to the regal seat,
Where now the wife and brave in synod meet,
Call'd by the anxious king to high debate,
Who fears perhaps too far the frowns of fate:
Awhile in silence all their counsels hear,   225
Till, breaking in their sight, thou shalt appear,
And pour thy speech in every wondering ear.

   He said, and ceas'd; no more the warrior stay'd,
But enter'd, with his guide, the gloomy shade:
Darkling they far'd through paths conceal'd from
      view,   230
And, as they pass'd, the cavern wider grew.
Ismeno now unfolds a secret door,
They mount by steps long-time disus'd before:
Here through a narrow vent, from upper day,
Appears the glimmering of a doubtful ray.   235
Now from the seats of night their course they bend,
And sudden to a stately hall ascend,
Where, with his sceptre, crown'd in awful state,
Amidst his mournful court the mournful monarch
      sate.

Y 3

The

The haughty Turk, within the cloud conceal'd,
In filence ftood, and all that pafs'd beheld ;   241
Then heard the monarch in an awful tone
Addrefs the fenate from his lofty throne.

O, faithful peers ! behold the turn of fate !
The laft dire day how deadly to our ftate !   245
From every former hope of conqueft thrown,
Our fafety refts on Egypt's powers alone ;
But thefe muft join us from a diftant land,
When prefent dangers prefent aid demand.
For this I bade you here the council hold,   250
And each the purport of his thoughts unfold.

He ceas'd : and foon a murmuring found enfu'd,
Like zephyrs foftly whifpering through the wood :
Till, rifing from his feat, with noble pride
And fearlefs fpeech, Argantes thus reply'd.   255

What words are thefe to damp the martial fire ?
No aid from us thy wifdom can require.
O ! in ourfelves our hopes alone muft reft,
If virtue ever guards th' intrepid breaft ;
Be that our arms, be that our wifh'd fupplies,   260
Nor let us life beyond our glory prize !
I fpeak not this becaufe my anxious mind
Defpairs from Egypt certain aid to find :

Forbid

Forbid it! that my thoughts, fo far mifled,
Should doubt the promife which my king has made.
But this my ardent foul has long defir'd,   266
To find a few with dauntlefs fpirits fir'd;
That every chance can view with equal eyes,
Can feek for victory, or death defpife.

    Orcanes next arofe, with plaufive grace,   270
Who 'mongft the princes held the nobleft place:
Once known in arms amid the field he fhin'd,
But, to a youthful fpoufe in marriage join'd,
Proud of the hufband and the father's name,
In flothful eafe he ftain'd his former fame.   275

    Then thus he fpoke: Well pleas'd the words I hear
Which fpring, O monarch! from the foul fincere;
When the full heart with inbred ardor glows,
And generous threats the hero's warmth difclofe.
Should now, tranfported with a noble rage,   280
The good Circaffian's heat too far engage;
This may we grant to him whofe dauntlefs might
Difplays like ardor in the field of fight.
It refts with thee his fury to control,
When youth too far tranfports his fiery foul.   285
'Tis thine to view, in equal balance weigh'd,
The prefent danger with the diftant aid;

Y 4

The

The hoſtile power that on our city falls,
Our new-rais'd ramparts and our mouldering walls,
I ſpeak the dictates of a faithful heart :   290
Our town is ſtrong by nature, ſtrong by art,
Yet, ſee what mighty ſchemes the foes intend,
What huge machines againſt the walls aſcend!
Th' event remains unknown—I hope and fear
The various chances of uncertain war.   295
Th' unlook'd-for ſmall ſupply of herds and corn
That yeſter-night within the town was borne,
Can ill ſuffice ſo vaſt a city's call,
If long the ſiege ſhould laſt before the wall :
And laſt it muſt, though by th' appointed day 300
Th' Egyptian forces here their aid diſplay :
But what our fate if longer they delay ?
Yet grant thoſe ſuccours ſhould prevent in ſpeed
Their plighted promiſe, and our hope exceed :
I ſee not thence the certain conqueſt won,   305
Nor from the Chriſtians freed the threaten'd town.
We muſt, O king ! with Godfrey meet in fight,
Thoſe gallant chiefs, thoſe bands approv'd in might,
Whoſe arms ſo oft have ſcatter'd o'er the plain
The Syrian, Perſian, and Arabian train.   310
Thou, brave Argantes ! oft compell'd to yield,
Haſt prov'd too well their valour in the field :

Oft

Oft haft thou fled the foe with eager hafte,
And in thy nimble feet thy fafety plac'd.
Clorinda and myfelf have felt their hoft ;   315
Nor let a warrior o'er his fellows boaft.
Free let me fpeak, and unreftrain'd by fear,
(Though yonder champion fcorns the truth to hear,
And threatens death) my deep foreboding mind
Beholds thefe dreadful foes with fate combin'd : 320
Nor troops nor ramparts can their force fuftain ;
Here fhall they fix at laft their certain reign.
Heaven witnefs, what I fpeak the time requires,
Love for my country and my king infpires !
How wife the king of Tripoly ! who gain'd   325
Peace from the Chriftians, and his realms retain'd ;
While the proud foldan, on the naked plains
Now breathlefs lies, or wears ignoble chains ;
Or hid in exile, trembling from the ftrife,
Prolongs in diftant lands his wretched life ;   330
Who, yielding part, with gifts and tribute paid,
Had ftill the reft in peace and fafety fway'd.

    He faid ; and thus his coward-thoughts difclos'd,
With artful words in doubtful phrafe compos'd ;
Yet durft not plainly his advice declare,   335
To fue for peace, a foreign yoke to wear.

But,

But, at his speeches fir'd with just disdain,
No more the soldan could his wrath restrain.
To whom Ismeno—Can thy generous ear
Without concern these vile reproaches hear?   340
Unwilling have I stay'd, (the chief returns)
My conscious soul with just resentment burns.
Scarce had he ended, when the mist, that threw
Its friendly veil around, at once withdrew;
Dissolv'd in air was lost the fleecy cloud,   345
And, left in open light, the monarch stood:
Full in the midst his dreadful front he rears,
And sudden thus accosts their wondering ears.

   Lo! here the man you name, the soldan stands;
No timorous exile fled to distant lands!   350
This arm shall yonder dastard's lies disprove,
And show what fears his trembling bosom move.
I, who of Christian blood such torrents shed,
And pil'd the plain with mountains of the dead!
Left in the vale, by foes begirt in fight,   355
All succours lost! am I accus'd of flight?
But should this wretch, or any such, again,
False to his country, to his faith a stain,
Dare, with his words, to shameful peace betray,
(Do thou, O monarch! give my justice way)   360

This

This falchion shall avenge the hateful part,
And stab the treason lurking in his heart.
First in one fold shall wolves and lambs remain,
One nest the serpent and the dove contain,
Ere with the Franks one land behold our state,   365
On any terms but everlasting hate!
　　While haughty thus he spoke, with threatening
　　　　mien,
His dreadful hand upon his sword was seen.
Struck with his presence, with his words amaz'd,
The pale affistants mute and trembling gaz'd.   370
Then, with a soften'd air and milder look,
To Aladine he turn'd, and thus he spoke:
We trust, O monarch! welcome aid we bring,
When Solyman appears t' affift the king!
　　Then Aladine, who near to meet him drew: 375
How glows my heart a friend like thee to view!
No more I feel my flaughter'd legions loft,
No more my foul with anxious fears is toft,
Thou fhalt my reign fecure, and foon reftore
(If Heaven permit) thy own fubverted power.   380
　　This faid, around his neck his arms he caft,
And with an eager joy his friend embrac'd.
Judæa's fovereign then, this greeting done,
Gave to the mighty chief his regal throne:

　　　　　　　　　　　　　　　　　Himfelf,

Himfelf, befide him, to the left he plac'd,   385
Ifmeno next with equal honours grac'd.
And while, enquiring every chance of fate,
In converfe with the fire the monarch fate,
To honour Solyman the warrior-dame
Approach'd ; then all, by her example, came.   390
Among the reft, Ormuffes rofe, whofe care
Preferv'd his faithful Arabs from the war :
Thefe, while the hofts with mutual fury fought,
By night in fafety to the walls he brought ;
And, with fupplies of herds and corn convey'd, 395
Gave to the famifh'd town a needful aid.

  Alone, with louring front and gloomy ftate,
In filence wrapt, the fierce Circaffian fate :
So feems a lion, couching on the ground,
Who fullen rolls his glaring eyes around :   400
While low his head declin'd with penfive air,
The foldan's looks Orcanes could not bear.

  In council thus Judæa's tyrant fate,
The king of Nice, and nobles of the ftate.

  But pious Godfrey, victor of the day,   '   405
Had chac'd his foes, and clear'd each guarded way :
And now he paid his warriors, flain in fight,
The laft due honours of the funeral rite ;

                              Then

Then bade the reft prepare (his mandate known)
The fecond day in arms t' affault the town ;   410
And threaten'd, with machines of every kind,
The rude Barbarians in their walls confin'd.

The leader foon the timely fquadron knew,
That brought him aid againft the faithlefs crew:
In this the prime of all his friends he view'd,   415
Who once the fraudful damfel's track purfu'd :
Here Tancred came, who late, by wiles reftrain'd,
A prifoner in Armida's fort remain'd.
For thefe, to meet beneath his lofty tent,
Before the hermit and his chiefs, he fent.   420

Then thus he faid : Let fome, O warriors ! tell
Th' adventures that your wandering courfe befell ;
And how you came, by fortune thus convey'd,
In need fo great to give fuch welcome aid.   424

He ceas'd ; when, confcious of his fecret blame,
Each hung his head deprefs'd with generous fhame :
At length the Britifh monarch's deareft fon,
The filence broke, and thus fincere begun.

We went (whofe names, undrawn, the urn con-
    ceal'd)
Nor each to each his clofe defign reveal'd,   430
The darkfome paths of treacherous love to trace,
Lur'd by the features of a guileful face :

                                        Her

Her words and looks (too late I own the shame)
Increas'd our mutual hate, our mutual flame :
At length we drew to where, in dreadful ire,   435
Heaven rain'd on earth of old a storm of fire,
T' avenge the wrongs, which nature's laws endur'd,
On that dirè race to wicked deeds inur'd ;
Where once were fertile lands and meadows green,
Now a deep lake with sulphurous waves was seen :
Hence noisome vapours, baleful steams arise,   441
That breathe contagion to the distant skies.
In this each ponderous mass is thrown in vain,
The sluggish waters every weight sustain :
In this a castle stood, from which there lay   445
A narrow bridge t' invite the wanderer's way :
We enter'd here ; and, wondering, saw within
Each part present a lovely sylvan scene ;
Soft was the air, the skies serene and mild,
With flowers adorn'd the hills and vallies smil'd :
A fountain, 'midst a bower of myrtle shade,   451
With lucid streams in sweet meanders stray'd :

Ver. 436. *Heaven rain'd on earth —*] The country of
Sodom and Gomorra. Aristotle and Galen both mention the
lake here described by the poet, and give the same reason for
its supporting any heavy substance, the grossness and den-
sity of the water.

On

On the foft herbage downy flumbers lay;
Through whifpering leaves the fanning breezes
    play;
And cheerful fongfters warble on the fpray.   455
I pafs the domes our eyes beheld amaz'd,
Of coftly gold and polifh'd marble rais'd.

   There on the turf, with fhade o'er-arching grac'd,
Near purling rills the dame a banquet plac'd;
Where fculptur'd vafes deck'd the coftly board, 460
With viands choice of every flavour ftor'd;
Whate'er to different climes and funs we owe,
Which earth, or air, or ocean can beftow;
With all that art improves! and while we fate,
An hundred beauteous nymphs in order wait.   465

   With gentle fpeech and foft enticing fmiles,
She tempers other food and fatal wiles;
While every gueft receives the deadly flame,
And quaffs a long oblivion of his fame.

   She left us now, but foon refum'd her place, 470
When anger feem'd to kindle in her face.
Within her better hand a wand fhe bore;
Her left fuftain'd a book of magic power:
Th' enchantrefs read, and mutter'd fecret charms,
When, lo! a fudden change my breaft alarms!   475

Strange

Strange fancies foon my troubled thoughts purfu'd,
Sudden I plung'd amid the cryftal flood :
My legs, fhrunk up, their former function leave ;
To either fide my arms begin to cleave ;
A fcaly covering o'er my fkin is grown,   480
And in the fifh no more the man is known !
An equal change with me the reft partook,
And fwam, transform'd, within the limpid brook.
Oft as my mind recalls th' event, I feem
Loft in th' illufion of an idle dream!   485

   At length her art our former fhape reftor'd,
But fear and wonder check'd each iffuing word.
As thus amaz'd we ftood, with angry brows
She threaten'd added pains and future woes.

   Behold (fhe cry'd) what power is in my hand! 490
I rule your fates with uncontrol'd command :
My will can keep you from the ethereal light,
The haplefs prifoners of eternal night ;
Can bid you range among the feather'd kind,
Or, chang'd to trees, with rooted fibres bind ; 495
Can fix in rocks, diffolve in limpid ftreams,
Or turn to brutal form the human limbs.
It refts on you t' avert my vengeful ire ;
Confent t' obey what my commands require :

Embrace

Embrace the Pagan faith, my realms defend,   500
And your keen fwords on impious Godfrey bend.

  She faid : the proffer'd terms our fouls difdain'd,
Her words alone the falfe Rambaldo gain'd.
Us (no defence avail'd) fhe ftrait conftrains
In loathfome dungeons and coercive chains,   505
Thither was Tancred led, by fortune croft,
Where, join'd with us, his liberty he loft.
But little time, confin'd within the tower,
The falfe enchantrefs kept us in her power.
'Twas faid, an envoy from Damafcus came,   510
To gain her prifoners from the impious dame ;
And thence, difarm'd, in fetters bound, to bring,
A welcome prefent to th' Egyptian king.

  We went, furrounded by a numerous guard,
When Heaven's high will unhop'd-for aid prepar'd.
The good Rinaldo, who, with deeds of fame,   516
Adds every moment to his former name,
Our courfe impeding, on our leaders fell,
And prov'd that valour, often prov'd fo well.
He flew, he vanquifh'd all beneath his fword,   520
And foon again our former arms reftor'd.
To me, to all confefs'd the youth appear'd ;
We grafp'd his hand, his well-known voice we heard.

Here vulgar tongues fallacious tales proclaim,
The hero ftill furvives to life and fame.   525
Three days are paft fince, parting from our band,
He with a pilgrim travell'd o'er the land,
To Antioch bound : but firft he caft afide
His fhatter'd arms with ftreaming crimfon dy'd.

  Here ceas'd the knight. Meanwhile his ardent eyes
The hermit fix'd devoutly on the fkies;   531
His looks, his colour chang'd; a nobler grace
Shone in his mien, and kindled in his face;
Full of the Deity, his raptur'd mind
With angels feem'd in hallow'd converfe join'd : 535
He reads in future time's eternal page,
And fees th' events of many a diftant age.
He fpoke; while all intent and filent gaz'd,
Much at his looks and awful voice amaz'd :
He lives! Rinaldo lives! (aloud he cries)   540
Then heed not empty arts or female lies !
He lives! and Heaven, whofe care his youth defends,
For greater praife his valued life extends !
Thefe are but light forerunners of his fame,
(Thefe deeds that now o'er Afia fpread his name) 545
Lo ! after rolling years, I plainly view
His arms fhall many an impious power fubdue;

His eagle guards, with silver wings display'd,
The church and Rome beneath its friendly shade.
Succeeding sons with equal virtue shine,   550
And children's children crown his glorious line !
To pull the mighty down, exalt the low,
To punish vice, or virtue aid bestow;
These be their arts ! and thus his dazzling way
The bird of Esté soars beyond the solar ray :   555
To guard celestial truth his flight he bends,
And with his thunders Peter's cause defends :
Where zeal for CHRIST each holy warrior brings,
He spreads, triumphant, his victorious wings :
The chief recall'd, must here his task resume,   560
Such is the will of Fate, and such th' eternal doom !
   Here ceas'd the sage; his words each doubt
        appeas'd,
And every fear for young Rinaldo eas'd.
All, fill'd with transport, spoke their joys aloud;
While, fix'd in thought, the pensive Godfrey stood.
Now had the night her sable mantle cast   566
O'er darken'd air, and earth around embrac'd :
The rest, retiring, sink in soft repose;
But, lost in cares, no sleep the leader knows.

END OF THE TENTH BOOK.

www.ingramcontent.com/pod-product-compliance
Lightning Source LLC
Chambersburg PA
CBHW032144110726

47902CB00003B/690